F
GRIFFIN NI Dizzy
Griffin, Nicholas, 1971-
Dizzy city : a novel /
FTBC 1073168468

D0014773

TEMPORARY BOOK COLLECTION

On week of: 11/01/07   On week of: 05/01/08
Send to: JOAQ   Send to: FRB

On week of: 01/01/08   On week of: 07/01/08
Send to: TRAN   Send to: KMAN

On week of: 03/01/08   On week of: 09/01/08
Send to: MEN   Send to: BKF1
              Run C45
Return to FHQ on week of: 11/01/08

DIZZY CITY

NICHOLAS GRIFFIN

STEERFORTH PRESS
HANOVER, NEW HAMPSHIRE

Copyright © 2007 by Nicholas Griffin

ALL RIGHTS RESERVED

For information about permission to reproduce
selections from this book, write to:
Steerforth Press L.C., 25 Lebanon Street,
Hanover, New Hampshire 03755

Library of Congress Cataloging-in-Publication Data

Griffin, Nicholas, 1971–
  Dizzy city : a novel / Nicholas Griffin. — 1st ed.
     p. cm.
  ISBN-13: 978-1-58642-132-8 (alk. paper)
  ISBN-10: 1-58642-132-8 (alk. paper)
  1. Swindlers and swindling — Fiction. 2. United States — History — 1913–1921 — Fiction. I. Title.

PR6057.R49D59 2007
823'.914 — dc22
                                    2007023906

First Edition

For Adriana

PART ONE

————⟫•⟪————

Mr. Benedict Cramb
November 1915

I'm not one of those, thought Ben, looking back along the lines of sameness all dressed as he was, in drab green, dull as you like, a country visit on a day of rain. That's what they were now, the color of moss and mud, thousands and thousands of soldiers walking in one another's footsteps. I am different from that lot, thought Ben. If I was back in London, I'd be in a wool suit, the one with the chalky lines down it. I'd have my white shirt on, my shoes gleaming, my hair would be just cut, tapered to the neck and run through with Macassar oil. My mustache would be waxed and the ladies on the Strand, balanced in their heels, would be tapping their pretty little parasols at their sides, pretending not to look at me.

Then I'd be meeting the gentleman I've come for, beside his club with its slit-eyed porters. I'd be talking, as ever, and the man I'd be talking up would be nodding in agreement. We'd have met before, but now he'd trust me and he'd be reaching inside his jacket and out would come his wallet. It'd be pigskin, monogrammed and worn down by the passage of pounds, and he'd part that fleshy cleft and would dip in and pluck out a dozen notes for me. He'd have that confidence in me and then he'd never see me again. I'd be on the tram to Harrods, going with his money to buy myself a silk tie. I'd not be telling the boys about this little job on the side. This one I'd spend on myself.

The sergeant blew his whistle and Ben breathed in the wet air and stared up from his daydreams at the blank French horizon. What the hell am I doing here? A thousand pairs of boots in the damp mud, the soft pop of their lifting, the slap of their descent was all that Ben could hear. This is temporary, Ben swore to himself. War is a passing thing, but other men's money will be needed every day of my life.

Chapter One

THEY WERE LYING on their fronts in the mud. There were two games usually played at night: Birthday, where a man named his favored food, and Perfect Girl, where each contributed a body part of a woman known to all until they conjured an ideal.

"Birthday or Perfect Girl?" whispered Douglas, breaking an hour of silence.

"Both," said Ben.

David giggled nervously.

"I don't want to play," whispered Chimer, his skinny body shaking from the cold.

"I'll go first," said Ben softly. "Mashed potatoes with lots of butter served off Ellen McNabb's bum. With the French silk pants on. The blue ones."

"You've never even seen them," said Chimer in a hushed voice.

"A roasted chicken," whispered Douglas, "held between Catherine Ellis's thighs. With her stockings on. And garters."

"Come on, Chimer," whispered Ben, "why don't you play?"

"You're all fucking lunatics," whispered Chimer through chattering teeth.

That morning, after the march, Ben had been standing in the trench, still tasting the taint of rum and bile at the back of his throat and then the whistle blast and he was over and running. They were together at least. And they went over together that morning, Ben and Douglas, and Chimer and David. Best friends who had taken their shilling together at the Duke of York's on the King's Road, had done their square bashing at Aldershot, running and drilling. Again, it was the noise that shocked him once he was over. The artillery had stopped, so there was no more thunder, just screeching and whistles and thuds and screaming. The Germans had hurried up from deep beneath their ordered trenches and set up their machine guns. Ben had looked to his right as he was trying to run and he could see them going down ten at a time, more. And he couldn't move fast, they had said to run, and Captain Traven was blowing his whistle, but Ben had mud coming over the tops of his boots and he didn't know about the rest, but he had trouble seeing out, had tears coming down his face. Crying, just the nerves, the body doing strange unconscious things. So he had moved with his own lot right on the eastern edge of the push, and everyone was going down, so Ben dived too and his lot followed. They always followed him.

His friends thought he was lucky. Twice in London Ben had been taken by the police, but they'd all been done five times and more. Of course, thought Ben, his wounds were relatively fortunate, the deep scar on his hand, but that was where a man got lucky wounds, out in the open, the only reason anyone ever volunteered for patrol. Stay in the trench and it was all head shots and shells, but on patrol or out in the open there was the blessed chance that a man could be shot in the leg or arm and packaged home.

Ben had dived into a shell hole. One of theirs, one of ours, Ben didn't know, but twenty feet deep and more. Ten days in a trench and earth on all sides and then up and running and feeling nothing but naked and exposed and in truth, there was comfort to be back down in the mud. First thing he did was to leave his rifle on the edge of the crater, pointing back to their own lines, because he knew he'd have the sense not to stick his head back over until darkness had fallen. By then they'd all have forgotten which way was which.

We're all right, Ben thought; no one knows we're in here. At the bottom there was thick mud, but none of them cared with the sound of what was above. There were bodies at the bottom, Germans from a push two days before. And there too was the body of Captain Traven. Ben's friends were trying to get purchase, using the other rifles to dig in so they wouldn't slip down. No one wanted to slip down into the deep mud with the dead.

Once secure, they looked at one another and found that they were, to a man, untouched, barely a scratch. Nothing wrong with any of them that rum rations couldn't have cured. They were shaking, but they'd been shaking all that morning waiting for the whistle. Ben remembered that Chimer hadn't been able to stop himself. Even when the fire had dwindled to silence, he was muttering, his thin frame shaking, "Fuck, fuck, fuck, fuck. What the fuck are we doing here?"

Ben knew the answer: they had always followed him, from the theater, through the streets, right up to enlistment. He looked away from Chimer, useless to think about what could have been done differently to avoid the present. If they were to blame it on anything, then blame it on the fact that they had ever met. In London, in the theater on Old Street. The boys "acted" from time to time, bribed by their parents, brought on stage as orphans or acolytes. They were pointed to, drew an *ahhhh* from the mothers in the audience, and were given a little copper afterward to save for the penny candy store.

Sunday afternoons, after the matinee, the mothers and fathers would walk across the road to the Pig and Bell and the children would be left to mischief. Always to the prop room, Ben in possession of a borrowed key. Always soldiers. Redcoats, cavalry, Roundheads. And they were only caught once, when they had played too hard, breaking the cardboard swords.

"They look real," said Chimer.

"They are real," said Douglas, and brought one down on David's head.

"To the battlements," shouted Ben, and off they ran, parry and thrust, and when all had marched up and down, played the roles of good and bad, they found that their swords lapsed at awful angles, creased and wobbly.

"What do we do?" asked Chimer.

"Just put them back," said Ben, as if he thought that a night in the prop room would restore them to strength.

Ben had been summoned by Chimer's mother the next afternoon and bent over her knee. The shame of it, no real pain, just surprise and crying and red-eyed in front of your friends at the grand age of eight, too old for such babyish humiliations. Far too old to react with tears. Ben laughed now, little silent wisps of heat escaping from his lips in the half-light. How long had they been in the shell hole, he asked himself. An hour? Three?

"I'm the Romans," Ben said, age ten, standing in ill-fitting armor.

"What?" asked Chimer, swinging his shield around his head. Thin now, thinner then, all rib cage and wide eyes.

"I'm the emperor," said Ben.

"Of who?" asked David.

"Of you lot."

"And who are we?" asked Chimer.

"Whoever you want," said Ben.

"I'm a king," said David. Thick blonde hair, a mop until the army cut it. Always a comb in his back pocket, right up to enlistment. Look at him now across the shell hole — blonde sideburns, flecked with mud to the side of his helmet. "There was a King David, right?"

"We can all be kings," said Chimer breathlessly, his shield still held above his head.

Three kings against an emperor and they always knew that Ben was supposed to win. Their deaths could be long and imaginative. David and Chimer and Douglas twirling and shouting and making last, violent lunges at the emperor as they fell, but Ben was always left standing amid the bodies in the center of the stage. That was the way it always was. Ben remembered the sensation of their still bodies lying around him. They'd never dared to turn on the theater's floods, so there had never been any warmth from stage lights, none of the heat of the audience, and Ben had always felt he was alone in the dark, his friends at his feet, with no one watching from the wings at all.

"Can we get up now?" Chimer would always ask when they had died, exhausted and happy, lying in the middle of the stage.

"Not if you're dead," said Ben.

"Fuck off," said Douglas, and got to his feet. Always swearing to make the stagehands laugh, to get a reaction from their fathers. Ben turned from one side to the other, feeling the stiffness of one shoulder ease up as the other pressed against the muddy side of the crater. Chimer was staring at him.

"You come here Ben Cramb." Chimer's mother again. Always trying to curb him.

"Stick a finger up your arse," he would shout. Aged what, thought Ben, aged all of eleven. And spanked again, always by Chimer's mother. But no tears, not now, and his father dead and all of the company amused by him and soon a little wary. Ben's mother didn't come there anymore; she let him run wild. By then, only Chimer's mother felt she could discipline him. The rest let him stay. And then came the card playing, and then came the little thievery, the learning and the leading of Chimer, Douglas, and David. They all loved him, even their mothers deep down, even when they called him a cheeky monkey and he called them daft old windbags. But that was it; he was good looking even then. He'd learned to seduce as a child, could persuade them all, even Douglas eventually. He looked up at Chimer, still all bones, even in uniform, with his pack on, muddy puttees. Bet he doesn't weigh a hundred pounds, thought Ben. Never did.

>●<

"And what are we going to do?" asked Chimer, now thirteen. Past playing dress-up. Wanting to be older, little mustachy wisps guarding their mouths. Not Ben, of course. He had stolen a razor and made a morning display of shaving. Smoking, all four of them, out the back of the theater on the steps, watching the girls pass by in their stockings. "What are we going to do when we're old?"

"When?"

"I don't know, in five years then?" asked Chimer, a little cough at the rough tobacco.

"Make money," said Ben.

"Doing what?" asked Chimer.

"Football," said Douglas. "Five pounds a week at the Arsenal."

Ben shook his head. "Five pounds a week," he said. "That's for the monkeys. You don't have to work." He reached into his back pocket and pulled out a wallet.

"Whose is that then?" asked Chimer.

"Point is," said Ben, "I don't rightly know. Point is, it's got twenty pounds in it. That's four weeks of David running in the mud with your Arsenal getting cold. And that's if you could kick a ball."

"Which you can't," added Douglas.

And the laughter and they're laughing at David, with his boyish dreams and his blonde thatch, and Ben did worse than that, he thought now in the mud. He gave them all a five-pound note, a fortune to his friends. They're not going to be able to show their mothers. It'll make them like him, apart from their parents. It'll make them *like* him. And did he *like* them? God yes, he now knows, not Douglas perhaps, too often against him. But David, and his winks and open heart, and Chimer, and his secret ties with Ben. Chimer's mother knew him well. Chimer knew him well, too. Knew Ben was still a little boy, that there was a thick layer of posture in Ben and what then? What was behind that? A shortcuts man, a con artist in schoolboy knee pants? Was he always this way?

>●<

"You awake?" murmured Chimer.

Ben nodded.

They began to whisper the time every other minute. Douglas had four wristwatches from picking in English graves. No luck in that, Ben had thought. They had smoked everything they had that afternoon, for they knew they couldn't smoke at night. There was nothing going on by then, all silent, except for those who'd been shot and hadn't made it back. Ben could hear them calling. The Germans were usually good with stretcher bearers, letting them come and go. He supposed most had made it back, but no one had thought to look in their hole, and they weren't about to look out.

"When the hell are we getting out of here?" Douglas whispered.

November and dull clouds and no sun, not that day. It was getting dark and they knew how cold it would be. The mud would harden, a crust of frost, and no food, no drink, not a cup of tea to warm them.

David said, "We'll get out tonight."

"What if we're shot by our own?" Ben asked. They didn't know the password. Why should they? They were supposed to be in one trench or the other, not in between.

"So what do we do?" David asked.

"Wait for the end of the war," said Chimer and that had brought the last shared laugh. "Or Ben'll think of something?" he added grimly. "Right Ben, right? Don't you always think of something?"

Ben looked down into the darkness behind him. The day before they had all been issued short pieces of rope to help pull one another out of shell holes should they fall from the duckboards. He sat upright beneath the lip of the crater, rubbed his hands together for warmth, and tied the ropes together, then signaled that he was ready to be lowered down the crater's side, to strip greatcoats from the dead. The earth was chalky and the depths of the pit emitted a creamy froth of phosphorescence.

><

Ben slipped down the shell hole toward Captain Traven's body. It lay atop the others. The German snipers had been picking the officers off, noting them by the gleam of their shoulder pips, and though Traven had been free of such identification, Ben recognized the fur-lined collar. Balancing with one foot in mud and the other on the back of a German corpse, Ben began to pull the coats off the bodies, then throwing them up to Douglas. They'd been issued badly cured fur jerkins that still reeked of the goat, sheep, or horse they'd been stripped from, but had been ordered to remove them for the attack. Germans overcoats were thicker than theirs but none was as fine as Captain Traven's: leather cuffs, fur collar. Ben kept it for himself. There was a small book of some kind in the inner pocket that Ben decided to return as identification. Douglas and David hauled him back up the slope and the four men sat miserable in the darkness together, urging the sun to rise.

Still, they could not warm themselves. Chimer wanted to crawl back to their lines, but Ben insisted they'd be shot. "Stretcher parties'll be out again at dawn," Ben said, pushing his hands under his armpits.

"What if they don't find us?" asked Chimer.

"They don't have to," Ben had answered, explaining that if Chimer, as the smallest, played dead, they could use two rifles as a stretcher and put one of the greatcoats over him, create their own stretcher party. There was only one small issue. There were only four of them. In thick mud, the RAMC always used four men per stretcher, sometimes eight in double shifts. They knew it would be hard, but still, better than creeping through the dark with one of your own taking potshots at you. Muddying their helmets first, they pissed on the firing mechanisms of their guns to free them of muck, then held them close and threw a coat over Chimer. David and Douglas had one end, and because Ben was the biggest, he stood alone at Chimer's legs.

At dawn, they made it all of twenty feet from the shell hole, and it had been silent. Ben had a Sunday morning feeling, like he was walking over a field to church and nothing else was stirring. He was with his best friends in the world, but his hands were so cold, they'd been bare to the wind all night and the mud was like black ice, slippery, and he was trying to keep hold, but he couldn't. One of the rifles slipped and out came Chimer. He fell to the ground, sprang to his feet, and immediately began to wipe his muddy hands on his puttees. And it would have been funny anywhere else, a face full of mud and your best friends there to laugh. There was nothing but silence, but Ben sensed something else; he knew they were being watched. There must have been some sun that morning, because Ben's last memory was of a rapid shadow moving across the mud, and he could hear it coming, one of those barrels coming through the air and he was farthest and he saw it so he could turn his back and let Chimer block its path.

And when he could not see, could not hear, he could smell the overwhelming, cloying scent of almonds. He lay there in the mud, ears deafened, blood flowing from his body, and had the absurd thought that he was covered in marzipan like a Christmas cake. That paste the Germans used, the pink paste, and Ben remembered a piece of red china in the mud beside him, because the Germans filled up those explosive barrels with everything they could get their hands on. Teacups and old clocks and nuts and bolts, anything that'd rip through a man. Ben couldn't hear a thing; the explosion had knocked a hole through the air.

Douglas, was it Douglas, yes the wristwatches on the arm. But there's nothing above the shoulders, no head there. Nothing to see, no eyes to look into. David, where are you? Next to Douglas, face-down in the mud, helmet off and blonde hair showing. Both your legs are snapped backward, one is almost torn off, your guts are on the backs of your thighs, there's a hole in your flank the size of your canteen. And Chimer, where the fuck are you? Ben tried to turn his head to the side. Right beside him. As always. With a hand missing, and a piece of metal driven deep into his cheek, splitting the teeth, now scattered in the mud. Chimer's choking and twitching. Is that

really you? It's you, and you're dying like a bird, all tics and con-
vulsions. Look down, there's nothing left beneath your knees.

Ben reached up to push the blood from his eyes. I want to see it all,
he thought. I can help. But something was lying on top of him; he
could feel it now, something wet, heavy, and meaty that he did not
want to see leaking through his greatcoat. He could feel its
warmth. Ben stared straight up at the sky and did not say a word.
He was found lying in the mud, mute, clothes in rags around his
body, identified by, of all things, the fur collar of another man's
coat.

Chapter Two

WAKING, BEN KNEW at once that he did not belong. The sheets told him so, as crisp and starched as the English voices around him. No roughness, no swearing, no mud, no rat scuttle, no laughter, nothing but the polished sounds of educated doctors and patients. No Chimer, no David, no Douglas. But he could not think of them yet; he must think of himself, ensure safety, absolute safety. All he wanted to do was talk, but he knew he would be betrayed as a private by his first words and all of this, the wonder of cleanliness, the absence of worry, would disappear at once. Back he would go to the front. And no, that was settled the moment he woke into this other world. He would never go back. The boys were gone. Silence was the obvious, the best approach.

Doctor Willis introduced himself within an hour. He walked under the large chandelier that dominated the night nursery, past the Corinthian columns, and stood before Ben, as wide as the bed, with a long flaccid mustache that hid what Ben believed was a sympathetic smile. He ignored Ben's silence as he detailed his patient's wounds, rolling him over, indicating Ben's great fortune with gentle pushes, how the different pieces of shrapnel had avoided all that was important. He added that he was not strictly a doctor of the body, but was a specialist in neurasthenics. Ben had no idea what Willis was talking about but nodded and kept quiet, trying to glance out of the window to see what heaven he had ascended to.

"Isle of Wight," said Willis, following his stare. "You're in one of Queen Victoria's palaces, Osborne House. She died here, so if you follow you'll be in good company. Can you nod?"

Ben nodded.

"Can you remember anything?"

Ben shrugged, uncommitted, but in truth, he knew it all and what he did not know, he suspected.

"Do you remember your name?"

Ben shook his head.

"Captain Jonathan Traven," said Willis.

Every day nurses came to wash him and he liked the feeling of the sponge, felt the thrill of being rubbed up and down. He had barely seen a woman in over a year. David would have liked this; Chimer would have been muttering in a corner avoiding their eyes. These women were older, better bred. His irresistible erections would go unmentioned. He wanted to apologize, but still, no words to betray it all. He watched their hands push the white flannel against his skin and could not believe any of it. That he was breathing calmly, that danger was a hundred miles away, that this was *his* skin tingling. Or that every friend he treasured in the world had been buried, or worse, scooped into a burlap sack and added to the list of missing.

Officers talked to Ben in the Billiard Room, though he was relieved to find that there were stranger men than him there: stammerers who did not stop talking, screamers, lots of them, outbursts of uncontrollable fear. He thought he was comparatively normal. He sat in the shade of an enormous porcelain urn and avoided their eyes. They must have been used to similar behavior, because it didn't seem to disturb them at all. They handed him a notebook and pens, but he refused to write a word. He could talk fancy of course, all his friends could, to make fun, to imitate, they could sprinkle their sentences with *old chaps* and *what a firecracker*, and all the other things that lords said to earls, but that would make it worse, wouldn't it? Douglas was good at it, could do the Prince of Wales pat. Ben should keep himself quiet. They would think he was making fun of them, and that wouldn't do at all. Back he would go.

He lagged at the rear of walking parties, all of the officers identical in their blue pajamas and dressing gowns, meandering in slippers through the palace grounds along the dead queen's favorite walks. At first they plagued him with questions, What school did he go to? Where was he born? What club? Did he hunt, shoot, fish? Did he know Dicky Thornton-Blyth? Such a wonderful presumption of shared experience. Happily, silence was considered a response, and best of all, he had the bandaged wounds to excuse him. Down they would walk to the gray water off the beach and then back up to Osborne House. The officers mocked the palace. Italianate, a pile of bricks, stinking of Lysol, far inferior to friends' estates. Ben was awed by the size alone. Every time he passed between the front gates he felt alarms would ring, detecting in his blood an absence of education and money.

It took Ben one full day outside of the night nursery to understand how unlike the other patients he was. There would be a communal jump should a forgetful attendant slam a door. Up they would all start like crockery when a fist slammed a table. But not Ben. Quite the opposite. He was always the one to wind up the gramophone, insist on another disc being spun. Take a nurse for a sway and a dip.

"And when I tell you how beautiful you are," crooned the disembodied voice, "they'll never believe me."

The nurses liked him. They told him he looked an Italian Douglas Fairbanks. They may have thought of him as outgoing, a prospect for rehabilitation, but Ben knew he was not well, knew that he did not simply look forward to the gramophone, but needed to hear it if he was to keep the thoughts of Chimer and Douglas and David at bay. And it was not simply the gramophone records. It was the sound of the bath running, nurses chatting. Anything but the silence his fellow inmates desired. He was very different from them all, thirsting for noise. He felt that if silence came, the boys would come to him too, wondering why they were in one place, Ben in another.

On Monday morning the nurses were grinning. The doctor smiled when he shadowed the foot of Ben's bed. "Just wait till tomorrow," said Dr. Willis. "Your family is coming to remind you who you are. It will probably feel a bit strange, like being handed the wrong coat at a hat check, but just be patient with yourself."

Ben's eyes must have shown the panic, for the doctor continued. "Your fiancée will be up from London first thing in the morning. Your parents should be down from Leeds by five or so. We'll put aside some tea for them."

After breakfast, in came this young lady, about twenty or so, a fine-boned thing, wearing a hat shaped like a dandelion's beard, and the nurses left them alone and he said nothing and she said nothing because she couldn't, because it was tears and tears because he wasn't Captain Jonathan Traven. He wanted to say something of comfort to her, to apologize for the deceit, but the best he could do was eventually join her, weeping. He wanted to say, *I'm sure that you'll find him.* But it was a lie, for Traven had lain beneath him in mud a month ago, peeled of his overcoat, dead and ripped.

He wanted to say more. *I've lost too. My friends, my only friends, they're all gone too. There's not going to be a man left, I swear to you.* But he said nothing of course. A nurse poked her head in and smiled in sympathy at the weeping lovers and walked away. Five minutes later, the young woman had put her hand to his cheek and composed herself, kissed his head and said, "I'm sure someone will come for you." She hadn't suspected the extent of his fraud, just presumed him lost, dazed, some other lover's lucky find.

But Ben could not wait for Traven's father and mother, could not wait for their sympathy to turn to outrage. Ben knew what they would eventually unearth. He wasn't like the captain. He didn't have his schooling, his money, his family crest, or even a family.

As a child everything seems normal. The theater, their gang of children, they had always been together. Pianos, the boys, applause were all he could remember until the age of seven. Then there were doctors at home and then a father gone and Ben had known that wasn't normal because all the other dads were still around. And Mother, never one with words, all silence now. Ben would go out to play with Chimer and Douglas and David; he'd run to the theater as if his dad still sat at the piano. When he left, Mother would be scrubbing the dishes. Ben would come home, sometimes for tea that might or might not be there, sometimes later after the theater had emptied. And she'd still be scrubbing dishes, as if she hadn't moved at all. He'd kept a year of it to himself, told no one about her. But someone must have figured it out. Mother went away, and off he went to Aunt Kath and his six cousins, just down the road. All Aunt Kath had said was "Your mother's resting for a while." Which didn't mean *resting*, it meant his mother was still staring at walls. And *a while*, that meant forever. Staying with Aunt Kath only made the walk to the theater longer and that was that. Chimer, Douglas, David. They were it. They were family.

Traven's girl had made him wonder about his mother. What had she been thinking after her husband had died? What had she seen that had taken her out of the world? He knew he couldn't have done anything for her back then. And she'd never come looking for him, never written him. Still resting for *a while*, sitting in some government-run house lost deep inside herself. She'd never learned to pretend, had she, he thought. Hadn't known that the inside and the outside can be different worlds.

At lunch, when all were gathered in the dining room, Ben stole a uniform from a fellow patient, complete with the insignia of an officer in the Essex regiment. In the breast pocket was a wallet containing thirty pounds. Ben walked out of the front gate of Osborne House, the fresh-stitched stripe of the wounded on his shoulder and all the propriety of a man who had deserved his leave. After returning the salute of the guard, he traveled, courtesy of the government, up to London. There he changed into civilian clothes stolen from a laundry, wrapped the uniform in a bundle, squeezed rocks into the pockets, and threw it in the river from a railroad bridge. He took the next train to Liverpool.

Carrying twelve loaves of bread and a rucksack filled with eighteen quarts of water, Ben walked aboard a steamer covered in steve-dores, seamen, and bursars. Unquestioned, he descended, past the fo'c'sle, into the engine room, through to the coal bunkers. In the darkness that first night, Ben could hardly tell the difference between empty dreams of sleep and the mechanical void of consciousness. Both were polluted by the grinding roar of the engines. He knew neither the name nor the destination of the vessel.

What cargo they carried, he did not know, only that the ship ran on coal, for he breathed the dust day and night. At first, every piece of bread he ingested returned. He could not measure a day at sea but knew he had been there long enough for the water to begin to taste stale. When Ben's lips got dry his tongue had no dampness to wet them and sat fat in his mouth. Finally, when he lit a match, he saw that his bread had turned black. Endure anything, he commanded himself, to stay away from France.

The ship shifted uneasily. Back and forth, up a sudden wave and then rushing down. A sickening sway that brought first one lump of coal and then another racing toward him. He could do nothing to protect himself in the dark, only turn his back to the assault, arms wrapped around his water, bread pushed inside his jacket, and every now and then take a step above the lumps crowding his ankles.

In a night of swaying, flinching and tumbling coal, he lost his blanket. The churning noise of fuel burning, the whistling cargoes of steam in pipes, the clanking of hot ash buckets, the distant heat brought no comfort. The ship moved forward. He lit his last match to confirm that the present still existed. Nothing. Nothing to fight for, no friends, no family. War had come and war had won and was eternal.

➤●◄

Now, on the ocean, there was nothing to do but think. When he had lain in hospital, Doctor Willis explained to him how amputee patients suffered sensations in their absent limbs. Now that Chimer, Douglas, and David were gone, Ben did not know why he remained. He had waited for the same banishment, but even that ache was receding. He no longer itched for the absent but understood that he was what had been lopped off, not what remained.

Chapter Three

BEN HAD NEVER been so cold as in the bunker of the ship — not in trench water, not marching through November rains. Blackness and memory, shivers and swollen tongue, patience, stores of it. Ben sat, listening but not hearing, fighting all the tricks minds play in constant dark, the leaps of time, the muddy dreams that try to uncap the skull and creep out to sit beside you. And all the blood that he had seen, spilling and sloshing in the bilge. The scraping sounds of shovels as coal was taken out from the bunker far beneath him.

Soon, it seemed soon when it finally came (though a minute before, time had stretched limitless as the ocean), Ben heard the wonderful sound of engines dying and cranes working. He tried to laugh, but coughed, then wiped at teary eyes. There came English cries of the coal drags and firemen and stokers. He could not tell where he was. He tried to listen for voices from the port for some clue to his destination. More patience, just a trickle, just until the cranes stop and the voices fade.

Must provide my own noise, he thought, once it had grown quiet. Accompany myself with foot crunching on coal, boot on iron bars. His weakness staggered him. The struts of the ladder were hard enough to negotiate, but the door above seemed so heavy that at first Ben thought it was locked. Trying again, he ducked his head and pushed his shoulders against it and it rose slowly. There was nothing resting on top, just a normal resistance, close to impenetrable in his weakened state. He crawled over the lip and lay on his back for five beautiful minutes, not caring who saw him or what they would do. Standing with the aid of a steel bar, Ben found a niche behind a door and sat and listened for the crew, gathering his strength for an exploration of the steamer.

There was silence on the main deck. Ben could hear voices from the docks and movement beneath him in the main hold. He tugged his boots off, hung them from their laces about his neck, and walked along the narrow corridor barefooted. The ship astounded him; he felt as if he had walked aboard a relic, destined for a maritime museum of disgrace. In the dim threads of light that slunk through the porthole, Ben could see that the first low cabin he entered was scattered with scraps of sackcloth. Tatters of old clothes were employed as mattresses. There was nothing to steal. He could hear his own breath, nothing more. He backed out of the cabin and turned in the corridor.

Moving quickly along, Ben's heart hammered when he saw the rough reflection of a Negro mirrored in the metal siding, but it was just a corruption of his own filthy shadow.

He took a fresh gulp of air and crept to the galley. The noise of the men beneath him increased, but tempted by hunger, Ben entered. There sat a kettle, still warm, an inch of watery vegetable soup with a thick layer of fat upon it. He spooned it up greedily, then found little jacketed potatoes in a pot and chewed through the remaining dozen or so. Glancing at the door for a second, he then peered inside a second kettle, sniffed, but coal was all he smelled. Was it coffee, tea, or dishwater? The rusted spout did not move from his lips until the kettle was empty.

Keeping to the port side, Ben stole along the gangway, past the ash tubes that led down to the stoke hold. Footsteps came his way. He reached for the nearest door handle, twisted it, stepped quietly through and shut it behind him. The footsteps passed by. Light from the docks seeped through the porthole. Apparently the captain's cabin. As a soldier, he had had respect for some of his officers. They fell beside their men, but now it was a time of necessity. The world was painted an English red. The port might well be His Majesty's, and under the Crown ran the government in its glorious and intricate layers, and there would be police, port authorities, and the military. All would be anxious to make the acquaintance of a man who had granted himself an indefinite leave.

He relieved the captain of one shirt, one sweater, one pair of socks, underpants. Trousers simply too short, far too broad for his slim figure. He stripped and entered the captain's head and prayed for five minutes of peace. There, with a beige towel, Ben set about turning himself from black to white. It took three separate washes. The coal had worked its way into his skin, the slim fold of his stomach where he had hunched, the creases from smiling that ran down either side of his mouth, the lifeline along his palm. His beard was stiff with dirt. Soon, he began to feel human again. Still weak, but a dozen times the man he had been just two hours before. He retched suddenly, vomiting a thin streak of gruel onto the cabin floor. Wiped his mouth on his cuff. Concentrate, he ordered himself. It's all for nothing if you don't. They'd want you to. You want me to, don't you lads? You'd curse me if I was caught now. Think man, think. He removed a pen and papers from the captain's desk, folded them, then pocketed matches, loose change, a pair of handkerchiefs, and closed the captain's door softly behind him.

He waited by the door to the main deck for an hour, nothing compared with a night at a listening post in no-man's-land. Waited until he saw the last of the crates removed from the hold, swung by the crane to the dock, heaved by silent longshoremen into orderly rows. Then all disappeared down toward the fo'c'sle, save the man Ben prayed was the captain, standing talking to another sailor. The crew reappeared within minutes, and accompanied by the captain, walked along the short plank to shore. Two had been left behind on watch. He cursed them both until one passed by Ben's door and around to patrol the port side of the ship.

Ensuring that the lone watchman was still turned toward the piers, Ben stepped quickly into the night, onto the gangway to shore. Then he turned about to face the ship and called out to the sailor on deck.

"Is this the *Yorrick*?"

The man started, then swiveled to study the pale apparition about to board his ship. "Never heard of her," he called.

Ben gave him a quick nod, walked down to the pier, and for the first time stared up at the city before him and breathed out in relief, attempted to digest the scene with false nonchalance. The lights that came from the city tapered upward, a silver hem of a skirt that rose to impossible heights. And then Ben realized he had seen it before, on postcards. He was in America, in the city of New York, with its vertical audacity, its thousands and thousands of windows, some lit, some quiet, all staring down at a stowaway. Endurance and the stars he had not seen for a fortnight had combined to deliver him to neutrality. America and her isolated reluctance, embracing neither side of Europe's war. English-speaking America. New York, flooded with foreigners. He could hear the city's low static buzzing, a permanent hum that seemed to rise from that fleet of buildings before him, as if each were a ship run by stokers. Fuck lads, he said to himself, it's America.

Ben had left behind the remains of his bread, his stale water; brought only his stolen sterling. He looked about while walking. In the dark, hurrying away from the huddled ships of the pier, he hoped that to the casual eye he would appear a decently dressed sailor late for leave. To the north and south lay other piers cutting into the water, suckled by ships and tugs. A group walked slowly a hundred yards in front of him. Ben followed, between large warehouses, their walls advertising shipping lines. Just through those gates, he said to himself. Watch them pass. They are not stopped. Walk on. You are lost in thought. Do not look.

"You," said the gateman.

Ben walked on.

"I said *you*," repeated the voice.

Ben stopped a yard from the gate. He could see a taxi, an American taxi passing by empty. The rattle of wheels over cobbles. He could have hailed it. He could run.

"Papers," said the man.

Ben turned to face his examiner. The man had emerged from a minuscule station constructed from corrugated iron. Ben could see that behind him, in the shelter, were two others, blue uniforms and high hats of police. He went through the motions of looking for imaginary papers.

"Can't seem to find them," he muttered.

"Then back you go to look for them," returned the man with a sarcastic smile.

"Can't I just get them for you when I'm back on board?" asked Ben. "Bit of a thirst on me."

"Back with you," said the man. "You're not passing here without them."

Ben smiled, then turned around.

He walked back between the warehouses, then skirted to his left looking for another exit. He was met at all points by a high, wire-mesh fence. In his current state, he deemed climbing impossible. Instead, he followed it about. At one point it seemed a dog, or desperate hands, had begun to dig under. No strength, but he was not going to be kept in there, not with the nighttime silence coming, not with the boys waiting inside his head. He walked on, keeping away from the lamps. As he walked, he collected broken pieces of boxes and shards of splintered crates from the ground.

Back toward the gatehouse stood a stack of wooden containers marked CEYLON TEA. Ben made a small pile of tinder against their base, then struck a match to scraps of tarred rope. He held the wisps to the tinder, and the fire took, running up the side of the first crate. When Ben caught his first pungent sniff of dark, concentrated tea, he walked backward into the shadows and circled about to the gatehouse. It took ten long minutes for the shout of *Fire!* to go up. Out ran the keeper and the policemen, one carrying a bucketful of sand, the other calling for pumps. Ben slipped calmly through the gates, accompanied by the aroma of a thousand English drawing rooms.

Chapter Four

NEW YORK, ESPECIALLY in the cool April weather, was a city of coal dust, invisible grime that rose in the air, trailing from chimneys or else sprinkled by the rushing elevated trains that cranked north and south past second-floor windows. Eventually, the dust would settle in black visible smears on every white windowsill, on every gentleman's stiff collar, and on the leaves of every potted plant. Still, April had much to recommend it. Snow had been banished; summer had yet to arrive with its condensed reek and suffocation. April was, despite its indecisive weather, a time for true New Yorkers to revel in the in-betweenness, ignoring the winter past and denying the coming heat.

That first day brought what Ben would always consider "American" weather: the simple surprise of a Northern European to find that there are parts of the world where rain is not a daily occurrence. He had been to London, passed through Paris, but this city had no comparison. Its skyline reminded Ben of harvest, when all the hay was cut and bundled into high mounds, then bathed in sunshine. Bright promising skies and a park, Central Park, which he had come to after stumbling north.

That night, beneath Belvedere Castle, he had found a calm patch with little rings of daisies that brushed his cheek as he slept. He woke up twice, nobody there, no friends, and twice cried himself back to sleep, angry at his tears. Not one man disturbed him during the day, only the wonderful sounds of chatter, barking dogs, chugging distant engines. He tipped his hat and slept and did not dream and did not think at all, until the next morning when the tip of a policeman's boot moved him on and he complied without speaking.

Ben did not wish to convert all of his currency immediately, just ten dollars' worth for food. He vowed to make no definite appointments until he had understood the city's patterns. He did not take a room at a hotel, but asked advice of a newsboy and walked back down south, past Grand Central, finding himself in the middle of the morning surge, amid volumes of suits spewed up into the city, a flood of faces that made the sidewalks indistinguishable from the street. He tried to stand still among the paperboys, the shoe shiners, and hawkers of sheet music. The crowds blocked the trams and carts and horses and automobiles that were fighting for supremacy of the street. Neighs, horns, brays, Klaxons, shouts, and in the middle of it all, Ben, thanking the fates for putting him here above all cities of the world. Best was the preoccupation of every face, as if each person believed that he reigned in this city. He could have been shaking, stammering, and slavering as badly as any of Osborne House's cases and he knew not one glance would have been cast his way.

He chose to walk west until he reached the famous Broadway, an endless stretch of glass windows. Ben wandered, grinning, mesmerized by the abundance of artificiality, thrilled at the noise of it all, at the distance he had put between himself and the war. Shops sold bright wax fruit and false flowers made of taffeta and muslin. The baby in the beribboned crib was made of porcelain. He stopped by a mannequin advertising hats and stared, until she winked at him and he tipped his hat, laughed at himself, and kept moving. New York City. He would not even have thought about it, but it was joy, genuine good fortune to have landed here, luck a distant memory in itself.

The farther south on Broadway he walked, the larger the signs became and the cheaper the goods. Poor haberdashers, tinny jewelers, and nickel tobacconists dominated south of Forty-second

Street. But once past Union Square, the windows were filled with live models: young men in gymnasium clothes demonstrating the virtues of exercise, young women rolling cigars, gentlemen exhibiting on-and-off patent reversible collars. Ben tipped his hat to each of them and was roundly ignored.

He turned east and after a few blocks found himself under the shade and occasional roar of the Second Avenue el. The Salvation Army was easy enough to find; you had only to look for the dirtiest, most unfortunate characters and follow them awhile. His captain's clothes were better than all of his companions on that afternoon's line as it wrapped itself around the Bowery block, but his gaunt face, still ashen from the bunker, ensured that no questions were asked.

It was odd, he thought, to find himself back in an army of a kind, but he realized that he was drawn to people, that he had a need for their noise. The more time he spent in the company of these faceless crowds, the more conscious he became of what might happen if the sounds evaporated, if the company was swept away by the wind and he was left alone on a city block, with only the echo of his own voice, with only his memory. He wanted the clamor of the city that morning, he wanted to hear others breathe before he slept, as he woke. He wanted to wait in line for his bath, have someone waiting when he emerged. People, noise, motion, noise, conflict, noise.

But it was a comparatively silent army in New York, not the jostling camaraderie their company had experienced before they had seen action. There, Ben had held the popular position of company rooster, who, come the arrival of any mailbag, was guaranteed a half dozen letters. No father to write to him, no mother, but instead a clutch of different women, all in some state of swoon, each well deceived into thinking she had possession of his heart. Ben liked to give a great display of not even needing to read a letter, just staring at the handwriting and passing it to any empty-handed man. Only Chimer disapproved, for he'd have happily given his heart for a single girl, though he'd yet to do so. Would never do so. Was dead.

Ben knew where most of his letters ended up. All but the most treasured were destined for the latrines. Most of the youthful declarations he received, all those unread poems and scribbled little hearts, ended up rubbing against the arse of an unknown soldier. Now, months later, Ben felt he might swap all he had left for a friend of any kind. The Salvation Army drew only the desperate. The men were allowed in at seven in the evening. Three hundred places. The line began to form as early as two in the afternoon. They were fed a thin supper of undetermined meat, shown to vast wooden bunks to lie as close as cutlery, and were woken at half past five. Above their heads hung a sign: GOD DOES NOT SEND US MORE THAN WE CAN BEAR.

Ben spent his days exploring the immediate neighborhoods, keeping himself busy, away from his own thoughts. The Bowery was an acrid place that reeked of chlorinated lime, sprinkled over garbage stacks and gutters to stem an outbreak of infantile paralysis. The same chemical Ben had smelled as it had been dusted over the lines of the unburied south of La Bassée.

The streets were crisscrossed in washing, already tainted by city dirt in the encroaching darkness. Having seen fragments of uptown, Ben recognized this as immigrant America: poor, bursting, and bristling with intricate rivalries that Ben began to decipher after days of eavesdropping. He learned that neighboring Greenwich Village had achieved a form of social recognition, if only for endless talk and protest, and that the Bowery was its shame-faced brother, the one who had not learned to talk, to dress, to clean himself. For every Iowan and Ohioan in the Village, there were five Poles, ten Russians, and a score of nationless tramps in the Bowery. And while it had settled from the raucous and dangerous capital it had been not twenty years before, the reputation of danger remained.

He thought he had been doing well, that there was a difference between his appearance and his thoughts that no one could broach. But then, at dusk on his fourth day, a young woman who smelled strongly of jasmine stopped him on the street and asked for a light to her cigarette. No beauty, to be sure, but he began to smile at her like he might have done back in London, and she smiled back at him, and then suddenly his confidence evaporated. He fumbled in his pockets, mumbled an apology, and walked off.

"Not going to bite you," she called after him in laughter.

When was the last time a woman had disturbed him? Years ago. Far away. Back in London, before Ben knew much of a thing about women. It had been the jasmine that had done it, Ben told himself. From fourteen onward, all the boys had talked about was the perfume of certain girls who would lay it on thick enough to turn men's heads. Chimer's sister, Eileen, fourteen months older, as tall as Ben, as pretty as he would be handsome. No one can be a man at fourteen, and handsomeness is still a childish beauty. Girls aren't quite ready to deem it worthy. They're looking upward, thought Ben, just like the boys, at the men and their motorcars and their jobs and opinions.

Eileen had auburn hair, tied it in a blue silk Japanese ribbon borrowed from the prop room. She had large eyes, dark as a rabbit's, and breasts strapped tight under a corset. He'd touched other girls, paid for the pleasure with little gifts or coins, and some had let him touch it for nothing, that moist partition unseen beneath the skirts. But Eileen was Chimer's sister. Chimer didn't like the attention she got wherever she walked. Especially didn't like the glances his friends cast in her presence. Ben would wait until the other boys weren't around, and then, once a week from the age of fourteen, he'd ask her out.

A year later, he was still asking.

"Can I take you out?"

"No you can't Ben Cramb."

"Why not?"

"Because you're still a boy."

"You'd rather go out with the girls then?" said Ben.

"No," said Eileen. "I'd rather go out with a man."

"And what's he going to give you?" asked Ben. "He'll want a ring on your finger, put you in his mother's kitchen." He was shaking his head at her foolish resignation.

She laughed a little to encourage him. "And what are you going to take me out with?"

"The riches of the world," said Ben. "Nothing in London I can't afford for you."

"Is that right?" she said, beginning to see him as separate from her brother, noting the loose good looks. Not the child her mother had once put across her knee.

"I was thinking the theater," said Ben. "Not ours. A proper theater. Like the Strand or the Shaftesbury."

"And then what?" she asked.

"A meal," said Ben.

"What's in the meal?"

"You'd have to use your own imagination," said Ben. "That's your limit."

She met him in the middle of Piccadilly, far away from the eyes of their neighbors. They attended the Shaftesbury Theatre off St. Giles. It was by far the grandest building he had ever entered, a thousand seats, nary a poor view, and most in evening clothes. The two of them tucked away in the last row of the balcony, close to the brilliant gilt ceiling and bright chandeliers. Ben waited for the lights to dim to hide his poor clothes. The show was called *The Arcadians* and meant nothing at all to Ben, except he could remember the final act took place in a restaurant, which made his stomach begin a quiet rumble. He spent most of his evening casting casual glances Eileen's way to see if she was enjoying the play, yet she seemed more concerned with trying to peer at the fashions about her.

"That was wonderful, Ben," she said afterward, pronouncing the word wonderful with a deep, affected accent. He wasn't sure if he should laugh or not.

"Glad you liked it." Motorcars were all about them, attendants and drivers picking up their employers, ladies in long silk dresses brushing past the couple, gentlemen calling goodbyes over their heads.

"And where now?" asked Eileen, still staring about her, giddy-eyed at the passing jewels.

"This way," he said. He took her to a teahouse he had often seen young men enter. He could not tell what Eileen thought, impossible to tell if she knew this world, or was impressed at his knowledge. As they were led to a table next to the kitchen door Ben made a brief assessment of his wallet. It was still stuffed with stolen bills. She ordered lamb, mint jelly, new potatoes, and carrots. He had a shepherd's pie and slathered it in savory sauce. They talked briefly about the play — she had adored the heroine's pink dress — but Ben was too nervous to direct conversation. He paid and left a large tip for their waiter.

He remembered now, walking up the Bowery, no one on the block ahead, the feeling of hope he had all those years ago when she had laced her arm through his. Puffed up, he remembered, on parade with Eileen, their faces aglow as if they were a couple stepped fresh from the stage.

"Where now?" she said.

"A promenade?" he said, very proud of the word.

She directed him along Drury Lane, past the haberdashers and milliners. She made him pause before each window.

"Isn't that lovely?" at the first.

"Just the most adorable thing I've ever seen," at the second.

"Wouldn't that be the finest?" at the third.

It took Ben almost until the end of the street to interpret the unsubtle squeezes on his arm.

"Would you like to try one on?" he asked.

"Can I?"

In they went. The ashen-faced assistant looked askance at them, but Eileen was a pretty face, prettier still with a pink hat perched upon her auburn hair, staring deep in the mirror, turning her head to the left, to the right, asking Ben's opinion again and again.

"Would you like it?" he asked at last.

"I would you know," she said. "I really would."

It was wrapped, it was boxed, it was carried out the door by Ben, cheeks now as pink as the hat itself. Eight pounds for a hat with a feather, as much as either of their fathers had ever earned in a month. Ben's wallet of notes, down to the odd coin.

"Where next?" she said.

"Wherever you like."

"Oh, I don't know," she said. "Why don't we just take a bus home then? We'll get off a stop early so no one will see us."

"I don't mind being seen with you," said Ben.

Still, they hopped off the bus ten minutes from home.

"It was lovely, Ben," she said, standing by the bus stop as the motor chugged away. "Really lovely."

"Thank you."

"You're quite the little gentleman."

He'd done it before, but not like this, not when it counted. He leaned in and stole a kiss from her, just a brief touch of the lips before she pulled back.

"Why would I kiss you?" she said, and looked about her as if her mother might be walking past.

He remembered still thinking that all was not lost. He kept his good humor, tried his charm.

"Because it's a case of love."

"Go see a doctor then."

She turned to walk off, clutching the hatbox.

"Shall we go for a walk tomorrow?" asked Ben.

She turned around.

"It was a night out," said Eileen. "We had a lovely time and it's never going to happen again." Ben stood there, aghast, mouth open to catch the falling soot. "And you say a word of this to my brother or Douglas or David and I'll never speak to you again in your life."

"Of course not," said Ben.

"*And* I'll call you a liar. *And* my mother'll want to know where you got your money from."

She turned away.

"Can I walk you back then?" he asked, taking the first few steps after her.

"No." And off she went.

"Goodnight," said Ben, the last of his hope dwindling. But still, just a flicker. "Hope you like your bonnet."

She kept walking.

He couldn't remember why he had felt like crying back then. Was it the end of the money, or because he felt love and forgiveness and that hot murmur of anger? She had ignored him the next day, and the next, and on the third he saw her on the arm of Joseph James, an automobile mechanic. He remembered turning red and trembling with some unutterable sense of shame. There she walked with the pink hat upon her head, its feather sticking straight up into the sky. Joseph James, nineteen years old and in a suit, walking past him with Eileen, about to enter the Pig and Bell.

Of course he was hurt. He still remembered it now, ten years later. That choking realization that you meant nothing to one you thought so well of. Ben had begun to walk away for a moment, but then followed the couple across the busy street. He tugged at her skirt and they both turned toward him. Joseph, all scrubbed up for his night, a lingering smell of grease despite the suit. He took a half step back, seeing Ben's eyes on Eileen.

"That's a beautiful hat you're sporting," said Ben.

She flashed warning eyes at him. "Thank you."

"Funny though," said Ben, "to take it off one man one night, then step out with another fellow a day later."

"Pardon me?"

"The hat I bought you."

"You bought that did you?" asked Joseph, edging forward.

"I did."

"With what? A shilling from newspapers?"

"She's not true," said Ben, directly to Joseph. "She'll wait till your wallet's empty and that'll be that."

"Little liar," spat Eileen.

The speed of the slap surprised Ben, such a sting. Through the water welling up in his eyes he could see the couple turning away toward the pub, stepping between a pair of factory boys.

"Good luck," Ben shouted after them, knowing that since the audible crack of the slap the eyes of the street were on them. "A guinea will get your hands up her skirt. You'll know you're doing all right when she hits a high C."

Ben saw Joseph continue walking, but there it was, a quick glimpse at Eileen's hat, and Ben's heart warmed. Words, that was all it had taken to make a man change the way he had been thinking. No more tears for the girls, he'd promised himself, and that was the way it had been.

Ben was almost smiling now, recovering from his quake in front of that New York girl and her welcoming smile. He'd get better, even though the block he walked along was reminding him of his London. Tenements and brothels, fading music halls; the Bowery seemed split between the Jews and the Irish. The perfect place, thought Ben, to earn an invisible living, the last place they would ever look for him. Ireland, still seething at the enforced recruitment of two divisions and more. Fifty thousand men, called to an English war and promised their return in six months. Already a year ago. A country beginning to choke with anger against the

grinding Empire. And the Irish Republican Brotherhood rumored
to be stirring. Whispers through the trenches, England is stretched
thin, why not strike when she is weak? Why would an Englishman
look for work in the Bowery? Why would he be given it?

Ben's strength was returning; muscles that seemed to have atro-
phied after two weeks in the coal bunker flexed again. He ate four
times a day, twice at the mission, twice outside. More than any man
in the place. As he waxed, they waned. He sat on stoops with his
food on his lap, sandwiches of fresh meat, still rare and exquisite to
his army palate. Before chewing, he would suck the beef in his
mouth, draining it of juice, then bite down, slowly, tasting it, swallowing with reluctance. He sought out sounds to accompany his
lunches. The Victrola shop on Eighth Street that piped its music
out onto the street, loud enough to bray above the motors. The bar
off Astor Place that brought a pianist down at lunch. Ben's fingers
would tingle with the need to run back and forth across the keys.

He knew what he longed for was to create his own noise, to talk.
Chimer, Douglas, and David gone, no man to talk to. How could a
single friend be too much to ask for? Ben had found himself
playing piano just because his father had, not thinking, but imi-
tating, and it was well enough, the vaudevillian existence that had
taught him everything, given him every friend. All those third-rate
card players and second-rate musicians, a lowly estate that their
fathers had passed on to them. Easy enough, once an option had
been presented, to imagine that war would lead to a better world.

That evening in the mission, Ben passed inside the gate just before
seven. They were taken in groups of five for showers. In and out in
under a minute, cold feet on the rough cement floor, no electricity
in there, just the weak city light leaking through a frosted window.
Tip the head backward, thought Ben, let the water run through the
hair, then spill along the length of the spine. Not much more than
a cold trickle, but still enough to induce revitalizing shivers. Keep
your hands up, cover your scars. Ben was the last man out. He
slipped back into his clothes and patted his jacket for the com-

forting bulge of the wallet. It was a comical terror, the patting of one pocket, the searching of others. Ben knelt and ran his hands along the floor, back to the step that led down to the shower room, but there was nothing there. Douglas would have laughed. *Him*, Ben, ablest of all, having his own wallet slipped.

An announcement was made that evening at dinner.

"It appears," said a minister, "that a wallet has been found. It contains money. We would dearly like to reunite it with its owner. Please do not come forward if it doesn't belong to you. We'll need a precise description of all its contents."

There was a common look of amazement, followed by a huff of ridicule. Who in the mission, in this land of fleas and scratches, who had the money to buy a wallet, let alone fill it? Ben watched five men make attempts to claim his wallet during dinner. But he could not stand. It burned him, but he kept his eyes no more or less interested than those about him. Twenty-five pounds sterling, four months' rent, sitting in the minister's office. He could not claim it, and all the implied ties to England and questions that would be asked.

Ben would have liked to have said that he felt freer without a pound or dollar to his name, but that would have been a lie. He could not stay on with the threat of a minister poking at his past. Poor without a hope of a mission roof over his head, Ben found himself without a job, a home, a friend, a single dollar. That night, he no longer stood in the circling line of the dispossessed. Sleep? A half hour in a doorway, but too cold. Winds were strange in the city; they came down one avenue, then paused, then came again from a side street. Ben had not noticed them before. He had to sit up. The subway gratings were warmer. I have not survived to sleep on streets, thought Ben. He resolved to head back to the edge of the Bowery, among the Irish, and look for a job where the English would not find him. Perhaps the army still considered him dead, but luck was nothing Ben wished to rely on.

><

Just before sunrise Ben washed his hands and face in the common cup by the public drinking fountain at Astor Place. He waited until an early commuter threw his newspaper into a trash can, then fished it out and began to read carefully, scanning for opportunity. With the last of his change he bought steaming coffee and fried dough and watched through the diner window as men passed on their way to work. Across the street, a building was about to rise. They seemed to be rising all about the city suddenly, as if thrust upward by seismic shifts, but it was the work of men, individuals who now streamed past the window. Ben left and followed them.

Structures were not built on empty lots. Their predecessors were demolished, two, three at a time, walls pulled down, walls going up, huge steel girders handled by cranes that could span a city block. All the men with mortar-whitened shoes, covered in fine dust. Against the morning sky Ben watched scaffold hangers walk the thin girders. Below them, trucks pulled up and away from this promise of a building, all the laborers huddled in their groups: Negroes, Irish, Italians waiting for work. Six months ago, Ben had hidden in a crater for less than a minute and when he had emerged, the church ahead of him was no longer there. What Europe knocked down, New York could build up. Ben was filled with a strange optimism. This was the place to live, to hide, to earn, and all about him they would build, hundreds, thousands of men, digging subway tunnels below or perched on girders like pigeons above. Ben spent an hour listening to the mortar and concrete mixers, the squeak of cranes and the clank and punch of riveters. Even the curses of the foremen sounded as sweet as birdsong.

But he would not be ground down by manual labor. A man could work with his hands and not be rewarded by calluses and union struggle. In New York music was a basic need. It was as close to a common tongue as existed. He had passed Italian theaters, Yiddish and Polish, but now they were melting toward the shared language. Newspaper in hand, shaking out his dirty jacket, he walked down to an address not two blocks from the mission. The facade of Miner's Theater on the Bowery retained a distinctly Irish flavor, all fading greens with a battered sign swaying in the April wind.

The door was open, letting the air dry the sodden boards and cleanse the scent of cheap cigars from the seats. The manager, Mr. Farrell, was on the stage, shifting a papier-mâché column of ancient Rome when Ben entered. He put down the column and turned to face the intruder. Receding red hair, arms crossed before him, Farrell wore a brown suit that bagged about the knees as if he were still hoping to grow into it.

"Good morning," called Ben.

"Where you from?" the manager asked him at once.

"England."

That alone resulted in a noticeable silence. A second head popped up, a man who had been slouching in the front row, older, well dressed, an overcoat draped over his shoulders. He didn't say a word, just turned and looked for the manager's reaction. Ben could feel Farrell watching him, and his black mustache gave a slight twitch. He had taken extra care that morning, using water to part his hair, still glistening and chill against his scalp. He presented Farrell with his advertiser's profile, the noble nose, the square chin.

"What's it you play?"

"Piano," said Ben. "You advertised." He waved an envelope. "I have a recommendation here," he said, giving the letter he had completed that morning a quick flap to attract the man's attention.

"Give it here then," said Farrell. He ripped it open, licked a finger, and ran it over the fresh ink, smearing it. "At least you can write," said Farrell. "But can you play?" The older gentleman in the front row laughed and shifted on the bench, not saying a word, as if he had paid for a ticket and was watching the opening scene of a play.

"Of course," said Ben, straight-faced.

"Then take a seat," said the manager. Ben entered the shallow orchestra pit, lifted the lid of the battered piano, ran his fingers across the keys and found it surprisingly well tuned.

"'Coax Me,'" ordered the man. Ben played.

"'Coon, Coon, Coon,'" he said. Ben played.

"'God Bless America.'" Ben played.

"'Piccadilly Rag.'"

"I'm not sure I know that one," said Ben.

"Good," said Farrell.

Ben thumped a *har har har* chord, which made the manager smile.

"You ever played anywhere like this before?"

Ben nodded. "In London. It's what my father did for a living."

He saw the stranger in the front row nod to himself in approval.

"Not exactly a large inheritance," said Farrell. "Where'd he play?"

"At Old Street."

Farrell nodded in recognition. "Be here Sunday at seven to meet the boys."

He pointed down at the scar on Ben's hand that ran in the perfect semicircle of a bite mark.

"Where'd you get that?" asked Farell.

Ben shrugged uncomfortably. "Years ago."

"Who bit you?"

"A dog."

Farrell nodded, but obviously didn't believe him. It was the size of a human mouth.

"Why would you hire an Englishman?" Ben asked, changing the subject.

"You not heard?" asked the manager. "There's a war on. Now what would an honest Englishman be doing in America?"

Ben remained silent, though it was the very thought he had counted on.

"Besides," continued Farrell, "if you really grew up in a place like this, you can't be as straight as you look. Come in a half hour before the shows, play and leave. If you don't talk, then no one's going to be hearing where you're from. Just make your noise on the box. Any trouble, see me."

Ben made a theatrical bow over the piano keys, rose. "Any chance of a dollar or two till Sunday?"

"None at all," said Farrell. Ben smiled and headed back into the day. He hadn't even inquired as to pay. He unfolded his *Herald* from beneath his arm and scanned for information for how an honest man, or a dishonest one, might make enough money to eat by nightfall. He was certainly too excited by his own performance to notice that the aging stranger from the front row had slipped out to follow him.

Chapter Five

THAT EVENING, BEN sat in the middle of a small audience above a makeshift boxing ring in a theater only three blocks from Miner's, his stomach protesting in rumbles and dramatic thunder. He was surrounded by the warm, alcoholic breath of men who had been drinking through the evening. Was Ben really thinking of partaking? It was for fools, inebriated blowhards, those with outsized opinions of their own abilities. Ben's stomach was insisting he wear the gloves.

And who will last one round with this old Negro warhorse for twenty dollars? The onetime sparring partner of the great Jack Johnson. Jack Johnson has the money, thought Ben in his seat, the only Negro with film contracts, roadsters, and titles. If I were a sparring partner relegated to some poor theater I'd be an angry man. But twenty dollars would keep me from the streets for a week, thought Ben. The first challenger into the ring was a bearded giant, leveled by a single punch. The Negro's manager had not been amused. You needed a dollar to challenge for the twenty, who was going to put another dollar up if you knocked them down like that? You don't have to hurt them. Help lift up the bearded man, thank God he can stand. See? No harm done. Brave fellow and who's next? The veteran dealt well with a stumbling drunk, avoiding the wild swings, tapping punches against the man's shoulders, playing a minute, then delivering a half punch to the man's chest that sent him straight over backward, landing unhurt, but with a thump that appealed to the audience.

><

He was simply too hungry not to fight. Ben stepped forward, stripping to what had once been a white vest, yellowed now with sweat. He looked as if he had spent the winter beneath the woodpile, skin pale, but a well-kept mustache and tall. Ben moved well. He let some of the boxer's first jabs glance off his guarded fists. Ben's feet were dancing, little hops that moved in and then out twice as fast, eluding the fading punches, making the boxer look like what he was, yesterday's man, out of shape, a sideshow traveler. The veteran's lunges grew angrier by the second. A hard blow in his midriff, but not down.

Ben wasn't trying to provoke him. In fact, he had barely thrown a punch, just accepting the boxer's efforts, not trying to rouse the crowd who might, in turn, rouse the boxer. Three minutes. With only seconds to go, the veteran moved in and tried a combination to Ben's face. He never moved his gloves. The Negro wound up and swung a roundhouse at Ben's right ear, but he saw it coming, ducked six inches, and the blow went sliding off the sweat of the hair. Two more punches, hard in the midriff, and the bell rang. Ben bent double and touched a knee to the canvas.

No credit to the manager, who kept a smile wide across his face as he refused Ben a cent for his pain, claiming correctly that Ben had not yet provided the dollar fighting fee. A chorus of boos. But credit to the veteran, who bounced his own gloves off Ben's in appreciation. Credit to Ben for the way he had fought.

"I'll take nineteen," said Ben to the manager.

"That's not the way it works. There are rules. You never had the entry fee, so how can you presume the purse?"

"I'll put up my nephew's buck," said a small well-dressed man approaching, overcoat draped over his shoulders, a dollar already folded neatly between thumb and forefinger. Ben recognized him immediately. It was the silent stranger who had been so interested in his audition at Farrell's music hall.

"Your nephew?" asked the manager in disbelief.

He turned to see if he could expect support from the veteran, but the boxer was already pulling his robe over his body, uninterested in the outcome.

"Very well," muttered the manager, and counted out the nineteen dollars one by one.

Ben turned to walk off, the little man in tow. Now that he was closer, Ben could see that the stranger favored a veneer of shabby gentility that suggested a moneyed family, a college club, that creamy fraternity that ran to the top of every city. Ben was now at least sure that he was American and not an employee of the British Embassy, not a military man or a threat to his freedom. Indeed, he looked more like a pantomime's impression of avuncular respectability, gray-haired, creased forehead, eyes both blue and kind. Yet Ben remained suspicious. He thought the man too thin; he had the amicable approach Ben had used on junior officers in the mess halls on his way to negotiate rations.

"So what do you think a loan like that is worth?"

"I'd say a double on the money," said Ben.

"Julius McAteer," said the stranger as they walked.

"David Johnson," said Ben.

"So double the dollars on the money *out* or the money *in*?" asked McAteer, speaking quickly while retaining the languid air of a country gentleman. "I mean, if I'm not there, you've got a zero and we know that half a nought is none. Then you could say double the dollar, and that would be two. Paltry. Then you could say, half the twenty at stake, being a nice round number, like a ten."

"Which is steep."

"Of course, I was thinking eight."

"Three," said Ben.

"Six."

"Meet you at four."

"Five."

Hands were shaken, and money passed.

"So you're English?"

"You Irish?" asked Ben.

"If you're meaning at the moment I came here when I was lower than my mother's knee, then I am. Though I'll consider myself part of this city and nothing more. How about you save some of that money for the moment and allow me to buy you a steak dinner?"

"Steak?" asked Ben, and his stomach rumbled to swing the vote.

The two men took a streetcar uptown to Browne's Chophouse on Thirty-third and Eighth. McAteer paid their fares, and Ben sat staring at all those walking on the streets, as if once he had been among them, and now he was raised a short step, not on a subway, nor a taxi fare, but a tram rider. In the restaurant of dark woods and sawdust floors, he stared at the walls lined with photographs of actors and actresses, their fame proved by framed playbills. Both men selected the thickest chops on display and asked them to be cooked through. Waiting patiently with full mugs, they sat over their plates, marked only by a pickled walnut, until the steaming slabs of meat were slapped down before them.

"You're a friend of my boss, Mr. Farrell?"

McAteer shrugged. "Irish and Irish, all friends and favors. Go by there once in a while to see what he's got going. A bit shabby for my tastes, but you never know what you can dig up. You didn't box as well as you played."

"I didn't have to," said Ben.

"An Englishman your age," mused McAteer. "You a conchie?"

"An objector?" Ben shook his head and reached for his beer. "Was demobbed."

"Why?" probed McAteer. "The war's not exactly over."

"Is for me," said Ben. He pointed to his chest. "Wounded. Useless to them."

"That's funny," said McAteer. "You looked pretty good in the ring."

Ben stared at him. "That's the way it is."

McAteer held his hands up in surrender. "Not pressing. I'm with you pal. We're all with you."

"That's the way it is," repeated Ben, turning his attention back to his food.

Coffee and tea were slapped down before them in pots. Ben said nothing.

"Say," said McAteer, "what you told Farrell this morning, that your father played in London. That true?"

Ben nodded.

"You grew up like that?"

"With my ear to the side of a piano."

"He taught you to play?"

Ben nodded again.

"That's how you earned a dollar?"

"Sometimes."

"But mostly you were an improviser?"

Ben didn't answer.

"You made up your living? Floated? One job, then another?"

Ben smiled. "That sort of thing."

"You must be good at cards. Growing up in that kind of place."

"Made a penny or two."

"Where are you staying?" asked McAteer.

"Bowery."

"I got a bed I could rent you," he said, "in the room above my wife and me." The man was fast talking, inquisitive. Wanted something indefinable from him, but Ben couldn't grasp it yet. Meanwhile, why not? Another night on the street, the unaffordable cost of a hotel, but a room, a room so unexpectedly gifted where no one would know where he was, that he would not know where he was, the appeal was strong.

"Sure," said Ben. "I can pay."

"Of course you'll pay," said McAteer.

He stared at the pin on McAteer's lapel and smiled to himself, thought of Chimer, Douglas, and David. It was a pleasure to think back, through the war, out the other side to the time before all he had seen and smelled was the dirt of men. The scheme had worked for the better part of the year. The four of them would go drinking together, in a posh place, somewhere in the West End.

They each had a specific outfit. A Sunday best suit, with gaudy fob watches and garish ties and too-stiff collars. They were hard to place. Sitting amid club men, the odd tourist, here were these theatrical types, all bluster and noise, always the right side of exuberance. If they were challenged as to occupation, they called themselves actors, not far from the truth. Often they were subjected to stares, but they ignored them, knowing the British depended on silence as a withering retort and relied on fate to provide comeuppance.

They would talk loudly and run up a bill of champagne. At the end of the night, Chimer, Douglas, and David would throw their smeared napkins on the table and wait outside for Ben to pay the bill. He would make an appropriate show of searching for his wallet. When it couldn't be found, he'd offer his diamond pin. Not *his* exactly, borrowed on the pawn out in Braintree, ten pounds for a month's use. No London owner would trust an actor on the look of the pin. He'd always be walked to the local pawnshop, and there, in plain sight, the pin would be valued at one hundred twenty pounds, more than enough to cover their thirty-pound evening. Ben would revisit the restaurant the following morning with the thirty pounds, reclaim his pin, and return again with his boys by the end of the week. By now the owner presumed Ben was some kind of theater swell, with his polished mustache, his good looks, his diamonds and champagne tastes. They'd drink again all night and once more Ben would offer the tiepin as collateral, and ask for another fifty pounds to be borrowed on top of it. Of course the owner would comply; he knew the worth of the diamond pin. Only he didn't have the eye to know the difference between one pin and another, and was left holding a two-pound fake, Ben and his lads buoyed by their free meal and cash in hand.

Their scheme had worked all over London until someone snagged just off Piccadilly and all four of them were turned over to the courts. Of course, they had done little wrong, merely offered up jewels as collateral that turned out to be near worthless. Yet their judge took it upon himself to interpret intention and was in no mood for forgiveness. The country had been at war two weeks, and the frivolity of young men was discouraged while others waited in winding queues to enlist. They were told bluntly to either join the front of the line or face three years' imprisonment. Ben did the internal calculations for the four of them — a few months in the army, a war come and gone, and they'd be back in London with soldiers' stripes. It had been an easy decision.

Chapter Six

MᴄAᴛᴇᴇʀ's ʙᴜɪʟᴅɪɴɢ ʜᴀᴅ in common with its King Street neighbors the inner appearance of a rickety nest, where each apartment's trash was left beside the fire buckets on the central landing by the doors. Even in April's chill, small clouds of flies departed and reassembled with the passage of the two men. Light came only when a door opened, the windows of the stairwell blocked by rusted bars and buildings close enough to touch.

Despite the roofs that Ben had recently slept under, he was still surprised by the roughness of McAteer's spare room. It was the way the man dressed. He wore his money. Barely a dollar was invested in his surroundings. No electricity, only a gas mantle. A stack of books in the corner, a narrow bed, a table and a pair of chairs. Old newspapers lay on the floor. The pillow was stained by hair wash and the sheets had the stale, sweaty smell of alcoholic excretions, but all in all, it was a safe lodging, and more importantly, chosen from an act of randomness. If Ben had little idea where he was, then how could any British official? And sheets, pillows, Ben was not long enough out of France not to take pleasure in the simplicities.

"The wife isn't one for spit and polish," explained McAteer. "Five dollars a week to you." He pointed to the window. "There's a school to the left. Sewing shop the other side. If you don't get the screaming, you get the yammering. You all right with that? And the el train, it comes down Sixth, rattles with a boom."

Ben nodded, withheld the smile. When McAteer shut the door behind him, Ben lay down, sore, exhausted, but content at the day.

><

Not bad boys, not bad, he said to himself. He had woken on the street
with immediate necessity before him. Now he might think harder on
a future. Too tired now. Here comes sleep, four walls about him, a
blanket, a mattress, breakfast to look forward to. Drifting deep and
silent throughout the night. And when he woke early, Ben leaned out
the window into the morning's hubbub and smiled.

What's wrong with noise?, thought Ben. With wanting to live
down close to the street with the sound of metallic cranks being
turned in engines, of herds of children chasing the water trucks to
clean their feet, of families and open windows, of tram gongs and
steamship calls and chattering stoops? This is a city isn't it? A real
city, a big city is where you can't escape noise, it comes up the hall
in metal cap shoes and shrieks through the windows in fire bells
and thuds overhead with neighbors' boots and leaks through the
walls in muffled conversation. Ben wanted thoughts that might
cohere to be dissolved by a street shout.

   He wandered down the corridor to the bathroom, ran water into
a shallow tin basin, and brought it back to his room to shave. For
the first time since France, he was excited by the thought that he
might be able to talk openly, even revive some part of himself
numb from over a year of soldiering. It was the prospect of friendship that he anticipated as he ran the blade carefully either side of
his mustache, the opportunity to move outside animal self-con-
cern. He felt a little guilty at the thought and hoped the boys
weren't listening, or if they were, would be able to forgive him.
Above all, Ben wondered how well he might imitate the normal,
and whether a sharp man would look at him and know in an instant
how different he had become.

McAteer knocked and entered the room. He wore bright white
trousers and a neat blue blazer, rubbed thready at the elbows. He
stood before his new tenant and clapped his hands together softly,
surveying the room.

Ben ran his eyes up and down his landlord's clothes. "Where'd you moor your yacht?"

McAteer wasn't listening, but looking about again. "You didn't have anyone up here last night did you?"

"No," said Ben.

"Christ what a noise. Howling like a loon." He gazed into Ben's eyes. "You know, if that was just a dream, you should really be in some kind of a hospital."

Ben made sure that McAteer's words had been accompanied by a smile. He looked him up and down, in those white trousers and his fading blazer, a different size altogether from him.

"I was thinking," said Ben. "My rent's, what, twenty a month?"

McAteer nodded.

"Now say," said Ben. "If we were to go shopping and I was to get you a couple of hundred dollars of clothes, how many weeks could we write off with that?"

"Well clothes, as soon as they walk out a store, they're second-hand, say a third of the price. A third of two hundred is sixty-six, so I'd reckon you could push that to four months. But that would be if I needed some clothes, which I don't, making it a needless luxury, the sort that drives us in this city, so we'll knock a month off and call it three."

"Shakes," ordered Ben and the two men pressed their hands together. "I'll need a small loan, repaid by the end of the day," added Ben. "Well, in truth, not that small."

"What makes you think I'd have dollars about me?"

"The yacht," said Ben, running his hand across McAteer's blazer.

Lord and Taylor could be sniffed a block away; the sweet scent of perfume leaked out the department store's doors every time they opened. The smell just sat on the block, like valley fog, waiting for a wind strong enough to disperse it. Ben stared at the windows with their elaborate showcases of female mannequins, women, more women, none real. Each of the windows reflected the Eden of imagined America. Ohio's wheat fields, California's orange groves,

Rhode Island's gentle ocean, each of them inhabited by a pair of mannequins walking under parasols. Not the old fashions of Europe, with their layers of crinoline and bustle and bows resting on exaggerated bottoms, but slim fabrics, close to the skin, reflecting, amazingly enough, the shape of a woman. Not a hint of the war, not the merest suggestion that the world is alight. So perhaps it is not, thought Ben, perhaps it is Europe that is deluded. For if you do not hear the guns, do not have your streets populated by the gray and the limbless, why would you dress for a funeral? They turned their bodies to allow a wave of women to exit the store.

Through the lobby with the aisles of mannequins draped in satin dresses and topped with saucer hats and ostrich plumes. Past the ladies' department, full of women dipping their hands in and out of powdered gloves searching for the snuggest fit. Ben browsed the aisles of the men's department with McAteer, accompanied by a breathless young shopgirl with a pencil behind her ear, all hair flicks and encouragement of the wallet. Two forty-dollar suits, a sixty-five-dollar tuxedo, two pairs of twenty-dollar shoes, four shirts, four ties.

Ben paid for the clothes with McAteer's money, two hundred twenty-two dollars in cash. He put the receipt in his pocket and glanced about to see if the assistant's floorwalker was near.

"What time do you get off for lunch?" he asked the girl, leaning toward her as he pushed his wallet back within his jacket pocket.

"One," she said.

Ben paused for a moment and gave her his finest, most open smile. "I was hoping you'd join me for a walk?"

"I don't know," she said, never breaking eye contact. "I only get an hour."

"Just you and me." McAteer looked the other way as Ben talked. "I'll meet you at the library, right between the lions."

Outside, Ben and McAteer crossed the street to a drugstore and cooled themselves with two iced seltzers, enjoying the stir of the fan.

"How are you going to pay me back?" asked McAteer.

"Patience," said Ben raising a cautionary finger.

Ben was struck by the number of women in the street uptown. Pushing prams, walking in pairs, gloved, tilted hats, all dressed in white. McAteer explained that they were rare below Forty-second Street. Ben watched them pass, a different species from the shop-girls and shirtwaist workers that surrounded them downtown. They were unblemished by paychecks, walking the streets with petite purses cuffed to their wrists by little gold chains. He wondered if the four of them would have had a chance with girls like that.

Just past one o'clock, Ben saw the shopgirl head north toward the library.

"Excuse me," he said to the counterman. "Could you keep this bag for me?" He slid the morning's shopping across the counter along with a dollar bill. "I'll be ten minutes." The man nodded and stowed the large bag beneath the counter.

McAteer followed Ben through the doors of Lord and Taylor. They rose in the elevator back to the third floor, where they were greeted by a shopgirl at the start of her shift. With her assiduous help, Ben began to order exactly the same items that they had bought not an hour before, coming to the identical total of two hundred twenty-two dollars.

Announcing that he wished to continue shopping in another department, they headed down to the ground floor and walked to the returns department, where Ben presented his new goods along with the receipt from their earlier visit.

"I'd like to return these," said Ben, handing the clothes back to the assistant, a slim, sharply dressed man with the wide-set eyes of a cat.

The assistant sat up in his seat and looked at the large bag now sitting in front of him.

"All of them?" he drawled with discontent, accepting the receipt from Ben.

"Everything," said Ben.

"Was there a problem with them?" asked the assistant, pushing himself to his feet so that he could stare down his nose into the bag.

"Don't ask me," said Ben dismissively. "They were a gift for my friend here."

McAteer, surprised, managed a brief nod. "I'm known for my particularity," he huffed. "Never let a thing near my skin that wasn't hand-stitched in England."

The assistant smiled faintly and looked back up at Ben, unamused. "Will that be credit?"

"Cash," said McAteer on Ben's behalf.

"I'm not sure I have that much right now," said the man, staring at the receipt. "I'll just write out the credit slip."

"I'm sure if you actually have a good look," said Ben warmly, "you might be able to find it."

The assistant looked up, resentfully dipped a hand into the till, and laid out a mixture of tens and twenties before them.

They crossed the street, reclaimed their bags from the counterman, and in high spirits, full of laughter, walked west, until turning south on Sixth Avenue.

"You know," said McAteer, "when I saw you punching, I thought, now I could make a dollar or two off fists like that. It's why I had you in. Now I'm thinking altogether differently."

"I'm rising in your opinion?" asked Ben.

"Like yeast."

By the end of his second week Ben was almost beginning to enjoy himself at Miner's. He was in a comforting maelstrom of noise. The kindly McAteer came to watch him every now and then. Always alone, never with the wife. But he soon felt that other eyes were studying him, ones that fixed upon him for minutes at a time, ones that made him hot and ill at ease. Ben knew well the danger of the game he was playing. To be discovered by the British authorities would be to be shipped home, face court-martial. Despite the wounds, they would shoot him. It had happened before. What other options were open to them? At such a distance, Ben had sympathy with power. Should he presume the worst and run? But then where to?

The stranger was always the first to open his applause for the orchestra. The string section was convinced he was from Tin Pan Alley, or a recruiter from one of the hotel orchestras. But he looked only at Ben and Ben knew it. When Ben spoke after the shows he de-emphasized his Englishness, hoping that should the man be standing close, all he would hear would be that strange New York mixture of short a's and slurred brogue. He didn't confess his fears to McAteer, didn't want to be exiled from the comfort of his room, his first place of peace and privacy since enlisting eighteen months ago.

Every Friday came the most dangerous evening at Miner's, amateur night. Aspirants who could afford to pay Farrell a dollar before lunchtime were permitted to step on the stage to be judged by a critical and inebriated audience. The more experienced members of the orchestra wore wide-brimmed hats. Entering their pit, Ben would watch the gallery policeman wave his cane at the groups of young men that crowded the pews. "All of youse now, hats off." There followed a palpable rush of air as two hundred derbies, boaters, and flat caps were swept from the crowns of heads.

The first note of the night came from Ben's fingertips, the signal for the artillery of noise. Everything rushed and hissed, ringing in Ben's ears, noise without threat, the shudder of the timpani without the quake of the roof above his head. Once he was under the drum thunder, he barely noticed the weight of the stares. There followed the parade of characters, desperate to take that evening's five-dollar purse. Few made it through their act. The last Friday, a gap-toothed girl who had begun to warble through "Won't You Dance with Me?" was greeted with a unanimous, thundering "No." She left in tears. The house policemen did their best, tapping talkers with long canes, eyes out for the over-inebriated, the pugnacious.

Potbellied waiters, white aprons and muscled arms, prepared for resistance. They would help me, wouldn't they, thought Ben, if the English should come?

For they could prove a sentimental crowd. That night, a saccharine newsboy quartet raised the roof. Ben and his piano were caught in a hail of pennies, hitting his head, getting caught in his lap. All the musicians protected their instruments, flute under jacket, back shielding violin, Ben's body draped over the piano, listening to the clinks and pings of the bouncing coins as Farrell handed out the evening's purse. Ben looking up after the financial artillery had eased and met that continuous gaze from the first row, unblinking eyes of calculation undisguised by the sweetness of the smile. McAteer was waiting for him outside the theater, a battered boater perched on top of his head, an old and favored hat. He was gesturing urgently for Ben to move from the stage door.

Chapter Seven

BEN TROTTED QUICKLY across the street and they strode together through the night, toward Washington Square, ignoring the few streetcars that clattered along with men hanging out the back for the benefits of the breeze. It was the fifth day of May and a prelude of summer warmth had descended across the city.

They entered a bar off Fourth Street, a mean-looking place with a row of stale lunch sandwiches sitting on a table in the middle of the room, covered by thin linen and studded with a turbulent pattern of flies. It was one of the last bars in Manhattan yet to be electrified. The old gas lamps shone their dull halos against the black-and-white wall tiles. McAteer led them through, shook a man's hand, headed through a darkened basement, along a narrow corridor, and then back up into an alley.

"What exactly are we running from?" asked Ben.

"You know you've got another admirer. In the theater," said McAteer huffing, finally slowing his trot to a more considerate speed. "You know who he is?"

"No," said Ben. "He seems to leave me alone."

"Is that the right way to be looking at it?" asked McAteer.

"At what?"

"What if he's a civil servant?"

Ben shrugged.

"An English civil servant," said McAteer.

Ben tried to keep his eyes steady. Of all things, it was what he feared the most, even while refusing to admit it to himself. That his arrival in New York would set off some invisible network of bells, jangling from the Bowery to the halls of a consulate. That there might exist some special squad invented to apprehend deserters before they leaked all their knowledge and infected other countries with the truth of what they had seen.

"How can I know for sure?" choked Ben.

"You can't," said McAteer. He patted Ben on the back. "It's all right. You don't have to be certain, you just play the cards don't you? When the dealer's got a strong hand, you change tables. Just don't go back to Miner's."

Ben nodded.

"Can't imagine going back to the war?"

Ben closed his eyes and gave a brief shake of the head.

"So you were a deserter?"

Ben looked straight at him. "Hadn't you guessed?"

"Just need to know what we've brought into the house."

"You and the wife?"

"A very opinionated woman," said McAteer. "She'd approve of desertion, believe me. As do I. For differing reasons of course. She's a socialist, thinks war is a poor man dying for a rich man's quarrel, but in my eye, I think of fighting as a playground business. And this country's not fool enough to join in the fists. Mexico yes, small enough to go down there and bang a few heads about, but Europe, entirely too big, too messy. Could dizzy yourself trying to sort that one out. I'd have sat it out, same as you."

Ben was looking back over his shoulder. A man came toward them. Ben could smell herring, and saw he carried his fish wrapped in Yiddish newspapers, nothing to do with the presence at Miner's. He looked back at McAteer. "I didn't exactly sit it out."

"You must relax a bit," continued McAteer, "You're a corked bottle. Was a soldier myself once. Two years of marching. It changes the way a man walks."

"Were you really?"

McAteer considered it. "No, no, in truth, I wasn't. Did think about it, but the army seemed too dull a place in peace and nowhere a man should be in war."

"How about Farrell?" asked Ben. "If it's an embassy man nosing around, will he talk?"

"And tell him what?" asked McAteer. "That you gave him a wrong name, that he doesn't know where you live? Besides, he's got no love of the English. Whatever he thinks you are, he likes you for it." He motioned for Ben to start walking beside him. "I think we're going to have to find you another line of work."

"I suppose so," said Ben.

"Lucky you met me, lucky you are. So you'll not be working tomorrow then, will you?"

"A holiday," said Ben relaxing. "We'll call it May Day."

"Then let's make a real day of it," said McAteer.

That Saturday, for the first time in America, eyes studied the white shriek of Ben's scars. The Englishman pulled up his swimming costume to cover them. McAteer continued to stare. Ben had endured. Ben knew that McAteer had wanted to put him up for a fight, like a spurred cock or a collared dog, but last week Ben hoped he had proved there was no point. Had he not already repaid him with a fine suit? Did they not already look like members of the same gang, dressed in their identical department store clothes? McAteer could look at his scars all he wished, for of all the scars on Ben's body, the only one that shamed him was the white crescent on his hand.

A month before Chimer, David, and Douglas had died, Captain Traven had chosen Ben for a patrol. It was the first time he had ever been selected apart from his friends. For two days they had been subjected to the cries of a wounded English soldier shot through the stomach while on reconnaissance. It was a fatal wound even if he could be dragged back to the trench. During the day, the man's cries had elicited every reaction from compassion to ridicule, but he had plagued the entire company in the darkness with low constant moaning, a living ghost from some penny dreadful that had unnerved them all. No one could stand another night of it. The day before, in the early morning, Chimer had whispered, "I might have to go out there and shoot him myself." Douglas had answered, "They'd have range on him wouldn't they? You'd have to knife him." They'd dropped into silence, accompanied by the constant groans.

It was the unnaturalness of it all that perturbed the company. Normally the Germans had been impeccable in allowing stretcher bearers to attend the wounded. There were rumors that two German prisoners had been taken by the English but when they'd come under fire heading back to their lines, the officer in charge had shot both captives in the head. True or false, it explained the German reaction to the one wounded English soldier. They had collected their own dead, then fired at the British bearers sent to collect the wounded man. It seemed to imply some sort of wrong-doing, but the implicated officer had denied everything. Captain Traven shared his dugout.

Traven would not be accompanying the party. Ben reported at ten in the evening outside Traven's post, where he met with his bald-headed sergeant, who always smelled strongly of Keating's insect powder. They nodded in recognition of each other, but there were no smiles swapped. Traven's batman was cooking the captain his supper on a small gas stove. Ben could hear the bacon sizzling in the dark. To their surprise, each of the waiting men was offered a rasher. Ben kept the bacon pressed inside his cheek and sucked the flavor from it, all the while studying the sergeant's shiny pate. He had no idea what tied the two of them together in the task, though he knew Traven had access to all their records and this sergeant knew of his past arrests. He could only imagine that the two men had decided a criminal record qualified him for the night's task.

The sergeant was called inside the dugout and emerged not two minutes later. "We're cutting wire," he said curtly, and pointed down the trench, indicating that Ben should follow him. Ben knew it was a lie; they weren't even carrying a pair of cutters. He had sensed from the moment he had been summoned that they were headed toward the shrieking man.

The two men slithered through the muck, not a trace of grass beyond their wire, just different degrees of solid and damp dirt. Ben could feel the imprint of horses' hooves and the deep ruts of wagons, and the looser fetid earth of filled-in latrines and soil churned by artillery. The lines rarely changed. They were always digging where someone had dug before. The moans of the soldier grew louder as they approached. They came at him from behind. The sergeant touched Ben's shoulder to stop him, then slid something cold into his hand. The blade had been muddied so as not to catch any reflection of torch or starlight. Ben raised the knife and looked at his companion. The sergeant jabbed his finger toward the soldier and ran a finger across his own throat.

Ben knew he'd be cursed if he did it. Like a good dog he'd accepted his scrap of bacon from Traven. He thought of the sins he'd committed before, bilking men of small amounts, cheap card tricks, rewarding sleights of hand with diamond pins. And Traven, or this sergeant, had thought murder was his next step. He held the knife, but shook his head. The muttered moans were very close.

The sergeant pointed at the soldier and prodded Ben with the hilt of his own knife. Ben shook his head again in silence. The sergeant slithered up beside him and cupped his hand over Ben's ear. "Do it," he whispered. "Or you and your lot are on *every* patrol, *every* night, and you'll be over first *every* fucking time."

Ben had been on the line long enough to know that life was simply luck. To have fortune removed from the equation, to be placed deliberately in harm's way, meant death for all four of them. A sudden swell of impotent anger fueled him. For a moment he wondered if he could kill the sergeant instead, plunge the knife straight between his eyes hard enough to crack his skull.

Ben slid away from his superior. It took seconds. Four movements to get within reach. The soldier turned his head from where he was propped against the rough stump of a tree and smiled weakly. Ben hoped the man was in a state of delirium. He pushed himself quickly to his knees, held his hand over the man's mouth, and drew the blade across his throat. The soldier bit deep into the fleshy part between Ben's thumb and forefinger. The pain was extraordinary. Ben clenched his own teeth in silence. And when the soldier did not loosen his savage grip, Ben took the knife and angrily stabbed him twice through the throat. The teeth opened; Ben pulled his hand away. The soldier slumped over and used the last of his strength to pat the ground softly. Ben lay on his back, breathing hard, cupping his good hand over his mouth for silence. After a minute, he crawled back toward the sergeant, who patted him on his back. Ben ignored the gesture, holding his bloody hand to his own mouth, and headed back toward the gap in their wire.

When Ben returned to his unit, Chimer saw the handkerchief tied about his hand. "You all right?"

"Caught it on the wire," he said in a voice so free from emotion that none of them had ever inquired again. But the teeth marks were still there. All Ben had to do was look down on the Coney Island beach and see the little ring of white scars to remind himself that some things would not let themselves be forgotten.

McAteer turned his eyes from the scars of Ben's torso to scan the shores of Coney Island, while Ben listened to the high-pitched sounds the wind carried, the whine of the Wurlitzer, that low, rumbling murmur of a great Coney crowd beyond sight. There was no one else in the gray Atlantic. Ben had never seen the ocean before, save for his few days at Osborne House. When they'd shipped to France, all the portholes had been blackened, all lights dimmed or extinguished. No smoking cigarettes. The first beach he had stood on was at Calais, under thick fog. They had been handed a ground-sheet, a jackknife, and two hundred rounds of ammunition. The lads had looked at one another and weighed the shot in their hands. Chimer had barely been able to lift his pack. "All this for a shilling a day," he had moaned. Douglas and Ben had each carried part of his rations. Then they had boarded a train, and Ben remembered looking about him and understanding for the first time how others saw them, a company made only of men, all the same age, same haircut, all uniformed and carrying identical equipment.

He marched down to the edge of the water, let the frigid first wave shock his body, and then waded into the next assault. The scars were hidden beneath his costume, and there he was minutes later, walking back up the beach to Coney Island, with its thousands of day-trippers and flocks of young women, and carnival noise and prizes to be won and fortunes guessed, and the fading percussion of the waves. Is this, can this possibly be the same earth as the one I've left behind?, thought Ben. What did it demand to join this new world?

Ben and McAteer ate at a hot dog stand, chewing through their nickel meals then wiping their mustaches free of mustard. After sunset, Coney Island was switched on and stood out against the night. The towers of Steeplechase and Luna Parks, set just behind the Coney beachfront, were studded with thousands of lightbulbs, so bright they hurt the eyes with their blatant illumination. Ben was thrilled, and the thought of being recaptured remained deep at the back of his mind, well behind the Coney glare and the presence of women. They walked among rich and poor, citified and country-clad under the vast glass dome. The noise came at Ben, and all seemed to call to him — boosters, shillabers, spielers, barkers, ballyhoo men. We want you. You, you, you there, yes sir, most likely, Mr. Gentleman, head this way, over here, no here. Here.

He rode beside McAteer on the largest of the Ferris wheels, swaying gently back and forth, pressed close to his seat by a metal bar. Ben stared out at the lights of Coney in amazement. Beneath them swarmed a city, a dense army of people pushing for entertainment and diversion. He did not sense the warmth of humanity or goodwill but a panorama of distraction, noise, and ignorance. So many languages were spoken beneath them that Coney seemed more like some biblical city of madness than a heaven to balance the hell of France. And yet Ben felt strangely settled amid the cacophony, happy to have one friend.

"You need to get yourself a girl," said McAteer as they moved up and over and down again. "You like girls don't you?"

"I do."

"Good looking lad like you, can't be so hard."

"That's not it," said Ben.

"What is it then?"

"I don't know. It used to be easy."

McAteer nodded. "Just think of it as starting again then."

But what if they can see inside me?, worried Ben.

He didn't worry what McAteer thought of him. He presumed theirs a mutual attraction. That McAteer was willing to make deals, to hang around the places that they had met, boxing rings and music halls, meant that despite his gentlemanly clothes, he was well acquainted with the lower rungs of life. At first Ben had thought him retired, but then he reconsidered, suspecting McAteer was akin to him, not entirely aboveboard, a man who perhaps made his money on the side, a card player, a grifter of some sort.

Once Coney's lights were dimmed, the two men retreated to the Oriental Hotel. Their room was, to Ben, unbearably quiet. They rolled into their beds, but Ben could not stand the silence of the deep night. It was never so still in Manhattan. Coney had gone quiet as quickly as the flick of a light switch. While McAteer slept, Ben dressed and went for a walk next to the surf. The evening had brought in a salty fog to shoo the wind and rain. There was nothing to be heard apart from the lick of small waves. All Coney's guests were gone, and the uninvited had come up from beneath rickety piers, the small huddles of poor families lying on their mattresses of newspapers. Three in the morning was too late to beg, only time to doze, entrenched in sand beneath the blanket of fog. A sleeping army in the mists, vulnerable. Ben sat cross-legged and watched the sad sight, pulling a cigarette from his pocket, wondering at the ways of the world and his own sudden change in mood. Between the deep sea and the cheap entertainment scuttled those on the edge, trying to work their way back in. A voice beside him. Smelled the smoke. Have a cigarette? Of course. Money for me sir? Of course, said Ben. He pulled a dollar from his pocket. You're a kind man. No, said Ben, I'm really not.

At four in the morning, Ben returned to the room. He sat on his bed, pillows bunched behind him, watching McAteer sleep. His father's death in London, his mother's disappearance had always made him eager for friends. Very skillful at gathering them, putting them together, all his lads. He and Chimer, he and David, even he and Douglas were close, seated about the pub alcoves, orchestra seats, mess tables. Until they came apart, no longer together, separated from one another, from their own hands, their fingers, their kneecaps and noses, helmets and heads. Bodies could be close, bodies could be scattered. Past, get out of my head, thought Ben. Too quiet in here.

"Julius?" he said. Then, much louder, "Julius?"

"What?" mumbled McAteer, groaning to attention. "What's the matter with you? Can't sleep?"

"No," said Ben. "No chance tonight."

McAteer swung his feet over the side of the bed and sat up.

"Old man's bladder," he huffed, and left in search of a plumbed bathroom. When he returned he sat on the edge of his bed, and instead of swinging his feet back under the covers, faced Ben and asked, "Have you ever considered a career on the stage?"

"As an actor?" said Ben, glad for the conversation.

McAteer nodded. "Without an audience and paid, well paid as any Broadway lad. Fortune without fame. In my own experience, entirely preferential. I've been thinking about how I'd include you, use you, so to speak. I want to adapt your talents, what you did at Lord and Taylor, that sort of thing."

At that, Ben turned on his side to face the old man.

McAteer talked at Ben for the better part of an hour. He wove his words slowly, making sure that Ben could follow every step of his intentions. Very simply, McAteer had admitted to being what, in this new country, was called a bunco man, a flimflammer, a con artist, but either way, Ben recognized him as a consummate professional to his erstwhile amateur.

Ben stared at the flaky paint on the ceiling, amazed at what he had heard. Most decisions to come to New York were concoctions of desperation and reason, and in this respect, Ben knew he was little different from other immigrants. He had come to hide and to appear, to forget and to contrive, to run away yet cease to move. I will be, Ben had thought, whatever I wish to be, anything but what I was. McAteer was offering him an extension of his desires. He had witnessed the legal world; what was war if it wasn't legal?

"What's the wrong end of this stick?" asked Ben. "What if I mess it up?"

"It's not for everyone," said McAteer. "Takes nerves, a calm, calm stomach. But for you, your particular case, I think it's a riskier wager. Play me the wrong way, I'll march your embassy to your door. They'll swing you, you know."

Ben said nothing. McAteer stood and Ben could see now that he was other people as well as the man Ben had taken him for. He looked into McAteer's eyes, then offered him his hand. "In the morning write to Farrell," said McAteer. "Tell him you quit. Tell him you're leaving for the West, in case anyone should ask."

"Fine."

"So you want to know more?" McAteer walked over to a small portmanteau that he had carried out from the city. He clicked the lock open and withdrew a sheaf of papers.

"You just happen to have brought all of this with you?" asked Ben.

"I'm a flimflam man," said McAteer smiling. "We don't believe in coincidences. I was going to wake you early anyways."

><

The first thing McAteer showed Ben was a half-page newspaper advertisement torn from a midwestern daily: "Looking to invest in solid business. References necessary. Low rate of interest." The return address was a New York bank.

"I place these in a dozen papers. Asking for a reference'll discourage most of them," said McAteer. "The rest will write you. Most of them are honest enough men, but they want you to know it, and they'll send you more than you ever wish to know. I've had letters from pastors and mothers. Brings a tear to the eye. The best ones, the ones you're looking to respond to, are the ones with a major ambition. They get invited up to New York, at their own expense. Two cents a word of advertising. That's all it costs to meet your mark."

"And then?" asked Ben. "How do you take them?"

McAteer put some more papers before him, this time a filled-out application for the imaginary loan that he was offering.

Ben read, "Henry Jergens. The Paseo, Kansas City, Missouri."

"This man," said McAteer, "is a cattleman. If we want him, he'll be coming to the city next week. Not a cowboy, not a rancher, but on the bloody side of the business. Family owns a string of abattoirs."

"So you sell him on that? On meat? On real estate?"

"That's the bait," said McAteer, "but then you switch. You look for something he likes but doesn't know the ins and outs of. I got a friend out west, done some work for each other over the years. He sent me these."

McAteer put a series of newspaper clippings before Ben. They were various accounts of social events attended by the Jergens family. Everything from state fairs to funerals.

"Are they rich?" asked Ben.

"Of course," said McAteer. "Maybe we can take him for twenty-five, thirty thousand."

"So what do you take him on?"

"Look at that clipping," said McAteer, pointing at a description of Henry Jergens's own wedding. "He had a band take a train all the way from New Orleans. What does that tell you?"

"He's partial to music?" asked Ben. "How on earth do you take a man on music?"

McAteer tapped the side of his nose and proceeded to explain.

"It sounds a little complicated," said Ben when McAteer had finished. "Better if I just stick to my own graft."

"Fifty dollars there, another hundred here, sure," said McAteer. "Keep at it. You'll be worth a thousand dollars by the time you're thirty. Or maybe you can make that with me in the next month. Maybe more."

Ben seemed unconvinced. Anything that might involve him further with the law was anathema to him.

"Don't you think I have a little much to lose?" Ben asked. "If there are agents already tracking me?"

"What you've been playing is checkers and I want to teach you chess," said McAteer. "How to think ahead. Five moves, ten moves ahead. Everything I do I know before. Even for me to make this play to you. Ask yourself, how do I do it? Why are you going to say yes? Because I took time to weaken your position."

"Really?" asked Ben, a small smile upon his face. "And how did you do that?"

"By undermining what you were beginning to consider normal," said McAteer. "I befriend you. Then I help you get your job at Miner's, then I take your job away. Send a pal of mine to see you every day of the week at the theater, making sure you note him. I bide my time, tell you he's working for your government. And you can't go back, you're open to my suggestion."

Ben smiled. "So why not go back to my job now that I know? Why would I trust you now?"

"You shouldn't," said McAteer. "You should never trust me. But you can like me. A very different prospect. And I can teach you more than a piano can. I already have."

Ben nodded. "So why do you need me?" Intrigue was cause for distraction. Everything he had done before the war seemed slight and transient compared with the game McAteer had laid out.

"Like I said," said McAteer, "I can see ten steps ahead. You're the most perfect convincer for what I have in mind. I saw you play a boxer, I saw you perform the humble applicant in Miner's, gentleman of sorts for the shopgirls. You're raw, I can see that, but I can make you better than good."

Chapter Eight

THE STREETCAR STRIKE did not slow down the return from Coney Island. McAteer and Ben rode on the open-top deck of the bus under an indeterminable gray sky with Ben's bundle of wet swimming gear wrapped in a towel. The only wind was manufactured by the speed of the vehicle, threatening to whip their hats from their heads.

Sunday evening, Ben did not write a gracious letter of resignation to Farrell as McAteer had directed, but opted to visit him instead. The Irishman was in the back office, behind the evening's take, a sky rise of coppers and small silver stacked above tenements of dirty dollar bills. Ben sat when he was asked to, and immediately informed Farrell of his intention to head to California.

"I'm sorry to see you go," said Farrell, standing to shake his hand, but instead of releasing him, he motioned for Ben to sit again. "This may not make much sense as a question," he said, "but I've been thinking to myself, the day you first came to me, there was another man visiting. The kind who likes to get involved in a man's life. You ever meet a Julius McAteer?"

Ben shook his head with an overdose of insouciance. "Don't remember the name."

Farrell smiled. "If you should ever come across him, just watch yourself. Not the kind of man who'd have been laying the molasses on me or you, less there was a point to the sweetness. That's why he was here, poking around for over a month. Be wary of trusting a man like that." Farrell put his hands on the table before him and huffed. "What do I know? Maybe you're the same kind of man. He's a flimflammer; he'll turn on you, he's dropped men before. Man like you needs a safe hole, someone to trust. This may not be much, playing a box in the Bowery, but it's the straighter line. Don't find yourself trusting a man like that."

"Why not?"

"Chances are, young London, you've got a lot to lose. Careful where you put your trust." Farrell was trying to pierce him with the stare of a schoolmaster. "But we're both forgetting; you're heading out to California."

"That's right."

"And should any man come asking, that's where I'll tell him to look."

Ben nodded, knew the understanding was reached, and stood again to reach for Farrell's hand.

Free to play a thousand roles, whatever McAteer asks of me. Now that's freedom, that's getting lost, isn't it? They're not going to find me when I'm not even me. Besides, he thought, McAteer was a fellow flimflammer. What greater regard could one professional have for another? He could only admire McAteer for having picked him up and identified him so quickly, long before Ben had thought to look back at him.

It was May the twelfth, the first hot day of a hot year. The stairwell was even more sloughy than the room. By the time Ben reached the ground floor he found himself a sudden victim of the oncoming summer: moist armpits, sticky dryness of salt set on skin, a dank suit, shiny clefts of flesh. Sweat started on his brow, dripped down the side of his nose, pooled above his lips waiting for his tongue or the back of his hand. Air so hot Ben got the odd sensation that he was breathing in someone else's exhalations.

McAteer appeared from the doorway and took a seat next to Ben on the stoop, where the Englishman sat smoking a Turkish cigarette.

"What a day," moaned McAteer, flapping his hat to create a

breeze. "Let's go find you some more of your free clothes. And don't think I'd never seen that one before. You ready for this? You going to appreciate my pearls of wisdom?"

"You know," said Ben, smiling broadly, "I'm actually looking forward to this."

After a profitable hour in and out of Stern Brothers' Department Store on Forty-second, they were swept by the crowds down Sixth Avenue, hopping between taxis, buses, and cars that honked their way around horse-drawn wagons. The high walls of the buildings threw the city noise back on itself. Calls and business, cries and insults and on Twenty-eighth near Broadway, windows open and an extraordinary cacophony of piano notes ebbing and flowing, fragments emerging for the ear, then dissipating, an eternal discordant succession.

"Tin Pan Alley," said McAteer. "Every music hack in the city."

Ben nodded eagerly.

"In a day or two," continued McAteer, "when you meet this man, Henry Jergens, he's going to be interested in two things: cattle and music. This is all the education you're going to get, give you a basis for conversing. Talking. I just want lots of happy talking."

As they walked, McAteer pointed out pianists positioned in many of the lobbies on the block, some playing, some resting, some smoking, legs crossed and idling as sure as any office clerk.

"Pluggers," explained McAteer. "Paid to sit, paid to play, but only songs of the house. If they think you work on Broadway, you're taken in, tied down, they give you whiskey or coffee and they make you sing one of their songs your next night out. You sing their song, maybe they'll cut you a piece of profit. Aim is to get your song out of this street and move it north or south. Take it to the Bowery or to Broadway, but just make it heard."

Ben nodded. "The pluggers write the songs?"

McAteer shook his head. "Pluggers aren't crazy. Songwriters, any bar within a dozen blocks of here, spit and you hit one. They only write when they're thirsty. Maybe they get twenty, thirty bucks a song. Maybe it won't make a dime, maybe it'll make a million. Same thirty dollars."

McAteer stopped in front of a brass plaque that declared HAMM'S MUSIC AND PUBLISHING CORPORATION.

"See this?" said McAteer. "Second floor, first door on the right. That'll be me. Remember, okay?"

"Our company's called Hamm's?" asked Ben.

"*My* company," said McAteer. "You're going to be a songwriter. One *of* a thousand. I'm a manager, one *in* a million."

A million dollars from a song? How do you get your entertainment? You do not live in Cleveland but in Devon, Ohio, explained McAteer. You do not live in Manhattan, but in Saranac Lake, New York. Where is your movie house? Where are stages teeming with actors and penny-cheap museums? Yet, every other man plays the piano. And if you don't, said McAteer, you can lift the lid and place your roll into the player piano and gather round the phantom keys. There are Victrolas waiting to be wound, wax discs to be placed softly on their wheels. Music is still America's entertainment. It is a business that has grown large enough to be housed next to Broadway. It booms and reverberates across the nation. You can buy sheet music, purchase wax discs, pay to listen to revues. The only things you can do for free, insisted McAteer, are hum, whistle, or sing.

"And how do you get Mr. Jergens involved?" asked Ben.

"Convince him to buy into a piece of my business," said McAteer.

They walked farther downtown, past the chasms opened in the city streets by steam drills. If you paused to peer in, you could see the tunnel rats digging for the new subways. One race above the ground and below, immigrants working up by digging down. Every now and then, blocks would close for small, controlled explosions and the coffee in your cup would sway and nobody would pause, not even Ben, who absorbed the city sound without hesitation.

➤●◄

McAteer plied Ben with information, then quizzed him to check the facts had sunk in. "'After the Ball?'"

"Sold four million," said Ben.

"Who wrote it?"

"Chas Harris."

"Best show on Broadway?"

"*Robinson Crusoe, Junior.*"

"Who's in it?"

"Jolson."

McAteer said, "Not bad, soldier," and steered the Englishman uptown until they passed under the sharp twin steeples and stained-glass eye of St. Patrick's Cathedral. Inside, the different-colored light met in mosaics in the aisles. McAteer marched Ben through the marble glow and paused by one of the thick columns.

"Here's your one true lesson of the day," said McAteer.

"I hadn't marked you as a papist."

"Not the cross," said McAteer, pointing upward. "The glass. Look at that." Ben followed the trace of his finger. "Sixtus the Fifth. Look at his eyes. What can you see in them?"

"I don't know," said Ben. "Nothing much."

"Exactly," said McAteer. "For forty years, he hid the fact that he was a zealot. The bishops elected him pope and found themselves under a reformer and they never knew. Never knew at all. That's the game."

"Is that really Sixtus the Fifth?"

"It doesn't matter as long as you know the story," replied McAteer.

"What do my eyes say?" whispered Ben.

"Too much happening in your eyes. If you look like you're looking twice at everything, everyone's going to look twice at you."

"How do you empty your eyes?" inquired Ben.

"What company were you in?" hissed McAteer viciously. "What was it like in France? Why'd you run and leave the rest of your boys out in the line?"

Ben didn't break McAteer's glare, but could feel thought, anger drain from him, and his eyes emptied accordingly. My boys aren't out on the line, he thought. They're not exactly anywhere.

"There," smiled McAteer, "you have it already. You want to know how to empty your eyes in front of a man, just think about your war. But when you drift off just do me a favor and purse your lips like you're thinking, and not some vacant loon."

A short walk downtown found them among the imposing columns of Pennsylvania Station and its canopy of steel and glass, the sun throwing the chessboard grid of the roof girders to the floor. Oddly, to Ben it felt more holy than the cathedral. McAteer checked the large clock that hung at the end of the waiting room, then pushed his way through the crowds toward track number five. They paused amid the crush and bought lunch from a pretzel vendor sitting cross-legged by his basket. Ben followed McAteer down the metal stairs that rang from the steel in his heels and onto the tracks, where they boarded the Jersey-bound train. McAteer finished his pretzel and licked the salt from his fingertips.

The train pulled from the arc lights of the station into the subterranean pitch, all heat and compression. Close to Bergen stood the stockyards, acres of bleating, snorting, and lowing animals brought straight from the prairies of the Midwest to within a mile of the five million hungry mouths of New York City. Ben and McAteer stood on the lowest rung of the fence and watched a flock of sheep pressed tight to one another, prodded by two men in dark work suits capped with hats. "Ante-mortem check," explained McAteer, slapping at an insect on the back of his neck. "Trains come in here, feed them right into the abattoir. Sheep, cows, don't do hogs here, don't know why. If Jergens asks you tomorrow, blame it on the Jews."

"Is it automated?" asked Ben, waving mosquitoes from his face.

"Sure," said McAteer, "Henry Ford's the hatcheck girl."

Amid the sheep stood a black goat.

"You know what they call him?" said McAteer. "The Judas goat. That little sap tells them, don't worry, follow me, it's okay this way."

Can I remember all of this, thought Ben. Can I really persuade this Mr. Jergens that I work in his business?

They entered the neighboring building, a churning noise of chains and bellows.

"This," said McAteer, "is how Henry Jergens makes his money."

The room echoed with the dull violence of execution. The cow at the front of the line was dragged forward. A poleax was brought down swiftly and efficiently, punching a hole in the skull. The cow slumped to its knees while one of the men drove a cane into the opening in the head, stirring the animal's brains. The dead cow's legs were attached to chains; a windlass drew the carcass off the bloody floor. Legs were cut off beneath the knees, skin stripped, offal removed, blood drained, only the edible remained. The body was swung along a chain apparatus so it might be cleaned and set a dozen yards away. Blood ran down the gutters, under the feet of the waiting herd. Ben knew horses could smell blood and the way the cows stood, wide-eyed with tails tucked between their legs, he could not doubt they knew the certainty of what awaited. I won't forget this, thought Ben. Entirely too familiar to forget.

He remembered a night march that had cut through the center of a seemingly untouched French town, hundreds of them in resounding step through the tree-lined streets. In the central square they were greeted by the strange sight of a group of uniformed road sweepers at work under gaslight. And Ben had wondered at the strange conscientiousness of the French services until he grew closer and could make out a few shattered stalls from the day's market. The sweepers were pushing a black stew into sacks, the remains of civilians who had been packed close together when a stray shell hit. They pushed with wide shovels, flesh and the day's newspapers soggy and dark, wallets and cloth, all gathered together.

Chimer had been staring too and they had said nothing but looked at one another. A month later, when they had passed by a tin-plated shack, blackened by fire, they moved from silence to blindness. Whoever had been inside the building had been broiled to a low pool of fat that had leaked out to form a ring about the structure. The place reeked, of burned meat and singed hair. A swarm of orange butterflies had descended to suck strength from the congealing liquid. "Probably horses inside," Chimer had said. "Horses," Ben had agreed, but by then they both knew the difference in odor.

"Nothing," said McAteer, pointing to a barrel of eyes, "nothing goes to waste. Not even bull's balls. Even the blood, the guts — they make fertilizer. You all right? You look a little green my boy."

Back at the station, McAteer pulled a small envelope from his pocket and slipped it inside Ben's coat. "You've got five tickets to a first-class carriage. I've arranged it so you'll find Jergens has the last seat. There'll be no one to disturb you. Take your time; let him talk first. Bring him in slow. You're to be on the one-thirty from Chicago, so don't be late, all right? If you're late, you're going to ruin six weeks of work."

Ben nodded.

"You'll find a suitcase in the station," continued McAteer. "Everything you need. Tags on it from the White Star Line like you're fresh off the boat. You've got five hundred in your pocket. I don't want to see a red cent of that jack. Okay?"

"Easy enough."

"Don't let Jergens loose of you," said McAteer. "You can't steer him till you've roped him. Once you got him, keep him close. I'm giving this one to you."

"Meaning?"

"You think people in this game start where you're starting?" said McAteer, taking a small step backward. "You're starting halfway up the pole. Normally you've got to rope, find the man to begin with. Next time out, you're going to rope. Everyone's got to pay their dues."

They shook hands. Ben looked down at his palm.

"What is it?" asked McAteer.

"Just counting my fingers," said Ben.

"Strange day," grinned McAteer. "Still friends?"

"Better friends," said Ben.

Chapter Nine

THE FOLLOWING MORNING, Ben found himself in Grand Central, boarding the Twentieth Century Limited on the all-water route to the great western hub of Chicago. It was a sleek line of steel cars and muted upholstery, with Pullman sleepers to ease the twenty-hour journey. A half hour of leafing through the newspapers, ignoring the war news, the meaningless numbers of casualties, the unchanging line of the front. Instead, Ben concentrated on Broadway tidbits, the names of American teams — Indians, Braves, Cubs — and the gilded froth of city society. But the war was even hidden in the Sunday picture section. Right there, above "A Charming Picture of Miss Elsie Janis at Her Summer House in Tarrytown," was a photograph of British soldiers near Ypres. Ben quickly turned the page.

The hours passed slowly. America, thought Ben as he stared out the window, kept on going and going, an infinite land of endless, tan-colored fields, the loose earth currying in the dry wind with the sweep of the passing train. Every now and then, big ugly horses and flitting larks turned their heads to watch Ben's passage. Irrigation ditches, blood-red barns, rail tracks, and the occasional smudge of a town passed them by. Ben was surprised again. He found, staring out at the end of the afternoon, that he was filled with a nervous anticipation, the slight dizziness he had experienced in Miner's as the orchestra tuned before the curtain rose, the same strange sensation that had accompanied the march to the front. And for the first month in France, they had talked of what they were feeling and then they didn't talk at all, for they were either dead or deadened.

>●<

Eating alone in the dining car, Ben eavesdropped on four sides at once, making sense of nothing but at ease in the chaos of crossed conversation. He drank three straight scotches. Despite the alcohol, Ben recognized the signs of tension. He was not grinding his teeth so much as pressing them together. His arms were half numb from tiredness. He was not breathing deeply, just looking about him, listening, drifting.

Ben reached out beneath him and jumped straight to his feet in the middle of the dining car. All heads turned to the sudden movement. Sitting down near La Bassée, in the dark, sitting down next to his friends. Chimer was smoking and only when Ben had put his hands down to push himself back to his feet did he realize they had been sitting on the bodies of the dead, stacked three deep. David had laughed at his jumpiness. "It's not fucking furniture," Ben had said. They'd all laughed at him. So good to see Mr. Imperturbable thoroughly perturbed.

Ben was spinning. A waiter was coming up to him. Ben looked in horror down at the sofa and reached to touch it. The fabric was green, had felt like the canvas of a British uniform. Horsehair, he told himself, not cold flesh. The waiter was in front of him now, asking him a question. Ben couldn't hear it. He was walking past the hospital tent with Chimer, the day they came off the front. Walking past two boxes of amputated limbs, pale, dirt beneath the discarded fingers. They were laughing. Usual jokes. "Wouldn't hurt a fly," Chimer was saying. "What?" asked Ben. "They're 'armless," said Chimer, grinning.

The lady who had been sitting to Ben's right touched him on the sleeve. He flinched at the contact and turned to her. Her lips were moving. The waiter was standing beside him. Ben looked about and saw all the faces in the dining car looking back at him. He tried to wave them off. He couldn't hear a thing. The silence overwhelmed the sounds of the train. It was like knowing the gramophone was on, but being deaf to the music. Where have you gone? Don't leave me. Tell me what to say? He couldn't hear a voice.

Don't worry, said Chimer. We're right here. Ben started to cry. Easy boy, easy, we're right here for you. I thought you'd left me, said Ben. Just say you're fine, said Chimer, ask them what they want.

"I'm sorry," said Ben, wiping his sleeve against his face. "Gone there for a moment. Nodded off. How can I help you?"

The waiter looked at him strangely. "Just asking if you wanted another scotch."

Ben nodded. "A double."

He could hear the voices inside, thank God. But where was the pat on the head, or the hand of a friend to help him back to his feet? Not ready to be alone. Not ready at all. Ben didn't even wait for his drink but retired to his compartment, embarrassed, frightened by his behavior. What if he could not do McAteer's job? How could he pretend to be another? In the army, he had always had the option of returning to who he was and the comfort of friends. Private Benedict Cramb, sir. He could tumble backward into a space of belonging, regiment, company, platoon. Now, he was positioning himself as a man who did not exist, and when such a man fell backward, he tumbled into nothing.

They reached Chicago the next morning. Ben, as ordered, checked into the Congress Hotel, shaved, bathed, dressed in his new blue suit, and headed back to the station within the hour. He caught the one-thirty sleeper to New York City, holding five first-class tickets, but showing the conductor only one, knowing that his compartment would contain the lone figure of Mr. Henry Jergens.

Ben entered and closed the door behind him.

"Afternoon," said the man opposite, one leg crossed over the other. His voice was unnaturally loud, a foghorn of confidence that surprised the Englishman.

"Good afternoon," returned Ben. He took his seat and pretended to read his copy of the *Chicago Tribune*. He had delivered the simplest words and to his great relief, his voice had held. He had heard no quiver to betray the anxiety that roiled him. He stole the occasional glance at Henry Jergens. Fuzzy black eyebrows, squirrel eyes, the sort that scavenge the landscape for scraps, and a heavy body, stout about the chest. An attractive enough man, but still perked by the remnants of baby fat, as if life preferred to coddle rather than erode him. His suit was extraordinary, a bright gray plaid with orange lines that Ben believed would make Jergens as conspicuous as a giraffe in New York.

"In Chicago long?" asked Ben.

"Week or so," boomed Jergens. "You?"

"Just since Monday."

"Where'd you stay?" asked Jergens.

"The Devonshire."

"Had a steak there last week. Not such a bad joint."

"The steak or the hotel?" asked Ben smiling, beginning to relax.

Jergens cracked into thunderous laughter. "Where are you from, my friend? Where *are* you from?"

"England," said Ben.

Jergens leaned forward. "Now that is a lovely country. I went to Windsor once. Had a look around."

"Wonderful," said Ben, finding himself speaking more softly to balance the blare of Jergens's voice. "Afraid I've never been invited there. Had a couple of weeks down at Osborne House by the sea, but no, never Windsor." Ben was feeling a little overwhelmed by the force of Jergens, yet also suddenly amused at his own participation. He'd have bought our diamond pin, thought Ben. He'd have taken a half dozen and come back for more.

Jergens smiled and offered Ben his hand. "Henry Jay Jergens," said Jergens. "From Kansas City, Missouri." He squeezed hard.

"Ben Newcombe," said Ben. The name had been on his White Star ticket and his luggage, McAteer's little joke.

"You're a long way from home."

A long way from home. Did Jergens really say that? Yes, strangers did these things, thought Ben, of course they did, they leaned into conversations, used inoffensive phrases, the harmless, the banal. Especially the ones in such suits. Ben shrugged and affected to stare out the window a moment. A long way from home.

"Business?" inquired Jergens. Ben noticed that Jergens's voice had a slight drawl that Ben had been told indicated the southern states. "Is what you're doing . . . ," continued Jergens, lowering his tone to what Ben guessed he equated with a whisper, "has it got anything to do with the, the war?"

"I suppose it does," said Ben calmly. "But not munitions or anything. We're farmers."

Jergens nodded. He said nothing. McAteer said you'd bite now, thought Ben, growing a little nervous. He twisted the little finger of one hand with the thumb and forefinger of the other. Come on, thought Ben. He said you'd bite, now bite.

"We farm cattle," persisted Ben, a little more loudly, as if Jergens might respond to a change in volume. "Not dairy, I'm afraid."

"Don't be afraid," blurted Jergens congenially, "I'm in the same business myself."

"How about that," said Ben, and breathed out, amazed at the prospect of having to tie himself to this man. At least there would be no chance of quiet. Ben's mouth was a little dry, but otherwise he was surprised at himself. Extended acting was not beyond him. From the orchestra pit he had marveled at the skill of deception on stage, but without a crowd it seemed so much easier.

"I'm not a breeder," said Jergens, leaning forward to tap Ben on the knee. "I'm on the other side of the fence. My family owns slaughterhouses."

"Tell me," inquired Ben, "in killing a cow, are you a proponent of Bruneau?"

"Hell no," laughed Jergens. "We use what you'd call the Greener method. A man on a long plank with a carbine, cows beneath him. Pop, pop, pop, back of the head. Our abattoir's less than two years

old, best in the state," continued Jergens proudly. "Less sweat for
the same steak. What's your breed?"

Ben was drifting a little. Six months ago, back in the reserve
trenches. You didn't expect to see much there, just hillsides smoth-
ered in parked wagons and timber, ammunition dumps, tents and
bivvies and the odd observation balloon swaying above. It was a
place of relative recuperation, but that morning, shells were
pouring over the top, coming back deep even beyond their own
artillery, to where all the horses were tethered. He had almost
thought of it walking through the abattoir in New Jersey, but had
pushed the memory away. And Captain Traven had chosen volun-
teers, the four of them, as ever together. Each issued a revolver.
Most of the horses were lying in the mud, squirming and
screaming. The wounded were thrashing and slithering about,
some missing legs, stomach wounds spilling guts up over their
manes. One horse's eyes had rolled back in its head, and yet the
whites of his eyes seemed to watch Ben as he shot it. So much
worse than the common trench sights, because it was a fresh inven-
tion from hell. Not easy to get in position to shoot a horse in the
head, not easy to pull the trigger, to pull it twice if the horse still
struggled. And Captain Traven was helping too, and they were all
red-eyed and teary, never for the men no, just the horses.

"What breed?" repeated Jergens, even more loudly.

"Hereford, exclusively," said Ben, with pursed lips and a smile.
"A soldier won't eat most anything else."

"Bullied beef?" said Jergens. "You supply the army?"

Ben nodded.

"I read," said Jergens, "they get London deliveries from Fortnum's
pretty much all day long at the front."

"Hardly," said Ben. "It's not like that at all I'm afraid."

"Were you out there?" asked Jergens.

How could Ben hide it? He did not have the skill to cloak such
experience, despite McAteer's warning that such a question might

be asked. An obvious pause would have betrayed him anyway, a loss of lines.

"Yes," said Ben simply.

For the first time, Jergens looked uncomfortable. Ben didn't acknowledge the sudden absence of conversation; the wheels of the car, the chatter from the corridor was enough. He hoped he hadn't scared the man off, destroyed McAteer's plans with one moment of truth. The train seemed to have speeded up. Ben thought he could hear the increase of the piston's exertions. Speak, he thought, before the boys come around, speak.

Jergens leaned forward again. "I'm going to apologize. I had no idea. Let me atone. Come join me for lunch." Ben was relieved, even warmed by the change in tone. The man had an underbelly of sincerity to him.

"Only," said Ben, presenting a sudden benign smile, "if you will be my guest for dinner."

The white lace curtains of the dining car were drawn to veil the movement of the train but every now and then the salt and pepper pots would shiver in a private dance, betraying their speed. They talked of the Kaiser and the process of war. Ben sat back and let Jergens lead, his voice carrying through the car, turning heads. "Order well," McAteer had warned. "Eat a lot. A small appetite *looks* cheap." They finished a large lunch with one brandy and then another, dozed off together back in their car, and then swapped papers and rustled through the news before repairing to the dining car again for dinner. A martini helped relieve their dry whiskey mouths and Ben chose a fine Bordeaux to accompany their lamb. The Englishman didn't flinch when paying the bill, nor when he overtipped the grateful waiter. And when Jergens suggested that they should lodge in the same hotel in New York, Ben concurred and gave the considered nod of a man who has heard an unexpectedly sharp piece of logic.

"You a married man?" asked Jergens over a final scotch, a stubby cigar clenched between his teeth.

"No."

"Where was I when God was ladling brains?"

"Children?" inquired Ben.

"Six," said Jergens. "Exactly six too many." He grinned and took another large swig of scotch. "No, really I love them."

"Of course you do," smiled Ben.

"Damn, I should give you one."

Ben laughed. "I've room for a brace."

"I'll tell you what," said Jergens, raising his glass. "In New York, we're going to find you a wife. On my honor, I'll find you one, if we have to trip up every club in the city."

"Maybe we'll find you a mistress," ventured Ben, laughing, in case Jergens was not so inclined.

Despite the alcohol, Jergens straightened up into an impression of sobriety. "No sir," he bellowed. "I like to look as much as any man. But Lord, let only my *eyes* be tempted. I made an altar vow, so now it's God's business. I have no wish to see His wrath."

Ben was more shocked than worried and hoped he hadn't insulted the Missourian beyond redemption. Not like I was. He's a bit like Chimer. Takes his girls very seriously.

"Of course," he nodded.

Jergens laughed loudly at Ben's apparent discomfort. "You're not a married man. Why *should* you know?" He leaned over and gave Ben a pinch on the flesh either side of his knee. The Englishman flinched. "All the ladies of the world before you." He leaned back again and repositioned the cigar in his mouth. "You believe in God, Ben?"

Ben hesitated.

"Of course you do," answered Jergens on his behalf. "You've been on a battlefield in the middle of God's hurricane, the center of God's choosing. You came through." He looked at Ben, jabbed his cigar once toward the Englishman. "The good come through."

Ben tried not to listen, tried not to think of them. Ben took McAteer's advice — pursed his lips and nodded.

"A good man needs a good wife," said Jergens, and taking his glass in his hand, reached across toward Ben.

"To my future wife," said Ben, and they clinked their glasses.

During their ride from Grand Central to the Bristol Hotel, Jergens sat in the back of the taxi and cursed the population of New York, beginning with the driver of the streetcar in front of them. The avenue was narrowed to the width of a single car, the rest occupied by a deep rift in the ground where subway tracks were being laid. The two men seemed to quake to the rhythm of the steam drills. Jergens spent the remainder of the ride peering up out of the windows, following with his eyes the bundles of telegraph and telephone wires as they looped from pole to pole. Over intersections, wires crisscrossed, dozens changing direction, most heading north or south. They cast their own serpentine shadows across the street.

"It just gets me every time." Jergens clicked his tongue against the roof of his mouth, his head still tilted toward the skyscrapers, staring back downtown at the ridiculous, incomprehensible height of the Woolworth Building.

"That's just showing off," shouted Jergens out the window, turning the heads of passing New Yorkers.

While Jergens soaked in his bath in the adjoining suite, Ben investigated the modernities in his room and pondered the puzzle of Henry Jergens. There was an electric fan on the ceiling. An electric percolator, refrigerator. Ben turned every appliance on. Clicking on, clicking off, trying to generate noise in his new home. The window was stiff and sealed with paint. Ben jimmied it open, letting the sounds of the city wash over the room. He rang for a bellboy and sent him out with ten dollars to change into dimes and quarters for tipping. McAteer had warned him that he was in the only city in the world where a five-dollar hat could run a man another twenty a year. Lying full clothed on top of the sheets, Ben spent his afternoon wondering if McAteer had any idea what kind of man Henry Jergens was. The lads would have hated him — far too much talk.

Did such brashness make him a better or worse mark to fleece? Ben supposed the exterior didn't matter. Just because he dressed like a vaudeville barker did not necessarily exempt him from shrewdness. He just hoped the man had enough money available and had not spent it all on either his vast family or wardrobe.

At ten to five, loaded with silver, the Englishman descended in the elevator, clipped across the floor of the lobby, marble, carpet, marble, carpet. He leaned over the desk to whisper to the concierge.

"I was wondering if you could do me a favor," said Ben. "I'm having a small spat with my friend, Mr. Jergens, just arguing about where we should go tonight. He's insisting on this awful spot on Sixth Avenue, and I won't budge either, so we said we'd compromise and go whereever the desk advised." Ben pushed two dollars across the desk. "That's for Reisenweber's by the Empire."

Reisenweber's was a gaudy establishment on Fifty-eighth and Eighth, with a large canopied roof garden and doors thrown open to the warm night. It was decorated in cream and gilt edges, from the walls to the napkins that came folded as swans. Ben greeted the maître d' like an old friend, slid him ten dollars, and secured a table close to the stage. The steak was stringy, but the whiskey was smooth and Jergens drank copiously, until he began to enjoy himself. The music, when it finally started, was played for laughs, an all-white "jass" band, doing their best to squeeze farmyard noises from their instruments, the trombone of a bull, the porcine squeal of a clarinet, all worked higgledy-piggledy into a free-form rag. Jergens's tuxedo was a disaster, poorly cut, trousers hoisted too high about his belly, blue socks drawn to the eye by his shiny patent-leather shoes.

"You like music?" Ben asked Jergens after the end of their first session.

"Rag man myself."

"You play?"

"Hell no," said Jergens, ordering another round of whiskeys. "Music of my youth. Every cathouse in Kansas City had a stride player ten, maybe fifteen years ago. You listen to rag in London?"

"Of course," said Ben. "But this, well, it strikes me as false."

Jergens, who had been howling with laughter along with the rest of the audience at the animal lampoons of the laboring orchestra, paused and said, "How so?"

"I write a bit, you see," said Ben. "Music, that is. Just for fun, but I know what I'm hearing and I'll be damned if this is the best New York has to offer. Who played your cathouse music? Men like this?"

"No," said Jergens. "Negroes, most every one."

"We'll go and find some Negro music tomorrow," said Ben, signaling for a black busboy to come over.

All that counted, McAteer had explained, was the one moment when information was gently slipped to the mark, like an envelope passed under a door. The busboy politely followed the predetermined pattern of conversation. Recommended a club in Harlem, he said, "Up there the sounds are breathing, but there aren't any songs. Everybody plays what they feel like playing, whatever comes in their heads, so you never hear the same tune twice. Someone sets a pace, rest of the band runs to keep up." Harmless information, thought Ben, but it was all that it took to push the mark along. McAteer was right when he compared Ben's role to that of the sheepdog, he reckoned; it was a nudge, a growl, and a drive toward the pen.

"You really want me to go to a nigger club?" asked Jergens as they headed back to their hotel. "Come on now man, I know you don't have niggers in England."

"You said they played all your cathouse music."

"Yes," said Jergens. "In a *white* man's house. Niggers are just there for entertainment. I think you might go on your own."

"You're afraid of Negroes?" asked Ben innocently.

"Course not," said Jergens. "It's a question of hygiene. I'll go with you if you want, keep you safe, but we better keep our gloves on. And I'm not drinking from any nigger glasses. Taking a whole bottle for myself. I just wouldn't want to catch anything."

Chapter Ten

AT NINE, BEN struggled from clean sheets into a room with wallpaper on walls, paint not peeling, fan stirring above his head, carpet thick and luxurious beneath his feet. Everything dream-like in its perfection. Ben didn't like it, not at all, he thought as he ran the bath. The purpose of a hotel was to deceive guests into believing that their rooms were untouched, unspoiled, without trace of another.

When Ben emerged in his towel, the boy had left his tepid eggs waiting on a table by the window. He ate them cautiously, waiting for his stomach to rebel, but it held and he dressed in his blue suit and new straw hat, swallowed a second cup of coffee, and headed through the doors of the hotel, thrilled not to be Jergens's chaperone for the day.

He took a streetcar south, hopping off near Washington Square, then walked south and west to McAteer's apartment. He kept to the shadows. In the middle of the street men were peering into the mystery of a broken, steaming engine, awaiting revelation to the bleats of car horns. Walking up the stairs, he found his employer descending with a noticeable trot in his step. The smell of cologne stopped Ben just before McAteer said, "At the bank then, is he?"

"He is."

"And you've no other friends to amuse your afternoons with?"

"Not as yet," said Ben, shifting on a stair.

"None from Miner's?"

"Probably not a good idea," said Ben.

"Then we'll have to be socializing together," said McAteer, and gestured that Ben should turn around.

They walked up the metal steps to the Third Avenue el and headed north to Fifty-ninth Street.

"What if Jergens gets his loan at the bank today?" asked Ben as they sat side by side.

McAteer laughed. "The officer of the bank in question is an associate of ours. Jergens'll be played for time, then dismissed."

"What if he leaves beforehand?" asked Ben. "I can't believe he's a patient man. What if he gets bored of New York?"

"A legitimate concern," pondered McAteer. "A mark will rarely last past three weeks. Should be plenty of time. Why, how did he look? How was he last night?"

"Exhausting," said Ben. "And a drunk. And deafening." In truth, Ben thought Jergens was like a shaken bottle of soda: impossible to tell if he would produce a mild fizz or explode in your face.

McAteer nodded. "I heard a fine report of your own behavior. You did well with him."

Ben cocked his head, then smiled at the compliment.

"Well," said McAteer, "you must always expect a *small* audience."

"Will I have one tonight?"

"In Harlem? Of course. You'll be on a Negro block. You used to them?"

"Me? Not a worry. Not so sure about Mr. Jergens."

McAteer shrugged. "Missouri born. Not necessarily fond of them. So keep him at ease. What you're looking for tonight is complicity. Involve Mr. Jergens in the music. You know ragtime and the rest in a way he doesn't, so get him thinking on the lyrics."

"And then I come to see you?"

"At Hamm's Music," nodded McAteer. "Bring him in before ten on Wednesday. But don't let him be drinking too much tonight."

Ben could not describe his gratitude to McAteer for sharing the company of his day. If Ben had not been so intent on the pursuit and conquest of women all his life then perhaps he would have had friends other than Chimer, Douglas, and David. He became more at ease as their walk progressed. Outside of the hotel room, he was comforted by the crowded paths. It no longer seemed to be the walk of an employer and his employed, but uncle and nephew with no sniff of business.

McAteer was acting as a guide to the houses of the wealthiest of New Yorkers, walking Ben up Fifth Avenue, pointing with admiration at the mansions. The more turrets that pierced the sky, the more ivy that was trimmed obediently over the curtained windows, the more impressed McAteer was. French Renaissance seemed to kindle a particular admiration in his breast, and he frequently brought their walk to a halt to direct Ben's attention to slight details in design.

"Do you think the rest of us are uncivilized?" asked McAteer.

"Who?"

"Americans."

"Hardly," said Ben. "Besides, I'm not really one of the *civilized* English."

"You mean you weren't sent away to school at five?"

"Never sent away to school at all."

"At least you had a loving mother then," said McAteer. "Much better than an education."

Ben smiled at the thought. He thought of the chaos of his own childhood, raised somewhere between home, Aunt Kath's, and the Old Street stage.

When they were all fifteen, the same year he had bought Eileen her hat, Chimer's father had acted as the accompanist for a mentalist from Wapping who wore a thick turban and called himself Achmed the All-Seeing.

Ben, Chimer, Douglas, and David were shills, wandering through the audience before the curtain rose, eavesdropping on any slithers of information that Achmed could use in his act. But what impressed the boys most were the different tales that Achmed would start the evening with to warm up his audience. They were all torturous or sentimental sagas, but the boys were the right age to appreciate them. Their collective favorite was the story of a Hindu prince, Abu Abu, who had died on his twentieth birthday. When his father, the Maharaja, urged the court doctors to cut him open to see what his son had suffered from, it was found he had no heart. Some of the audience laughed at the deadpan delivery, some paused for thought, but it had provoked long discussions among the lads on what organ they could do without. Only Ben had argued that the prince had had the right idea, and from then on, especially in the presence of women, they had always referred to Ben as Abu.

"Do you have another woman?" asked Ben as they continued their northern walk.

"Awhile ago," said McAteer, looking closely at Ben as if to find where the question came from. "Lost the one I loved."

"What did she die of?" asked Ben.

"Infidelity," said McAteer. "She ran off west with a boy your age."

"At least you've still got your wife."

"As great a comfort as a bed of nails."

There was more in common between them than Ben had first thought. He guessed McAteer was as glad for his company as he was for McAteer's. Perhaps he's like me, thought Ben, better with his past, talking to friends long gone. Once, Ben had been very good at talking to the living. Not with the young girls who just fluttered into his bed, swooning into what they were convinced was love, but the older ones, those who knew what he was. Those married to someone much better than he, like Prudence and her Member of Parliament. Talking her into bed the first time, now that was enjoyment. And then things changed. She was much older, thirty-five to his twenty, all breasts and buttocks. She liked to laugh and laugh as they made love. Every time he made her come she couldn't stop her laughter. And yet, whenever they were through, the gaiety would disappear for a moment.

"I'd do anything for you, you know that?" she said one day.

"I know."

"Would you do anything for me?"

"No," said Ben.

She laughed. "I know it. You know what Oscar Wilde says. You know who he is don't you?"

"I grew up in a theater my lovely," said Ben. "Give us a bit of credit every now and then."

"Sorry," she said. "He says that every man wants to be a woman's first love and every woman wants to be a man's last."

"I'm twenty," said Ben. "No rudeness intended, but I hope you're not the end of my road."

"I'm sure I won't be," she said, and lay back on the bed, her large breasts each drooping toward the mattress. "I'm sure yours will be a very long road indeed." She ran her hand over her pale belly. "You can be very cold you know."

"At least my hands are warm," said Ben, and traced one up her thigh to prove it. Her laughter started again.

Ben and McAteer walked along the eastern edge of the park on Fifth, turned in toward the carousel with its hand-carved horses, watched the children spin slowly in their circles, and gazed at the parents standing proudly by.

"Do you have children?" asked McAteer.

"No," said Ben. "No children, no wives, no friends. It's all very simple really."

"Don't worry about the children," said McAteer. "Just adopt a younger fellow like yourself. Much safer than the risks of natural selection."

They continued north, past the boat pond and the cherry trees with their promises of summer, among the nannies with princely prams and five-pound shampooed dogs. Ben stared at the privileged in silent aspiration, listened to those clean American voices call out for one another, blonde disheveled hair, exasperated nurse-maids, tutting mothers. He suspected that even Henry Jergens sprang from some lower rank.

Chapter Eleven

THAT EVENING BEN escorted Jergens to Harlem. It had London beauty to it, thought Ben. The buildings did not shoot from the earth; they were in more orderly rows than the fairy-tale beanstalks farther downtown. The faces changed back and forth, one block white, dominated by Jews, the next black. Their taxi came to a stop on a black block. Music seemed to be rising from below the ground.

"I can't believe I'm doing this for you, Ben," said Jergens.

They looked suitably out of place at Sensie's. Jergens was wearing an English tweed with flecks of bright yellow, entirely inappropriate for Harlem, let alone New York, or even America. As they walked to the door, Ben imagined Jergens at a Savile Row tailor his last trip to London, smirking cutters standing behind him, winking at one another as he made his choice in cloth.

Having paid fifty cents to enter, they checked their hats and descended a staircase covered with a well-worn red carpet. The room, throbbing with people, threw up a noise and vibrancy that one would expect in a city only on payday. Negroes in their finest, energy abounding, the early competition for women, the sounds of ice served in glasses so thick they fell without breaking. Where walls and booths were viewable between the shifting crowd and dancing couples, the same deep red as the carpet, just as faded. Eyes prickled their backs, everyone wants to know who's down here, who's come to a place they don't belong.

><

Upstairs it was May, but in the subterranea it was August. Shirts clung to backs and all skin, black and white, glowed in the orange light. The music owned the club, not the liquor, not the dancing, not the best-cut suit nor thigh-high creeping dress. They were directed to a booth, angled so that they could be seen only from the stage, hidden from the rest of the audience.

"Christ," whispered Jergens to Ben as they slid into their booth, "the smell in here." He dabbed the sweat from his neck.

"You might be a little overdressed," said Ben with concern.

"English cloth," said Jergens. "Let them know the lords from the lackeys. Way you've got to be."

They called for whiskey and Ben waited a drink or two, watched as Jergens mopped his forehead with his purple silk handkerchief and ogled women and tapped his feet and drank some more. Ben could see that despite his grudging entrance, he was entertained. Finally, Ben drew a pen out of his pocket along with a small notepad. He wondered what he was listening to — bass, piano, drums, clarinets, coronets. There was a harmony among the eight musicians, sweating in their suits on stage. He imagined the band as a murder of crows, and every few beats one would circle to flaunt his skills.

"What are you doing?" asked Jergens.

He reminded Ben of a bossy child, only happy when distracted.

"Nothing," said Ben. "Just writing some of this down. I just thought it a bit of a shame. It comes and it goes and they'll never have it again. Such a waste."

"Ant and the grasshopper," said Jergens, thrumming his fingers against the table in time with the drums. "They can't help themselves." Jergens poked his finger over at another table. "Look at them. Bet it's their first time here too."

Ben looked over his shoulder to where another two white men slouched against a red banquette, hats still on and tipped down, so that only their chins emerged. One was slim; the other had blonde sideburns. For a moment, Ben thought he was looking at Chimer and David, but then where was Douglas?

Ben turned back toward Jergens, keeping half an eye on the others. Perhaps it was an innocent coincidence and they too were wondering what other white faces would be doing in this Negro nightclub. Was it wrong to worry? What if they were either watching Ben because of his flimflamming, or worse, because of his desertion? What if they were English?, thought Ben. The irony of having McAteer reveal his own subterfuge and then being arrested by true agents ten days later.

If you'd been there, thought Ben. Do you know my record? Have you read of my wounds and do you still wish to drag me back? One of the men slid down in his booth, away from Ben's open stare, as if he were slipping back into a trench, just the flesh of his nose peeking out between hat and collar. Raise your hands, thought Ben, please raise your hands if all your friends are dead. Raise your hands if you have seen lines of corpses laid out beside a muddy track. That's who one of these men reminded him of — that night, when Ben had been on sentry duty and not even seen him crawling until he was spoken to. The English sniper had slithered over the parapet in muddy overalls, a sackcloth mask pulled down across his face with arrow slits for eyes, a slim cut for the nose and mouth. The flesh of that nose, poking out like this stranger's. If the figure hadn't spoken English, Ben would have thought he had offered a cigarette to the devil himself. The man had pushed his mask back across his face and they had smoked in silence beneath the flares.

Where are you now? Such a pile of horrors, such unexpected horrors. Who among them had dreamed it was possible? Not him, not any of the boys. Who among you here know that men can build an abattoir without a market? Who among you know the incredible humiliation of standing in that line, waiting to be buried as bones and splinters. Like Chimer and Douglas and David. They'd have been shoveled into sandbags, dropped into a hole, sprinkled with lime. That was what lay beneath you, bones and rotting flesh, wherever you marched. That's what you thought about when you were alone and it ate at you, day by day, it broke you. There was not an impenetrable division between the courageous and the cowardly, simply a slope down which they all slipped.

Boom boom boom goes the bass. There, thought Ben, I'm all right. The high weeping trumpet sound waning. Two guitars strumming through, *snare snare drum snare. Boom bass boom.* Noise, that's all, thought Ben.

"Hey Ben, you all right?" asked Jergens.

Me? Of course, thought Ben. I'm fine. We're fine. All of *you* are troubled. *This* is not normal. *That* was normal. Ben smiled. Jergens stared at him and nodded as if he knew the spinning thoughts of the Englishman. Ben looked over at the other white men. You are the most deluded of all, he thought. You have the most useless existence. You are sent out to hunt deserters, destroy them before they affect the innocent. Then, to his utter relief, he saw one of the men drop his hand under the table and rest it on the other man's thigh. Not embassy men, nor police, but daisy boys up from Manhattan, seeking a little solitude in touching. Ben laughed aloud; they had probably been staring at him all evening, worried that he would be from a department of morality, coming to send them to hell.

Just as McAteer had forewarned, after the second set the leader of the band pulled a chair up to their table with an aggressive sense of propriety. Jergens bristled immediately, pushing himself upright. The cornet player was dark-skinned, eyes deep set and bulgy. Wide shoulders strained at the suit, a musty hound's-tooth check.

"What in the hell are you doing?" asked Jergens.

"Whatever I want," said the bandleader. "I own this club. What in the hell are *you* doing?" he asked, pointing at Ben's pad and paper.

"Listening to music," said Ben, calmly. "No rule against that now is there?"

"Looked to me from up there like you were writing down music. Is that what you were doing?"

"Yes," admitted Ben. "I was writing down music."

"What in hell does it matter?" said Jergens in Ben's defense. "Free country. You remember that don't you?"

"Can I see what you wrote?" asked the bandleader, ignoring Jergens.

"Surely," said Ben, and pushed the pad toward him.

"Seems to me," said the man, studying the paper, "that this is something I was playing. What do you plan to do with it?"

"Play it myself," said Ben.

"You want it for free?" laughed the bandleader.

"Don't pay the boy a dime," spat Jergens to Ben.

"Forty dollars," said the Negro.

Ben smiled. Not the twenty dollars McAteer had described. The Missourian and the cornet player glared at each other. Ben raised his palms in peace. "I'll give you thirty for it."

The bandleader nodded once and Ben counted three tens from his pocket, pushed them across the table. Jergens scowled and downed his drink, abruptly stood to leave.

"God almighty, they've some strange ideas here for what passes for politeness," said Jergens as they reclaimed their hats and made their way up the stairs. "Niggers asking for money," he muttered, staring down drunkenly at his feet. "I tell you, they're going to have talking dogs and dancing mules before this year is out. You mark me."

Outside in the warm Harlem night it was three in the morning and there were no taxis in sight. Across the street were the stables of a dairy delivery service. The smell of horses was so strong Ben could have licked it from the air.

"Why'd you pay him? A boy like that," said Jergens.

"Perhaps," said Ben, "it was worth thirty dollars. Perhaps it's a steal at the price."

"If it was me," said Jergens, "I'd've whipped the son of a bitch."

They wove their way south, Jergens kicking dried manure until his shiny leathers were worthy of a distant farmyard. They shared the contents of a silver flask the Missourian removed from his jacket, regained their buoyant moods and sang. Since the tunes of the evening had never been accompanied by voices, the two men were forced to conjure lyrics.

"*A sweet little girl from Kansas City,*" sang Ben.

"*Did you ever, ever see one so pretty?*" sang Jergens.

"What's next?" asked Ben. "*Sweet little girl from Kansas City, did you ever, ever see one so pretty* . . . What's she called, Henry?"

"Henry's an odd name for a girl," said Jergens.

"No," laughed Ben. "I said 'Henry, what's her name?'"

"Her name," mused Jergens. Then breaking into song again, warbled, "*She went by the name of Elsa Lee.*"

"*With the prettiest lips you ever did see,*" followed Ben.

"Yes," said Jergens, patting his friend on the back, "yes, we're getting there."

And so they walked, the alcohol providing the momentum for the first forty blocks of drifting, but as much as Ben tried to prod Jergens toward the song, his drunkenness lent him a wandering mind.

"Uppity nigger," he muttered.

He bent down and picked up a pebble from a gutter, threw it up at an apartment window.

"What are you doing?" asked Ben, sober enough to know how drunk Jergens was. Speech slurred, logic blurry, argumentative. Slipping uneasily between smiles and scowls. He's worse than Douglas, thought Ben, realizing that he had failed to keep him calm. He's going to be wanting a scrap soon, looking for an opponent and if he doesn't find one, he'll try it on with me. Jergens's trousers had made their way a few inches south, covering his blue socks but exposing the pregnant whiteness of his belly.

"Where's your sense of fun?" said Jergens. "I am looking for Juliet." He picked up a second pebble and hurled it upward. There was a sharp crack in the night and a hole in the pane.

"Oops," said Jergens.

A face appeared at the window. It peered down toward them. Shouted no complaint, but shrank away from their stares in fear.

"Sorry," shouted Jergens. "So sorry. How about we come up and have a drink?" He smiled broadly to show his innocence. "You don't have to be like that," shouted Jergens far too loudly, so that

Ben tried to take him by the arm. Jergens shook himself loose. "What's the idea?" he hissed at Ben before turning his attention back upward. "I'm sorry about the window." He turned back to Ben and smiled. "I'm trying to be very, very polite here. Take this man out for a drink. Wrong window, you see. But the son of a bitch ain't very sociable."

Jergens unzipped his fly and walked over to the building's stoop.

"I hope you're looking," he called upward. "I am ur-ig-inating on you." His piss hit the third step and began to flow back down toward his own shoes.

"Sir," said a voice. "Can I help you?"

Ben turned to see the high hat and white gloves of a New York policeman. Big buttons on his coat shone in the streetlight. It made Ben catch his breath. To be taken in for public drunkenness, to risk being identified or handed over to the British Embassy, was far more serious than being associated with Julius McAteer.

"Can I help you?" repeated the officer.

"You could shake this here thing for me," said Jergens as he looked over his shoulder. He laughed when he saw who he was talking to.

"I'm sorry Sergeant," said Ben.

Jergens put one arm around Ben and offered his damp hand to the officer, who looked at it and declined the invitation.

Ben shrugged and smiled for the officer. "My friend has had a few glasses."

The policeman pointed up to the window above and kicked a shard along the sidewalk. "And broken some as well."

"He thought it was a friend's window. I think we're on the wrong block."

"You seem straight enough," said the cop, "but I'm going to have to take him in for the night."

"Naturally," said Ben. He didn't want to do it. Didn't see what else he could do. "Officer?" inquired Ben, and as the man turned to face him Ben drove his fist into the man's jaw. He crumpled. One shot and down he went. Ben checked, out cold.

1073168468

Jergens laughed out loud and walked over to sway uncertainly over the policeman's body. "You can hit boy!" he cried in drunken amazement. "That a good strong right."

Ben shook his hand loose, testing to see if he had done more than crack open the skin of a knuckle. His white scar gleamed in the lamplight.

"That was for me?" asked Jergens, a small bubble of emotion rising in his voice.

"I suppose so," said Ben.

He looped his arm over Ben's shoulder. "You shouldn't have to do that for a friend," he said earnestly. "You're a good friend, Ben. You really are. A fellow should be glad to have met you."

Ben helped carry him down the street. "*Sweet little girl from Kansas City,*" sang Jergens.

By the time that they reached the Bristol Hotel at just past four in the morning, milk and ice wagons were groaning over the cobblestones, drawn by horses that barely dared the street during the day. They sang their song together over a goodnight drink, Ben writing down every word:

> *Sweet little girl from Kansas City, you never ever saw one so*
> * pretty.*
> *She went by the name of Elsa Lee, with the prettiest lips you*
> * ever did see.*
> *Carried her east to New York town, gripped her hard,*
> * couldn't put her down.*
> *Going to marry Miss Elsa Lee, Missouri girl's good enough*
> * for me,*
> *Oh Miss Elsa Lee, Miss Elsa Lee,*
> *I'm down on my knees, marry me, marry me.*

They fell asleep to the thrum of an electric suction cleaner working its way down the corridor, Ben's swollen hand resting in a bucket of ice.

Chapter Twelve

THE MORNING AFTER his visit to Sensie's, Ben stumbled to the sink and buried his hangover in a basinful of cold water. Normally it would have shocked him enough to withdraw, but today he stayed under as long as he could hold his breath. Emerging, he dried his hair with a clean towel. He used a small comb to run wax through his mustache, then shaved with his safety razor, cutting himself on the chin. He dressed and headed out for the papers. The knuckles of his right hand were swollen and red. They were supposed to be with McAteer within the hour.

At a breakfast of eggs, bacon, ham, and buttered toast, Jergens and Ben flapped and folded their newspapers. Apart from a greasy pallor, Jergens looked and behaved as if he had had half a bottle of weak wine and an early night. Over coffee, Ben pushed his finished paper under his empty plate and said, "I was thinking of getting my money back."

Jergens stopped and looked at him.

"My thirty dollars," explained Ben.

"We'll need a damned lynch mob."

"Not from Sensie's," said Ben. "On Tin Pan Alley."

"What do you mean?" asked Jergens.

"Let's sell the song."

Jergens laughed.

"I'm serious," said Ben. "Okay, so we were a little high when we wrote the lyrics, but I think they're rather good and the tune, well, I think it might be worth thirty dollars. Will you come with me?"

"Hell, no."

>●<

Ben went back into his own room while Jergens shaved. He returned with a piece of sheet music, originally provided by McAteer.

"Here," he said, and handed it to Jergens. "This made a mint last year."

Jergens studied it for a moment and asked, "So what?"

"So nothing," said Ben. "But it has the publisher's address on it. Hamm's Music and Publishing Corporation. We might as well start at the top." Ben knew there was no meeting that morning between Jergens and McAteer's man at the bank.

"We can always have a drink afterward," suggested Ben. "You could wear something sharp, musical."

He watched as Jergens weighed his options.

McAteer, as he had told Ben, had occupied the empty office space on Tin Pan Alley as of two weeks ago, a small favor from a friend in realty, and had furnished it cheaply with borrowed chairs, desks, and tables. Altogether, the illusion of Hamm's Music and Publishing Corporation had cost him less than three hundred dollars. Apart from the piano that stood in the lobby of the second-floor office, it could have passed for any staid business. It was neat, freshly painted in a dull white, and had a pair of desks, behind which sat two pasty youths. Four chairs, which waited for those who waited, completed the furnishings. In the back of the room, a spiral staircase wound upward to the unseen.

"Afternoon," said Ben. "Who would we see about the sale of a song?"

"Have you been here before?" asked the boy on the right, speaking from beneath a mustache so wispy that Ben thought it was coffee waiting to be wiped away. He glanced at Jergens. With Ben's help, he had chosen a yellow shirt, dark suit, black tie, and boater with a matching black-and-yellow band. Sartorially speaking, Jergens had never looked better. Perhaps it was because he was humming, but Ben thought that he resembled a bumblebee.

"No, never," said Ben.

"One moment please," said the boy. He wound tight circles up the staircase, the long awkward legs of a grasshopper. A minute later he called down, "Mr. O'Keefe will see you now."

Ben ran a hand over his own mustache and marched upward. Jergens huffed after him. The secretary was standing by an open door at the end of a short corridor. Jergens and Ben walked past him and into an office where Julius McAteer sat, rifling through an assortment of papers. He had manufactured the air of an exasperated clerk: tie loose, fingertips stained with ink, hair wavy in back-office humidity, looking like he had a million things to do, all of them more important than chatting to a pair of amateurs. Ben wanted to smile at the beauty of his performance.

"What can I do for you gentlemen?" he sighed.

"We have," said Ben, "a song we've written that we'd like to sell."

"Really now," breathed McAteer with a patient smile. "And what makes you think I'd buy it?"

"We hear you buy only the best."

McAteer laughed. "You English too?" he asked, pointing a finger at Jergens.

"No," said Jergens. "From Kansas City. Henry Jergens."

"O'Keefe," said McAteer, offering them both his hand.

"Newcombe," said Ben.

"You don't look like a pair of songwriters," said McAteer. "Is that what you do?"

"Not exactly," said Ben. "We're new at it."

"It's our first song," admitted Jergens.

"And before that you were?"

"We still are," said Ben. "Actually, we're both employed in the cattle industry."

"And maybe you should stay there," advised McAteer. "You know what a songwriter earns? They work to drink and drink to work."

"We do that too," said Jergens, laughing. "On a grander scale."

"Okay," said McAteer, and held out his hands. "Let's see what you've got."

Ben handed him the piece of sheet music.

"Is that it?" asked McAteer. "Only the one?"

Jergens and Ben nodded and then McAteer became silent, his eyes scrolling downward and then over.

"Neville," he called out.

"Out to lunch," came the cry of a young voice downstairs.

"Sorry boys," said McAteer. "The plugger's out to lunch."

"I could play," volunteered Ben. McAteer looked up, apparently impressed.

Downstairs, Ben looked at his own music and laid his hands on the piano keys. McAteer stood poker-faced next to Jergens. It took Ben and Jergens one run-through to remember exactly where the words of the song had belonged at four that morning, and though Ben's head still bore the eggshell hallmarks of a hangover, Jergens belted out his basso with all the conviction of a Sunday churchman. McAteer seemed to be smiling by the end of their third set.

"Not bad," said McAteer once Ben had finished. Jergens was looking expectantly at McAteer.

"I'll give you fifty for it."

"Cochran's said they'd give us one hundred for it," said Jergens immediately. Ben looked up in surprise.

"Well why don't you take it back there?" said McAteer coolly.

"Very well," said Jergens, and plucked the sheet music from under Ben's nose.

"We can always try Timmons and Company," blurted Ben. "Weren't they interested as well?"

"I believe so," said Jergens, and the two men turned to go.

"Fine," said McAteer. "I'll give you eighty. Can you write another like this? You know, one that hops a bit."

"Perhaps," said Jergens turning around, waiting for Ben's acquiescence.

"Michael," said McAteer, turning to his secretary. "Draw up a B-11, one-song contract. What do you want to call this song?"

"'Elsa Lee,'" said Jergens. Aggressive, thought Ben, even decisive. Ben was beginning to see how the facade of a garrulous dandy might be fronting a man of some determination.

Chapter Thirteen

BEN AND JERGENS returned to Sensie's Thursday night, resolving to remember as much as they could of one particular tune, then leave while they could still hum it, thus avoiding the bandleader's thirty-dollar surcharge for scrawling during songs. As a result, both men remained reasonably sober. It was comical, thought Ben. There they were, humming their way back to the hotel, through the doors, in the elevator, down the corridor, and into Ben's room, whereupon Ben rushed over to his desk and began to draw a loose arrangement of notes across the paper while Jergens hunched over him. Then came time for the lyrics. Jergens's first effort was about a girl called Yvette, wanted for murder in the *Police Gazette*, then Yvonne, operator of a telephone, and at about two in the morning came Lillian Hollers, who married a man worth two million dollars. Ben kept dismissing the ideas and pouring Jergens whiskey, amused to see what he would come up with next. Finally, they settled on the title "I Know What's Good for You."

> *I know what's good for you,*
> *what's good for you is me,*
> *you'd like a little milk in your coffee,*
> *I'd like a spot of tea.*
> *You think that you know best,*
> *better than all the rest,*
> *and at your behest,*
> *I'm willing to take the test*
> *to find out what's good for you,*
> *since what's good for you is me.*

>●<

In bed, Ben found that he was still humming to himself. Born into theater, born into music, he had thought it was poor luck that he hadn't inherited a finer voice. His father had a somber baritone, his mother a thin nightingale trill, but Ben was for the better part flat. In pubs, he would play the piano and rely on Chimer and the others to drown his voice out. Ben would only sing loudly on the trains. They would all sing on the trains, the preposterous memory of whole carriages of happy soldiers in chorus. He wondered what those fleeing the front had thought of their melodious wake of sound as they were carried toward the lines.

The day that they had taken the train to Folkestone, the platform had been thick with families and well-wishers. A band was playing "Home Sweet Home." And Ben's reputation, long cemented among his friends, spread through the rest of his regiment by the day's end. Not one, not two, but three admirers showed to press mementos into his hand, and to hang about his neck. The little bald sergeant had looked at him and laughed, and each of the girls had their turn of a squeeze and a hug and Ben behaved the exact same way to all three, which, he now thought, must have hurt them all equally. But he couldn't blame himself for his absence of heart that morning, since, just when eyes were already upon him, there appeared a maître d' from a Leicester Square chophouse, demanding Ben's arrest. He was a red-faced Italian, crossing back and forth between languages, raising his hands against Ben as if to strike him, flapping an unpaid bill in front of his face. Ben recognized him at once; they had taken him for about fifty pounds with a fake diamond pin. His sergeant intervened, pushing the man backward. Ben had bowed politely. No, he thought to himself, you played it up. You got a laugh from the girls, from Chimer and David and all the watching troops as the Italian was removed from the platform. And the boys have paid, above and beyond, for every petty crime and each stolen pound, and perhaps I haven't, thought Ben.

>●<

McAteer was waiting for them the next day, this time with Neville, his plugger, a jaundiced, thick-lipped pianist. McAteer held up his hands in surrender after the first performance, and Neville made a little bow of compliance that Jergens seemed to take some pleasure in.

"How about a drink?" said McAteer as they signed their second contract. "On Hamm's Music, of course."

"I don't know," said Ben curtly.

"Positively, absolutely rude not to," said Jergens with great humor.

"Neville, come with us," ordered McAteer.

McAteer slunk his arm through Ben's and led the Englishman out the door. As they walked down Twenty-eighth Street, Neville chatted intently with Jergens about the joy captured in his lyrics.

"All good?" asked McAteer.

"Are we fast enough?" asked Ben. "Should we speed things up?"

"Not at all," said McAteer. "All on track. Didn't get a chance to apologize for your policeman. Should have taken care of that before he even got to you. How's the hand?"

"All right," said Ben. "I'll play again. He just drinks too damned much. Hard to know what's going to happen."

"Glad you're fine," said McAteer, ignoring Ben's concern. "I thought I'd bring in Neville to play today just in case. You're doing well boy, you are. Take the day off tomorrow, we'll fix Mr. Jergens with more bank business. Go out to Coney. I'll take you if you want. I think you could do with a bit of unwinding."

"Why?" asked Ben, a little shocked that McAteer should blame anything on him, rather than on Jergens's tempestuous character. "I'm well enough."

"Your policeman," said McAteer. "You broke his jaw. Just calm yourself a bit. There's such a thing as being too eager, too ready. Find yourself an amusement tomorrow, all right my boy?"

McAteer walked their group to Gallagher's, a local establishment filled with those who had left work early for the day and those who had yet to make it back from lunch. Publishers and pluggers, songwriters and pitchmen, gathered out of the early-summer sun.

There was a fan whirring over a bucket of ice, circulating a dribble of cold air. The white paint on the ceiling had yellowed from smoke. McAteer waved at an old gentleman sitting alone in a corner. The man squinted, unsure of who was greeting him, raised his hat politely.

"Simmons," improvised McAteer. "Grand old man."

He directed them toward a booth in the back of the bar and ordered four whiskeys. When they arrived McAteer raised a toast to the Cattle Industry, which the four men happily clinked on.

"If I thought you men were just songwriters, we probably wouldn't even be having this conversation," laughed McAteer, almost to himself.

"Why's that?" asked Jergens.

"Songwriters," said McAteer, "they're the foundation of the industry, God bless them. And like every other foundation in this city, they spend their days being stepped on. You see," he continued, "I know I can't lose money on your songs. Cost me less than a penny to print the music, but you turned over every right you have to that song for a lousy eighty dollars. I might turn over ten thousand on 'Elsa Lee.' Maybe more on your other."

"Is your intention to mock us?" asked Jergens. "Because you're heading there fast."

"My intention," said McAteer, "is to explain my business to you. I'm just an employee, same as you get your eighty, at the end of the week I get my check whether I've sold a hundred or a hundred thousand songs. Same damned check. The money in this business isn't in songwriting nor acquisitions, and it's not in playing, nor bandleading. It begins and ends in publishing." He dabbed the back of his neck with his handkerchief and continued. "You know how many sheets of 'After the Ball' sold in this country alone?"

"A million," said Ben.

"Almost four million," said McAteer.

"So why tell us?" said Ben.

"Because," said McAteer, "I'm not a rich man. But the only way to make real money, and there's plenty of it, is to move *into* publishing. To buy in. Now Neville here's never been wrong. If he says it's going to sell, it sells. I don't doubt him. What we need isn't a hit, but a piece of the hit. I've been saving for eight years to buy a piece of Hamm's and I've got plenty put away, but what I need is money *now*. We could have a hit on our hands, and we won't see another red cent. We could make our money back in one song, maybe two. Hamm's has got a deep enough catalog anyway. We've been turning over forty thousand dollars a year for the last five years. Worst we'll have is a dull deal. Best, a money machine. If you come in with me, we could do it together."

McAteer took a breath and ceased to talk, leaving the silence hanging among them. Ben looked over at Jergens. Jergens looked back at Ben.

"Out of interest," said Ben, "what would a stake in a firm as prestigious as Hamm's be worth?"

"For a hundred thousand, maybe even ninety, we could have a large controlling interest. What's that in England, Mr. Newcombe, twenty, twenty-two thousand pounds?"

Ben nodded and was about to speak when Jergens interrupted.

"Mr. O'Keefe," said Jergens, "I've got a lot respect for you. You're good at your job and I'm not saying you aren't." He paused to drain the end of his glass of whiskey. "I'm a cattleman. It's just not my business." Ben almost liked Jergens for taking a stand.

"You don't want to think it over?" asked McAteer, his voice steady.

"Thank you kindly," said Jergens. "Writing a song is a pleasure but next week or so, I'll be back west again."

"It'll practically run itself," pleaded McAteer. "Stick around for a month, you'll see."

"Thank you," said Jergens. "But no thank you. I'm sorry, I didn't mean to speak for you, Ben."

Ben had no room in which to maneuver. "No, my friend," said Ben. "I think we're in agreement. Mr. O'Keefe, you're a good man, but it's just not our game."

McAteer slapped the table and broke into a smile. "You can't blame me for trying." He put the money for their drinks down on the table and seemed entirely unperturbed by what was, to Ben, a straightforward rejection of their entire scheme.

The following morning, Ben took his time brushing his teeth. McAteer had explained that his decision to take a day off was made partially for Ben's own good, but mostly to let Jergens stew in his own loneliness. What McAteer had failed to recognize was that it was not simply Jergens who did not know what to do with himself in New York, but also Ben. Waking, Ben knew that the entire extent of his day was planned about feeding himself at lunch, and how to stretch that task out to occupy his time. He sat on the edge of his bed and slowly slid his hands inside his shoes, feeling the thinness of the soles.

Without family, without friends, Ben knew he was confronting a yawning vacuum. He wanted to look backward, to remember his friends, but there were none left who could share his memories.

His thoughts were interrupted by a knock on the door.

"Come along, pal o'mine, come along," shouted McAteer from the hallway. "You're not too busy, are you?"

It was one of those clean May days where the brightness of the sunlight is revealing, making familiar city blocks new again, illuminating previously unnoticed flourishes as if directed by theatrical footlights. Even the cloudy smudges of coal dust on white brick were granted a natural beauty. The streets were crowded, as if all New Yorkers had risen, opened their windows, and declared it a fine day for walking. They paused as a pair of horses with bright white sweat stains dragged a cart heaped with secondhand clothes past them. McAteer didn't want to go to Coney, too crowded on such a day, he said, so they walked along the piers on the Hudson, accompanied by the deep bellows of the liners and the busy skirting of the tugs.

It occurred to Ben again that he was not the only lonely man. Surely if McAteer had better places to be on a free afternoon he would not be willing to spend the day with him. He could imagine that McAteer's was a business of many acquaintances and few friends. He remembered what McAteer said. He should like him, but did not have to trust him. They passed a group of well-dressed ladies in white summer dresses and lace frills. In tandem, the two men paused and swept their hats from their heads, receiving a passing giggle in return. When they continued their walk, McAteer asked, "Did you leave a girl behind?"

"None in particular," said Ben.

"England must be crawling with desperate women," said McAteer, as if he were suddenly plotting a transatlantic journey. "There can't be all that many good men still in the country."

"I don't suppose there are," said Ben. He remembered the train pulling out for Folkestone and meeting each of his sweethearts' eyes and blowing three kisses of identical proportion and knowing now he'd never see any of them ever again. The moment of thought meant a moment of silence. At the corner of Seventy-second Street Ben paused, uncertain which direction they wished to head in.

"Geography not your strong suit?" asked McAteer.

"No," said Ben. "Though I can read the stars."

"What do they say? Money on the cards? Sudden wealth steaming your way?"

"No," said Ben. "Astronomy, not astrology. If I'm lost I can read the stars."

"Have you ever?"

Ben nodded. "In France. Compasses didn't work out there. So much metal in the ground that the needle couldn't tell east from west."

"Is that so?"

Ben nodded. He didn't know why he was telling McAteer this. He wanted to be open. How open could he be? There was no harm in it, he told himself. It wasn't a betrayal, he thought, nothing given away about the boys. Ben understood that by confessing things to McAteer he was, in a sense, asking for help. Not like a child, not instinctive grasping, but more flattering still, for he had sought him out, could tell him things that the rest of America did not yet know.

"We'd wait," said Ben. "Just lie there in the middle of nowhere, in mud, with the odd flare going off and wait for the clouds to pass, hope that they passed. Nights could be so quiet. When you're listening to yourself, when you're laying wire and it's the loudest sound in the night."

"And if the clouds didn't pass?"

"You'd wait through the day."

"You did the right thing coming over here," said McAteer. "I can tell you that."

By the end of the day, Ben felt light. He was surprised at himself. He had come from chaos to a state of merry diversion in one day, and the black whirl in his mind was receding. The past was no longer stalking him. His friends were patient with him, allowing room for new worries over Jergens. Perhaps, he thought, he had found a way to live where he could dare to look into the future. He liked the odds of working for McAteer, of the twenty percent that roping might earn; he even thought he might find a pocket to pick, given half a chance.

The difference he felt before his talk with McAteer and after was as stark as bone on blood. What he needed now was friendship, particularly that of a woman, outside the competitive step of men. Despite a liking for McAteer, he did not wish to end up with the hated wife, the lost mistress. One day he would want nothing to do with money, just the simple American pursuit of happiness. And out of all variations of happiness he knew that what he really missed was the contact of making love. But no more of what he was before, no more pretending that his own actions were of no consequence. He knew better than that now, was willing to admit it, and wanted to find a woman to trust.

Chapter Fourteen

AT FOUR O'CLOCK on Tuesday, Ben had the easy task of persuading Jergens to step from their familiar Broadway stroll into a well-appointed bar off Fifty-third Street, walled with misted mirrors and brightened by polished brass fixtures. They sat sipping cold beer, discussing the possibility of taking an evening tour of the Bowery, when the house pianist began a familiar tune. Ben stopped in mid-conversation and smiled, eyes widening. "I don't believe it," declared Jergens loudly.

"How about that?" said Ben.

Both men stood and walked over to the piano player, who, despite the fact that a toothpick hung from the side of his mouth, accompanied himself with a whistle.

"Excuse me," said Jergens.

"Sure bud," said the piano man.

"Could you tell me what you're playing?" asked Jergens.

"Course." He peered at his sheet music. "'Elsa Lee,'" he said.

To their great disappointment, McAteer was out, but his secretaries were surprisingly courteous. Neville shook their hands warmly and asked if they'd been working on anything new.

"Do you know how 'Elsa Lee' is doing?" asked Jergens.

Neville shook his head. "You'll be fine on it. I didn't know you'd taken a piece."

"We haven't," explained Ben.

"Oh," said Neville. "Then you've nothing to worry about either way." Ben wanted to laugh. Neville was good.

"Just tell O'Keefe we'd like to see him," said Jergens. "Tell him unless he's anything fixed, we'll swing by and pick him up tomorrow around lunchtime."

"Have you changed your mind?" asked Ben as they walked back down the stairs.

"Not sure," said Jergens. "But it would be nice to know how our girl's doing."

At least McAteer had replanted the seed of consideration, thought Ben. He led Jergens up Broadway. As the sun dipped behind the buildings, the signs seemed to grow brighter, until New York was dominated by the lightbulbs of chophouses, lobster palaces, theaters, and the headlamps of passing cars.

"How about a show?" asked Jergens, pointing to his left, up at a board advertising the *Follies*.

"I'm not really dressed," said Ben.

"Well I'm dressed for two," said Jergens.

"As always," said Ben.

"You don't like it?" Ben looked him up and down. Pink shirt, black-and-white-striped tie, a brown suit pinstriped with jade.

"No, no," said Ben. "I think you dress very exclusively."

"I just don't get a chance to wear things like this back west," said Jergens. "My wife doesn't approve."

"Well then," said Ben. "What would you like to see?"

There was neon all around. Electric women clutching umbrellas. Neon cats playing with balls of burning wool. Just up the block was a sign flashing last month's big production, *The Happy Ending*, farther down Forty-second Street was *Boomerang*, and closest to them, the week-old and well-reviewed new play by Max Marcin, *Cheating Cheaters*.

"*Cheating Cheaters*," said Jergens. "It's new this month."

The theater was hot and cramped, all the orchestra seats occupied by men broiling in their tuxedos, women whose perspiring palms were absorbed by their long evening gloves. Both of their hearts stopped somewhere near the beginning of the third act, when a figure stepped from the wings, dark bobbed hair, pale face, and lips full and red under the lights. She was full-figured, breasts promi-nent, calves shapely, arms long and lithe, playing the small part of a gangster's girl pretending to be a high-society maid. Jergens nudged Ben, but Ben was already resting his chin in his hands and his elbows on his knees. She walked as if the stage were made from eggshells. It made her seem dainty yet feline, a predatory kitten.

"That," whispered Jergens, "is your wife." He flipped through the program and pointed to her name.

When she spoke, the two were silent, when she twirled before her beau, Jergens meshed his fingers together in irritation, and when they kissed, Ben found himself smiling. As a child he had thought he loved the theater his father worked in, but later realized what he adored was the knowledge of artifice. The wooden balls rolling down tin chutes for thunder, chains clanking, bats agitated at the end of strings. This one, this actress, had the perfect combination of artifice and innocence.

They saved their applause at the curtain only for their favorite, standing for their own private ovation so she could not help but notice them. She broke into the sweetest smile, as a person, not an actress. She smiled only for them. As they exited the theater, Jergens rifled through his pockets. "We must send her flowers."

They bought a bouquet from a street vendor and waited expec-tantly by the backstage door. In small groups, the performers filed out, and when finally Miss Katherine Howells emerged, it was on the arm of a man perhaps twenty years her senior, dressed in an immaculate tuxedo. Ben looked at her and hid his disappointment. She wished them a good evening as she passed, and Jergens con-cealed their bouquet behind his back. The elegant couple got into a shiny Thomas Flyer, and the chauffeur cranked the car. The engine purred happily as the car pulled away from the curb. Miss Howells did not give her two admirers a backward glance.

>⋙⋘

"Perhaps it was her father," said Jergens.

"Perhaps you're mine," laughed Ben. She's a money girl, he thought. The hardest to prise away, the hardest to keep hold of. As a rule, in London, they'd all steered clear of them.

"Shall we follow her?" asked Jergens. He pressed the flowers into the arms of a passing girl, then reached out a hand for a taxi that was lolling slowly down the street.

Miss Howells and her companion drove straight to the Hotel Astor and rose in the elevator to the restaurant on the roof. The two men followed them up, and Ben's ten-dollar tip resulted in a twenty-minute wait under the green-and-gray-striped awnings. Herds of white-coated waiters bustled past while Jergens stared down from the mansard roof, dizzy among such elegance. They were the only two not in evening clothes. The maître d' hid them at a romantic table hemmed by a grove of palms. Finally seated, Ben had a partially obscured view of the actress. When her escort reached over the table, she took his hand. She held it tenderly, but she was an actress. She looked prettier in the candlelight. Lips very red, perhaps done for her by the makeup artist. The face lacked a perfect proportion, the eyes just a little large, combining with her crescent brows to give her an expression of childish awe. He strained to catch the sound of her voice, but couldn't pick it out from the rest of the dining room chatter.

Jergens called over a busboy.

"You see that couple over there? You keep his water glass filled. What's he drinking? Good, give him a beer on the house, put it on our bill. Don't tell him where it's from."

They waited patiently, Ben amused, Jergens drinking two doubles, intent on his plan, until the gentleman stood to excuse himself for the bathroom.

"Hello there," said Jergens approaching the young woman. She looked up with the puzzled gaze of one rifling her memory for slight acquaintances, her eyes widening at the glare of Jergens's attire. "Am I very much mistaken or were you not on stage at the Eltinge tonight?"

Katherine Howells smiled pleasantly as her face relaxed. "Yes," she said. "That was me."

"You were just wonderful," said Jergens. He turned to Ben. "Could I introduce my old friend, Ben Newcombe? I'm Henry Jergens."

She offered them both her hand.

"We're not disturbing you, are we?" asked Jergens.

"Not yet," said Katherine, "but I'm in the middle of dinner." Ben was happy to notice that even though Jergens had initiated the conversation, she shared her glances between the two of them. Her lips shone underneath the electric chandelier. He had been afraid she would be stupid, but the eyes were sharp and flinty. He didn't feel like running away. He didn't want to move much at all.

Jergens didn't turn away. He looked up quickly and saw no signs from the direction of the bathroom.

"Do you know Gregory Schultz?"

"The producer?" asked Katherine.

"An old friend of mine," said Jergens. "I'm sure he'd be glad to meet you."

"You're very kind," said Katherine.

Jergens pulled out a card, offered it to her. She took it, thanked him, and slipped it into her purse.

"I'll tell you something," said Jergens. "After you're through, maybe you'd like to come over and join us for a drink?"

"Come on," said Ben. "Come over for one drink. Last of the French champagne."

"You're very kind," said Katherine, "but I happen to be with someone."

"You can bring her too," said Ben.

"Him."

"The man you're with?" asked Ben. "Why not. I'd be happy to buy your father a drink."

She laughed.

"Mr. Newcombe's only in New York for a week or two," continued Jergens, flowing freely in his alcohol. "A genuine hero. From the war in Europe. Really, you'd make him so happy."

Ben wished Jergens hadn't said it. It gave him a quake. He stood there between the tables, falling back into the long stare of the soldier. He remembered the girl on the street asking for a match and how he had fled and how she'd laughed at him. "Perhaps we shouldn't inconvenience the lady," he interrupted, taking Jergens gently by the arm. "It was a pleasure to meet you," said Ben. "I trust you'll enjoy your evening."

He heard Jergens's stage whisper as he turned away, "Painfully shy."

"Hello," said a voice behind them, and Ben turned to face Katherine Howells's dinner companion, a few years older than Jergens, distinguished by a white skunk streak that ran down the middle of his hair. They muttered an awkward introduction, and in less than a half minute retreated to their own table.

Once they were reseated, Ben began to breathe more easily, but wondered why he had panicked. Not exactly myself, am I, he worried. Not with women, at least. Jergens was sipping his drink, hadn't noticed a thing.

"Gregory Schultz?" Ben asked.

"Read his name in the paper today," said Jergens in one of his louder whispers. "Tiniest white lie. On your behalf."

"Wasn't that a little direct?"

"Would I tell you how to approach a woman in London?"

"It's not Kansas City," said Ben.

"She'll always remember you my boy," said Jergens. "The tall, handsome, almost silent lamppost." Jergens bleated laughter at Ben, and in spite of himself Ben joined in, seeing the amusement in his newfound maladroitness, knowing that he would have to change should he ever wish to defuse his loneliness. The days of Abu Abu seemed long gone.

Chapter Fifteen

AFTER DINNER, JERGENS insisted on a visit to the Bowery. Ben was not worried about being recognized. He had always obeyed Farrell's original advice and moved quickly about the streets, never making a friend outside of Miner's. On such a damp night the Bowery was a land of dark corners under shattered street lamps, home to every tramp and outcast from steamships, rail yards, and open roads. The dispossessed, with their split lips and stubble, cabbage ears and bleeding gums, flocked to the main stem and her all-night missions. Drunken floppers stood in groups outside shabby lodging houses, peering with red-rimmed eyes at passersby. Jergens, in his pink shirt and black-and-white tie, seemed to get more uncomfortable with every step of his patent leathers.

Ben found his only discomfort was in Jergens's company. Everyone had a friend they'd rather see in private; a friend too ugly, too foolish, too brash or irritable, one who turned heads for all the wrong reasons. Jergens was simply too conspicuous for Ben to feel at peace. It was like walking through the Bowery at the head of a garish parade. He hoped that McAteer or Neville moved somewhere behind them, one eye on their well-being. It may have been his old neighborhood, but then his shabby suit had been little better than the street sleepers.

"Isn't this the most extraordinary city in the world?" asked Jergens. "A half hour ago we were in the finest restaurant in New York and now look at us. Moving unnoticed through the underbelly of the beast."

A month ago, Ben had smiled when local boys pelted the tourist buses with fruit. He'd felt like one of them, but now, if he was stopped, he would be guilty of too many crimes: of being wealthy, being English, being a slummer. A group of men were standing around a large pushcart filled with shoes, one using a friend's shoulder to balance, hopping up and down, sorting through the odd collection, keeping a bare foot from the filthy sidewalk.

Ben turned the other way. There was a crowd waiting outside a door, reasonably dressed young men and women. Jergens paused and said, "Need a drink."

Ben thought Jergens had probably meant to ask a question, but the words had come tumbling out as an order.

"I'm not sure we should," said Ben, looking at the banner draped across the door announcing that tonight was a hop in honor of the Clover Social Club.

"Suit yourself," shrugged Jergens, walking toward the end of the line. "I'm getting the hell off this street." Ben followed reluctantly, remembering McAteer's warning that there would always be moments of improvisation.

The gathering was not as proper as they had thought. The clothes that had looked good enough in the dark were revealed to be ratty and second-rate in the arc lights inside. Rather than suaveness, pride was taken in too-tight jackets, bowlegs, and biceps. These were Irish shopgirls and boot boys, dressed up for a dance. We've just walked into fucking Dublin, thought Ben. Every girl had her floorwalker, and every floorwalker held a per-fecto between thumb and forefinger, puffing smoke to the roof. They took turns in two-steps across the floor, and all about was the sense of mock gallantry. Ben didn't think these were men of knives and guns, but figured that most knuckles were chafed. Jergens stuck out like a lone candy cane on an empty Christmas tree, blissfully unaware of his impact. He seemed fascinated by the rituals of the Social Club and stared at the pairing off, the plainer girls with their backs against the wall, the knots of boys and their rising brogue.

"We're in another country," said Jergens as they made their way to an improvised bar to order whiskeys. "I wouldn't take that actress in *here* for a drink, I tell you that straight. Wish I'd have worn more green. I've got the perfect suit back in the hotel."

Ben spoke softly, but Jergens seemed ignorant of danger.

"Are you thinking of investing?" he whispered, taking a sip with his head down. "I just don't see how it's such a bad investment. A company with steady income, a possible bright future, that we, you and I, might be partly responsible for, and we're not to be intrigued? It's betting on yourself." He tried to steer Jergens away from a table of younger men.

"Perhaps you're right," said Jergens. He looked about him. "In Missouri, you'd be hard-pressed to find a place like this."

"Really," said Ben softly.

"How about in England?" asked Jergens. Ben winced, but only disconcerted glances were thrown their way. Neither of them even attempted to ask a woman to dance, and to Ben's relief they seemed to be either tolerated or ignored. An hour after their arrival, a short man approached, no more than twenty-one, with a sweet freckled face.

"Gentleman," he said, "you've been asked for a drink in the back rooms by Mr. O'Sullivan."

Neither Ben nor Jergens responded immediately, so the youth added, "He'd be the leader of this association."

Mr. O'Sullivan was sitting on the edge of a desk talking to various men, each of whom had taken off his coat; the room looked like muscles and smelled like a gymnasium. The windows were shuttered, the rough wooden floor bare. In the corner an umbrella stand was filled with baseball bats.

Three years ago, in east London, they'd walked into an Irish pub. Chimer had asked for a whiskey. "What kind," they'd asked. Chimer had said, "The cheap kind." And the big bastard in the corner had said, "There's no cheap whiskey here, only a cheap Englishman." Chimer had had the good sense to tell him to fuck off and the fists flew, but then there were four of them. Even so, Chimer gained a broken nose and a gash in the back of his head.

"Strangers among us," said Mr. O'Sullivan to their orchestrated intrusion. He made no move to greet them formally, to shake their hands, or even stand. He gave extra attention to the mysterious figure of Henry Jergens, attempting to interpret his manner of dress.

"And who would you be, now?" he asked. "It's an Associated dance and I can't remember you being associated at all. Unless you're someone's brother or uncle and have a family tree to show us, I'm wondering what your business is."

"We were just coming in for a drink," explained Jergens.

"You're not hawking anything now, are you?" he asked suspiciously.

Ben was loathe to talk, to admit to his Englishness.

"What's your name?" asked O'Sullivan.

"Henry Jergens."

"A Dane?"

"Once upon a time," Jergens replied.

"And you?" asked O'Sullivan, pointing his finger at Ben.

"Ohio," said Ben quickly.

"I asked for your name."

"Newcombe."

"Have I seen you before?"

Don't say it, thought Ben, scared again, but in another direction, Don't say Miner's Theater. "There must be a few things you've never seen before," covered Ben, his attempt at an American accent faltering.

"Yes," said O'Sullivan, "like a conchie in the Clover Club." He turned to one of the men standing beside him. "Terry," he said, "is it just the one you heard?"

The man on his left pointed a stubby cigar at Ben. "Just him."

"So would that be *London*, Ohio, you're from?" asked O'Sullivan, smiling and casting a glance toward the stand of bats.

Ben shrugged, ready to take a beating. He would not fight back, would go down quickly. He presumed they would not be so hard on the Missourian.

"Would you like to join our association?" teased O'Sullivan.

"How would we do that?" asked Jergens, his voice a little shaky.

"They say it costs an arm *and* a leg."

There was a snort of suppressed laughter from the man closest to the window, but the others kept puffing on their cigars. The inquisition was interrupted by a knock on the door.

The same small man who had walked them to the office peeked around the door and said, "Just to say that there's a man by the name of McAteer downstairs."

Ben reddened for a moment, as if the name would ruin their illusion, then calmed as soon as he saw the thankful blankness of Jergens's face.

"Julius?" asked O'Sullivan. "And he's so busy he'd like me to interrupt my business?"

"Says it'd be worth it, pocket-wise, to stop whatever you might be doing to see him."

O'Sullivan laughed. He jabbed his finger toward the door. "You can both go." His colleagues stepped away from the two interlopers as Ben and Jergens turned for the door. "But you can leave a contribution on the table."

"Contribution?" protested Jergens weakly; Ben was already placing twenty dollars before O'Sullivan, silently thanking McAteer for his intervention.

Chapter Sixteen

IN THE MORNING, Ben wandered next door and poked about Jergens's room while the Missourian bathed, looking for the signs of attachment that would mark him as one of them, those with friends and families. A wardrobe of rainbow selections, nearly thirty ties and as many collars, studs, and handkerchiefs. There was a picture of Jergens's wife and six children by the bed. Ben squatted to look at it closely. The woman was a sturdy figure, prematurely aged. Her children were lined up at her feet like a hunter's game at the day's end. Wife and kids, Ben asked himself. We were never ones for all that, were we?

On their way to Hamm's, Jergens insisted on stopping to use the bathroom of a coffee shop. Ben propped himself against the counter and looked around him. There, in a booth by the door, sat the actress. Doing what he did for a living meant Ben was all but immune to coincidence. He looked at the signpost through the diner window. They were barely four blocks from the Eltinge Theater.

She was engrossed in the *Herald*, and Ben was at leisure to examine her. He liked the intensity given to such a quotidian task and wondered what she was reading that held her so rapt. Probably theatrical reviews. He was still considering whether or not to approach when Jergens came bustling out of the bathroom and followed his gaze to the window.

Jergens tugged at his arm. "What was her name?"

"Kate?" said Ben.

"Katherine, that's right," said Jergens. "Go on then, say hello."

Ben looked at him closely. "Why would I do that?" What if he talks me up in the war again, thought Ben. He'd do it, wouldn't he?

"Because you're flesh and blood," said Jergens. "Go on."

And when Ben hesitated, Jergens did not. He wondered just how innocent Jergens's attentions were. The photograph in his hotel room, of six children and the horse-faced wife, could be interpreted as a reason for either fidelity or a need to stray. Ben drifted after him.

"Do you remember me?" asked Jergens loudly.

Katherine squinted, folded her paper, then smiled and nodded. "The close friend of Mr. Schultz, the Broadway producer."

"That's right," said Jergens.

"I happened to meet him at a party last night," said Katherine. "Isn't that just the strangest thing? I told him I'd met a friend of his. I even had your card on me. Jergen, right?"

"Jergens," he corrected.

"And he'd never heard of you."

Jergens looked abashed.

"He was merely guilty," said Ben, stepping forward, "of trying to impress you on my behalf."

Katherine nodded. "And you're the wounded soldier? What war?" she asked. "The Civil?"

Jergens interrupted. "You can't blame Ben," he said. "I'm just a fool ma'am, you can see that. I may be a liar, but he *was* in the war."

She looked Ben in the eye. "Is it true?"

Ben did not flinch from the gaze. "It is."

"Then you'll have to accept my apologies. I just made the assumption of birds of a feather."

She paused, placated, seemed to be weighing an idea. Finally, she spoke again. "Maybe you can redeem yourself." She held out a small card to Ben. "In a few weeks we're auctioning war bonds at the theater at intermission. Show them this and you're my guests. But I want to see some hands raised."

Ben took the card from her.

"Don't look so worried, soldier," she teased. "It's on behalf of the English."

Ben laughed. "Very happy to know we're on the same side."

"We'll be there," said Jergens, peering over Ben's shoulder, "with pockets bulging."

At Hamm's, details were discussed. McAteer had introduced the concept of the putative owner, a Mr. Hanlon, who only visited the office once a week to sign the paychecks. McAteer was left alone for the most part, in charge of acquisitions *and* finance. Hanlon, for instance, had no idea that a song called "Elsa Lee" had sold seventeen hundred copies in its first week. A first-week sale that strong might change a man's mind about selling. According to McAteer, his boss was a bean counter. Burned in the stock market in '88, Hanlon was anxious for cash in uncertain times. McAteer mentioned that he had saved eleven thousand dollars for his own investment. Jergens looked pleasantly surprised. It left seventy-nine thousand to be divided between Ben and Jergens. There followed a brief, over-polite period of haggling. Ben began aggressively as instructed, claiming a majority stake, then slowly backed down, letting Jergens wade in for a commitment of thirty-five thousand dollars.

"Say we were to do this," asked Jergens. "How much time do we have to raise the money?"

"The problem is this," said McAteer. "The quicker we move, the better. Hanlon'll be hot for the deal, but if 'Elsa Lee' should break before we close, he'll know what I've been up to. Hell, he'll kick me across the Hudson. How long will it take you to lay your hands on the money?"

"It's a bit of a problem," said Ben, "coming all the way from England. I'd say the best part of the week. I'll have it wired; it's just that it'll have to go through my bankers in Shropshire. They're not exactly city-quick."

"Mr. Jergens?"

"About the same as Mr. Newcombe. Have to sell a couple of stocks, would need my father's signature if I'm not there. Might be quicker to jump a train myself. Two days there, two here, a day of business. If I left Friday, I could be back next Wednesday."

Jergens could not travel alone back to Kansas City. He must be followed, from train to house, house to bank, bank to station, station to New York City. McAteer described it as the dreariest part of the job, allowing no straying, rationed sleeping, and a constant heightened alertness. Ben, he said, should be counting himself lucky that McAteer had men available for the journey. Should Jergens confess their scheme to his wife, or worse, his father, the investment would most likely be questioned. While assembling thirty-five thousand dollars might now make perfect sense to Henry Jay Jergens, there was no doubt that it would raise eyebrows throughout his circle of friends and family. McAteer could not prevent such an action, but a detailed report would help him calibrate how Jergens might be best played on his return.

McAteer's cons presented the lure of deceiving another. Would an honest man buy into a business, knowing that company assets were hidden to the seller? Would he not think he was taking money from another man's pocket? Or would he justify it to himself, calling it a simple matter of business, putting value on his own creative involvement, dismissing his knowledge of their manipulation of company accounts?

McAteer's man rang long distance from Kansas City to confirm that he was taking his only amusement in his long journey from the furtive movements of Henry Jergens. He noted how Jergens had waited outside the bank before it opened, greeted the clerk at the door with a nervous tip of his boater, and then proceeded inside. McAteer passed the information on to Ben, doing an impression of Jergens as a man hunching his shoulders close to his head, as if a turtle-like neck might somehow disguise the truth of his business. Most importantly, Ben now knew that Jergens had emerged from his bank clutching a pair of thick envelopes and had taken a taxi to two double whiskeys at a nearby bar. Heavy money, explained McAteer, always changed men. It made their eyes dance fast, their pace increase, their brows sweat.

"Wait till you see it," said McAteer. "Maybe it'll do the same to you."

For four days Ben and McAteer were freed from the constraints of their roles. Ben went to the cobbler's and had his shoes resoled, took his lunches alone, but in the middle of movement. He sat on either the white marble steps of the public library, between the two stone lions and the street-colored pigeons, or down on Broad Street, watching a building rise. The steel skeleton was being covered in the meat of concrete and still the trucks arrived with lumber, pipes, and bricks. If he waited till the end of the day, just before the foreman blew his whistle, the dipping sun caught the cement dust on the air. Ben thought he could see promise in the golden haze.

On the Sunday, they made the ride out to Northport in McAteer's rented Knox Runabout, both wearing summer suits, McAteer's a sky blue, Ben's a seersucker yellow. At the beach, McAteer rented an umbrella and chairs. Ben swam alone in the cold water, looking back at McAteer staring out at him. After a brief lunch of sandwiches, Ben went for a walk. He liked it down on the water's edge, where he was never met with silence, always the accompaniment of the waves. On his return, McAteer was standing ankle-deep in the swirling water, trousers rolled up.

"What are you doing spending your days with an old man like me?" asked McAteer. "You should be chasing little lambs up and down the beach."

Ben shrugged. "I have my eye on a certain young lady."

"Good for you, pal o'mine," said McAteer, with just a trace of regret. "Well then, who is she? Where did you meet her? When will you two meet again?"

Ben smiled but said nothing.

"What is it?" asked McAteer. "I'm too American, am I? Don't know you well enough to ask such a thing?"

"No, no," said Ben. "It's just that I probably think more about her than she does about me. She's an actress," he explained. "As a rule, I think they have a lot of admirers."

"When will you see her?"

"In a few weeks," said Ben. "At a benefit for the war."

"Are you speaking?" smirked McAteer.

"Maybe I just shouldn't go." Ben had suffered a minor quake at his own mention of the war.

McAteer gave Ben a slight slap on the back. "I think it would be good for you if you did."

That evening, they rode back into the city in the pollen-dusted Knox with Ben's wet suit tied to a door handle, whipping in the wind. The sun wrapped the skies in summer gold. Manhattan had been gifted a set of low orange clouds that looked like airships tethered to her peaks. At dinner Ben tested the limits of McAteer's generosity, bringing along a farmer's appetite from his day of exercise. Do I trust him?, Ben asked himself. What if there came a time when it was more profitable for McAteer to call the British Embassy than to pay Ben his deserved amount? Even tonight's dinner: was it a claim for a more parental role, or was it a way of establishing control? But the thing is, thought Ben, I've no one else to lean on.

On Wednesday morning Ben visited the coffee shop opposite Grand Central where he and Jergens had encountered Katherine Howells. He drank three cups of coffee, waiting, wondering if she would appear again, not wanting to wait till the following week for another glance as a spectator. Finally, he wrote his address on a napkin and slipped the waitress a dollar, on the off-chance Miss Howells was a regular. Then he hurried back to the hotel to await the arrival of Henry Jergens.

PART TWO

MR. HENRY JERGENS
June 1916

Chapter One

HENRY JERGENS WAS snoring soundly on the train, albeit with one eye open. He knew he was being watched, had been followed all the way from New York to Kansas City, stalked quietly, as much the presence of a guardian angel as a ghost. In Kansas City, he had stayed at the Cumberland, dressed drably, and wandered only between hotel and bank, checking now and then from dining room tables that his shadow had not strayed. All through his brief journey, his gait had been as hurried and self-conscious as a child with stolen sweets heading through a dime store's doors.

Back in teeming Grand Central, Henry understood that the brief trip to his native Midwest had not so much relaxed him as made him aware of how little he belonged there. Nor had he any great liking for New York, with its towering oppression, all the preposterous presumption of equality and opportunity, when all he saw was beggary and dirt. He was still not sure where he would move with his wife when there was more money in the bank, but it would be far from the dizzy verticality of Manhattan.

Henry checked to see if his ghost followed in the next cab then ordered his driver to take him to the Bristol Hotel. Ben was awaiting him in the lobby, reading the *New York Herald*. He rose and offered a hand, but Henry pushed it aside and grasped him with a friendly hug. He gripped him hard, felt the vague shivers of an Englishman resisting contact, but finally received a couple of awkward pats on the back and separated himself.

"Good to see you Ben," said Henry loudly. "Good to see you. God, feel like I've been gone for weeks."

Ben laughed and pointed a finger toward the ceiling. "Shall we go up for a drink?"

"Lots to discuss," said Henry, and they turned to the elevators.

"Four," said Ben, and they traveled up in silence, interrupted only by the accordion squeeze of the doors opening. Henry could feel the suspicion of Ben's look, the slight glance directed at his beaten portmanteau and the dollars within.

"So," said Ben, opening the door and allowing Henry to enter first. "How was the trip?"

"Good, good," said Henry, walking lazily across the room and placing the portmanteau on the table next to the Chesterfield. "I was thinking, you know with all the miles I've traveled in the last three weeks I could have made it to England." He collapsed into a chair with a theatrical sigh and took the glass of scotch that Ben offered. "Have you seen O'Keefe?"

"Yes," said Ben. "My money came in yesterday, so I went by to tell him we were pretty much there. Just waiting for our lyricist."

"God," said Henry quickly, "where the hell are you keeping it?"

"In the hotel safe."

"Guess I should do the same," said Henry, pointing at the portmanteau. "Not as heavy as yours, but it can burn a hole through leather."

Ben laughed. "Coming back from the bank I don't think I've ever walked so fast."

"When are we on for it?"

"Tomorrow afternoon," said Ben.

"I have a small problem," said Henry, leaning toward Ben.

And when Henry reported that checks larger than eight thousand dollars required his father's signature, he imagined that Ben's report to McAteer would make the old man's cheeks bulge with foul air. And what could a rich business partner such as Ben Newcombe do but the obvious, to hesitate for a moment or two, then propose that he pick up the difference until a time when

Henry could muster the rest of his investment. Their money sat side by side on the table the next morning, Ben's neatly packaged, Henry's in eight loose piles that he counted and recounted, making sure that every last dollar was there. Henry knew that Ben would be using a boodle, a mixture of real and fake money. He picked up one of the packets as if to weigh it by hand. He saw Ben avoid the wince, enjoyed his moment of causing the Englishman anxiety, then put the money back down on the lacquer table.

Ample amounts of cash are rarely seen, thought Henry. Ben must have thought he dealt in large enough figures, the accounts that Henry had originally submitted to McAteer when applying for his loan showed that he regularly signed checks for between five and twelve thousand dollars, but the sight of cash had a visceral effect on all men. It was no longer an intangible series of figures that traveled between bank accounts and budgets. Cash is anybody's, thought Henry, green and immediate.

It had been clear to Henry from his very first meal with Ben that he was dealing with a good amateur, unwittingly out of his league. Appearance, of course, was of paramount concern, and in that respect, Ben came well equipped. With or without thought, all humans were adherents of the nineteenth-century science of physiognomy. The untrustworthy were thin-lipped, shifty-eyed, sharp-nosed, and shirking. And there Ben had sat in the chug of that railroad car with healthy cheeks, warm blue eyes, a patrician mustache. All in all, the face of anyone that he chose to present himself as. A confidence man and more amazingly, a veteran of the war. What could be better to convince a man that you had a past? Yet Henry knew that he had an unfair advantage, after all: he had been creating schemes for the last twenty years of his life.

At least Ben had been able to think on his feet. Henry thought of his drunken playing during their first Harlem night, how Ben had swung and knocked a policeman clean off his feet. Extremely effective, but a giveaway. No bunco man would use a fist where a word would suffice. Henry would have gone to the station and spent his night in the tank and laughed it off with his mark. Which meant that Ben was either a roughneck, which Henry doubted, or at that moment had been acting in his own personal interest.

Henry had seen Ben shake every now and then, minor tremors running along his body. Often, he seemed on the edge of a stammer. That was the strength and weakness of Ben as a professional bunco. The experience of war was an absolute first-class convincer, but how fragile a man had he become? When would he crack, and was he strong enough to carry a con off? So far, good enough, thought Henry. If he could carry the music con, then Henry concluded that he would put his confidence in him, so to speak. It meant, of course, that Ben really had seen war. A man who was protecting himself, apparently able-bodied, and a soldier, could therefore be only one thing: a deserter. That knowledge could be a powerful particular to hold over a man.

Different shops worked in different ways. And it was an original experience for Henry to be surrounded by, performed for, by such a full cast. He was much impressed by the intricacy of the music approach. It had a combination of tradition and modernity that appealed to him, and of course, the questions had occurred quickly to him. Where can I run this? When? With whom? But Henry knew that he was derived from a rare breed, and was unlikely to play any scheme with more than a cast of two. Always the same two, husband and wife. Such an ensemble as Ben ran with would be for distant days when he no longer had the energy and motivation to cover half a continent.

The following day proved a solemn occasion at old man Hanlon's town house, the small group having huddled around the corners of a great mahogany table in a tenebrous dining room. McAteer, Ben, and Henry sat on one side, with Hanlon and his lawyer facing them. Embroidered lace curtains soaked up any danger of sunlight. The only color in the room came from Henry's own pale blue shirt, electric pink tie, and pyrite cufflinks. He looked about and nodded in appreciation. The walls were weighed with a series of landscapes in ornate gold frames, the fireplace mantel draped in red damask, anchored by a large silver clock. Even the smell was perfect. The musky odor of a damp cellar added to the sense of oppressive opulence. Papers were passed around for signatures along with a fountain pen as thick as a man's thumb.

Henry spent the remainder of the day waiting patiently for the beginning of the turnoff. The art, and it was an art, was to force the victim into a position where he would leave town of his own accord, without suspicion that he had been conned. The best turnoff resulted in one of two outcomes: one, you'd never hear from your mark again; or two, he'd come back with a bag of cash and want to play some more. A well-executed turnoff was considered a courtesy to others who plied the same trade in different cities. A mark may not come back to the source, but maybe he'd be picked up for a game in Denver, or Sacramento. You may be doing a favor to a brother you've never met.

Like many new owners, they spent an inordinate amount of time around the office on Twenty-eighth Street. They were there as the telegraph orders for songs were supposedly delivered to their secretaries and there as McAteer read them aloud.

"Craine's Music, Boise, Idaho — two hundred fifty copies, 'Elsa Lee.'"

Henry particularly liked the famous Mr. McAteer. Among the flimflammers that Henry had encountered, he believed he had never met a man so concerned with detail. As Mr. O'Keefe, his hair was seldom washed, always exhibiting the slightly greasy exterior of a man who cared more for his business than himself. And the ink stains on the fingers was a clerkly touch of honesty, proof of the hard work that had brought him to his position of trust. And Henry did trust McAteer, thought that he would be entirely capable of making considerable money off the right man.

><

The orders got bigger in the first two weeks. Three hundred from a store in Cincinnati, McAteer would explain, more from stores on the West Coast, also selling well in Chicago and Boston. At the end of two weeks, Henry helped McAteer run the numbers and estimated that their songs alone were responsible for almost fourteen thousand dollars in profit over the first month of release.

"First we sliced the pie, now we bake the cake," McAteer would say with relish as the three men treated themselves to long lunches.

Henry's only insistence in the merry dance was that they pass a photographic studio and order a print of the new triumvirate, one for each of them. They posed in their best, complete with watch fobs and hats. Henry's suit was so shiny, a vague reflection of the photographer's bulb would be seen in the print. He'd also kept a cigar poking from his pocket. What a jolly bunch of hypocrites we are, thought Henry, but at least all smiles are genuine. On their way out, Henry had tipped the photographer twenty dollars and told him he wanted another three copies of the print for his private use. Later in the week, Ben hung his copy of the smiling men over Henry's desk.

"Well that is something now, isn't it?" said Henry. "What a trio. What's going to stop a threesome such as that?"

With only the eight thousand reaped, Henry could tell that McAteer was tempted to adjust their expenditures, but in all his experience, he knew that there was little point in skimping on twenty dollars here and there. McAteer would know that, thought Henry, so he continued to drink, ordered steak at every opportunity, occasionally a dish of oysters or lobster tails for the middle of the table.

"You like lobster, don't you boys?"

"Sure we do," said McAteer.

"And the English?"

"It's a delicacy," said Ben.

"One more plate then," ordered Henry, wiping the butter from his smiling mouth on his purple silk handkerchief, "and another glass of champagne. And the bill for Mr. O'Keefe."

At the end of every week, it had been the newly established routine of the owners to collect the week's payroll together. On Friday, June 16, they walked through the doors of the Second National Bank on the corner of Twenty-ninth and Fifth, tipped their hats to the young cashier, and made their usual request.

"I'm very sorry, sir," came the reply, "but your account has been sequestered."

McAteer laughed.

"It's not a personal account, sunshine," he said. "We're the owners of Hamm's Music and Publishing Corporation."

"I know who you are, sir," said the cashier. "That's the account I'm referring to."

McAteer said softly, "Is the bank manager here?"

"I'm afraid he's left early."

"Christ," said McAteer. "It's payday. Can you make us a loan against the account?"

"I'm afraid not, sir, the account is sequestered. Besides, only the manager could do that."

"I know," said McAteer, "and he's left early." He turned to his two co-owners and shrugged. "I don't know," he said. "Obviously some clerical error. Let's not worry about this too much. Have our weekend and come back in here first thing on Monday."

"Sequestered?" said Henry as they left, raising an arched eyebrow.

"An error," said McAteer.

"Let's hope so," said Ben.

"How long have I been here?" asked McAteer. "About fifteen years. I know this bank. They go screwy every now and then."

Conversation had already cheered by the time they turned the corner of Twenty-eighth Street and began the trudge up the stairs to their office. Henry was talking about the World Series and the chances that the Brooklyn Robins had to recover from their poor start when they opened the door to find a small man sitting waiting for them.

"This is Herbert Fording," said the secretary.

"Herbert Fording, *Esquire*," corrected the man. "Would you mind if I spoke to you gentlemen in private?"

"Not at all," said McAteer, and showed him to the spiral staircase, which they ascended one by one.

Henry followed, fascinated by the process, the players, and the sudden acceleration that had been made on his behalf. Obviously, they were upset with only eight thousand and were now trying to hurry him from town. It was real enough money that Henry had given them, had taken three months to save. To invest it, as it were, with McAteer was a risk, but Henry remained thrilled by the audacity of his intentions.

"You are Mr. O'Keefe?"

"I am," said McAteer.

"And these gentleman?"

"They are the co-owners of Hamm's Music and Publishing," said McAteer defiantly.

"I represent Irving Berlin Incorporated," said Fording. "They've filed a suit against your publishing house under the charge of plagiarism."

Fording took a sheaf of papers and spun them one hundred and eighty degrees on the desk to face McAteer.

"Plagiarism?" laughed McAteer. "How many suits like that are there on this street every week? It swings one way, it swings another. How many have been won? Maybe, *maybe* one a year. And you can tell that Jew boy that everyone knows some little nigger writes everything he ever does."

"Sir," said Fording. "If you let me speak, I can then leave and you will be free to contact your own lawyers, who, I am sure, will urge you toward settlement."

"Knock yourself out," said McAteer.

"The case is *Berlin versus Newcombe and Jergens*, two writers of yours, I believe. Hamm's Music and Publishing Corporation and its owners have also been named as co-defendants."

There was a sudden silence in the room. Henry took a half step backward and raised his hand to his mouth. Ben cast a nervous glance his way. Don't worry, my boy, thought Henry, won't say a word.

"You will find as evidence in my deposition a copy of a song they wrote entitled 'Elsa Lee.' On the ensuing page, you will see my client's original composition, 'Only Me.' I believe you will find the similarity quite disconcerting."

Fording stood. "I only came to serve you papers, but thank you for your hospitality. I should also warn you that the case has been filed at city hall with Justice O'Neill. He has decided, owing to the strength of the case, to immediately sequester all of your company's accounts. Only today, a check of thirty-two thousand dollars for my client's song was to be deposited."

"Thirty-two," said Ben.

"Goddamn it," roared Henry suddenly, "what is this?" Henry had spoken even more loudly than he had intended and seemed to rock the intrusive lawyer back on his heels.

"Good day gentlemen," said the shaken Fording, and withdrew from the room.

"Please," said McAteer, "just take a seat and let me look this over."

He opened the sheaf of papers and leafed through them until he came to the two sheets of music, "Elsa Lee" and "Only Me." McAteer took a moment to study the compositions and then looked closely at the dates that the material was copyrighted. He turned back to the typewritten front page and sighed.

"A suit for two hundred thousand dollars," he said. "Plus ensuing royalties."

"Preposterous," said Henry.

"Coincidence," said Ben.

"Exactly," said Henry.

"Look at it," said McAteer coldly, and passed them the music.

Even to Henry's untutored eye, the notes appeared to be in the same place on both sheets. He looked over both songs twice and couldn't find a misplaced quaver to confuse them.

"How exactly," said McAteer, barely keeping contempt from his voice, "did you write that song?"

Ben shrugged.

"Gentleman," said McAteer, "this suit outweighs the entire worth of this company. The truth might be defensible."

"I paid a man," said Ben. "Up at a club in Harlem. I paid a man thirty dollars for the rights to the song."

"And sold it to me for eighty?"

"Yes," said Ben.

"It was a Negro club," said Henry, a distinct note of whining entering his voice. "They weren't playing the same thing twice. How was Ben to know they were playing someone else's songs?"

"Because *Ben* writes music."

"The lyrics," said Henry. "I can assure you the lyrics are entirely original."

McAteer slammed both his fists down on the table so hard that all the papers jumped into the air. "Idiots!" he shouted. "Idiots." He wagged his finger at Ben. "A pair of fools. This is my *life*. My goddamned *life*."

Ben had his hands up in the position of surrender. "Mr. O'Keefe," he said. "I know a very good lawyer in the city. A friend of my family's. I shall go and see him. I shall. I shall go and see him now."

"*Shall* you?" said McAteer. "And what's he going to tell you? That you're a fraud? That you've buried a company?"

"Mr. O'Keefe," said Henry patting the air. "Surely you should stay calm."

"Neither of you see it! This is indefensible." With one hand he thrust the entire collection of papers into Ben's lap. "If I was half my age I'd throw you down the stairs."

Ben gathered the papers to his chest and stood up. "There's no need for that."

"Get out," roared McAteer.

"I shall go and see my lawyer," said Ben. "I'll show him these and I'll come back tomorrow."

"I look forward to it," snapped McAteer as Ben removed himself from the office.

McAteer looked up at Henry, who had now assumed a stony-faced demeanor. Henry shrugged in the echo of sudden silence and then followed the Englishman down the stairs.

Chapter Two

"JESUS CHRIST," SHOUTED Ben into the bustle of Twenty-eighth Street. All the tinkle of pianos pouring from the windows seemed to tease the two men, and such a beautiful day was not half as rare as the look of deliberate bemusement on both their faces.

"Who's the lawyer?" asked Henry urgently. "Is he good?"

"The best," said Ben.

"I've got a lawyer too," said Henry. "Let's see him." He pulled his wallet out of his breast pocket and began to rummage for a card. "Damned good lawyer."

"Mine's right around the corner," pleaded Ben.

"So's mine," said Henry, continuing to test Ben.

"I can charge mine to my father," said Ben quickly. "He'll never know it was me."

You're sharp enough, thought Henry. You and your occasional shakes and twitches. As long as they remain occasional, you'll be just fine.

"Jesus, Jesus," Henry muttered to himself as they walked. He is wondering what I'm thinking, thought Henry. Does a mark consider the actual dollars, the stacked bundles that felt so weighty in his hand? Does he think of his bank manager and how to disguise the shortfall? Surely he does not think of his wife or children, the amount's not large enough to think of them. Maybe he thinks of his father, or partners and their confirmation of his own foolishness. Henry settled his expression into a private trance, and Ben apparently decided on silence. That's it, Henry's thoughts ran on. He thinks I'm thinking of myself. It's enough money to only think of yourself.

Ben paused for a moment in the street.

"What is it?" asked Henry.

"Nothing," said Ben. "I just feel a little sick." Henry noticed he was good enough to convince himself. Ben bent double and cupped his hand over his mouth, producing a slight retch.

"Jesus, Jesus, don't," said Henry. "Come on, man. Unnecessary."

"Just money," said Ben with recovered spite, and on they marched, in their own worrying limbos, toward the law firm of Humbell, Carrow, and Sampson.

Mr. Humbell looked very lawyerly for the precise reason that he was a lawyer. A lawyer, his name stenciled on his own door, with a room rented from a group of practicing lawyers. A lawyer who reeked of rich clients, from the cut of his suit down to the box of Cuban cigars that he offered the two anxious men. A large shiny Dictaphone sat beside his desk, a threatening representative of modernity.

"Charles Newcombe's son?" said Humbell. "Now that is a pleasure."

"Unfortunately not," said Ben, and with Henry's occasional interjections the next half hour passed in a hurried telling of their sorry tale. Humbell nodded sympathetically and asked astute questions, then spent a silent fifteen minutes analyzing their papers. Henry took the opportunity to look about the room and study the details. First-rate, very impressive, he thought, well worth an investment; the sort of outfit you could trust to get things right.

"I've got two pieces of news for you, gentlemen," said Humbell at last. "First, I won't take your case."

Henry groaned and slunk farther in his seat.

"The second piece of news," continued Humbell, "is that you don't even need a lawyer. That's free advice."

"What do you mean?" asked Henry, suddenly sitting up.

"The suit has been filed with the city and the state of New York," explained Humbell. "Neither of you gentlemen appear to

be residents of said state. My inclination, if I were you, would be to
head home and give this city a wide berth for a while. The suit is
against all owners, so it will be addressed in court, but by Messrs.
O'Keefe and Hanlon. Their liability is certain, Hanlon incorporated Hamm's almost twenty years ago, and both men appear to be
residents of the state. There's no doubt that if they contest this,
they'll lose. If I were their lawyer, I might try to knock something
off the suit, but they'll be settling. Any jury would convict. *Adler
versus Smith*, 1912," said Humbell, "copyright suit that was con-
tested. Smith actually served jail time." Humbell waved their stack
of papers in front of them. "Same sort of thing."

"Jail time?" whined Henry loudly. "But it's an *intellectual* matter."

"It's a money matter," corrected Humbell. "It's outright thievery."

"Jesus," said Henry.

"And our initial investment?" asked Ben promptly.

"You can stay, ask O'Keefe to buy you out, to which he'll say no.
You can stay and contest the suit and be liable for more money than
your original investment if you lose, which you will. You can cut
your losses and say your goodbyes to O'Keefe. I know you're gentlemen, but let me ask you a question: out of the three principal
investors, which one was most familiar with music publishing?"

"O'Keefe," said Henry.

"Absolutely," agreed Ben.

"Isn't the recognition of previously published material really
O'Keefe's responsibility?" asked Humbell. "A lot of songs are published every year, but you'd think that a house as respected as
Hamm's wouldn't make this kind of amateurish error. If you ask
me," said Humbell, "they've tripped on their own laces."

"It's a valid point," said Ben, sitting up. Henry nodded eagerly
beside him.

Humbell got to his feet. "Gentlemen."

Emerging back into the afternoon, the two men felt better. The air
seemed to soothe their skin, sounds registered where before they
could not hear beyond the echoes in their own heads. The eternal

city Klaxons relented for a moment. Henry followed the passage of a pair of young women as they walked ahead. The two men bore a sense of mutual contentment in the comparative manner of a prisoner whose sentence has just been commuted.

"What do we tell O'Keefe tomorrow?" said Ben.

"Do we?"

"What?"

"Tell him anything?" asked Henry.

"Do we even see him?" asked Ben. Well played, thought Henry. A quick touch, well beyond your years.

On their way back to the Bristol, Henry purchased a copy of the *New York Times* and checked the week's manifests. He found that the *Alexandra* sailed the following evening for Southampton, England.

"I'll put you aboard the *Alexandra*," he said, wondering how a deserter would react to a prospective trip to England.

Ben asked permission to borrow the paper. "There's a train for Kansas City tonight. Why don't I put *you* aboard?"

"Wouldn't dream of it," boomed Henry, the grin kept deep inside, only concern apparent. "Better to see you on your way to England. International law; hate to see a man deported."

"Exactly," said Ben. "But it's a state matter, not federal. Isn't that how it works over here? Terrible to see the local authorities get ahold of you. Best we both go at the first opportunity. So you go first, I'm afraid."

Not bad, thought Henry, he's still thinking quickly. He relented, and that evening they packed their bags and arranged for their porters and taxis, then headed out for one final meal together. It was outwardly a somber occasion, where both men took turns as stoic and humorous, neither succeeding. They wrote their false addresses for each other and swapped their small pieces of paper, blotted and folded. Ben insisted that he would accompany Henry to the station.

>●<

Henry paid his bill, undertipping the concierge and bellboys and leaving nothing for the night porters. Ben took care of the taxi to Pennsylvania Station and followed Henry's porter as he wove his way among the passengers lining the platform.

"What do you think will happen to O'Keefe?" asked Henry.

"I don't know," said Ben. "He lost less than us, but I suppose it meant more to him."

"Listen," said Henry. "I was short in the deal. If you can give me a year, perhaps I can pay you back."

Ben stretched out his hand. "We're both gentlemen," he said calmly. "I know I can trust you."

"Your lawyer was right," said Henry, tipping his hat to the Englishman. "The truth is that if O'Keefe really knew his business, he should have recognized the damned song."

"Either way," said Ben. "He's good at what he does. He'll find work again."

They clasped and patted each other's backs.

Henry couldn't resist leaning out the window and waving at Ben all the way down the platform.

The train let out its shrill signal and eased slowly from the station. Goodbye, Mr. Newcombe, said Henry to himself. You are not a bad man, not a good man, but not a bad man. Your authorities shall be most pleased to meet you again. Take care of my money, he thought, for I shall be back soon to reclaim it and every other dollar that you have. Then he sat back in his seat and pulled his pink tie from his neck, rolled it up, and pushed it into his jacket pocket.

Chapter Three

THE NEWPORT BOARDINGHOUSE lay in the slim district between the grand cottages and the clapboard houses of those who worked in them, the footmen and ladies' maids, the gardeners, undergardeners, and boatmen. It was run by a widow whose strict adherence to Rhode Island morality was foundering under financial concerns. At the loss of friends, a sense of humor had emerged. She had become proud, not only of her seven bachelor tenants, but of their romantic escapades, and she observed, but ignored, the nightly comings and goings.

Her latest tenant had arrived from the West. A cheerful businessman from Cleveland, who introduced himself as Henry Jergens, black-haired, slightly porcine, with an admirable taste in clothes and flattery, who proved immediately popular at the dining table. Henry's first night had brought a generous contribution to the liquor cabinet and tall stories of red-cheeked mirth, but his mood seemed to be precarious. His second night, for example, he had taken supper in his room. When a house begins to gravitate toward one guest, his absence can cause a lack of conversation. They had all been aware that the light had not shone quite so brightly without Henry Jergens at their table.

It was hot in Newport. The benefits of the ocean, so adequately described in advertisements in the *New York Herald*, had apparently vanished. Henry had seen Lake Michigan, seen whatever waters New York laid claim to, but this was his first prolonged taste of the ocean. From his room in the boardinghouse he watched the lolling waves slap the rocks with the same absorption reserved for winter fires. He would wait and wait. Newport was his only chance of seeing his wife before the end of July and, more importantly, was the summer home of the British consul, whom he would soon visit on Ben's behalf. Sitting only in his undershorts, he worked his way slowly through a pack of Turkish cigarettes. His seersucker suit hung over the back of the bedstead. Henry had no more wish to don it than crawl under a bearskin rug. Atrociously hot, as his landlady had described it.

He came from an extreme climate. Up near Marquette, Michigan, with its mosquito summers and six months of iced ground. In the children's room he had been raised in, a half dozen pairs of snowshoes hung from the walls. There had been two big beds for the eight brothers, and life was a general struggle to contain the exuberance of the pack from the unreadable moods of their father.

Henry reckoned that they had been the only family in three hundred miles with a tennis court. When it emerged from under the snow in early May, his father would dredge a heavy roller out from the back of the barn and push it back and forth for a week. Then new grass would be planted and by late June it would be mowed to perfection, measured with a school ruler. Summer of 1892, Mother's billowy white dress, walking along a green tennis court in July sun. She said it was as close as a lady could come to reliving her wedding day.

Father and mother had both come from Chicago money, and lost most of it in the crash of 1883 in railroad speculation. They had given up the city, holidays, carriages, most everything except their family and their tennis court. It had not occurred to Henry at that time that there were others of his father's ilk who had not simply kept their money, but made more, much more. Nor had it occurred to him that his father was still famous in Chicago as one of its greatest failures, a living Aesop's fable, to be faithfully recounted to every ambitious young man in suit and tie.

><

Henry's father had become what was politely known as a "gen-tleman farmer," a euphemism reserved for farmers who knew nothing of farming. The children's suits and coats were taken from the great store of clothes that their father had worn in his own youth. The hand-me-downs had the strong scent of lavender sachets mixed with the acrid pinch of mothballs. They said in the schoolhouse that Henry and his siblings could be smelled before seen. Twice a year a seamstress traveled out from Marquette to work on their clothes. Henry's mother remained the only promi-nent lady in the district, so few ever knew that the fashions she wore were not simply last year's, but the fashions of her own youth. She was not ashamed. On her visits to Marquette, she walked in purple silks and whalebone corsets, stuffed birds balanced on her bonnet. They may have lost a few feathers over the years, but they lived on. The whole house was like a museum to the wealth of an age long past, and while much of America had struggled upward, Henry slowly came to realize that his own family was in a gentle free fall, an autumn leaf amused by its own spiraling descent.

Henry remembered the skies of his childhood, the wide blueness of a Michigan summer and the swirls of high wispy clouds. And yet here, at thirty-eight, was a glimpse of the ocean, from the second story of a boardinghouse. He remembered the itch of Marquette mosquito bites, the hum of insects even louder inside the house, the dead flies that gathered by the windows.

It had been his first dream in Michigan, to see the sea, to ride out storms, to leave his footprints beside Crusoe's. Two miles from home, on the side of a dirt road, was a disused telegraph pole that rose from the green grass. For Henry, it was the center of a great ship, the mainmast. He used to go there with two of his brothers and give them his sugar allowance to shake the pole back and forth once he had climbed to its top. Swaying, storm-tossed, locked in the imaginary boiling seas of Cape Horn, surrounded by angry white froth and screaming winds. The day his father caught him he was banned from his mast and all works of fiction and adventure, as well as August's traveling carnival.

Almost every memory, Henry realized, came from summer. Winter was a numbing whiteness best forgotten, but the hot months were about neighbors. His father would be exhausted from work, but smiling, and the local farmers would gather on their porch, sipping iced lemonade, waiting their turn for his family's machines. But Henry remembered summer best of all, because, at thirteen, it was when he had first met Gallon James.

Few of his father's friends came to visit, so each was remembered well, but Gallon James was the first who ever arrived by automobile and certainly the only fat man they had ever met with one eye. Besides, only Gallon James had all his jackets lined in red silk and wore socks to match. Only Gallon James employed a man as chauffeur and mechanic, by the name of Julius McAteer. He spent so much time under the hood of the car that until Henry had shaken his hand a month ago, he could remember little except the sight of the back of the man's head. Twenty-some years had passed, and McAteer was all but unrecognizable. Time had made him smaller, more impeccable, and garrulous where before, at least in Gallon's presence, he had preferred silence. But then Jergens had changed to a greater extreme. Through his teenage years he had been scrawny, plagued by acne, with thick blonde hair always sticking up mop-like, despite his mother's attentions. Even his name differed, his family's Livingston jettisoned in favor of Jergens. Johnny discarded for Henry.

Gallon, he slowly gathered, was not exactly a friend to his father. Supposedly, they had done a modest piece of business together, and while neither had exactly lost his money, they would spend long hours discussing where it had gone and what sort of increase in funding it would take to recover the original investment. It would be another two years before Henry would learn that Gallon James had fleeced his father not once, but on almost a dozen occasions for varying amounts of cash.

None of the brothers had ever seen a man as large as Gallon James. Had there ever been a larger, more delicate bunco man? Gallon had been blessed with a gravel voice, a bovine face of honesty, and little arms that hung from his sides like flippers. The three-hundred-pound grifter could make armchairs groan, axles squeal, and hostesses look with concern at protesting floorboards. Henry remembered his smell, the over-application of rose water and the sprig of mint kept in his handkerchief. It was always chewed before approaching marks. That a man the weight of a dairy cow could ever be thought charming had made a deep impression on the youth.

When their parents weren't in the room, Gallon would pop his false eye from its socket and roll it across the table, sending the children into delighted shrieks. He hid it among meatballs, under loops of spaghetti. They loved him for it and when he left that spring, not only Henry but all his brothers begged their father to invite him back. He returned the next October, the following spring, again at the summer's end, and the last time at the passing of the snows, always accompanied by McAteer. Henry remembered vague dinner conversations, remembered Gallon's ability to sell bogus life insurance when more complicated machinations were going awry. He would tap his eye with a spoon and plop a question into dinner. "Should a Christian man trust only in God's benevolence?" He would receive defensive answers, and then McAteer would sigh and say, "But can a Christian man neglect a duty to his family?" And Mother would look at Father and Father would sigh, too, and the men would retire to the study, and pen would scrawl across check.

On that last journey to their homestead, Gallon had stood with Henry during the breaking of the horses. He had leaned against a sturdy fence and watched the boy work at a man's job, using trickery to replace the familiar brawn. Henry would use his body, watching the horse, turning his head away, walking in one direction then another, until the horse began to do the same, until Gallon could understand that the horse had been subdued by thought and understanding and not whipping scars and frothing mouths. Obviously it was appreciated. That night Gallon made an offer to pay for Henry's education in a Chicago school. It was not something that Henry's parents could afford, but it was something they could desire. They may have left behind tea parties, the collection of museum funds, and stories from the East Coast and Europe, but the idea of recovery existed, albeit through the next generation. Could they deny their child such an opportunity? Only McAteer had looked more surprised than his mother.

"You a sharp-eyed pea?" asked Gallon the following morning when they were alone after breakfast.

"Yes sir."

"If a sheriff was to need a deputy, if a captain was to go looking for a first mate, would you be the kind of man they'd go searching for?"

"Yes sir."

"Then maybe it's time you embraced your family farewell."

They lined up on the porch for him, his brothers, his father shaking hands with him. His mother hugged him close, holding a handkerchief, though no tears emerged. The truth was that in a family of ten Henry had never thought of being more than one-tenth happy, until he found himself riding from his parents' house in the backseat of the car with a pop in one hand, Gallon's beer in the other, McAteer driving. The day was hot and the windows were down and Henry realized that there was nothing better the world could have offered him than what he had at that moment.

Henry had never doubted that Gallon would, in the end, do as he said — take him to Chicago and enroll him in a private school — but the man had no such intentions. Henry had promised his parents to write every month so he did, taking dictation from Gallon for two years, until his seventeenth birthday. He only thought about running away from Gallon their first week together, but never once tried. Life was too good; Gallon quickly figured his favorite foods, and nursed him through a short period of homesickness with ice cream, popcorn, and Wrigley's gum.

Henry could remember his voice. "You going to like the city," said Gallon. "Nobody stays a country boy." Henry must have looked unsure, queasy at the thought of leaving the country behind; he had only the faintest memories of Chicago. Gallon had given him a soft punch on the shoulder. "You think I'm all eastern city? I'm pure Indiana. When I was a boy, and my limbs would ache, my mother'd put a little jenny pig in bed with me to draw out the pain." Since McAteer was almost always absent on what Gallon called "prospecting ventures," Henry had been tempted to occasionally forget his existence.

It did not take Henry long to be sure of Gallon's strange tastes. On drinking nights, Henry could feel Gallon's eyes on him and his meaty hand would rest on his knee and his minty warm breath would come too close to his face. But never, never more than that. The man never laid a hand on him otherwise, but there was no mistaking the succession of visitors to their hotel room — young men, bored or vain, always penniless, who made their way to the big man's bed. They looked at Henry as he was sent from the room on errands, calculating what he was to Gallon. Henry was not sure himself. Gallon called Henry a protégé, a boy he wanted to teach all that he knew. Innocents, he always said, appealed to marks.

Occasionally Henry had wondered why, when all these boys who passed through his room were good enough for Gallon, was he ignored? But he knew their look at departure well enough to remember that Gallon was sparing, not rejecting him.

>●<

He could still remember McAteer's words. Perhaps because it was
the only time he could remember being directly addressed by him.
One night, when McAteer had returned from a prospecting trip, he
had suddenly grabbed Henry by the wrists while Gallon was in the
bathroom. "You'd better watch yourself. Get out from under
before that big son of a bitch splits you down the middle." The next
morning McAteer had gone, with all of Gallon's savings and their
automobile and every prop and paper they possessed. Gallon's
anger had been slow to emerge. He just shook his big head as if to
say, truly, there was no one in the world a man could trust.

They had to begin again. With the very last of their money gleaned
from wallets and pockets they traveled by train to Detroit, where
Gallon introduced Henry to an engraver who stamped the words
FOURTEEN KARAT on a box of dollar watches. Henry helped Gallon
sell them throughout the state, then helped sell silver-plated
spoons for real silver dollars. Anytime that Gallon was forced to
walk to sell, he'd curse the name Julius McAteer.

Once they had gathered what Gallon called their "financial foundation," Gallon set up a brokerage house in Chicago, declaring an
intimate knowledge of horse racing across the nation. He printed
an expensive brochure, mailed it to investors asking them to send
in a hundred dollars for the insider's report. He took a ten-dollar
bet from one client, put it on a horse that had already won. At the
end of the month, Gallon borrowed from the growing account and
sent the investor back his meager winnings with a note saying that
the volume of business was too large to handle such a small
account. Henry helped with the correspondence as investors wrote
back, wanting to know the minimum for continued investment.
Gallon settled for a thousand dollars. All he did was push money
around, paying off one client with another's investment as the business rapidly grew. Exiting was the key, as always, he told Henry.
The post office always grew suspicious of new businesses that
relied so heavily on mail. Three months after they started, Gallon

took his profit of over a hundred thousand dollars, bought them a car, and moved on again. "Who needs that shit rat McAteer?" he'd say every ten miles that passed.

Perhaps because he was still the age of a schoolboy, Henry saw his travels with Gallon as an education. Better than an education, since education had never been so fascinating and mutable. For Henry soon realized that Gallon demanded change more than wealth, that he grew bored very quickly, that he was happiest when pretending to be someone other than a three-hundred-pound, one-eyed grifter.

Only once did Henry question Gallon's continued contempt for McAteer.

"Why?" asked Gallon of him. "There are rules, boy. You're what now?"

"Seventeen."

"He wasn't that much older than you. I gave him a hundred ways to make a living off this land, like I'm giving you. Would you treat a man the way he treated me?"

"No sir," said Henry.

"And that's not to mention affection," said Gallon, his huge body leaning toward Henry to stress his disappointment. "I had an affection of great proportion, watching that man grow. The same affection I now have for you. I don't like to see it spurned. Would you want to see a friendship spurned?"

"No sir."

"*No sir* is the right answer," he said. "Handshake." It was their formal shake, once a week and always with a wink from Gallon. The wink said, Forgive me for my sins, shake my hand, and admit that what we are together is better than what we were apart.

They shared a favorite con. Together, they would buy dozens of spare eyes at a dollar apiece. Gallon would dress immaculately in a three-piece pinstripe, walk into an upmarket tobacconist, and make a great show of his knowledge of cigars. Henry was to wait on the street, out of sight. Gallon would buy only one cigar, rolling the Cuban close to his ear with a touch heavy enough to test it but light enough to leave the paper undamaged, then pay with a hundred-dollar note. While collecting his change, he would sneeze and bring his head up swiftly. There would follow the strange sound of a marble bouncing twice against hardwood and then rolling to a stop. Gallon would bend down quickly and retrieve his eye, palming it into his pocket, then pop his head back over the counter.

"Rather embarrassing," he'd say, pointing to the empty socket that scarred his face. "Do you think you'd help me look for . . ."

The owner would obediently scurry around the floor in an unsuccessful search.

"I can't understand," Gallon would say, smiling. "It must be around here."

"I'm sure it will show up," the proprietor would say from the floor.

But Gallon would explain that he was late for an appointment, leave a card behind, and confess that it was a very expensive eye, imported from Holland. If the proprietor was to find it, Gallon would reimburse him the full cost of two hundred and fifty dollars.

Gallon would crisscross a city, trailed by Henry, "losing" an eye at every tobacconist. The next morning, Henry would fold Gallon's numbered list of businesses in his pocket and begin his rounds. In his right hand, he would hold a cheap leather briefcase where a dozen glass eyes nestled. He would approach the businesses in the same order as they had the day before. He would say a warm good morning to the proprietors, then bend over to tie a loose lace and place the blue eye against the foot of the counter. Perusing a line of Turkish cigarettes, he would inch slowly across the floor, until he'd interrupt his inspection with the words "What the hell?" and bend down to retrieve the shiny glass oval.

This was how it always worked. Henry in possession of the coveted eye, the shopkeeper seeing his two hundred and fifty slip away. Then bartering would begin between a seventeen-year-old, who wanted to return the eye to its rightful owner, and the tobacconist, secure in the knowledge that it was worth a small fortune. A deal would be struck and Henry would emerge with a hundred dollars or more. And it always worked that way, until one day when it didn't. All had been going well until Henry, rushing around the city of Cincinnati, had entered Baines' Tobacconist with his briefcase of spare eyes. As ever, his foot touched the eye and he bent down in surprise.

"Ah," Mr. Baines said, "there it is."

"There's what?" Henry asked, cupping his hand over the eye.

"My eye," said Baines.

"Looks to me like you've got two already."

"It's not mine," explained Baines. "It belongs to a customer."

"Well give me his name," said Henry. "I'll be happy to drop it off."

"Just leave it with me," said Baines. "He'll be coming in later."

"Why would I want to do that?" said Henry. He looked at the eye sitting in the palm of his hand. "Looks like a good piece of work to me. Looks like something a man would be glad to have back. Probably doesn't look too good without it."

"I suppose he doesn't," said Baines.

"What do you think a thing like this is worth?" said Henry, rolling it in his palm. "Couple of hundred dollars?"

"I doubt it," said Baines.

Henry looked out the door for a moment, made to leave, checked himself, turned back.

"Listen," he said. "I've got a train to catch. I don't have time to go finding one-eyed men. What say you give me something for it. He'll pay you back. Say it's worth two hundred, I'll take one-fifty."

And at that point, as Henry placed his case on the floor to argue, it tipped, hesitated for a moment, and then fell sharply to its side. A series of clacks echoed through the shop as the eyes in the bag slapped into one another. Henry made the mistake of looking down at his briefcase. Baines, bigger than Henry, moved around him and locked the door, then took three steps toward the bag, opened it, and spilled the eyes across the floor. Henry looked at them all as they came to rest. They looked back blankly.

"The likes of you," said Baines, and pushed Henry hard so that he fell back against a case of imported cigarettes. "What'll it be then?" he asked, raising his hand. "A beating or a few months of jail? Maybe we'll find out the name of your fat bastard friend?"

Henry darted toward the door, but before he could twist the lock open, Baines was on him, pushing him around and slapping him hard to the ground.

"Not so easy, boy," he said.

There was a tap at the glass. Both men looked up to see a middle-aged lady at the door. She saw the scene and turned about, her mouth open to shout, but then it broke into a look of eager relief. A second rap at the glass revealed a Cincinnati policeman. By now Henry felt panicked, afraid of jail, afraid that Gallon would leave him behind. He sat in a corner while the policeman made his report, gathered the evidence, listened to a description of Gallon James.

"Shouldn't be hard," said the bluecoat. "A man that large, with the one eye. We'll have him by dark."

Henry was marched out of the shop, arm behind his back, around the corner. Two humiliating blocks, until he was guided into a bar where Gallon awaited him, his girth balanced neatly on a bar stool.

"There he is, safe and sound," said the policeman.

"Say thank you to Mr. Ruza."

Henry turned to the man dressed as a policeman. "Thank you Mr. Ruza."

Gallon looked up at Henry's nerves and confusion and laughed. "Don't worry so hard, my boy," he said. "Lad your age was bound to louse things up sooner or later."

Gallon stood to shake hands with his friend. Before Ruza left, Henry glimpsed the passing of notes.

"I'll pay you back," said Henry.

"Just learn your lesson," said Gallon, "and we'll make it back together."

><

Over their four years together, Gallon spoiled Henry thoroughly and demanded little outside of a few hours of work a week. Wherever they were, whether Chicago, St. Louis, or a three-street town, Gallon would order Henry to take a walk to the best hotel, to the best bar, to the best restaurant and let him know if he spotted his old colleague, Mr. McAteer. He never found him, but Henry tried so hard to remember what he looked like that he could barely imagine him. To lessen the weekly disappointment, he'd buy little gifts for Gallon — lead soldiers, or cheap clay cowboy figurines. It was the only routine that Gallon adored, and without realizing what he was doing, Henry had turned a part of the week that Gallon had reserved for revenge into a different ritual.

"You find him?"

"Yes sir," Henry would answer and remove the soldier, the statuette, or the figurine.

"You found him all right," he'd say, gazing at the object as if it might even be a clue to McAteer's whereabouts. Then he'd snap it in two and drop it to the floor.

At the age of sixty, when Gallon suffered a heart attack in a railway car halfway between Cincinnati and St. Louis, no one, not even Henry Jergens, had been surprised. It took eight men, a hacksaw, and a pair of cart horses to remove him from the train. His funeral in his hometown of Indianapolis had been well attended, but Henry did not go. Dippers and grifters came from across the country. Before the funeral, Henry had gone to Cincinnati and found Gallon's friend, the fake policeman Ruza. Just a favor for a dead friend, he'd said, and asked for an address for Julius McAteer.

"New York City," Ruza had said on his return from the burial, fresh with information.

Henry paid him, then paid him in advance for updates on McAteer's movements.

"Not necessary," said Ruza pushing his money away. "New York conners don't move."

"Why?" asked Henry.

"Because New York does. Always someone different coming along."

Henry had waited, patient through his twenties, receiving Ruza's occasional reports of McAteer's achievements. It had taken eighteen years until Henry was ready. Ruza tipped him to the placement of the advertisement in the *Kansas City Star*. Answering it had been like communing with the dead. Ruza sent McAteer bogus clippings of Jergens's life in Chicago through a mutual friend in the game, and soon Henry could feel Gallon James illuminating him with a smile from below.

Chapter Four

THAT MORNING, THE bell above the door had rung, and it was with relief that the widow heard the man ask if a Mr. Jergens was lodging there. Perhaps, thought the widow, a friend would lift his spirits. She asked him to wait in the parlor and walked up the creaking steps to Mr. Jergens's room. How strange Mr. Jergens looked when he heard he had a visitor. He had gone to look in the mirror and started to comb his hair. When he shook a bottle of rose water and dabbed it behind his ears, she felt duty-bound to elaborate.

"You're dressing yourself like you got a girl waiting in the dining room."

"I don't?" said Henry.

"A very nice-looking gentleman."

"I'll be down in a minute," said Henry, brushing the widow from the room. He pulled on his suit jacket and went down the stairs.

"Christ." Henry laughed and shook the proffered hand.

Michael Ruza rested his cane and bag against the wall and perched his thin frame against the dining room table. He would have looked like a heron at rest had it not been for his grand and manicured mustache. It lent him a false air of aristocracy.

The widow was still lurking. Ruza had long nurtured an air of gentlemanly helplessness, as if he were waiting for an orderly woman of a certain age to help him pass his final years. Henry Jergens had to see the widow gently from the room, then closed the door after her. Ruza corrected his slight hunch as soon as they were alone. When he slept, his body always began to curl, head arcing down to feet, the posture of a dormant weasel, a much surer indicator of his true character.

Henry used his key to open the liquor cabinet and poured them both a gin. He raised his finger to his lips and pointed, silent advice that a sharp ear was most likely pressed to the door. Ruza walked over to the Victrola and put on an old rag at a quiet volume.

"Like the hair," said Ruza, turning back toward him while pointing at Henry's neat black coif. "You do it yourself?"

"Barbershop," said Henry.

"Something else is different," said Ruza, examining him closely.

Henry swirled his tongue and removed two pieces of rubber from his cheeks. Without them, his face immediately lost its boyish plumpness. Ruza gave him a small, complimentary bow.

"Sorry there's no ice," said Henry, handing over the gin. "It's not Chicago around here."

"To be sure," said Ruza. "How's your wife? You got yourself children yet?"

"I'm trying."

"She trying too?"

Henry laughed. "Can barely remember what she looks like."

"I remember exactly," said Ruza. "A beautiful, beautiful thing." His tongue slipped out to give his mustache a quick lick. "And remember that the Hungarian male has a jeweler's eye for the fair sex."

Henry looked up and laughed at the old man.

Ruza peered about him as Henry walked over and opened the bag. Henry could tell Ruza had been surprised to receive his telegram. They hadn't seen each other in three years, and no one had asked for his money in twice that time. Counterfeiting had come a long way, and they both knew that on the wrong side of sixty, Ruza did not have the energy to adjust. The Treasury Department still sent out photographs and details of counterfeit bills to the banks. Ten years ago, Ruza could have claimed ownership of some of the finer plates in America. In fact, it had been so long since he had done any new engravings that perhaps they might pass lazy eyes again.

Ruza watched as Henry dug through the banknotes from the bottom of the bag, as thorough and untrusting as Gallon himself. Despite his doubts for the reception of his handiwork, Henry knew that Ruza would not stand between demand and supply. If Henry Jergens wished eighty thousand fresh dollars, it was his own regard. Henry leafed through it, happy. He'll think I've found a true dupe, thought Henry, to be willing to push such poor green upon him.

"Good," said Henry, and handed Ruza a slim envelope. "A drink and you're out of here."

"I was thinking more of a quick trip of business to Cincinnati."

"I'm not really in the mood," said Henry. "I'm waiting on an investment."

"How much?"

"Eight thousand, coming back maybe tenfold."

Ruza dipped his shoulders side to side as if to see whether he could bear the weight of eight thousand dollars. "Not so bad, not so good." He looked up to catch Henry's eye. "Why my money? We both know it's no good."

Henry nodded in agreement. "Second-rate. Maybe even third."

Ruza shrugged in confession. "Is it for McAteer?"

Henry smiled. "I'm working alone," he explained. "I don't have my own muscle, so I need to borrow it. How do I do it? I go to the feds with my story. If I say I've been taken for eight thousand dollars, maybe they'd shrug. What do they care about a Missouri butcher and a couple of East Coast bunco men? But I show them your money and tell them the buncos gave it to me and whoever heard of a fed turning down a counterfeit charge? I'm offering them a double play. Lock up the buncos for twenty years."

"Who's the agent?"

"I've been writing to a man called Lamb," explained Henry.

"Gentlemanly correspondent, looking into my case. I expect he'll wake up once I send him a bit of your poor green."

"You're Gallon's boy," mused Ruza, smiling.

"If that's not enough," said Henry, "one of the bunco is British, a deserter. That's three for one to a bureau man." It wasn't that Henry didn't like Ben. Despite the fact that his experiences in war had reduced him to tremors and twitches, he was still a bit of an innocent. A handsome man, that helped. His only mistake had been in aligning himself with McAteer, the only person that Gallon had never forgiven.

Chapter Five

WITH FEW FRIENDS other than his fellow boarders, Henry soon took to walking the Newport promenades, and passed the opening weekend of July in the company of cold beer and bratwurst sandwiches. He walked along the wrought-iron fences, the tended paths, between trees planted by garden architects and past garages of pampered automobiles that smelled of wax. Surrounded by swarms of naval apprentices and Boy Scouts peeking at the girls behind their parasols, Henry did little but stare at the face of the ocean and think of New York. All cons need bait. McAteer's eighty dollars for "Elsa Lee" was a small enticement. His own investment, eight thousand, was in expectation of a much greater return. He looked at his watch. His wife was to meet him within the hour.

The beauty of revenging himself upon McAteer, thought Henry as he walked toward the station, was in shattering one of the staunchest rules of their community. Not in conning the con; cons were fair game. The grandest rule of them all was to always operate within your own store. Never use another con's store without his knowledge. It had been that way for forty years. Your own city guaranteed police protection, offices, players, inside men at banks and hotels, all of which McAteer had. Probably funded initially by Gallon's money. Henry reckoned it was a little empire built up from his own rightful inheritance. This was the consolation in putting forward eight thousand dollars. He was sure that McAteer must have put up almost four thousand in expenses. Justifiably, Henry was only four thousand dollars down, not including champagne and lobster tails.

><

Henry remained impressed by McAteer. Gallon had always said he'd been good. The Harlem nightclub, even a genuine Englishman, not so easy to find in these days of war. His only fault had been in the selection of his mark. Henry had known exactly what to feed, what to hold back, had had fun tweaking Ben in the Irish quarter, had been pleasantly surprised by the speed of their rescue. He had loved playing the loudmouth, the hard drinker, the fast dresser. Henry's only regret was the fact that he knew he could not explain his ability to anyone other than his wife. To do so would be to destroy it. The money always melted away. Big conners were all guilty of that, the sharp suits, the ocean liners, the best suites, the cigars and perfection. They pretended it was necessary in order to find the cream of marks, but they were all accustomed to it, all guilty of rolling in money as long, as vigorously as they could. Except when they were in these purgatories, the unmemorable days or weeks of in-between.

They met, as they often did, at the station as a train arrived. The temporary crowds gave them cover should one or the other need to discreetly drift away. This time, she waited until all the passengers were gone, till Henry was feeling that first tinge of worry, and then out she stepped from behind the ticket office, just yards from him. Katherine Howells, his wife of five years.

"Darling, darling, and light of nine lives," said Henry.

"Tell me you're surprised," said Katherine.

"I am, once again, surprised. Eternally surprised."

"Good," she said, and kissed him. He held her against his suit, forgot about the heat for a moment, and disguised his own sourness with the sweetness of her perfume and the familiar scent of cinnamon on her breath.

"I'm going to have to eat a horse," said Katherine. "Where are you taking me?"

"We can't afford the whole horse yet," said Henry. "You'll have to eat a pony. Or a part of the horse. We could scrape together enough for a nag's leg."

><

He offered his arm to his wife and walked beside her, noting the tidy bows on her white shoes, her slim, stockinged ankles. He believed he could feel the charge between them. Weeks without each other and all the tingling buried memories were being awakened by the prim contact of hand on arm.

That afternoon the world was amplified and isolated for Katherine and Henry Jergens. The sun, the waves, the summer wind were theirs. The sounds of a band playing within an invisible stand were sent to them. The place of contact, where white-gloved hand rested on an ordinary blazer, was glowing gold from anticipation. Had their time together not been so brief, perhaps the world would not have shone for them, but it did, and the boardinghouse echoed from emptiness. Even the widow had removed herself from her station on the day that belonged to them.

Henry looked at his wife, stretched naked upon the bed, lying on her side, painted toes curling up and down in some primitive form of exercise. The same position that he had seen on their first night together seven years ago, the most beautiful of women. Was that how it was? Henry knew that, concerning his wife, he was guilty of gross embellishment. When she was miles away and he closed his eyes to fantasize about her, she bore an uncanny resemblance to Mary Pickford. True enough, his Katherine was the fresh dollar bill compared with his rumpled note. The strength of their relationship was that it could only head one way, deeper and deeper, for the more they knew about each other, the more they did together, the further tied they were. He couldn't imagine tiring of her.

At first he had been cold to the role he had had her play. But she liked the changes, the challenge, the chumps, and as long as Katherine thought every game was different, then Henry believed she would be content with him. Love made no difference to work, but recently the balance between them had changed, in Henry's mind at least. Where before he had carried her along, now he would not have known what to do without her. He disliked her side of the game, said nothing for fear of losing her, but knew that if he managed their money a little better, he could move them away, lessen, but never stop, the amount they played. Or, as he had mentioned to Ruza, plug her with a child. That, if anything, might slow her down to his speed, stitching together the fourteen years that separated them.

"How are our friends?" he asked.

"Good," said Katherine, covering a yawn with the back of her hand. She rolled over onto her stomach to face Henry. He looked down her spine to the gentle curve of her bottom rising from the bed, then tried not to think of how other men had seen the same sight.

"How's Ben?"

"Damaged goods," said Katherine. "But then I specialize in damaged goods."

"Am I supposed to take that personally?" he said, smiling.

She laughed. "Don't be silly, silly. He'll be keen I think."

"*Love* keen or *like* keen?" asked Henry.

"Somewhere in between," said Katherine. "I think he doesn't know half of what he's thinking."

"What's he like?"

"Lonely," said Katherine. She saw the creased brow of concern that had accompanied the question. "Look at you. All worried."

Henry offered his wife a cigarette. She waved away the gesture and he lit his own, tapping the ash directly out the window as they talked. Henry ignored the prolonged call from the Fall River Ferry, cutting across his view.

"And Dent?"

"Absolutely in love," said Katherine.

"Really?"

"Maybe not in love," said Katherine and turned over onto her back to stare at the ceiling. "This room could do with a fan." She waved a hand in front of her face.

"Does he love you?"

"Dent's incapable of love, but he's *intrigued*."

"We better introduce them soon."

"Aren't you the impatient one?"

Henry motioned around him, as if Newport was too small a distraction. "I'm sorry. You know, it's just that this is it for me for a while."

"My poor husband," she said. "You've been shopping."

Henry laughed. "How'd you know?"

She pointed at the black bag in the corner. "What did you get me?"

Henry jabbed the cigarette in the direction of the bed.

Katherine dipped her head and reached to pull a large pink box out from under the bed. "What is it?" Her hands quickly pulled at the white bow, then up came the lid and out came a beige silk dress, with a dark fur collar and cuffs and a brown velvet pleat dividing the skirt.

"It's beautiful," sighed Katherine.

"It's French," said Henry.

"How did it get over here?"

"Maybe your Englishman smuggled it."

"He's not my Englishman," said Katherine, pulling the fur neck up to her chin. "He's *our* Englishman."

Henry laughed.

"It's a bit hot today for this."

"Summer seasons, fall styles," said Henry. "At least, that's what the shopgirl said. It'll look great in a couple of months."

She sprang to her feet and danced a two-step over to her husband. "You've got pretty good taste for a man." She nuzzled his neck, ran her hand through his black hair, and then paused to pluck a strand from his head.

"We need to get you to a barbershop," she whispered. "The blonde's coming through."

Henry smiled. "There are some things a man just can't see without his girl."

Katherine wrapped the arms of the dress around him and tugged him backward toward the bed.

Making love was their secret. As always, they whispered throughout, as if their time together had always been limited, that one action must overlap with another. Declarations of love were never made over dinner, but when one mouth met the other. Henry could tell by the way she touched him that she was still in love with him. Either that, he said to himself, or you just gave her a hundred-dollar dress. But then her fingers traced over his nipples and she bit into his neck, pressed herself back onto him.

"I love you," he whispered.

"Me too," she said. "More than all the world."

All he wanted was to please her now, push himself up as she pushed down, hold himself for her, wait so they could move together and if not together, then her first. Henry looked down and saw his view blocked by the rise of his own stomach, but he looked at Katherine's belly button, then her breasts, up the arched neck to the eyes closed in concentration.

My love, he thought, never leave me. I'll come back to you always. Would she see it for what it was, the utter declaration of dedication, where it would lead? They had talked about children before. She was not resistant to the idea. To Katherine perhaps it belonged to a rosy future ideal. But Henry knew how close they were now. Perhaps, now was the time. Perhaps they would have not just a new security, but a new family. He pushed upward with his hips and brought her down again.

Afterward, Henry watched her as she tiptoed her way to the bathroom and cleaned herself. Thoroughly, he reckoned, so that when she came to be with Dent he would not be able to suspect the passage of her husband. He hoped with all his heart he had impregnated her. Alone in the bedroom, waiting for his wife, Henry was thinking how he would never stand for being called a panderer. Freedom, they understood, was not a state of mind but of finance.

In the seven years that they had moved together, he did not think Katherine had had a single affair that had not served a purpose in their greater scheme. Henry, in turn, had remained faithful to his wife, except, he told himself, when playing more demanding roles. Neither inquired as to the other's level of enjoyment. But he saw that now only a child could end their awkward balance.

Their operation was neatly divided. Together they had identified the two divergent strands of the con. Mr. and Mrs. Jergens were residents of the city of Chicago. Of all the rules of bunco, there was one that even Henry would not corrupt. Never fish in your own lake. To live in the same city as a mark was taboo. Marks were, of course, moneyed. Moneyed men usually had an equal amount of pride, and, moreover, superior connections. They didn't think of themselves as easy targets and came roaring after you, if you could be found. So once you whacked the hornet's nest, it was best to retire across one or more states. Or better yet, have them scouring for the wrong man, in this case McAteer, and think the name Jergens an honest one.

For over a year, Henry had devoted most of his time, and much of Katherine's, to observing a man called Rudolph Dent, a member of one of Chicago's most prominent families, third-generation railroad money. Better, far better, he had managed an almost impossible feat, marrying upward, to Germaine Carson, daughter of one of the country's largest manufacturers of textiles. Dent was, in so many ways, an ideal mark. The marriage showed aspiration, but the newspaper clippings of social events showed Dent as a tennis player, a motorcar driver, so also a competitor, a man who was likely to have been provoked, rather than subdued, by the influence of his wife's family.

Katherine and Henry had trailed Dent to Newport, to New York, knew his circles, his friends, his business, his favorite hotels, his favored foods and drinks. Henry even knew that Dent had a man who came to iron his hats and gloves in the Hotel Astor. He knew that Mrs. Dent spent hours inventing theme parties to hold each December. Last year had been the Red and White Ball, the previous year had been called the Dreams of Africa Soirée. They knew that Dent preferred to be shaved at seven in the morning, and that Mrs. Dent was at home to visitors on Wednesdays. A man such as Dent would like nothing more than to establish himself financially independent, yet was entirely unaccustomed to hard work. McAteer, reasoned Henry, would not be able to believe his good fortune when Dent stumbled into his path.

It would be up to Katherine to introduce the concept of Dent into Ben's mind. Or rather, reintroduce the concept. For they had already met. Henry remembered it well. The night six weeks ago in New York when he had persuaded Ben to join him in the theater to see Katherine's production of *Cheating Cheaters*. They had dined at the Astor, he had interrupted Katherine's evening to introduce Ben, and then Dent had returned to his table and found it besieged by suited strangers. It was the first time Henry had seen Dent close up, his skunk streak running down the middle of his hair. Dent had had the look of a man who would always manage to seem more at ease than anyone he happened to talk to.

Ben, on the other hand, was awkward. Jergens had to admit to a sneaking liking for the man, perhaps because he had seemed to enjoy his company. He had liked him right up to the point where he had introduced him to Katherine. Henry had thought that he'd do anything to keep Katherine close to him. Anything not to have to watch his wife not just with her current lover, but with Ben, her next lover as well. He remembered ordering yet another drink to cover his sudden disgust. In hindsight, thought Henry, perhaps that was when the idea of family had occurred to him.

Henry had let Ben think in silence after introducing him to Dent. He would remember Dent when Katherine reintroduced them. And if Ben mentioned it but once, McAteer would know the Dent name, would sniff once and snap, so hungry and disappointed from Jergens's cheap payoff. And the stakes would be high, and never, ever, had Henry seen a more perfect mark than Rudolph Dent.

Eight thousand was a small investment as far as Henry was concerned. If McAteer took his time, played him well, he guessed Dent would go for as much as a hundred thousand, and while Katherine brought Dent to Ben's attention, Henry would be ensuring that not a dollar would end in McAteer's lap. He would have a Bureau man beside him with writs for fraud and counterfeit, and an embassy man for the English soldier, and he would hold his hand across his heart and say, "Officer, I was taken for a high ride. These men bamboozled me out of my savings. Eight thousand dollars."

Chapter Six

WHEN KATHERINE LEFT, Henry missed her. She'd accompanied him to a small barbershop at closing time and instructed the man in the dyeing of his hair, an inky flat black for McAteer, far from the blonde, unruly mop of his childhood. He drank alone that night, drank too much. When Gallon was gone, when he had worked the West but was in the East, when his girl was far from him, earning in another man's arms, then thank the Lord for the shape of a bottle. In truth, he knew that whatever character he had played in the last three years, they all happened to be fond of alcohol. Who trusted a man who didn't drink? He sat back, poured another, and wondered just how hungry McAteer and his men would be. Surely hungry enough to snap at the first wriggle of a big fish?

They had one last, aborted meeting and then resorted to letters. Never the full story within one letter, but in the four pages posted in four different envelopes, sent to four different addresses and then forwarded to Newport. No point in saying much of anything on the telephone, not just the expense but impossible to trust an operator. Within the letters, the codes were simple enough, each mark assigned a new name, money described as children. *How do you think the children are? Are they coming along well enough? Are you taking good care of them?* And the day later that month, among all these dull days, that would always shine in his mind. When she wrote, *Apart from the usual brood, perhaps I have an extra dollar to share with you.* If children were money, then money was children. She was indeed pregnant. It made him anxious to see her. He wanted to see the rise of her belly, wanted their work to be over, the summer to end.

Progress, introductions were being made in Manhattan. As Henry had predicted, Ben and Dent had behaved as magnets, placed close enough by Katherine so that they had been drawn together. He wondered if Katherine was enjoying this New York life. When the time came, it would be hard for her to move on. It would be impossible to move back to Chicago; Katherine would never be able to live in the same city as Dent. It never seemed to occur to the elite how far some people had traveled, that if you carried dreams, there was a glamour of intoxication in their silver place settings. And did it really mean nothing to Katherine? Yes, Henry thought, she'll know our game is better. The rich play only games of movement, a constant spinning, spinning around New York parties and dance floors until they were quite dizzy and had achieved absolutely nothing but a pleasant memory, enough to sustain themselves until the next event.

Katherine wrote that she believed that Dent was a good man. It made Henry laugh. Only in Katherine's opinion was it possible to be a liar, an adulterer, a layabout, and a louse and still be good. She wrote that she was worried about Henry, that he was alone too much, he was stranded in a summer resort filled with other people's money. "I think of you," she wrote, "as a kid in a dime store without a nickel to his name." She wished she could ease his mind, but knew they must both sit back and allow time to carry them forward. Henry knew it too. He would not even think of allowing anyone else to view his nervousness, only Katherine. She wrote back that she forgave him his anxiety and wished they were wrapped up tight on a bed together. He would hold her close, she wrote in her sprawling script, one big arm under her body, the other about her stomach.

If she hadn't kept mentioning Ben in her letters, perhaps Henry wouldn't have been so enthusiastic, so vindictive when he discovered that the British consul had finally arrived for the summer in Newport. Ben, Henry had read, had taken her to the movies, had tried to hold her hand, would not talk of the war. He was sweet but not smart, she said, not half as sharp as you. She had written for a half page on what she imagined the British must do to their soldiers. Henry knew that Ben was younger, more handsome, and he could feel himself bristling, knew how wrong it was to doubt her, but could not help himself. Ben was simply a more romantic figure than a husband of five years.

The same sort of paragraphs were repeated again and again throughout the letters, amusement in her approach to Ben, his seeming rapture with her, then a burnishing of her husband's esteem at the end. Worse to imagine what she dared not mention, what they never discussed between them, and never would. Why should she not take pleasure where she could? Why try to despise one's work? Temporary emotion, he cautioned himself, but he knew he had never felt so disturbed by his wife. She must have a little more respect for what she carried within.

Henry was informed of the British consul's arrival at dinner one night by one of the older gentlemen of the boardinghouse. Henry set out on a Wednesday morning and walked in the direction of the White Pearl Restaurant, where they had informed him the consul would be lunching. It was a place of wide beams and small stairways with an aura of expense, priced by its past, proud of the sawdust on its floors and the fading prints on the dark wood walls.

Henry could have recognized the consul with his eyes closed by the gin on his breath. A large, upright man, as broad as a coffin, the consul had military airs, an affectation Henry presumed was becoming more and more popular in England as the war continued. He guessed the conflict dominated conversation with strangers. Henry, too well dressed to be ignored, waited for a lull in the table's conversation then loomed over the group to introduce himself.

>•<

"Nice to meet you Mr. Jergens," said the consul.

"I hate to bother you, but I have something I think you'd be interested in."

The consul rose politely to his feet, excused himself, and followed Henry into the lobby, where they sat side by side on a cream-colored sofa. Henry pulled the photograph of Ben, McAteer, and himself from his pocket. He handed it to the consul.

"I'm afraid I've never heard of Hamm's Music," said the consul.

"The man on the left is English."

The consul squinted at Ben's photograph.

"Good-looking boy."

Henry shook his head. "I'm afraid to say that the man is a disgrace to your nation. A thief, who bilked me of a considerable sum of money."

The consul looked up, tired by the intrusion. "You've been to the police I presume."

"I'm working with the federal Bureau of Investigation on his apprehension."

"Good, good," said the consul, looking over his shoulder to where he had abandoned his wife. A waiter was approaching his plate, poised to remove the untouched food.

"Is there anything in particular I can help you with?" said the consul. "Just that you seem to have everything under control."

"I believe the Englishman is here illegally," said Henry. "I also believe he's a deserter."

"That's a different matter altogether," said the consul.

"I think he might be violent."

"We presume they will be."

"Really?"

"When you know there's a firing squad awaiting you," shrugged the consul.

"Ah," said Henry, genuinely surprised.

"A photograph is a rather difficult place to start," said the consul, peering again at the picture. "Do you have a name?"

"He calls himself Ben Newcombe," said Henry.

The consul scratched the name in pencil on the back of the photograph. "Presumably that is a pseudonym. Where does he live?"

"New York."

"A deserter," mused the consul. "Truly?"

"He told me so," insisted Henry. "You've more to work with than you think. I met him in mid-May, he hadn't been here long, didn't know his way around. So say he arrived a month before, left Europe the month before that. He's also wounded, so he'd have medals or a hospital record. I was talking to the Bureau," continued Henry. "They say when you pick a new name, you'll normally keep your first. So start with Benjamins and work through the B's."

"A wounded deserter?"

"I guess he'd figured he'd given enough for his country."

"Sad," said the consul. "But to leave friends to fight alone. Hardly exemplary. Did he say where he had fought?"

"No."

"What regiment?"

"No."

"Do you think he was an officer?"

Henry shook his head. "I don't think so. Not certain, but a bit rough in his speech. He doesn't sound like you."

The consul looked down at the photograph. "I don't suppose he does."

"I'll be going back to New York," said Henry. "He doesn't think I know. If I told him I had more money for him, a reinvestment, perhaps he'd agree to meet me."

The consul nodded. "I would love to say that we had the resources to devote to such a man right now. I'll take the picture and we'll wire England, but frankly, the easier it is for us, the more likely we are to respond. If you could tell us where he was, we'd be happy to pick him up for questioning."

"Good," said Henry and standing, offered the consul his hand. "You'll hear from me."

The blue skies were even more blinding after his half hour among the somber wood of the restaurant. Henry felt bad for a moment, but he was not to judge. He couldn't believe Ben's wounds wouldn't at least excuse him from execution; perhaps he would serve a little jail time and return to the army. But then perhaps Ben's wounds weren't even received in service, perhaps they had come from some civilian accident. Perhaps he was merely yellow and the scar on his hand was from biting himself in fear.

Chapter Seven

WHAT OTHER RECOURSE for the innocent? Henry knew as well as any professional that local bunco shops were only allowed to run in their municipalities on two conditions. First, considerable slices of the profits went to the authorities. Second, you were only allowed to touch up out-of-towners. Marks who pled their cases at local police departments were walked in circles, comforted with words, taken to the station, bought an out-of-state ticket.

And the only governmental department that might cross states lines was the Bureau of Investigation, formed only eight years ago. Henry knew that, at least while it was young, the Bureau would stay innocent, stocked with straitlaced, intelligent fellows. There were fewer than three hundred men across the entire nation, dedicated to exposing land fraud, to intelligence gathering, to apprehending smugglers. Henry knew that there was no specific training necessary to join the Bureau; these were all law enforcement officials or simply lawyers, united, presumably, by a dissatisfaction with city and state law.

He had once got a Bureau agent drunk at a gaslit bar in Madison, Wisconsin. Not for any particular reason, just to fill a hole in his knowledge of the opposition. It was in 1908, the same year the Bureau had been formed. He didn't know how much had changed recently, but the agent was furious with the disrespect the government had for his department.

"Eleven thousand dollars a year," the agent kept repeating.

"That's good money," Henry had sympathized. "I don't earn two thousand most years."

"For the whole fucking department," the agent had said before laughing.

It was good to know, but still, these were righteous men who kept working in spite of the low pay. There were probably some susceptible to greasing, but it would be hard to identify which. The others would be too proud of their pious poverty to have mercy on a grifter.

Much to Henry's relief, a visit to the Bureau's local field office required a trip south, to the inconspicuous storefront of a shabby five-and-dime in Hoboken, New Jersey, as if all they had to do was squint through a pair of binoculars to spy on all the vice across the river in Manhattan. "We prefer to work outside the city," Lamb, the special agent in charge, had written back. Henry guessed the truth of it — cheap rent. They would be willing to spend little on an investigation. Yet, if Henry offered them a conviction on a plate? "These men have relieved me of a lifetime of savings." If he were the sort of citizen who came with photographs of the suspects, who knew where to find them, who was a perfect candidate for a court of law? Lamb had pressed for more proof that the crime was federal. "What could be more federal?" Henry had written in reply. "I met the man in Illinois, he began on me in Indiana and had me by Ohio."

"Finally," said Lamb as Henry passed through the doors of the Hoboken office. "Enough letters."

"Very good to meet you," said Henry, swapping an enthusiastic handshake. He was impressed by Lamb's absolute physical banality. There was nothing at all remarkable about the man. An average height, mouse-haired, unmemorable.

"I've never seen a man pursue his own money the way you have," complimented Lamb.

"With respect," said Henry, "you don't have quite the same incentive as myself."

They exchanged weather talk as Henry hefted his briefcase onto the table. There is the difference in you, thought Henry. Lamb's voice and his eyes didn't seem to belong with his body. He was much sharper than he looked, the demeanor of a stockbroker, an advertiser, a salesman. It was unfortunate, thought Henry, that a man like Gallon James hadn't caught hold of him. Lamb might have earned a little more.

"This one." Henry held up the picture of the three partners from Hamm's Music and Publishing Corporation and pointed at McAteer. "Maybe I'm basing the opinion on age alone, but I'm thinking he's the leader of this particular lot."

"Julius McAteer. We asked around. He has no local record," said Lamb, shaking his head. "But with enough influence, perhaps he had one that's now expunged."

No matter, thought Henry, thinking of Gallon's extreme patience and his employment of justice. "Did you find anything for the one who called himself Newcombe?" asked Henry, tapping Ben's sepia chest with his finger.

"We've no matches," said Lamb after a while. Henry was beginning to feel distinctly like a suspect in his own bilking. It was the way the agent paused after a response, probably a personal technique, but these constant pauses and hard stares combined to such a degree that Henry believed Lamb could have made a cherub feel like Satan's child.

"Maybe you can't find him because he's English."

"So you wrote," said Lamb slowly. "We've checked with his embassy. They said you'd already been in contact. Mr. Jergens," continued Lamb. "I have every sympathy with your case. There are a lot of others like you too ashamed to step forward, or just don't know where to step. However, we are talking allocation of funds here. We'll have a very limited time to act. If I'm going to run this thing with you, I'm going to have to bring in state police."

"You can't trust a New York cop," said Henry. "No sir. They never did a thing to aid me, not a thing."

"I understand there are a few bad apples," said Lamb, after a moment.

"The whole damned orchard," said Henry.

Lamb smiled. "What I'm saying," he said patiently, "is that I have to know when."

"The when is easy enough."

"How?"

"I've got a Pinkerton man on it as well," said Henry. "Out of my own pocket."

"What's his name?"

"He asked me not to say," said Henry. "I'm not sure his license is in order." He rummaged back through his briefcase. "You asked to see this." He removed two hundred dollars of Ruza's counterfeit currency. "This is what they paid me for my song. I tried to use it back in Kansas City and my bank wouldn't take it."

Lamb looked it over. "Not bad," he said. "But not good." He examined it closely enough for Henry to know that he had piqued the agent's interest.

"Greedy sons of bitches," explained Henry. "Took eight thousand from me and rubbed rock salt in the wound with a couple of hundred phonies." He tapped the table to attract Lamb's attention. "It's a crime isn't it?"

"It most certainly is."

"Is it a state crime?"

"No, absolutely not," said Lamb, whatever interest he had had in bunco men now doubled. "I don't think you could find a surer federal crime."

"Can you trust your own?" asked Henry, looking about him. The problem with playing paranoid was that this time, Henry knew the role was not far from his truth. There was too much at stake, including, he was coming to believe, his marriage, not to be concerned with the minutiae of things that he would normally have considered outside his control.

"You shouldn't worry," Lamb assured him. "I stand by every man here."

"Can I meet one or two?"

Lamb nodded, took his keys, and walked Henry out of his office, down a short corridor of murky green carpet inherited from the previous owner. Lamb rapped at a door, opened it, and peeked his head inside.

"Nobody home."

"Unguarded?"

Lamb laughed, passing his keys from one hand to the other before putting them back in his coat pocket. "Out to lunch."

"Maybe they should take their work more seriously," cautioned Henry, brushing past him to look inside. "What room is it?"

"Steno pool, interrogation, evidence room, you name it," said Lamb. Henry backed out of the space, again brushing past Lamb, gently lifting the man's keys from his pocket. "We're tight on space," continued Lamb. "Most of the time they're guarding a roomful of papers."

Henry huffed, "Even so," and slid the keys into his trouser pocket, where they nestled safely in a handkerchief.

Lamb looked at him as if he wanted to shake his head but held his tongue. Any man who pursued his money as hard as Henry Jergens was obviously a stickler for efficiency and other people's hard work. He showed Henry the door.

Henry had sweated through his shirt. Lamb was much better than he thought. He knew the agent would have checked his story, traced money transfers and withdrawals. Lamb and his men would have found plenty on the surface, but if they chose to dig deeply into Henry's roots in Kansas City, they would quickly realize they were investigating a paper resident. No friends, no contacts, no business partners, no family.

As he passed back under the Hudson by train, Henry reassured himself with the fact that the Bureau would be happy to make the arrests. Henry knew that they would now also be concentrating on locating the counterfeit cash, their safest bet for prosecution. Henry's only duty would be in placing the package of counterfeit where it would be found by the agents so that they would connect it to the dealings of McAteer and Dent.

><

Three months ago, Henry had opened an account in Dent's Chicago bank with only a thousand dollars. Deposited one day, withdrawn a week later in singles, solely for the purpose of discovering exactly how the bank would package so many bills.

"Why do you need so many singles?" asked the curious teller.

"Tip money," said Henry smiling. "I'm touring in my Packard."

"Sure wish I was checking your oil, sir," said the impressed teller, packing the bills into an oversized leather wallet, one usually reserved for larger denominations.

The same wallet they would hand Dent if he was to make the appropriate withdrawal. The same wallet that Henry would switch from the real cash to the counterfeit that Lamb was expecting to find. Henry reckoned that he would have a minimum of two opportunities to make his switch. Perhaps on the night of their raid, amid any confusion arising during the arrest. It might seem the riskiest, yet sometimes that turned out to be the easiest. Second, presumably safer, was to use the keys to Lamb's evidence room. He'd copied them and then paid a delivery man a dollar to drop them behind a desk in Lamb's office a day later.

Chapter Eight

THE SUMMER WAS undoubtedly the hottest Henry could remember. He carried three handkerchiefs in various pockets and alternated his dabbers throughout the days. Everywhere, there was a general sense of helplessness over the heat. Even with the river breezes, Bayonne was a town desperate for relief, and no child spent the day more than a few yards from water, no house had a closed door or window, no dog moved from the shade. In the silent afternoon hours a man could have been forgiven for thinking he was down in New Orleans, rather than a stone's throw from New York City. He'd chosen Bayonne because it was a Standard Oil city, all workers, company men and immigrants, very unlikely to divert anyone from either New York or Hoboken. The downside was it was a sleepier abode than Newport, stagnant and small, the only life in the town coming from the river, where optimistic sailboats sat with sagging shifts.

He was kept alive by Katherine's letters, which revealed the path of the con. Staying away from Katherine and Manhattan was taxing. They made arrangements: he would telegraph her a time of the day and a block of the city; he would always walk on the north side of the street and she on the south. Wearing his cream suit and matching broad-rimmed hat, he sidled along the street and tipped his brim in Katherine's direction. He could see her smiling, his heart would settle, and he turned away to dream of the future. Odd to think that she might well be walking now with a child in her. Or if she had lost it, she would know and he would not. Yet no matter how much he wished to know, he remained a professional and never once stopped his wife for so much as a word. A glimpse, a half smile was enough, the knowledge that this game that they were playing was still entirely theirs. It boosted his sagging esteem and kept his misery at tolerable levels.

A man could crack in this heat, thought Henry on the ferry back to Bayonne. What constant pressure it put upon the simplest tasks. An hour of his evening was given to checking his head for stray blonde hairs. He just hoped that Katherine would not swoon into some dreadful mistake, that she would be able to see through Ben's handsome facade and find her way out of the deep pockets of Rudolph Dent.

A few days later, Agent Lamb telegraphed Henry up in Newport. His landlady promptly forwarded the telegram, which requested he head south. Their case was close to complete, Lamb had written, and they required Mr. Jergens's presence for identification. Lamb was not foolish. After Jergens reported to the Hoboken office, he was followed by agents. Henry was aware and focused. Once he had announced himself to Lamb he went nowhere during the day, did nothing. Lamb must never have seen a man who gave less of a hint of his character from his movement. It was as if all Henry thought of was winning his money back. Lamb confided that it had been hard to put a finger on the illegality of the gang they followed because their operation was too smooth. They seemed to dress for everything and do nothing. Having said that, Lamb found it hard to prove that Dent, their prospective victim, was any better. Was Mr. Jergens aware what these men now did for a living? Of course he was, Henry said to himself. Katherine was in full possession of the facts.

Lamb had invited Henry in on his own dollar, but lodging was provided by the government. To Henry's chagrin, he was required to share a room in a third-rate hotel with a federal officer. The man had little sense of hygiene and slept in the same underwear and vest he wore during the day in that July heat. Henry could feel that his own hair stayed wet during the night, and he flipped the pillow a dozen times, attempting to refresh himself.

Together, Lamb and Jergens staked out the places that McAteer was known to visit. Lamb kept Henry close. He knew that too often, when the Bureau had touched upon bunco cases, their witnesses became aware of the fact that convictions did not result in restitutions. Instead, they were tapped by friends of the men who had fleeced them, and settled on a percentage of their original losses for taking the next train west.

Henry could not have been more helpful. He had mapped out the city, and they picked up the trail of the one called McAteer. It led to lawyers, to bars, to the Englishman and a network of small-time associates. Lamb established two observation posts, and Henry claimed that he could smell the scent of his own money returning.

"What they did to you was bad," said Lamb. "But the way they've been dragging this new guy around town. To take him on this, frankly, I don't know where to stop the arrests. I mean, I can't believe it's all legal anyway, even for Mr. Dent. To do this in a time of war." Lamb clucked his tongue in disapproval. "But then, I'm from a long line of English."

"*Mayflower?*" asked Henry smiling.

"Give or take two hundred years."

Henry accompanied Lamb on a visit to St. Catherine's Church where they appealed to the priest and secured the use of the crypt as a temporary holding cell for the suspects. Lamb would not turn them over to city custody until the arraignment. It would give whatever ties the bunco men had in the local police little time to react. While Lamb secured the priest's permission, Henry went on a brief tour of the vestry and checked the lock on its door. Probably fifty years old, easy to pick. It seemed a logical room for the temporary stashing of evidence; perhaps, thought Henry, it might be a third option for switching the counterfeit money.

><

Lamb, it had turned out, liked to drink as much as Henry and carried a little flask of brandy in his pocket, sipping at it steadily despite the heat.

"Just wouldn't want to be these boys," he said smiling one evening over a gray cut of meat at a chophouse.

"Why?" asked Henry.

"Tides are turning over here," said Lamb. "You know, with this bunch, we've got them on fraud, bad paper, illegal entry to the States, probably gun licenses, and that's before we even squeeze them." He bit into his steak. "I was thinking," he went on, "you must have spent time with these men. You like any of them?"

"Liked all of them for a while," said Henry. "More I think about it, angrier I get."

"The Brit," said Lamb. "Say they post him back, into the war. Say he gets it."

"Say he gets it," said Henry. "That's war. All I know is he's dipping his nose in the wrong business in the wrong country."

Lamb took a swig of his flask and passed it to Henry.

"Are you really such a tyrant?"

Henry stared at him. "I want my money and I want to get the hell out of this stinking city," he said. "That's all I want."

"It's what everyone wants."

Henry judged it a sufficient enough endorsement to have Lamb stand beside him the next day as he telegrammed the British Embassy to invite them to send an agent up from Washington to share in Ben's arrest. They accepted the invitation immediately.

Henry had been very careful cultivating the image of McAteer and Newcombe as counterfeiters. The precise sum that they would take from Dent was not important. He had made the presumption, aided by Katherine's informative letters, that they would relieve Dent of between seventy and eighty thousand dollars. It was merely a question of salting and switching, all the easier with Lamb's insistence on Jergens's presence, whether it was in the church, in the Hoboken office, or on the night of the arrests. Lamb expected to find counterfeit notes, not real cash, and all that Henry had to do was ensure that that was indeed the case.

Sometimes, at night in his oven of a room, Henry was kept awake by the hot snores of the agent. He would study himself in the dark with his fingers, run them across the night's stubble on his face, across the paunch that lapped over the low-slung sheet, and wonder how Katherine still might love him. They both knew the importance of outward impression. But Katherine wanted only him, he wanted only Katherine. Do not let it slip. Odd to be only miles apart and not be able to be with each other. It was down to hours. He kept thinking that he saw her on different blocks amid the lazy sway of summer skirts. His eyes turned to follow the belly of any pregnant woman.

Time ticked fast and yet to Henry, everything slackened. There was no more patience for him to work through. He bullied the agent in his room, he bullied Lamb when he could, was generally ignored as an irascible necessity. Subways did not move fast enough for him, people stank, they walked idly in the street when he rushed and pushed past him rudely when he was lost in thought. He could no longer see the tips of the highest buildings, they were all shrouded in summer haze. A terrible, ugly city that he would be thrilled to be out of, as long as his wife came with him.

The last week was full of Lamb's promises, close eyes kept on the movements of McAteer and Ben and Dent, ready at a moment's notice to move in for arrests. The agents took to eating in their rooms so that they were ever-ready. Henry didn't know who was worse, he or his roommate; crusts of sandwiches on the floor invited neighborhood ants and cockroaches. He drank nothing but warm beer and his roommate looked at him green-eyed, but would not betray Lamb's trust and drink on the job. Henry hated him all the more for it. Hated them all, wanted out now, yesterday.

When he reasoned, which was becoming less and less often, he decided that his irritation grew principally from his lack of contact with Katherine. Everything else was in place, had gone reasonably smoothly. The roads to long cons were always cobbled, improvisation was to be expected. But he had not counted on such a close watch by Lamb; he could not even walk to a post office to collect his forwarded mail. What if Katherine had some vital piece of information to tell him now? Not a declaration of love, nor progress of her pregnancy, but an urge to call off their business, prevent a calamity? How would he know? Why did he doubt himself?

Henry was in and tied to the game and there was nothing he could do, and it was in that that he found his peace in the days before the arrests. He had organized the game and rolled the dice and now all he could do was wait. He went over the moves in his mind, could find no holes, could not fault Ben or McAteer for the direction of their new con. It was an obvious direction, considering their discoveries about the manner of business Dent was in. But who would have thought of it a year ago? Who would have known Dent himself was tied to such danger? Perhaps that's what is driving me to the edge of sanity, thought Henry. I don't need a war to madden me, he decided, just uncertainty.

He watched as the Bureau men considered their pursuit of counterfeiters, con men, and a deserter. The list of crimes, a list for salivation. And that was why it had come down to this heated talk on a hotter night. A pep talk by Lamb to his eleven men that belonged on an Ivy League football field, held instead in a rickety hotel. In amazement, Henry watched the other men strapping up. You would think that they were living fifty years ago in the western territories. Ankle holsters. Rifles in the back of their Fords. Henry was glad to see the government only gave them Fords. It was when Lamb himself tucked not one, but two service revolvers into his suit that Henry thought that there might have been a better, cleaner way to do this. Audacity was a wonderful thing, but he was not looking for the outbreak of a war.

>●<

They drove downtown in silence, parked their cars in the dull
shadows under the street lamps by city hall, and walked three
blocks west to Warren Street. Henry was carrying the counterfeit
money in its oversized wallet, tucked inside a weather-beaten portmanteau. Everyone was concentrating on their jobs, a little nervy
in the heat. Henry kept one eye open for Katherine. She had said
in the last letter that he had been able to pick up that she would try
to find a way to be near. His heart beat, in anticipation of her, of
their money, of the life beyond this night.

"Where do we stand?" asked Henry.

"You stand here," said Lamb, pointing to a lamppost behind him.

"And then?"

"You do nothing. Everyone gets the handcuffs, then you can
come forward and identify our suspects."

Henry took his spot just outside the arc of light falling from the
lamppost. He shifted his hat back on his head. He wanted them all
to see him. Ben, Dent, McAteer. Let them see him and let them
think on it. He wanted them up and out from beneath the city,
hands up, arrested, the whole lot of them. Most of all, he wanted
two years of work, two decades of desire to come to fruition for
him and Gallon James.

Henry was aware of all the anxiety; even now, with sweat and
thought, and double-guessing and improvisation, even now, it
could all unravel before him. Ben, for instance. When he had first
thought it out, he had not known that there was such a thing as a
bunco man fresh from a war. And if bunco men were exemplars of
flexible thought and planning and relied on their mouths, would an
unsteady tyro such as Ben crack when his dreams fell apart? Would
a soldier have carried a gun for the night when seventy-five thousand dollars changed hands?

Henry strained his eyes. Figures were emerging from the dark.
Although he hadn't yet felt a drop of rain, he thought he heard a

preposterously dramatic rumble of thunder in the skies overhead. There was the outline of Ben, the silhouetted elegance of Rudolph Dent, and the stooped McAteer. Wouldn't Gallon have liked to have seen this, he thought. Others seemed to follow the initial trio. Too many, he told himself, then glanced quickly at the government goons around him and shook his head. Almost there.

PART THREE

MISS KATHERINE HOWELLS
May 1916

Chapter One

RUDOLPH DENT WAS, to Katherine's relief and exhaustion both, a talker. He admitted that the only reason he had accepted the weekend invitation to Arch Grayson's house was because she had promised to be there. Perhaps not entirely true, she thought. Dent admitted that he accepted many weekend invitations. He was, he blithely confessed, one of the perennial invitees. The very wealthy could afford the palazzi with their harsh marble echoes, the sprawling oceanside properties of Newport, the sleek blue-hulled sailboats, but they could not buy friends. Not literally, at least. Houses must throng with admirers, but not with sycophants, Dent insisted, filled with those with taste who lacked the money to express it. Mrs. Dent, he elaborated, ran their Chicago circle in much the same way. He had looked hard at Katherine to see if she was perturbed by the clang of his spouse's name as it was dropped into the middle of the conversation. Katherine had only smiled serenely.

They had met in New York, standing at the bar in the Hotel Astor. Henry had escorted her there an hour before, bought her her first drink.

"Remember," he'd said, "you can have the spider, and you can have the fly. But nobody gets to eat without the web that brings one to the other."

"Great," she replied. "Now I'm a web."

Henry had bowed and then abandoned her to her work. They both knew Dent's reputation, that he felt no more fidelity to his wife than to a rented limousine. The trick for Katherine would not be in letting herself be seduced, but keeping Dent interested. He arrived an hour later in the company of two men. She caught his eye twice and was soon approached. Since she could see him struggling for words to create a charming impression, Katherine had simply asked him where he was from.

"Chicago born," he had said.

"Me too," she had replied, though her birthplace of Litchfield, Illinois, had two hundred miles of grazing ground between it and the closest Chicago suburb.

"And what brought you to New York?" he had asked. "An actress? Really? What restaurant?"

She had managed to laugh.

"On Broadway?" He had been impressed. "A new play?" A speaking part, no less. He'd have to come and inspect.

"I'd like that," she had said, studying him. Dent had a thick head of black hair with a white streak passing directly down the middle. Over six feet tall, his relaxed manner was projected by wide shoulders. He had kind lines about his face from years of smiling and enjoyment, smooth movement of his arms, developed, she guessed, by tossing tennis balls into summer skies or placing stoles over ladies' shoulders. She could tell immediately he was one of those experts in overt forms of charm.

Katherine watched him examining her, running his eyes up from her gold sandals over her emerald dress, noting her modest opal earrings and her smile that had said *experienced*, an encouraging smile, but the wide eyes that were in conflict. They were warning him, *Not that easy; harder than you think*. A woman would not have been in the Hotel Astor at midnight unless she had a desire to meet a certain class of person. He would not leave her be. He awaited her return from the bathroom, bought her cocktails. She knew it was nothing personal, that she was just a pretty opportunity that happened to be passing in front of him. After all, Henry had been keeping count: Dent had courted over a dozen on his trips to New York.

After his third whiskey and her third gin, Dent had invited her up to Grayson's Newport cottage for the weekend. There was a bit of business with Grayson that he'd need to take care of, but, he promised, the rest of his attention would be devoted to her. As Katherine had left, she had accepted. An even better start than Henry had envisioned.

A woman traveling on her own. Very modern. She wanted to be icy in anticipation of the weekend, but was, in truth, giddy at the thought of Newport. It was easily the largest role Henry had ever trusted to her. The train from New York had arrived early, a car had been sent to pick her up. They drove through the gates, sped up the half-mile drive, and the chauffeur tapped his horn in front of the cottage, a house the size of a New York city block. A young man came to retrieve Katherine's bag, and she was shown up the front stairs to what her weekend maid called the Blue Room, with its inlaid panels of sharp-beaked birds.

After a long bath, she finally descended for cocktails. Dent was waiting for her. Except for a singe of gray in the hair at the temples, there were few signs of the years. If anything, thought Katherine, he was well preserved, the look of a man who had just bathed in brine. Throughout the introductions, she felt like a plumed bird of paradise perched upon his arm and contented herself with nods and smiles and vacuous responses.

Katherine could tell that Dent was pleased she had dressed well. She did not look out of place, easy enough, since she soon discovered the guest list was a reflection of her hostess's whims. Hairdressers cavorted with stockbrokers, faith healers with pianists. A Broadway actress was hardly an exotic addition. At dinner, Katherine had been seated next to their host, Arch Grayson himself. He wasn't much to look at. When he smiled, his nose seemed to cock itself a snoot, as if it had just caught a whiff of something mildly offensive. And height, there wasn't much of it in Grayson's case, thought Katherine. You still couldn't buy height.

><

Katherine could feel Dent's eyes on her. He watched her study the confusion of silver cutlery, noted her hesitating for just a moment in her selection of spoon, waiting for another lady to lead, then following. When Dent turned his eyes toward her she made a special effort to smile and laugh at whatever Grayson was saying. Never once did she bestow upon Dent the meaningful glance of the favored.

After dinner, the men spent an hour puffing on cigars and pipes while the ladies withdrew in a high-heeled herd. When the men finally entered, Katherine found herself alternating glances between the small, hairless Grayson and the tall, dark-haired Dent. Grayson was interesting, solid with secrets, a distinct appeal of freshly acquired power. During the few minutes when Caroline, Grayson's wife, had excused herself from the ladies, conversation had immediately turned to stories of her husband's rise. Wealthy, always, but filthy rich two years and counting. Dent in comparison an airy, attractive figure, a familiar scoundrel to any actress, but not without charm. As he had plopped himself down on the cushion next to her, he had let out an old man's huff. She had barely acknowledged him, but now, a half hour later, he caught her looking at him and when he stared back, she smiled at him and gave the slimmest wink. A moment later, Katherine rose and walked out onto the terrace. Dent followed.

The May evening was too blustery to be outside, but Katherine pretended to take a girlish satisfaction in the way the wind kept trying to push her skirt upward.

"You find it all quite tiresome, don't you?" asked Dent. "I'm afraid you're not really enjoying the weekend."

Katherine smiled. "No," she said, "it's all very amusing."

"But?"

"I'm going to prove very bad for your reputation," said Katherine. "The strange actress you tracked to the terrace."

"My reputation is entirely based on such acts."

She laughed for him, but did not speak, a smirk creeping across her face.

"I am a rigorous follower of the Constitution's insistence on the pursuit of happiness," he continued.

"But only your own?"

"I figure if we each take our civic responsibilities as seriously as I do, then we'll all be just fine."

Perhaps there was something charming, to be able to say that, with all the desire she hoped he felt, with his drink in one hand and a cigarette in the other and eyes cloaked in innocence, and children and wife ignored. Transferring her cigarette and glass to the same hand, Katherine leaned in and kissed him.

A second later there was a cough from the doorway. They fluttered apart. Grayson stood there without embarrassment.

"Rudolph, we're having a chat."

"Now?" asked Dent.

"You asked me if we could talk."

Dent seemed almost anguished. It took him a moment to force clearheadedness. Katherine saw Dent's eyes flash quick calculations. Girls did not always lead to more money, but more money could always lead to more girls.

"You will excuse me."

"Go play," said Katherine Howells.

One kiss, a good kiss. That's all for now, thought Katherine. She watched Grayson close the door behind them and turned to rejoin the women.

By two in the morning, most of the guests had either retired to bed or departed. Even Caroline Grayson had said goodnight. All the motorcars had retreated, all the cloaks and overcoats were gone. Just empty glasses and teeming ashtrays and the overwhelming sense that an army had passed through, looting the place for liquor and cigars. The field of battle was still wreathed in smoke, enough to make the lilies wilt. Katherine took a long last look about and walked up to the Blue Room. Henry Jergens would have been proud, she thought, of how lightly his wife was treading, the languorous insinuation of a poor girl into a rich man's game. An hour later, in her sleep, she could hear the rattle of the doorknob. She smiled to herself and turned over, imagining the frustration Dent would be feeling to find the key turned against him.

Chapter Two

THE NEXT MORNING, walking in the gardens with Mrs. Grayson, Katherine listened as her hostess explained that she was very fond of the country, and she was, thought Katherine, insofar as she liked to own a lot of it. They returned through the back door with its extra coats for guests, an assortment of boots, the smell of wet dog, spare tennis rackets, a putter and basket of golf balls. Breakfast was a casual, English affair; guests came and went from the dining room, ordering their eggs, pouring their own coffee, choosing their own seats. Despite Dent's amorous glances across the table, she emitted a scent of distance, as if they had never kissed. Hopefully, he would suffer from a sliver of doubt.

Dent had agreed to stay on, but Katherine was resisting.

"I have a job," she said.

"How vulgar," he teased.

"How enjoyable," she corrected.

"I really can't persuade you?"

"Not unless you own a theater."

"Can't help there. Could ask Arch. He probably has a couple. Come on, just for the morning. I can drive you back down at two."

Dent remained distracted by the echoes of whatever conversation of business he had had the night before, but, assuming a reluctance, Katherine agreed to stay. Though genuinely worried she might be late for the theater, without so many guests about there was the possibility she might learn something of interest to Henry.

Mrs. Grayson, however, was on the verge of leaving for their house in California, and the mansion was awash in the hectic roar of packing. The campaign of preparation had begun and the advance party, headed by Mrs. Grayson's secretary, had already departed. There were pools to warm, electric wires to connect, bars and kitchens to stock, gardens to trim and edge, before a house might be ready for Mrs. Grayson, let alone her guests. A skeleton staff would garrison Newport, in case Arch needed it for business.

"Business, for most people, very sedentary right?" Dent asked Katherine as they strolled around the garden, doing their best to keep out of the way.

"I guess so," said Katherine. Then, "What's sedentary?"— just to please him.

"Desks and decisions," said Dent patiently. "No real movement."

"Sure."

"Doesn't have to be," said Dent. "Doesn't have to glaze the eyes over does it? Why don't you go upstairs and get changed. I've got a treat for you. You like treats?"

"Of course," she giggled.

"Caroline's leaving behind an outfit for you."

Upstairs the promised clothes were waiting, along with the smell of coffee and the gleam of a silver tray. Katherine picked up gloves, black leather trousers, boots, and long jacket. On top of the dresser was a helmet, and inside the helmet a pair of goggles. What the hell has Henry got me into now, she thought, and dressed quickly, Caroline's clothes a little loose about her.

A half hour later, they pulled into the side of a small airfield. Grayson walked Dent and Katherine over to a solitary figure attending to a ragged-looking conveyance.

"This is a Nieuport," said Grayson, tapping the side of the plane, addressing Katherine. "And this," he continued, "is my chief engineer and mechanic, Monsieur Glasson."

A blue-eyed Frenchman with a stray curl of dark hair that kissed his forehead offered Katherine a theatrical bow, which she returned with a prudish curtsy, feeling ridiculous in her outfit.

She was soon distracted by the contraption. A large metal chunk, resembling nothing so much as a car she had once seen crushed between the trunks of two trees. The wings were made from hide or fabric. She thought she might be able to peel them apart with a pair of tweezers or pierce them with a tapered lipstick. Katherine had seen planes before, seen them ripple through the skies high above, had shaken her head and smiled, but she had never actually approached one, never guessed at the sheer flimsiness of this supposed scientific advancement. The peeling insignia of an eagle glared at her from the fuselage.

"It's perfectly safe," said Grayson, looking at the worry seeping across Katherine's face. "We landed like a sack of cement last week and only snapped a wheel off. So who's going up with me?"

"Ladies first," said Dent.

With Dent's assistance, Katherine climbed into the passenger seat, squirming into the tight space. Though she was even shorter than Grayson, she felt cramped and pinioned, without a chance should she need to leap. To leap where? Tight can be snug, she tried to convince herself. Rust can be a sign of loyal service.

"*Coupe, plein gaz,*" called Grayson.

"*Coupe, plein gaz,*" echoed Glasson.

The mechanic put his bare hands on the propeller and drove it downward until the gasoline was sucked into the carburetor, then called, "*Contact, reduisez.*"

"*Contact reduisez,*" repeated Grayson.

What the hell does that mean?, thought Katherine, trying to hunker down in her seat.

Chapter Three

KATHERINE TIGHTENED THE strap of her helmet and tried pulling her gloves farther up her arms. Glasson spun the propeller, and the engine coughed once and lurched noisily to life, as did Katherine's stomach. Down the grassy flats, rattle and jog, and then, how to describe nothing? Air, thought Katherine. The first pitch of a thermal current and Katherine gripped her seat. For a moment she thought that she did not belong and then the wind rushed up into her mind.

Disembodied, free as she had ever thought possible. All the roar of the engine and the wind and still a silence. Up farther and a sudden loneliness such as Katherine had never felt before. Part of her longed to touch back on ground and part of her wished she never had to set foot on the ground again. It was too encompassing a solitude to actually be pleasant.

There, in the middle of nowhere, Katherine finally admitted it to herself. The life that Henry had created for them was not the life she wanted. Nor did she want Dent's world. What she wanted more than anything was her *own* world, free of the strings of men. True independence would take money. In this case, Dent's. Henry could do what he wanted, but Katherine would reap the reward. She had earned it a dozen times over. And Henry would be furious, but sooner or later, he would understand that big money was something that he knew how to earn and she didn't. Theft was the only route to her independence.

There was a hole in the clouds. Grayson wound the plane in tight circles until it approached the eye and passed through. The air was shrieking through the wings' support wires, clouds were enveloping them, Katherine was swallowing cloud, exhilarated by her self-confession. They had broken into a second world. The landscape was one of rolling cloud hills. Above, a new sky of impossibly vivid blue. Nothing here, not a single sign of man.

They landed so softly that Katherine's body touched down a full minute before her mind. Once the engine died, Grayson began to speak. They were both so deafened by their time aloft that their conversation could have been heard a mile downwind.

"What did you think?"

"Marvelous," said Katherine. She found that she was laughing. "I am just absolutely speechless," she said.

Dent approached and gave her a boyish pat on the back. "Was that your first time? You should have told us. Arch would have been much more gentle," he said.

And then he took his turn hurtling through the skies and came back, pink-cheeked and giddy as a child. They sat for a minute, enjoying the silence of the airfield once the engines had died, before speeding back to the house and trying to convince Caroline to join them for a brief lunch of oysters and crab. She waved them off, gave Katherine a premature kiss goodbye, and shouted down the hallway to stop a half dozen men in overalls carrying two large canvases in the wrong direction.

It was not even Dent's car, but belonged to a friend from Yale. He confessed to Katherine that he had never brought a car east, only his thick striped motoring coat that he wore about the streets of New York, as if he had just parked a shiny new Packard around the corner. She waited until they'd crossed the Rhode Island border in their southern sweep. Dent had paused to put chains on the tires before they attempted a rough uphill stretch of road, still a little soggy from passing rains.

Katherine whooped as they made it over the top. "What a couple of days, just wonderful," she said enthusiastically. But she wanted Dent's money, and it was time to work. "Have you ever flown down to New York? Can airplanes go that far?"

"Sure," said Dent. "Maybe you'd have to stop for fuel. I don't know."

"Do you own a plane?"

"I don't own one directly," explained Dent, as he overtook a milk truck on the downward stretch. "I just invest in them. Arch has a company that sells them."

"To who?"

"To Europe."

"Oh," said Katherine.

"We've got an arrangement with the Ecoles de Vol outside of Paris," said Dent. "We supply the engines for Voisins, Bréguets, Caudrons, Nieuports, you name it. All through a French holding company."

"Is it a good business?" she asked.

Dent laughed. "Do you know how long a *pilote de chasse* can expect to live on the front?"

"In the war?" she asked, hoping she hadn't overplayed her ignorance.

He nodded quickly. "Two sorties. Do you know how many planes he'll crash to learn the trade? Forty thousand dollars' worth, per head. We're beginning to manufacture fuselages too."

"How many pilots are there over there?" asked Katherine.

"They can't produce them fast enough," said Dent. "You get a week's training in a Penguin, two weeks flying about the country-side, and if you survive that, straight up to the front. It's a million-dollar industry until the war ends. And there's no sign of that." Dent shook his head. "Nothing doing, they say, no sign at all."

"You don't sell planes to the Germans do you?" asked Katherine sweetly.

Dent smiled. "If I did, would I tell you?"

"Depends on who wins the war," said Katherine.

"*We* will," said Dent. "Arch and me." He reached over for a friendly squeeze of her leg.

Katherine smiled. They were, for lack of a better word, warmongers. It did not bother her. But had Henry always known how Dent was making his money? She had thought of Henry, flirted with Dent. She had not used her body yet, though she liked the attention of men, loved how it brought Henry to a stop, made him look at her, made him aware that she had graduated from the role of simple tethered goat.

Katherine had noticed that Dent was slightly cowed in the presence of Grayson's self-made wealth. He seemed to know better than his blue-blooded contemporaries how useless empty names and respectable descendants were. Katherine had learned that Grayson was the son of a shirtwaist manufacturer. He had been to a decent enough school, a second-rate preparatory, but he had taken this insignificant beginning and managed to engineer his own propulsion into the stratosphere of American money. He had chosen his own wife, married for at least a semblance of love, and had not yet interrupted it with children. Where had Grayson made his money? No one asked aloud.

Obviously, Dent wanted some part of Grayson's success. To partake in whatever Grayson partook of. And that would be money earned by Dent, independent money, not inherited, not married, but earned through his own machinations. That was his weakness, Henry had said. It was Katherine's job to loosen Dent's concept that riding beside Grayson could be considered independent wealth. She should be gently undermining his character, so that by the time they offered Dent up to McAteer's shop he would be quick to see an opportunity unconnected to any social connections he might have. Undermine one man, she thought, then another, until she stood, for the first time, alone.

Chapter Four

DENT LEFT THE following morning for Chicago and his family, leaving Katherine with a large bouquet of peonies, a typed copy of Wordsworth's "By the Sea," and a promise to be back in two weeks. Katherine guessed the same flowers, the same poem, a similar promise had been received by countless others before her. It made her even happier to get back to the greasepaint. Broadway seemed all the more real for the extraordinary experience of her Newport weekend. She cleared the blue skies from her mind and submitted to the grub and muck of the city, the stage-door johnnies, the sarcastic comments of her fellow actresses.

She always smiled when she saw the sign on the dressing room door. NO MEN ALLOWED UPSTAIRS. Management clearly didn't think much of their morals. Katherine knew that whoring and the theater were not entirely unalike. Popular in the largest of cities, the businesses were run from the same neighborhoods. They were outward spectacles and private sweats, populated equally by those on the way up, those known about town, and those fallen. Afterward, the world had no use for any of them.

It had not been easy for Henry to help find her work. He had said that he had not known which card to pull until he had sat down with the manager of the Eltinge Theater. Posing as her agent, Henry had been about to offer the manager his wife's favors when he had realized the man was queer. Instead, he had pushed photographs of Katherine before him, pictures of high artifice designed to show an overdose of sophistication. Katherine as Little Butterfly from Japan, peeking out at the camera from behind a lush kimono and splayed fan. Katherine as the Rite of Spring, in decorous swaths of white cotton, holding a bouquet of pale lilies, exuding innocence. The day they had taken the photographs, Katherine had warmed to the prospect of stepping on stage. It was such a natural extension of what she and Henry did.

"These photos are from Chicago productions?" the manager had asked.

Henry had nodded and presented a small folder with five bogus reviews from Chicago newspapers, all of which singled out Miss Katherine Howells for lavish praise.

"A very pretty girl," the manager had said, looking at the Japanese pose. "The city is filled with very pretty girls. I really don't have the room."

Henry had said he'd been a little uncertain how to proceed, but he refused to stand and leave, insisting that the manager reread the notices.

"This is not a Bowery music hall. This is Broadway. You're supposed to sweat to get here."

"Horseshit," said Henry. "I'll do better than that. I'll pay you, directly. Whatever her first two months' salary is, I'll pay it straight to your pocket."

"And your cut is?"

"I'll make it up from the rest of the engagement."

"And if there isn't one? If the show folds?"

"Then I've established her in New York. You'll help her get a job, maybe in whatever you run next."

"Bribery," crooned the manager. "At least you didn't try blackmail. If we wait a little longer, do you think you'll have to rough me up as well?"

"I'll give you thirty dollars just to take a look at her," said Henry. "I'm not averse to a hustle, but for once, I'm offering you a real deal."

"I suppose I could have a look tomorrow," said the manager.

Henry smiled and stood to leave.

The manager held out his hand. "Cash up front."

><

The thing was, Katherine was good. She knew it, Henry knew it, and by the end of her audition the manager knew it. He had made swift calculations, knew that if he used her only as an extra, Henry would only pay him sixty dollars for her two months, but if he should give her a speaking role, he might clear at least one hundred and twenty. He nodded in agreement and offered her the smallest of the speaking parts.

"One more thing," Henry had said. "I'm going to need her for a weekend here and there."

"That I can't do."

Henry slapped down a hundred-dollar bill. "She's got a dozen lines. I think you can find a grateful understudy."

On June 17 she tried staring out into the footlights to make sure that Ben had indeed accepted her offer of free tickets, but did not find him until intermission. She had seen him before of course. The first time, three or four weeks ago, in the middle of the tenth row, alongside Henry. She had not gotten a good look at Ben until later that evening at the Hotel Astor when Henry had approached her table with Ben in tow.

Ben had a broad forehead, a modest mustache, olive skin, and very deep blue eyes, perfectly matched to his tie. Really very handsome, Katherine had thought at once, but whatever presence he might once have carried into a room had been stripped of confidence. She could imagine ladies still favored him, but how many more heads might he have turned had he known how to hold himself, or how to look at a woman. Instead, he had an uncertainty about him, a wobbly scurry of the eyes. It was still charming. Once you knew he was English, the presumption was almost immediate that here was some kind of troubled veteran, a man who had suffered something or other.

That evening, last month, looking at Dent after Henry and Ben had retreated from their table, Katherine had let out a small groan, entirely missed by her dinner partner. She had not been worried about what Henry thought of Dent; they had studied him for so long, he was as familiar to them as a corner shop. But neither had known whom McAteer might send their way as a roper. The fact that it was a young Englishman with his trim black mustache and sympathetic appeal of a soldier, with an elegant gait, a sadness to him, she knew what that would do to Henry. If he did not already feel it, it would begin to lend him an edge of green. He would begin not to trust her. It had happened once before, in Chattanooga, when Henry had put her up to tempt a handsome horse trader. She smiled at the memory. Henry could not bring himself to abandon the con, and they had taken the man for six thousand dollars, but more importantly to Katherine, it had propelled Henry to declare his love for the first time.

Finally, she spotted Ben sitting low in his seat on the far edge of an aisle. Of course, she thought. There she was, on stage at intermission, an officer from the Lifeguards beside her. They were about to sell war bonds to the audience. Ben, a deserter, must have been very wary to come that evening, but as long as he did not open his mouth, he could be no danger to himself.

"Miss Howells," said the director, "would you please introduce Captain Ethrington of His Majesty's Lifeguards."

"Didn't even know the king could swim," said Katherine, receiving a gentle patter of laughter.

She stood there hawking the bonds and hands were raised. Fifty, sixty, seventy, a hundred-dollar bond. And there was Ben standing, waving his hand at her. She smiled at him.

"How much can we put you down for sir?" asked the captain. Ben just nodded. "Can I take that for the full hundred?"

Ben nodded again and took his seat.

"A hundred to the fine-looking gentleman in the blue suit. Thank you, sir. Now who else?"

Katherine turned her attention away from Ben, but felt a sort of giddiness, all eyes on her; he was looking at her. And oddly, she felt free, her husband gone to Newport, Dent in Chicago, and this handsome man, a veteran who would dare come before a ranking officer. Henry had said he must be a deserter and she was flattered, very flattered, that he would come and stand before her and pledge money to a war he obviously wanted no part of.

At the reception afterward, held backstage, Ben drifted at the edge of Katherine's periphery, watching her react to the whispered jokes of other actors. She knew Ben was there; she gave him the odd smile, enough to keep him about. When she left, he followed. She got into a taxi, had it wait as Ben exited and climbed into the taxi behind, then ordered the driver to take her to her hotel on Irving Place.

Ben followed her back. The hotel bar was empty, save for the stiff-collared bartender and a quiet couple, nesting in a booth near the far window. Katherine was standing, a fresh drink in her hand, when Ben arrived. He smiled and approached her.

She turned to look at him, slightly drunk from the evening's celebrations. "Has the soldier gone and followed me here?"

"I thought tonight was in aid of England," said Ben. "Besides, I just came in for a drink."

"Sure you did."

"You must have a very high opinion of yourself." They were very good eyes, she thought. Perhaps he had recovered some of his confidence. Such deep eyes, they were hard to read, good for a bunco man. Henry was correct to think that Dent would trust him.

Katherine smiled. "Maybe you're right," she said. "It's just that fans are too dreary."

"I hope there's more to me," said Ben. "I could buy you that drink and we could find out?"

"You're going to have to do better than that," she said, and settled back on the bar stool.

"Unfortunately," answered Ben, "we're off the stage, the flies are hoisted, and I'm writing my own lines."

"Are you in theater?" she asked.

"Many years ago," said Ben. "Before the war."

"English?"

"I speak a little."

"Are *you* really English?" she laughed.

Ben nodded.

"Where's your friend?" asked Katherine. "The one with all the producer friends."

"Called back home by his wife," said Ben.

He was close enough to her to smell whiskey, greasepaint, dressing rooms, and skin creams, and above it all, the scent of clove chewing gum. "What were you?" she asked. "Too young to produce, too young to direct, too smug to have shifted scenery. My God," she groaned theatrically, "you're a fellow actor."

"No." He ran his hands across imaginary piano keys. "Orchestra player. You're very good," said Ben, "on stage."

"Oh, do tell me more," she whispered. "What's your name again?"

"Ben."

"Katherine." She stuck out her hand. "What are you doing over here?" she asked. "Don't you know there's a war on?"

"I've already done that," said Ben, lowering his voice and turning his eyes away from hers for the first time, gazing at his glass as he picked it up. Acting, she thought. He's probably played stoic hero for some, same old Ben for others, and now wounded veteran for her.

She stared at him. "Oh dear," she said, oozing sympathy. "I'm sorry. I remember now. The war hero."

"That's all right," said Ben.

"No, it's shameful," she said, and then laughed. "And wasn't it just the loveliest war?"

"Yes," said Ben, warming up again.

"And they've sent you here for what?" she asked. "Raising money, money and men and arms? Are you part of that? Isn't that what everybody's doing?"

"No, no," said Ben. "I've come here of my own accord. I have investments in New York, business to pursue."

"That's very Wall Street of you."

"How am I doing?"

"Wonderfully," said Katherine with a smile.

"Miss Howells, you are a very beautiful woman," said Ben suddenly.

She burst into peals of laughter, genuinely shocked. He smiled like a man who had risked utter honesty. She had the feeling that if she said the wrong thing, he might run from the room like a rabbit. Let's boost his confidence, she thought.

"And you, Mr. Ben, are a very beautiful man." She let the silence sit between them for a moment. "But that does not, not, *not* mean that I have the slightest intention. Tonight. Or at all. Ever."

She slipped out of her chair, and Ben watched her exit. She was flustered. She had meant the conversation to continue a little longer, but his declaration required at least a temporary retreat. To her surprise, it had increased her giddiness. She knew herself well enough to understand that it had nothing to do with Ben, only his appreciation of her. That a man so handsome might think so highly of her was like the softest, most seductive kiss to the nape of the neck, arousing her, marking her as desirable. At the door she swiveled to address him. "In another life I might have stayed for a drink," she said theatrically, "but I promised my paramour I'd be good tonight."

Ben rose to give her a small and distant bow.

Chapter Five

KATHERINE DIDN'T KNOW it quite yet. She and Ben were, in some sense, each other's orphaned half. He with no father and a mother he no longer saw. Katherine with a father who always called her Katie and a mother dead so long she had neither memory nor photograph of her. Despite this, Katherine considered hers far from a bad childhood, designed for the curious, for there were no limits. Her father was a harmless man unused to responsibility who would disappear into drink for the weekend and emerge on Sunday at church, daughter in hand and filled with black dog penitence. By thirteen, boys stared at her in school, men stared at her on the streets of Litchfield, Illinois, and before she knew what it was that she had, she knew it was something of worth. Her father was a lonely widower and all he treasured besides her was his Ford, his single extravagance. It was a Model G, driven softly, polished to a high shine. Even the crank was kept free of fingerprints.

The lonelier her father became, the more often he put his car up for sale. Men would come around to see it in the evenings. They would talk, maybe take a drink with him, then make an offer that he would reject. Katherine knew he was just testing its worth while sating his need for company, talking of his wife, taken in a week by pneumonia. And some of those men looked at Katherine too, flat-chested and flinty-eyed. Once, when her father had walked down the block for more ice, a man offered her a whole dollar to just look at, but not touch, her tiny breasts. She did it and laughed and took the dollar.

><•<

Katherine had a favorite blue cotton dress flecked with white daisies that she got to wear every single day because no one told her otherwise. At fifteen she stopped going to school because no one told her otherwise. She read a lot, mostly her mother's old novels about bad marriages and earnest wooers. She had always wondered what lay beyond the edges of Litchfield and the smoke of the candy factories. And when her father didn't come back to the house one Sunday, she didn't say a thing to her neighbors. For a week she waited for him, until she had exhausted the box of small bills and loose change that she had used to run errands. On Monday afternoon a man stopped by the house with an appointment to see the shiny black Ford. Katherine did something that she hadn't thought herself capable of. She told the man he could have the car for one hundred and eighty dollars in cash. It was more or less the sum that her father normally refused.

"Is that what your daddy says?" asked the stranger.

"Yes sir. One hundred eighty and not a red cent less."

"She looks well loved," said the gentleman, rubbing his thumb and forefinger against the bristles of his mustache and casting his eyes back and forth between Katherine and the Ford.

"She's like a sister to me," said Katherine gravely, and she hadn't meant to be funny, but the man laughed and went away and came back just before sundown with the cash. He cranked the car, waved, and chugged down the street.

She waited at home on Tuesday and prayed to God that He would send her a good explanation for the missing vehicle if her father came back. But God decided against testing her, for still, her father was missing. Katherine walked to the local haberdasher and spent fourteen dollars on a new dress, white, hemmed by tiny red roses, and bought a pair of slim tan shoes and a demure shade of lipstick. At home, she dressed in front of the mirror and waited downstairs for her father to return and for her punishment to begin.

On Wednesday, with still no sign of his return, she borrowed her father's beaten portmanteau, filled it with her clothes and two

novels, and lugged it for twenty minutes to the train station, perspiring through her new white dress, smearing the lipstick downward, toward her pretty chin. On the Chicago train women seemed
to either stare sharply and not return her smile, or else avoid her
eyes altogether. She remembered fretting, worried to the point of
tears that she had been incredibly foolish and that perhaps, outside
of her town, different rules applied to talking and making friends
and that she didn't know them. Finally, heaven sent, a man her
father's age approached and took a seat beside her.

George was a salesman for a manufacturer of electric suction
machines for cleaning the house. He traveled with great, impor-
tant-looking cases for demonstration. Katherine, so grateful for
even a simulation of kindness, required no encouragement to
accompany him from the train, to allow him to check into his hotel
alone, then smuggle herself up the back stairs to his room, bag in
hand. She knew that something would happen and was prepared
for it. She remembered being rather surprised by the nudity, but
the encounter had been less painful and briefer than the girls at
school had described. Either way, that minute or two was much
better than the next six hours, when George, twice her weight,
sprawled across her snoring. In the morning, when he rolled away,
Katherine began thinking about how he hadn't even offered her a
dollar. She knew she'd done a lot more than raised a blouse. While
George slept she plucked a five-dollar bill from his stuffed wallet.

When he woke, he still seemed keen on her and she began to feel
guilty about the five dollars. He insisted on taking her with him to
his next stop and bought them both a train ticket. It had all seemed
very adult to her, sitting in her good dress, smiling at a man her
father's age and ignoring the other women in the carriage, now not
caring what they thought. Ten minutes from Chicago, George
grew uncomfortable and Katherine knew he was going to tell her
something she didn't want to hear.
    "I live in Chicago."

"That's good," she said sweetly.

"I can't be seen with you, Katie," he said. "I've got my business here. And I already got a wife."

"I don't want to be a wife," said Katherine with great understanding.

"I just think the best thing is for you to stay on the train," he whispered, "or to take the next train back."

"I don't have a ticket," she said, trying not to tear up.

He reached for his wallet and Katherine blurted her confession. "I took five dollars from you this morning."

George looked up and smiled. "You're worth more than that." He pulled out a twenty-dollar note. "You ever do this sort of thing again with another gentleman, don't go thieving in his pocket. Just ask him outright for one of these."

One day and many tears later, Katherine took George's advice and spent the afternoon with an army captain returning east. She began to move about only in trains, rarely spending more than one night in any town. There wasn't a station within two hundred miles of Chicago that she hadn't visited by the end of the year. Trains and motion, always moving, and in fact, it wasn't until she met Henry Jergens that she had ever seen any man twice, save for conductors and porters.

When she first met Henry, he was thirty-one, a little chubby, like one of the three little pigs. He was young for her tastes. She had learned to look at suits, ignore rings and watches, listen to accents, and know the difference in smell between a good and bad cigar. She tended to concentrate on gentleman of about fifty, well enough on in their lives to appreciate their time together without getting hung up on her. The day she met Henry, she was with a bald Kansan milliner. To the milliner's great embarrassment, at a station not far from Litchfield, two men boarded and sat opposite them, one of them an old school friend. Katherine was introduced as a niece. The other stranger, Henry Jergens, seemed to look upon her act with amusement. All four of them knew how she made her money, but they were polite and she played well and all were thankful. That night she made her twenty dollars without ever having to touch a thing. And then, miracle of miracles, a night later, there was Henry on the same line, running back west.

Both were alone. Henry had walked straight over to her, doffed his hat, and asked, "What you make off that old man last night?"

"Twenty," she smiled.

He laughed at her.

She didn't know what he did, but because of the coincidence of him running on trains the same way she did, Katherine could only presume it was something equally shady.

"What did you make off *your* man?" she asked.

Henry looked about him, then reached into his pocket and pulled out a thick wad of notes. "I'd say about four hundred dollars," he said. "And *my* clothes stayed on."

"You probably don't look too good without them," she said defensively.

"What's your name?" he asked.

"Katie."

"No it isn't," said Henry. "You're older than that. You're a Katherine." He peeled off two hundred dollars and pressed it into her palm. "Why don't you take a few days off and spend some time with me?"

She had always loved and hated that about Henry. The spontaneous and utterly persuasive gesture that could make a person do what she had previously barely considered. That night on the train, she knew that for two hundred he'd be expecting something from her, something more than what twenty dollars bought. In retrospect, she realized that part of her immediate attraction to Henry was the relief of seeing the same face twice, of being able to build some strange thing together. She was grateful that he thought her worth keeping around. That week, when she had an upset stomach, he brought her hot water. Then to test him, she complained of a sore throat. He walked three blocks just to bring her a salted lemonade.

Katherine had never told Henry, but the few times that he had left her alone in their first week together, she had cried. Henry always said that when you left a dog it would bark and yowl because it did not understand that you would be coming back. She had wept and had waited, and when she had seen him again, it was like a dying fire had been stoked, right in the middle of her chest. She was seventeen years old and in love for the first time.

Chapter Six

THE FOLLOWING DAY at three in the afternoon Katherine received the following telegram:

"Mr. Benedict Newcombe leaves his address in case Miss Katherine Howells would like to apologize for her damning and dreadful behavior on night of June 17, 1916."

Katherine waited until six to reply: "Miss Katherine Howells will let Ben Newcombe know that she NEVER apologizes to men, especially when she has no memory of crimes of which she stands accused."

The same night, at the theater, she received the following answer. "Alcohol a terrible alibi. Mr. Newcombe asks Miss Howells for end to hostilities and suggests 11:30 PM at Halland bar for signing of accord, June 19, 1916."

Katherine was thirty-five minutes late.

"So sorry," she said. "Charming Mr. Ben. Couldn't find a cab for the life of me. Will you forgive me?"

"I'm not sure you deserve, or even need, forgiveness," said Ben with a smile. He seemed more settled, prepared for their meeting.

"You're a very bold soul, Mr. Ben," said Katherine with great seriousness, before suddenly breaking into laughter. "Am I being mysterious?" asked Katherine. "I told my friend Esther about you and she told me to keep an aura of mystery about me. How is it?"

"The aura?"

Katherine nodded.

"I have no idea who you are," said Ben.

"That's good," she said. "I think."

"How's your elderly friend?"

"My *elderly* friend?"

"The one you were with last month in the Astor."

"He's back in Chicago," said Katherine, "with his wife."

"That's very understanding of you."

"Very understanding of *her*," corrected Katherine.

"Your friend leads a good life."

"He can afford to."

"I don't think I could afford a girl like you."

"Why not?" asked Katherine. "I'm already paid for."

The tickets to the midnight show of *Intolerance* were two dollars apiece, an outrageous sum for a motion picture. Katherine was secretly thrilled. Henry rarely took her to the movies. The red velvet seats were clingy and spongy and stank strongly of cigarettes. Every seat was full when they walked in late. With the organ huffing and rising in front of the rapt audience, a storm of violence bristled over the screen. Soon, a fierce mountain girl was put up for sale at the marriage market in Babylon. Pretty girls were well paid for; the funds were then transferred to provide the ugly girls with dowries until they too had husbands.

"How much do you think they'd need for me?" whispered Katherine.

"Sacks of gold," said Ben.

"*Shhhh,*" from behind.

Ben swiveled in his seat and glowered at the offender. Katherine reached out and put a calming hand on his. He held it.

Emerging from the post-theater crowd, Ben directed them to a lunchroom on Forty-eighth Street. It was one of those restaurants that opened only late at night, running until the early morning, and was the primary domain of motormen, dragmen, and the young out until dawn in their dancing pumps. The vast menu was written across one entire wall, but Ben ordered only beer and ice cream.

>●<

Katherine quizzed him about his life before the war, the theaters he had played at, the roles he had admired. He had a gentle voice, eyes that met hers for moments then darted in apparent shyness, yet she didn't think him shy. There was much in Ben that confused her, which she laid at the door of professionalism. As a bunco man, she could not presume that the person being presented to her was the true Ben. When Katherine excused herself to the bathroom she could feel Ben's eyes on her and gave her dress a little downward tug, one last gesture of propriety.

On her return, she took a long sip of her beer, bending down to it rather than raising the glass, looking like a little girl sneaking a quick sip. When she sat up straight again, she wiped her mouth dry with the corner of her napkin and asked, "Tell me things. How many girls have you kissed? How old are you?"

"Twenty-five."

"Twenty-five girls?"

"Twenty-five years old."

"So you must have kissed a lot of girls."

"No," said Ben.

"Were you married?" asked Katherine smiling. "Was there some terrible accident? A fatal disease?"

"No," said Ben with a laugh. He leaned across the table and kissed her gently. She tasted the beer, the aftertaste of ice cream sweetness, and closed her eyes, feeling the softness of his lips.

"In public Mr. Ben?" she whispered.

"I'd prefer if it were in private," he said.

Ben left Katherine's bed once in the next twenty-four hours. He dressed, walked out the door of the hotel, bought two packs of Pharaoh cigarettes, clove chewing gum for Katherine, and stripped as soon as he closed the door to her room.

"Can you call in sick?" asked Ben.

"Can you?"

Ben smiled.

"I don't even know what you do," said Katherine.

"Good," said Ben.

"I know what you did, and I know what you did before you did what you did. But what do you do now?"

Ben crawled back into bed, brushed aside her hair, and nestled his lips against the nape of her neck.

"It's not very conventional," she said, "is it?"

"No."

"Once we leave here," she asked, "will it all fade away tonight? Will I see you again?"

"Of course," said Ben. "Don't be stupid."

"It's not stupid," she said into the pillow. "You don't know how many times it happens to me." She laughed and laughed.

"Oh really," said Ben. "And exactly how many times *has* it happened?"

"With at least twelve sailors," said Katherine. "And let's not talk about the union men."

Ben smiled at her and lit a cigarette. Perhaps he could tell she was barely joking. "I hate it," said Katherine quickly. "You're more mysterious than I am."

"It won't last," said Ben.

"It's destroying my confidence," she said, placing her forearm against her brow, screen parlance for despair.

Chapter Seven

OVER THE NEXT two weeks, Katherine realized that there was a predominant, exhausting theme to her life. Acting with Ben, acting with Dent, acting on stage. Who was she? Henry could manage. He had been taught by Gallon James. Famous, he said. A con man that no one ever managed to con, only thieved from once by his own pupil, the man now running Ben's shop. But Katherine wasn't like that. She wanted to be free from Henry's merry-go-round, his constant chatter of Gallon and McAteer, the numerous roles expected of her. It wasn't so much that she wanted to steal from a man she had loved; she wanted to thieve from a business she had loved. Katherine thought of it as a pension that she had already earned, and it was with this in mind that she accepted Dent's offer to head north again to Newport.

Ben knew she was going to see Dent for the weekend. Perhaps she was a little disappointed that he didn't seem to object. She had decided there was something virginal about him. Even the way he spoke to her, as if he were about to be stricken by first love. She had a genuine liking for his innocence, even if it was a facade, but she could not share it. She liked most everything about him: his tenderness, his surprising aggression between the sheets, the correct dose of attention that she desired, with just enough neglect to make her wonder if he was merely playing at love. But she would not return it. Sex was one thing, an available commodity between women and men. But love and affection were elusive creatures, and she hadn't fully pried herself from Henry. Still, it didn't mean she couldn't enjoy herself. As a couple, she loved the way they turned heads; there was something very vainglorious about being seen with him, a different reading in other men's eyes than when she walked with Henry. Henry, chubby and older, they presumed rich to be with her, but with Ben they presumed it a pure love.

When she arrived from the station, Katherine was surprised to find that Grayson greeted her like an old friend. It did not seem to take much to make an impact on the rich. They were predisposed toward kindness. Perhaps, she thought, it was simply the fact that she had been up to visit twice. In the spinning world of Dent and Grayson, perhaps that approached a deep friendship.

Over lunch, Arch Grayson delighted them all with long-distance stories from his wife in California.

"I wouldn't want to persuade you away from Rudolph," he said, "but movies out there are getting bigger than New York."

"One day," said Katherine, "I think I'd like the change."

"I'd be happy to get you a screen test."

She considered it for a moment — unattached to any man, up on the screen, money earned honestly.

"The thing is," Grayson was saying, "when a country goes to war, you get this sudden appetite for knowledge. The need to know what's going on. Especially the men." He laughed at himself. "We like to be armed with information at a dinner table. But then people get bored, they need diversion. A war that drags on more than a year is like a baseball game that hits the twelfth inning. Part of you wants to go home. People are going to turn to moving pictures, more and more."

"You think there's real money in it?" asked Katherine.

"Between you and me," said Grayson, "they're paying Chaplin ten thousand dollars a week. If they can afford to pay him that . . ."

Katherine was staggered by the sums they spoke of so casually. No one on Broadway made a tenth of that. She got the feeling that once she had the money from Dent's pocket, it was possible that he might not even notice it was gone.

"After lunch," said Grayson, "we're going to go down to the ocean."

"Should I put on my bathing costume?" asked Katherine.

"A bit more formal I should think," said Grayson. Dent smiled, and Katherine knew another surprise awaited her.

That afternoon, standing on the end of the painted pier, Katherine thought she was watching a ship easing into the harbor, but the gray metallic protuberance scratched a nagging memory. Last year the papers had carried such pictures for weeks. It was a German U-boat, merrily making its way up Newport Harbor, past the moored yachts, the pleasure boats sitting in silence against the piers. It was just a year since a similar craft had sunk the *Lusitania* and strewn more than a thousand corpses across the spring seas. One hundred and twenty-five of the dead had been American.

"It's a U-boat," said Katherine aloud.

"The captain's name is Hans Rose," explained Dent.

"What's he doing here?"

"Neutral port," said Dent calmly. "Perfectly legal."

"You didn't say that Arch sold planes to the Germans," said Katherine.

"He doesn't," said Dent calmly. "Not planes, anyway."

Katherine was most uncomfortable. She didn't read much about the war, but most of the newspapers she did read came down on the side of the Allies. Henry knew more. He said that England and Germany used to be friends, that German princes had become English kings, and that America itself was populated by great swaths from both nations. He said eight million Americans spoke German as a first language. But the sinking of the *Lusitania* had challenged Katherine's beliefs. She had been a vague acquaintance of Charlie Gruud, a friend of Henry's, drowned and buried in a closed casket. Did the sunken ship not raise a clamor? Hadn't it pushed them to the edge of war? What did Grayson and Dent understand that she failed to comprehend?

To all who watched, the sleek lethal fish was a potent symbol that proclaimed, Remember your wives, your husbands and your children, remember how they all bobbed in troughs and peaks, face-down. The *Lusitania* was sunk off the coast of Ireland, but look now, we can cross the Atlantic. Should you join a war, your vulnerability begins at the end of your beaches. Yet the arrival of Kapitänleutnant Rose on shore allayed Katherine's suspicions. A formal, punctilious man with a stiff mustache and narrow beard, a gentleman. He bowed with such great formality that the gleaming silver buttons of his jacket disappeared during his obeisance and flashed back upward into the sun. He wore a high stiff collar that would have corrected the deportment of the most sluggish of men. Very polite, inquiring after both Mrs. Grayson and Mrs. Dent. Katherine didn't even wince at being mistaken for Dent's wife, just smiled and asked him to called her Katherine. Dent winked at her when the German turned away.

The men spent the afternoon in talks while Katherine waited back at the house, where a dinner of welcome was being prepared. It was only going to be a small group, Dent had promised, with not one familiar face from their previous weekend, mostly just couples up from Baltimore or New York, Americans of German extraction. By the time the kapitänleutnant was escorted up to the house in the early evening, he had instructed his crew to swab and polish and then begin to show the submarine to any interested onlookers. Already, a line had begun to form along the pier.

Indoors, Rose began to ease his starched exterior, as if he had become so used to tight walls that he had not known how to communicate under open skies. He stared out of the window, down across the ocean, and complimented Grayson on the beauty of the views. Accepting the slim champagne flute, Rose raised a toast to friendship. The small gathering of men and women clinked their glasses.

"It is odd, no," said the kapitänleutnant as they stood in a circle, "that so many of us men should have German names?"

"Really?" said Dent. "I mean, I knew about Rudolph, but I didn't know Arch was German."

"Nor did I," smiled Grayson.

"Yes, yes," said Rose. "Archibald means 'very bold.' Rudolph is 'famous wolf.'"

The company tittered.

"I rather like that," said Dent.

"And Hans?" asked Katherine.

"It is actually a name we stole either from the Danes or the Jews," explained Rose. "I am 'the grace of God.' It was not very modest of my mother." Dent laughed enthusiastically. "And you, madam?" asked Rose, leaning toward Katherine.

Katherine understood that none of the others knew she had been introduced as Dent's wife. For all they knew, her husband was absent on business. "What was your maiden name?" persisted Rose.

"Schmidt," lied Katherine.

"Now there is an honest name. Our countries are tied in so many ways. Do you know where your family was from?" he asked.

"I'm afraid I don't," said Katherine. "We didn't really have much of a family tree. It was more of a shrub."

Rose nodded politely. "But it is sad, no, to lose the thread of one's family?"

"Common over here," said Grayson. "I'm afraid our ancestry had to be forgotten to ease the path of business."

To Katherine's surprise, it was the German, two glasses of champagne into dinner, who brought up the painful subject of the *Lusitania*. She presumed it would be a conversation saved for the men, but obviously Rose's was a mission of propaganda, and he probably thought of wives as quicker spreaders of information than husbands. "Yes," said Rose. "There have been regrettable moments."

"Nobody's pointing fingers," said Grayson diplomatically.

"My government's implications were clear: the zone of war has always included the waters adjacent to the British Isles, where the

Lusitania was sunk. However, I emphasize my sorrow for the loss of so much life. Am I allowed to speak as a civilian?"

"Of course," said Dent.

"Kapitänleutnant Schwieger did not behave well. I believe the sinking of the ship was entirely unnecessary. Had it been my own decision, she would not have been fired on."

"Don't take it so hard," said Grayson. "These are times of war."

"It is a miserable condition," said Rose. "But I would also ask you to consider a secondary conclusion. We must ask ourselves why this ship was not accompanied by British destroyers. We must ask ourselves why she was allowed to maintain her heading when the British knew well the position of our own boats."

"Do you really believe that?" asked Dent.

"Mr. Dent," said the kapitänleutnant, "the sinking of the *Lusitania* was not my government's policy. It was the decision of one man. But who is more cynical, the wolf who obeys his nature or the shepherd who abandons his flock?"

Katherine nodded in silence.

"Do you know what the Sanskrit word for 'war' means, when we translate it literally?" asked Rose. "'The desire for more cows.'"

After dinner, Dent and Grayson accompanied the kapitänleutnant as he paid his respects to the commander of the Narragansett Bay Naval Station. Arch ordered one of his cars to pick up the women and the company reconvened at the harbor, where they were invited to explore the confines of the U-53. With its slim body, sharp prow, and triangular conning tower, the U-boat resembled a large gray shark, hooked and drawn to the side of the pier. The party disappeared down the tower, Katherine's white dress brushing the metal sides. There was barely enough room to stand, and such echoing narrowness. Katherine was not prone to claustrophobia, but the falsity of the glaring electric lights only contributed to the sense that she had moved away from not only land, but air. How could thirty-six men share such accommodation? She bet the area of the U-boat was no bigger than her Blue Room in Grayson's cottage.

The kapitänleutnant turned to Katherine and another of the more adventurous women who had climbed down the hatch.

"You are among only a dozen women ever to have been aboard my vessel," said Rose. "And two of them were princesses."

Katherine gave a small bow of appreciation.

"What a machine," said Grayson, standing by the periscope. "What can she do?"

"Do?" asked Rose.

"How fast?" explained Dent.

"Over seventeen knots," said Rose. "A range of nine thousand miles. Halfway around the world."

"How many torpedoes?" asked Dent.

"Six," answered the kapitänleutnant. "Perhaps you would like to join us on exercises tomorrow?"

God no, thought Katherine. I wouldn't like to go a foot under the water in this grim canister.

"Not a good idea I think," said Grayson, to Katherine's relief. "We'll observe them instead. We'll have a day out on the ocean. Mrs. Dent, would that entertain you?" he inquired playfully.

"I should love it," said Katherine.

Chapter Eight

IT WAS AN odd day in Newport, full of contradictory winds and the tease of tepid sunshine. Katherine dressed for the cold, in a heavy tweed borrowed from Caroline Grayson's collection of winter coats. Their observation of U-boat maneuvers would take place from no less a vantage point than the USS *Birmingham*, a freshly painted white cruiser with golden prow, billowing a black smoke into the sky from its four thick funnels. Katherine felt quite ill dressed once aboard, standing amid a sartorial crew in their startling white uniforms, crisp peaked caps, and creased blue cuffs. The captain stood stiff, not amused at their presence on board his ship, especially the women, but apparently under orders to accept his guests.

They watched from afar as the U-boat came to life, spluttering out of the harbor into the open sea. Katherine could think of only one word to describe the ensuing maneuvers: dull. Once it dipped under the water there was nothing to see. Only the actual acts of submergence and surfacing were of any interest. Katherine began to think of Henry, probably sitting looking out at the sea, not a mile or two away. For three hours, she was lost in a web of daydreams, until suddenly confusion overtook the *Birmingham*. Only Grayson seemed utterly composed. Katherine didn't dare approach the captain. Instead, she asked Dent what was going on.

"Exercises," said Dent.

The *Birmingham* was lowering all her lifeboats. The sailors were dipping their oars in the water and aiming where? Over to the east.

Katherine hadn't seen it. A large, ungainly merchantman flying a Dutch flag. A half mile from them, the U-boat sat calmly in the water, waiting. Katherine watched in fascination as the lifeboats approached the ship, took two loads of crew, and began to head back to the *Birmingham*. Before they had even reached the ship, Katherine saw a white fissure streak through the water in the direction of the merchant ship.

The boat absorbed the hit and threw up a wonderful spout of water. Katherine traced the spout's trajectory, listened for the slap as the spray met the ocean again. She watched the ship list, roll, then disappear, the hull raised to the sky, the prow aiming, then plunging for the depths. For the first time in her life she was awed by what she was seeing. For a moment it seemed as if the surface of the ocean would follow the ship down. It rushed after it, creating a wicked whirl. To be caught, thought Katherine, to have dived and swum away, to be drawn back down. You hold your breath, you are still dragged downward, to feel the pressure squeezing your chest, your eyes are bulging as you follow the ship, a helpless escort until the last air leaves you in a burst of bubbles. For a moment you still see, but the ocean is dark down there, it is all black now. She didn't know exactly why, but she started to cry. Do we not do something?, she thought. Do we just watch ships sink? What would Ben think of all this? Neutrality. What an insipid word, what an extraordinary world.

The few times that she had discussed the war with Henry, he'd explained that both England and Germany had a facade, a gentlemanly code, which helped to swathe ambition under tradition, but this polite spectacle of destruction seemed perverse. She wondered if the trenches were like this. Official announcements of attacks that passed between the warring sides. Evacuation of targeted trenches. Perhaps they left packets of tea for one another, then returned to their own billets the next day to receive complimentary bottles of pilsner. No wonder they were in a stalemate. But then, how to explain a man with the scars, the nightmares, the variable moods of Ben Newcombe?

><

Over the course of the afternoon Katherine watched as the U-boat issued polite warnings of its intentions, as the American cruiser sent out her lifeboats, as they returned brimming with deckhands and passengers. The U-boat torpedoed the emptied vessels to the bottom of the sea. The most spectacular moment came with the sinking of the British liner *Stephano* in the early evening. The sun had already set, the Atlantic provided a background of perfect blackness, and Katherine almost managed to convince herself that she was seated in a comfortable movie house. Strings of electric lights ran along the great shadowy funnels of the passenger ship. They merely jiggled at the torpedo's impact. The lights tilted and then disappeared one by one until darkness returned again. She imagined that she could hear the fragile bulbs pop. It wasn't until the *Stephano*'s weeping children arrived aboard the *Birmingham* that Katherine was reminded that it was all real, but she did not cry again.

"Did you know?" asked Katherine that evening before dinner awaiting the other guests in the summer room.

"Of course," said Dent. "Arch wanted to see if the kapitänleutnant was a man of his word."

"Sinking ships?"

"Avoiding casualties," said Dent, checking the shine of his shoes as he took a seat on the corner of an armchair. "What you saw today was the perfect demonstration of the business of war. It was an economic act, not a bloody one. Who benefits? Germany gets to prevent trade, America replaces it. England suffers only in the wallet. As far as acts of war go, I can't think of a more gentlemanly conclusion."

"I don't get it," said Katherine. "What if these U-boats are so good nobody's willing to risk the run? I mean, they could sink everything that moves."

Dent smiled at her. "Aside from the owners, namely those who can afford the loss, when the crew are given the option of abandoning they're really not going to die protecting a vessel they know is about to be sunk. Why should it be any different from today?"

"So how does Arch get his planes to Europe?"

"It would be pretty tricky for a man without connections." Dent took a sip of his drink. "Neutral flags mean nothing anymore. England's been using them since the outbreak of war. But certain neutral flags will be observed by Germany. It's just a case of knowing which."

"But . . ."

"That's an awful lot of questions before dinner," said Dent, smiling kindly.

Katherine was horrified by her line of questioning, but it came from a genuine surprise and the wonder of what Henry might do with all the information. Her money might be at stake. "I've just never seen anything like it before."

"I should hope not," said Dent, smiling, as he stood to join Arch's guests.

Chapter Nine

SHE HAD TO admit that the true confusion of her weekend was brought about not by the sight of a U-boat, but by her visit in the morning to Henry while Dent and Arch talked business. Her decision to leave him had nothing to do with the usual matters of faith, but rather a slow realization that she wanted a life different from the one he craved. In the hour they were together she clung to him, and tried to imagine what it would be like to be seventeen again. Who else, she thought, would she ever trust with the story of her life? There would be much that she would miss.

Who, for instance, would have done what Henry did last year, driving her all the way home for the first time since she had left? It had been a five-hour marathon of poor roads, heavy dust, and the *tic tic* of brittle bugs dying on the windscreen. She had sat in the rear and worn her finest, an old-fashioned gown with protruding peach-colored bustle. For all the world, that afternoon she looked like a society lady mysteriously deposited on the outskirts of Litchfield, Illinois. She knew her own father wouldn't recognize her all prettied up like a Broadway star.

There on the corner of White Street was a new store, Marchesi and Sons. It had been empty except for a sturdy woman with a mole on the end of her nose who sat leafing through a newspaper behind the counter.

"I'm sorry to disturb you," Katherine had said, walking in softly, not so much a customer with money as an apparition of wealth. "My father's maid used to have a house up the road here when I was a little girl. This store wasn't here, was it?"

"No, miss," said the woman looking up from her paper and sitting up straight once she saw that she was dealing with a lady.

"I had a best friend," Katherine had said. "The only child of a man called Samuel Howells."

"Mr. Howells?" the woman had answered, breaking into a smile, either glad to have the connection, or happy to be able to offer information to so strange a sight. "Oh he's still here. Such a good man. So nice."

"And his daughter?"

"She lives in the East," the woman had continued, leaning forward.

"Does he ever mention her?" Katherine had asked, unable to disguise her interest.

"She writes him every week," the woman had said with pride. "She went to live with her aunt in Boston." She tapped the side of her nose. "Truth be told, Mr. Howells tells me, he used to be fond of a bottle. Best thing he could have done for the girl. A man isn't the same with a bottle in his hand."

"What a shame she's not here," Katherine had said, then thanked her kindly and retreated from the shop. She got back into the rear of the automobile and made Henry drive her slowly down the street, toward her house. It looked identical, only smaller and prettier, with fresh paint and windowboxes filled with pink blooms. The same elm tree towered in the front yard and there, parked beneath it, a gleaming black Ford. Henry put their car into neutral and let it murmur in front of the house for a moment.

"You want to go in?" Henry had asked.

"God, no," she'd replied.

Katherine stared out the window and almost expected to see herself come through the front door to approach their car. There was motion from within the kitchen, a sash brushed to the side of the window. A moment later, the door creaked open and there, in the doorway, stood a strange woman in an apron, a potato peeler in her hand, squinting against the sun to look at their car.

"Let's go," Katherine had said, and Henry pulled the car away from the woman, who, hands on her hips, watched as they retreated up White Street. Katherine had never been so shocked. Her father may have changed, may have given up drink and kept to his church, but the new car was there as proof to consistency of character. Katherine was sure his frugality persevered, meaning he would never have hired a woman to keep house. The apron-clad shadow could only be a second wife. Even if it was only the two of them within, Katherine had immediately recognized it as a new family. Perhaps that was when her belief that life could change had begun. Her father had prospered without her. Henry would survive the loss of her. She could build a new life apart.

She smiled for her husband, played him as she did Dent, as she did Ben. He'd brought her a dress and she'd made love to him with false enthusiasm. Conversation, disguised as business, was an expression of jealousy. Afterward, she'd washed thoroughly, scrubbing herself free of her husband's smell. More than anything she wanted to be out of his stuffy little room, finally persuading him that Dent and Grayson were in such deep conversation they could risk a drink in a humble bar after a quick visit to the barbershop. With only an hour left, Henry was more intent on business, listening to every little thing she had to report. When she'd finished speaking, Henry had thought for a moment and said, "There won't be any doubt on what they're going to try. It'll have to be something around and about the war. You've just got to push Dent along. Make him think he's not doing anything himself. Leaning too hard on his wife's money, or on Arch. Hit him low like that."

Katherine shifted in her seat. "But how much should I tell Ben about all of this?"

"The guy's a member of the walking wounded. Don't you think the war's in his mind every hour of the day? You say France, he thinks war, you say airplane, he thinks war, you say hello, he thinks war. Besides, he doesn't make the decisions. It's up to that son of a bitch McAteer."

"So I can tell Ben this week?"

"As much as you want," said Henry. "Maybe they'll take Dent for even more than we'd hoped."

"So how do I put them together?" asked Katherine.

"Take them both to the races," said Henry.

"Are you kidding?"

Henry shook his head. "You invite them both. Meet Dent there. Take Ben with you. Introduce Ben as just a friend. He'll play along for you. It's in his nature. Maybe Dent'll remember him from the restaurant. Races are good. He can see Dent make some bets, get a smell of the wallet."

"How do you know Dent will want to go to the races?"

"Christ Katherine," said Henry. "The man owns a dozen horses. If he likes you he'll do it. He'll want to show off."

"And if he doesn't go along with it?"

"Then you're not doing your job right." She could tell he didn't want to say it, nor ask the question that followed, but she shouldn't have doubted him aloud. "Have you fucked Dent yet?"

Katherine shook her head.

"Well maybe now's the time."

She nodded, crumpled a little. That's why, she told herself, you have to move on. "Take the train down with me," she said, testing him again.

"You're riding with Dent."

"I'll tell him I can't."

Henry let go of her hand and reached up to touch her face. "I love you," he said. "But go ride with Dent."

Back in New York, Dent dropped her straight off at the theater and arranged to meet her for lunch the following day. Katherine did not wait until the appointed time of two o'clock, but rode the elevator up to his suite in the Astor just short of midday. She rapped at his door.

"Yes," Dent shouted from inside.

"Three guesses," said the familiar, mocking voice of Katherine Howells. "And the first two don't count."

Dent's suite at the Astor off Broadway looked like the inside of a palace car, lustrous mahogany, Persian carpets, and brass fixtures, with sky-blue curtains monogrammed with the hotel's initial. It was the sort of suite where most people perched awkwardly on the edge of velvet sofas, dreading the spilled drink, the stray crumb, the nervous silence. Katherine presumed that his women were generally awed by it.

"Why don't you send your man out for a long walk?" said Katherine.

Dent's smile deepened. "I take it we'll be lunching here?"

Katherine guessed he was the sort of man who never kissed a girl for the first time without the benefits of alcohol. She could tell he felt naked before she even disrobed him. Katherine looked beautiful in navy chiffon. He looked a little puzzled, for they both knew it had been her decision, that she had thought on him, considered him while resisting him, and was now relenting. The timing had been her choice, as had the location. What could a man do but lean in and kiss her? She closed her eyes and this time she didn't want to think of Henry, or any man, but Dent was on top of her and she had to choose. She thought of Ben.

Perhaps it was the absence of drink, for Dent didn't last long. Afterward, he brought them both robes from the bathroom and awkwardly peeled off his socks. He wouldn't let her go, talked inanities until he felt himself capable again. Katherine felt in absolute control. His face was just an inch from hers and neither made an effort to kiss. She stared into his eyes when he was inside her, reached down and ran her hands over his buttocks. All the time smiling, letting him know what small movements brought her pleasure, all with her eyes. He was looking, he was paying attention. She could tell it fascinated him, aroused him further, and then it was over, but they didn't move for a moment, the sharing continued, and when he pulled away, she pretended to let him go with reluctance.

She explored his apartment as they dressed. There were switches everywhere for room service, for electric lights and fans. Dent explained every little thing as they walked from room to room. Opposite the Victrola in his drawing room was his desk, covered in papers. Katherine wandered casually over to it, but they mostly seemed to be handwritten letters. Beside it was a typewriter, and next to it, the cylinder, tube, and mouthpiece of a brand-new Dictaphone.

"You type?" she asked.

"God, no," said Dent. "Have a young man who comes here once a week when I'm in town."

Katherine picked up the Dictaphone's mouthpiece, flipped the switch, and spoke into it. "His name is Rudolph Dent, a very handsome gentleman of Chicago. America's second city."

Dent laughed and took the mouthpiece from her hands. "Her name is Katherine Howells," he dictated. "Broadway's best bet for the future." Katherine giggled when he slid the cylinder and played the recording back for them. "Shall we go now?" he asked.

Love was not to be believed in. It was hard enough to keep any man, anywhere, certainly in this city. Dent's eyes would turn elsewhere. And Ben, who was to know how he thought? A woman could never *rely* on a man like that. Outside, the wind had started to blow, and the taxi swayed as it passed through the streets. A small patter began to play on the green canopies of doorman buildings about them.

Chapter Ten

WHEN THE SUN finally returned to the streets that Wednesday morning, the people of New York found that their city had been dusted with thin red sand, carried by distant winds. The *Herald* said the night's gusts had sped faster than a roadster, and all about lay shattered flagpoles, cornices, and slate as proof. Refuse containers and mailboxes had been overturned, spilling their contents across the street. The temperature plummeted twenty degrees in less than one hour, lending the courtship of Rudolph Dent and Katherine Howells an ethereal coating.

They'd been walking back from the theater when the storm had hit, taking Dent's hat straight from his head in one mighty gust and hurtling it so fast down the street that there was no point in chasing. Instead, they leaned into the wind, pressing against each other, and held their hands up to their eyes to protect them from the biting sand. Any other woman would have been content to watch the storm from her window, but not Katherine Howells. To Dent's surprise, as soon as they entered his suite, she had handed him one of his umbrellas, took another, and back into the wind they went.

Dent's umbrellas, with their nickel silver springs, tulip wood handles, and mother-of-pearl buttons were sacrificed to the whims of an actress. Katherine lowered her umbrella against the wind and heard the sound of the sand as it strafed the black silk canopy. She imagined herself in France, tearing across a battlefield with Ben, with the *rat-a-tat* of machine guns pummeling their defenses.

><

Then a particular gust snapped the umbrellas' ribs and whipped the handles from their grasps and they raced back again to the suite, laughing at themselves through gritty mouthfuls of sand. She had made love to him standing up, her back to him, pressed against the cold radiator in the drawing room. Afterward, Dent had slumped, naked against the floor, trousers cuffed to ankles.

"Was your mother really called Schmidt?" asked Dent in the darkness of their bed that night.

"Of course not," said Katherine. "I just thought your Kraut would like it."

"That's what Arch said. That you'd made it up."

Katherine tapped the side of her head. "Pretty quick sometimes."

He turned on the electric light and lit a cigarette.

Katherine sat up, pulling a sheet from the bed to cover herself. "Have you and Arch always made your money together?"

"No," said Dent, putting a struck match to the tip of a half-smoked cigar.

"But now you just do with your money what Grayson does with his?"

Dent nodded. "You can't go wrong. Not yet, anyway."

Katherine nodded in an approximation of slow understanding.

"Aren't there investments on Broadway?" she asked. "You know, like investing in plays?"

"That's mainly for Jews like Ziegfeld," said Dent. "I'm not going to start a production for you, if that's what you're hoping." He wagged his finger, through his exhalations of smoke, trying to cover his comment in humor.

"I'm doing just fine on my own," said Katherine calmly.

"There are just better places to invest," said Dent.

"Like what?"

"The Jews aren't always right," said Dent. "On the other side of the ocean there's a war taking place. Every country at war has to push their production to a maximum." He exhaled a thick ring of smoke. "So let's say there are two countries pretty evenly balanced and both are pushing their hardest. No one's going to win. What one can do, the other can do. So what happens next? They look abroad, they start to buy abroad. And a country the size of America, a neutral country, is in position to sell to both sides. So next they try and outspend each other, and the only person to profit is the neutral supplier. As long as they continue to spend the same sort of amount, buy the same sort of things, then they'll continue to cancel each other out."

He tapped his ash in an empty glass on the night table. "You were born in the right country my dear. Trust me, another year or two of this in Europe, and all the ladies are going to have left are memories of dignity. Their men, if any are still alive, will be coming over here. The women will be whoring themselves for an evening's meal."

"Still doesn't sound like much of an investment," she said.

"You're objecting to the war?"

"No, not the war," said Katherine. "But isn't it a bit like being thrown crumbs? You know, from Grayson's table."

"You may call them crumbs," said Dent, smiling. "They're crumbs that can buy motorcars and houses."

"But it's still not your own idea," insisted Katherine, pushing him a little too far, knowing it would take work to bring him back again. "I just think that what makes this country great is when everyone does some thinking of their own, makes it their own way, on their own terms."

"How about you?" asked Dent, poking the stubby cigar in her direction. "You're an actress. You need a writer, a director, a producer, a theater to make your living. You have to depend on others."

"Sure," said Katherine. "I didn't mean people like me. I'm just entertainment."

That made Dent smile.

"Very good entertainment," he corrected her.

She giggled. "But you've got it all. You can do something by yourself. Without any help from a man like Grayson."

"Of course I could," said Dent. "And I intend to. Only a foolish man sits on his money."

※

Katherine slept well. Who needed the exoticism of the East when a sandstorm brought a desert to Manhattan? She peered out the window the following morning and enjoyed the semblance of change. You couldn't head east by ship, for Katherine knew what might happen. You would travel first-class for a few hours, but then, perhaps, you'd be rowed to the deck of an impotent American warship and carried back to your port of departure, your boat sunk beneath the ocean.

And yet, last night, Dent found a new way in which to appeal to Katherine, a small epiphany. Grayson and Dent were theatrical. Not so far removed from herself. Their stage was both society and business and they judged you not by what you were, but what you pretended to be and how you played their games. Dent kept a straight face, but Katherine knew that she had been studied throughout her meeting with the kapitänleutnant in Newport and immediately after her first ride through the skies. And possibly the same would be required of her again this weekend. She felt that she was earning her money.

Chapter Eleven

WITHOUT CAROLINE GRAYSON, that weekend the house seemed empty of the frothy distractions that had clouded Katherine's visions on previous occasions. Grayson hadn't opened up one entire wing. Dent had explained on the drive up that it was, essentially, a weekend of business. The men would be potential investors in Arch's airplane company that Dent had already invested in, Dent explained. So she should be especially gracious to them.

"Whatever you say," said Katherine. Only one other man felt comfortable bringing a woman along. Katherine didn't mind. She knew she fared better in the company of attentive men. She bet herself she could get half the guests asking her for Broadway tickets by Sunday morning. "Why does Arch need more investors? Hasn't he got enough money?"

Dent smiled. "What Arch has is a considerable ability to spend. What he has is considerable debt. Many assets, but many debts. So, more investors."

"They do that on Broadway too," said Katherine. "But the late-comers don't get the same returns, do they? I mean, you've got to pay more if you arrive after the appetizers."

Dent smiled at her. "That's quite right." He sped past a pair of old Fords, probably not doing more than twenty miles an hour. "Do you have a fear of failing?" he asked her.

"I suppose," said Katherine, and forced smoke down through her nose.

"Arch doesn't," said Dent. "He's happy to fall flat on his face. He doesn't give a damn about money."

"Is that why it seems to stick to him?"

"I suppose." Dent took his cigarette and flicked it out the window. "There was a time when what we call parsimony was responsible for the accumulation of capital. Those days are over. In this country all we've got now is faith. Better known as the bank loan."

Katherine had been teasing him the whole drive up. She could tell he liked it. Half the time his hand rested on her bare knee, giving it the odd, gentle squeeze.

"Do you have a lot of girlfriends?" she inquired, just before they got to Newport, cocking her head to question him. He had laughed and turned his eyes away from the road to look at her.

"I have a wife."

"And girlfriends?"

"Yes," said Dent. "And girlfriends. Come on, you're not going to tell me you don't have a few admirers, a pretty girl like you?"

"Sure I do."

"How many?"

"Just one."

"Is he special?"

"Yes," said Katherine. "And no. I mean, how special can he be if I'm here with you?"

"What's his name?" asked Dent.

"Ben Newcombe," said Katherine.

"Good name," said Dent.

"He's English."

As Henry had predicted, it caught Dent's interest. "Must be even older than me."

"Why?"

"The war. They send the young to fight it."

"Not Ben."

"He's young?" asked Dent.

"My age," said Katherine.

"A baby."

"But he got wounded. So now he's here."

"A veteran," said Dent. "Fascinating. What does he do?"

"I think he still works for the army," said Katherine. "He won't really tell me."

"Terribly secretive," said Dent, smiling. She predicted the thought process, a short pang of guilty panic that his counterpart had bled for his country while he sent munitions over to Europe. "Perhaps he's a spy."

"Spying on who? Me?"

"Broadway can be terribly subversive," said Dent, winking and promptly getting off the subject. Nothing more was said about her boyfriend all weekend, but Katherine knew the thought of Ben stayed with Dent.

Katherine could not imagine where Grayson had rooted out these investors. In person, they were disappointing. In size, in shape, in bearing, they were a combination of too short, too stout, too glib for Katherine's liking. All that could recommend them as a collective was their clothes. Katherine cast her eyes over their suits and made several inquiries as to their tailors. When this conversation ran dry, she inquired after their cooks. Anytime that business was brought up, she kept quiet, knowing that the only chance of learning lay in silent feminine acquiescence.

Katherine could see now how Grayson used Dent. If Grayson had the wealth of a nation, then Dent was a favored ambassador, not appointed for knowledge of politicking or business affiliations, but from social standing. He was there for his looks, for his outward charm, his education. He could talk smartly to the wives of great men, entertain and flirt, and if dinner conversation was turned his way, knew enough to pass it onward to greater minds without halting the flow. Nothing but a shill.

As Henry had often explained, Dent was the perfect mark. Reasonably intelligent without being an original thinker, a man who had survived off the skills and money of others, who would be eager to accept a similar deal on his own terms. Usually, Henry would

have avoided conning a man in the game he played, but the joy of
Dent was that he did not play the game of arms directly. He had
none of Grayson's intricate knowledge. Even better, Dent would
presume he *did* have the knowledge. Katherine smiled to herself.
She didn't see how either Dent or Grayson was any better, any more
substantial than Henry himself. It was comic to her that Ben, a
bunco man, a deserter, a thief, was the most innocent of the lot.

In the morning, the investors stood before Grayson's one true
extravagance, saved for unveiling at special occasions. He kept his
collection of carriages in a large barn adjacent to the unused stables. Walking the investors among the gigs and dogcarts, mail
coaches, road coaches, upholstered opera buses, buggies, and a pair
of spider phaetons, Katherine ran her gloved hands over the
smooth polished surfaces. For any man older than twenty-five or
thirty, such a sight was immediately reminiscent of childhood. Such
a nostalgic assemblage immediately suggested to the investors that
they were all from the same stock, with the same pasts, the same
memories. Only Katherine knew she was different.

The twelve men and two women piled into Grayson's opera bus
and accompanied their host to his airfield, where he introduced
them to his favored mechanic and personal *pilot de chasse*, Monsieur
Gaston Glasson. The Frenchman was deferential, peeling off a
glove to shake hands with each of the men and bowing to the two
women. Dressed in his flying leathers, goggles pushed high on his
forehead, Glasson stood apart. Katherine could see it now. Glasson
was the star of today's theatrics. He was to play the part of the
product these men should invest in. There goes the chug of the
engine, the props spluttering, then spinning into an abusive roar,
along and then upward, followed intently by all eyes.

Glasson was putting on a show of great skill, banking the plane,
rolling her, sending her into elaborate dives and groaning over
their heads. He would rise so that the plane would quickly be lost

against the sun, returning five minutes later from the center of the glare. The investors were enjoying themselves. Grayson looked calm, pleased by the attention. Perhaps he wished he too were up there, flying, thought Katherine. Glasson returned and breezed over their heads, waving at them as he rolled. And then, once more, he disappeared into the sun.

They sat on the folding chairs that Grayson's men had strapped to the back of the carriage and waited. They expected to see Glasson soon. They listened for the distant whine of the engine. They waited some more. After fifteen minutes, Katherine noticed that the investors were no longer looking at the skies, but at Grayson. Five minutes later, they were all disturbed by the sharp ring of the telephone from the makeshift air tower. Grayson held up his hand to his chauffeur.

"I'll get it."

He returned a minute later with a bashful smile on his face.

"Terribly embarrassing for Monsieur Glasson," said Grayson apologetically. "Bit of engine trouble. Thinks he hit a bird. He's over at a landing strip in Narragansett. He'll come over for a drink after dinner and answer any questions you might have."

There were assurances of general relief. Grayson pulled out two thermoses of chilled lemonade, well spiked with vodka, and they talked while standing in a circle, joking with one another as to who would be the first up the following day. No one looked too enthusiastic.

"Our friend, Miss Howells, has already been up," said Grayson.

All eyes turned to Katherine. "You're kidding," said one investor. "What was it like?"

"Absolutely breathtaking," she said, and saw Dent and Grayson smile as one at the collective laughter of their investors.

A half hour later, the group piled back into the coach, and Grayson trotted his team back toward the barn. He waved goodbye, then walked over to his Daimler. Dent opened the door on the passenger side and sat himself down. Katherine climbed into the back-seat.

"Why don't you go back to the house with the others?" suggested Grayson.

"He's crashed, hasn't he?" asked Katherine, closing the door.

"Why don't you go back to the house?" repeated Grayson.

"I just vouched for your planes, didn't I?" she said.

Grayson didn't answer, but threw the car into gear and pulled away from the barn.

The plane had gone down in a field of tall corn not far from the ocean, close to a farmhouse, a ten-minute drive from Grayson's airstrip. The young family were standing huddled, as if it were cold outside and not a day of blue glory. Another set of rutted tire tracks that had cut their way across the field. Grayson tipped his hat and talked briefly to the father.

"Ambulance left a quarter of an hour ago," he explained to them as the three broke away to walk toward the wreck.

It was easy to follow the course of the crash. The plane had cut the cornstalks, bounced back into the air, then thrown up a large divot of earth as it came to a sharp halt. One wing was crushed. Katherine peered over into the cockpit and wished she hadn't. The pale leather seat was stained with blood.

"I don't suppose he's all right?" asked Katherine.

Grayson pinched the bridge of his nose. "Neck broken. About the same as the plane. Not a word of this tonight."

Chapter Twelve

GLASSON'S DEATH COULD not shake either Grayson's or Dent's mask of good cheer. "Mourn in silence" was how Grayson had put it. Katherine looked at him peculiarly, impressed with either the shallowness or the depth of the man. It was impossible to tell which. Never had Katherine been more sure of her interpretation of business as a performance, the same as her marriage, her seductions, her friendships. What, exactly, fell outside the bracket? When, for example, could either Grayson or Dent afford to be himself? Katherine supposed it didn't matter.

Katherine spent a great deal of the weekend alone, and all the meals besieged by attention. Mr. Hayden had a lovely broad smile and a pair of hands that ached to stray south from her waist. Mr. Shackleford had already referred to his farm up the Hudson on several occasions in front of Dent, and made it plain that Katherine would be welcome there any weekend the family was absent. Katherine had expected nothing less, acting being among the world's oldest professions.

"Now when is that pilot of yours arriving?" asked Hayden.

Grayson looked up, waiting for attention. Despite his modest size, Katherine saw that he had a way of staring down a table so that even the candles seemed to pause in their flickering.

"I have been guilty of harboring a small lie," he said. "Monsieur Glasson will not be joining us this evening. He landed rather heavily."

"Not too heavily I hope," offered Shackleford, displaying emotion as a thrust to impress Katherine.

"No," said Grayson. "He's being kept in the hospital for the evening. They suspect he might have fractured his ankle."

There was a slight silence as the repercussions rippled about the table. No pilot, no morning flight. But, no morning flight, no heavy landing. How safe was such a machine? Katherine was also glad. She had felt a little sick that morning. Had, in fact, retched at the idea of being hurtled through the skies again.

"I'm afraid our *pilote de chasse* was guilty today," said Grayson. "Too eager to show off to you. Did things to that plane it didn't know it could do. Rest assured that not even pilots over France would attempt these things. He's paying tonight for his over-enthusiasm."

Grayson had organized a morning sailboat ride for his investors, with brunch served on the deck of a blue-hulled racing ketch. Katherine begged off, saying that she wasn't sure of her sea legs, thinking she would take the opportunity to see Henry. She did not know if she would be invited back to Newport again before Henry moved himself back to New York, and it might be the last time they could see each other until all was done. She thought Henry should know about the crashed planes. What if it was a serious defect that had caused the crash? What if it affected their investment? What if it made Dent more cautious with his dollars? Should she try to explain any of this to Ben? Or simply leave it to the people behind the Englishman?

Besides, there was a situation that she didn't know whether to call good or bad news, wasn't even sure if she should admit to herself. She believed she was pregnant. There was no way she would show for another couple of months, so she had a choice of either somehow using the information, or withholding it from Ben and Dent. Either way, she decided to ask for Henry's advice, although she was worried that his excitement would be so great, it would distort his thoughts.

She dressed herself for the summer in a flowing, light violet dress, a present from Dent for that very weekend. With her handbag in the crook of her elbow she turned toward the door to leave, only to find Dent himself standing there, watching her.

"Where are you going?" he asked.

She heard the jealous incline of his voice and smiled sweetly in return. Perhaps she had mentioned Ben's existence a day too soon. She twisted the strap of her handbag in her hands. "I wasn't going to sneak off."

"Yes you were," said Dent.

Katherine laughed. "I was going to go indulge."

"In what?"

"Newport fashions. Ladies' shopping."

"Can I walk you?" he asked.

"You can," said Katherine. "But I shall bore you terribly."

Dent shrugged. She walked to him and put her arm through his. "Why don't you walk me down to town, and if you get bored you can have a car come and pick you up?"

She borrowed a white parasol from the absent Mrs. Grayson, and they walked slowly down the gravel drive, through the gates, and along the open road down to the town, the wide blue sea calm before them. Their peace was interrupted by the odd, angry coughs of gasoline lawn mowers. The air was laden with the deep green spice of cut grass blown inland by a salty wind. Katherine had never been so irritated by the constraints of her profession.

"So where shall we go?"

Dent seemed so intent on spotting her Englishman that he did not even look twice when Henry stood before them on the promenade. Katherine flashed hot eyes at her husband; he read them at once and stepped off into the crowd. Soon Dent relented. She could tell he began to feel annoyed at himself, that he should even care enough to be jealous. He resolved things in his own manner, and bought Katherine a wonderful sun-bright hat, topped by the feathers of a Venezuelan parakeet. The touch of Dent's arm began to fill her with loathing and the smile on her face became wider and wider. Every now and then her hand brushed her stomach and she began to wonder what it might be inside her, boy or girl?

Chapter Thirteen

THE WEEK IN New York brought similar confusions with Ben. She told him it was the poor time of her month. In case he became insistent in bed, she ducked her head down beneath the sheets to please him, wanting to keep things away from her child. Her child. More than a hundred miles from Newport, without a chance to talk face-to-face, it was hard to think of Henry or any other man as a father. It seemed as if whatever was going on inside her was entirely her own creation, regardless of what had passed in her bed. The unborn was her responsibility alone.

On the few nights they had managed to spend together she noticed a remarkable increase in Ben's nightmares, a constant twisting. He would almost always wake himself up, half strangled in a sheet, shouting or swearing and then pretending he was fine.

"Are you all right?" she would say.

"Why?" As if it were normal to shout at the top of your lungs in your sleep, or sweat through the sheets without any semblance of fever.

Katherine wondered if she should warn Henry about him, but once dressed and outside, Ben seemed as sane as any New York resident. Katherine had also noticed his perpetual desire for noise. At first, she had taken offense. He never wanted to sit in some romantic restaurant and whisper compliments over candlelight, but slowly she understood that it was part of a permanent need to be in the middle of sound. He preferred busy diners and luncheonettes to any dignified restaurant of carpet and wood. It was exhausting just keeping up with him. He didn't like to sit for long unless it was in someplace you could barely hear him speak. It was as if his head were still at war, unwilling to make peace with itself. He might as well go back, she thought, for all the tranquillity he had found in the city. She was sure it was not a game, that despite being a bunco man, he was affected.

She had had to trust her news to the mail, sending news of her pregnancy up to Newport. His advice was simple. Do what you wish, although he had a course of action to recommend. Scrap the idea of the day at the races. Only Henry could always turn an unpredicted happening into an improvised improvement.

She followed Henry's instructions. First, he had told her to make sure she was close enough to Ben to be able to pass him on to Dent. "How?" she'd asked. There was nothing more convincing to a lover, said Henry, than a woman's past. Not her affairs, naturally, for, as Henry always said, women have no history and gentlemen no memory. He was talking about her family's past. Henry had organized everything. His friend Ruza, whom she had met once before, many years ago, was to play her father. She told Ben she was estranged from her parents. They were upset at her Broadway career. Could Ben please play at her fiancé and lend her a veneer of respectability? He looked overjoyed at the prospect. Henry had ordered her to take a train to Westchester, where she would be met by Ruza and a lady of his choice who would play her mother in a house rented for the weekend.

How Ben had struggled. Katherine had been unsure how wise the plan was, knowing his dislike for country quiet. Ben had been fine on the train, but then he had read something in his newspaper and his mood changed abruptly. Throughout the visit he had seemed preoccupied and edgy, talking far too much, uncomfortable out of the city in the gentleness of the countryside. Still, Katherine had been amused to see how much care Henry had taken. He had sent a photograph of her in Japanese costume to Ruza and her "mother," which they placed prominently in their front hall. But Ben liked the role a little too much, and when she took his hand in front of her faux parents, he squeezed it, kept it close, was reluctant to let her go. It was not a sexual gesture; more, thought Katherine, as if he had decided she was an amulet. Proximity to her guaranteed protection from whatever disturbed him during his nights.

As her husband instructed, she announced her pregnancy to both Dent and Ben in the same week. She almost wanted to laugh at their reactions. Since she had felt wonderful after returning from Westchester, she was forced to take a small dose of emetics two mornings in the same week to produce displays of morning sickness for them. On both occasions, she allowed her lovers to find her slumped over in the bathroom.

Ben had awoken to an odd sound, a cough and echo. He rolled over to wrap his arms around Katherine, but she was no longer in bed. He pinched his nose and sat up, swinging his feet to the floor. Crossing the carpet to the bathroom, he found Katherine sitting beside the toilet. She spat into the bowl and flushed it.

"What is it?" he said.

"What do you think?"

It took Ben a moment to understand. "What do you want to do about it?"

She had been weeping, using a little lemon juice to redden her eyes. "I didn't want it to happen," said Katherine.

"Is it mine?"

She shook her head. "I'm not sure."

"How unsure?"

"I don't know," she said.

"It could be Dent's," said Ben. "Do you want to keep it?"

She nodded her head, then shook it, still crying. "I don't know. Get me some water," she said.

"I'm sorry." Ben brought her a glass of water and bent down to kiss the top of her head. "Let me think about this. I'm sorry. I don't know. Whatever you decide." He had seemed simultaneously horrified and in awe of his own capability to create.

><

On the other hand, Dent had immediately rushed to solve her problem.

"What would you like to do with it?"

"It?" she said.

"Come on," he said. "Let's not try to be difficult. Let's try to be sensible. I presume that you don't want to keep it."

Katherine hadn't said a word.

"You want to have a baby without a husband?"

"Why not?"

"Well, I mean, where to begin? Your work. Your life. Your future."

"It may not even be your baby," Katherine said. "So what business is it of yours?"

Dent seemed relieved. "I know, I know," he said. He put his head in his hands for a moment. Katherine let him think in silence, wiping tears from her eyes.

"I suppose there's no reason it shouldn't have a father," Dent said.

"What do you mean?"

"Perhaps you'd give me the phone number or the address of your young man."

"Why would you want that?"

"Responsibility," Dent said. "Both of us have to take it. It's probably one of those things best sorted out by men." It was as Henry had predicted in his letter. For those with interests to protect, America was a land of law and paper, and together they constituted proof, and proof, Dent knew, could be bought. He would do anything to ensure that his name would not be appearing on the birth certificate.

Dent not only wished to meet Ben, but insisted that Katherine be present, if only to introduce them. Naturally, he wished the meeting take place at his hotel suite, to leverage whatever advantage he could bring to a process of negotiation. Katherine had sat there waiting, not worried but aglow with the future, feeling herself only part of an audience to an entertainment. When Ben arrived he shook hands with Dent, perceptibly taller than his host.

><

They were on the tenth floor, so far above noise that ears had to strain for the street. God, thought Katherine suddenly, it's too quiet for Ben in here. She felt foolish for not having thought of it earlier, not wanting to put Ben at any additional disadvantage. Thinking that he had established his superiority, Dent then did his best to put his visitor at ease, letting a Negro in a starched white uniform pour him a generous scotch. Dent seated his guest in the largest armchair, so voluminous that Ben's feet barely touched the ground.

Katherine watched Dent study Ben's suit. Not a bad suit, not the best. Very careful with his mustache, hardly deferential with his eyes, they looked directly into Dent's until Dent looked away. However, Katherine could see that Ben seemed gradually unsettled by the grandeur. He stood and edged toward the windows while they were chatting, and then of all things said, "Would you mind if I opened one?"

"Of course not," said Dent.

Ben tugged the window open. The sound of traffic rushed into the room, all the congestion and frustration of the street whipped up ten stories.

"Not too loud for you?" called Dent to her from his velvet chair.

"It's fine," said Katherine.

Ben shook his head. "I just like the air."

"I understand," said Dent, though he did not.

There were, in Katherine's opinion, three levels of deceit in the room. First, Dent, who would do anything to preserve his image of himself as a good man, as long as he could avoid all responsibility for his actions. Then Ben, who if he could still think straight would realize that one of the wealthier men in America had fallen across his path. And herself, an assistant orchestrator, who planned to use one man to rob the other for her exclusive benefit. It did, of course, hinge upon this meeting. All Ben had to do was notice the wealth of the man and report it to his boss. Was that too much to ask? Even of a muddled mind?

Katherine noticed small tremors in the Englishman's hands as he strained to open the window, a nervousness just a little short of desperation. A cheap hat had left a faint black streak from the ribbon across his forehead, and his collar was a little too high, giving the impression of a man struggling to keep his head above water. She could tell he was straining not to stammer. If anything, he reminded Katherine of a kettle on the stove, rattling in anticipation of the boil.

"How did you two meet?" asked Dent.

Ben wandered over to the Victrola in the corner of the room.

"How did you meet Katherine?"

Ben looked up. "At the theater. I stayed behind to introduce myself. Would you mind if I put on a record?"

"Help yourself," said Dent. "You know how it works, do you?"

Ben didn't answer, but selected "After the Ball" and started up the machine. He turned back to his host and apologized. "Sorry, it's just been awhile since I've heard this."

"Not at all," said Dent, indicating that Ben should retake his seat in front of the black lacquer table.

The Englishman sat and Katherine watched as Ben immediately began to fidget among a small pipe in the rack, cigars in a japanned box, and a Chinese bowl full of assorted cigarettes. He finally selected on one of the cigarettes and lit it. The disembodied voice from the Victrola had drowned out all sounds from the seat. Ben had turned it up too loud.

"Katherine, if you wouldn't mind leaving us for a bit?" said Dent.

She walked over to the desk where she'd left her bag. "Ben," she said, "maybe you should turn off the music."

Ben looked a little concerned but rose, and as he pulled the needle from the record, Dent looked to make sure Ben operated the Victrola gently. Katherine took the opportunity to flip the switch on the Dictaphone. She gave neither man a kiss goodbye, but slipped from the room. Her job, for the most part, was already done. All she had left to satisfy was her own interest. If she could offer Henry any other information, all the better, but in effect, Dent would now be passed into the arms of Ben's syndicate. By the time she returned to the Astor, an hour later, Ben had already gone and Dent was changing for lunch at the Cumberland.

"Do you mind if I stay here?" she asked, giving her stomach a tiny pat. "I just feel a little faint."

As soon as he was gone, Katherine flipped the cylinder of the Dictaphone and listened to the muffled conversation. She wished Ben had closed the window, but at least she had convinced him to turn off the music.

"She's a lovely girl," said Dent's distant voice, "but that doesn't mean that I'm going to trust her. I'm sending her to my doctor, just to make sure she's pregnant. I'd hate to be tied up for no good reason." It was his voice of intimacy. "You understand the precaution."

"I understand a lot," Ben answered, "except why you wanted to see me."

"The fact is," continued Dent. "This has happened to me before. It was all easily resolved and I'm hoping the same can happen again. We obviously have something in common. Listen, I live in Chicago. I have a wife there, and Katherine here, and of course she's going to get lonely and seek out another fellow. I'm just glad it's a fellow like yourself."

"That's kind of you," said Ben with a hint of sarcasm.

"Now she's pregnant," said Dent. "What do you make of that?"

"I don't make anything of it," said Ben. "She tells me it's yours."

Dent laughed, and Ben laughed along, a little too late, thought Katherine.

"Tell me, Ben, are you a rich man?"

"No," said Ben.

"That's what I thought," said Dent. He gave another familiar laugh as if he could now assume a new role, thought Katherine. "I've been to Europe a couple of times and know your country well. Katherine may think you're a *pas de deux* from a duke but your accent's different, isn't it? More of a butler, or a valet? Is that what you were?"

"I did a bit of most everything."

"Katherine says you still work for the army?"

"Something like that."

"Doesn't exactly pay well, does it?"

"Not particularly."

"They'll pin a lot of medals on you. Men do funny things for medals. But you can't start a new life on medals alone, can you?"

"I don't suppose you can," said Ben.

"What do you do for them over here?"

"Afraid I'm not at liberty to say."

"Trusted, always good to be trusted by your government. Very intriguing. Will they send you back to England?"

"I expect I'll be given that choice if and when the war ends."

"Awhile yet," said Dent. "That's what they say. What do you think?"

"Awhile yet," concurred Ben.

"How old are you?"

"Twenty-five."

"That's right," said Dent. "Marry the girl, or don't marry her, that's your own business. Either way, the kid should be yours. Maybe it is, who knows? Maybe it isn't, but I want the two of you to raise the kid."

"You want me to raise the child?" Katherine could almost hear the smile breaking across Ben's face.

"Between gentlemen?" asked Dent. Ben must have nodded. "I really don't give two tomatoes either way," explained Dent. "I'm a pretty casual kind of fellow. I'm here to make you a simple offer. If the girl makes a claim on me, I get dragged through the courts. My wife, my family get dragged along with me. What I'm offering you is a flat sum, two thousand dollars for signing on that birth certificate. Whatever she says, you and I know that you take full responsibility for the child. That's the end of it, according to the law. What do you say?"

There was a pause. "I'll tell you what I'll do," said Ben at last. "I'll sign that piece of paper for just a thousand dollars."

"Why do I feel a condition coming on?"

Ben laughed. It sounded very reedy on the Dictaphone. "That we meet once more. That you allow me to pitch, just pitch, a business plan your way. It's to do with my work for the army. Who knows, we might be in a position to help each other. Come meet my partner, and I'll sign any paper you want."

Well done, thought Katherine. Not so damaged after all. Well played.

Chapter Fourteen

IT HAD BEEN a week, and both Ben and Dent had suddenly become so busy they barely had time for her. Hardly coincidental, since she knew each was preoccupied with the other. She spent her own free time walking and visiting cheap cinemas and dreaming of life alone. No more travel, her baby, perhaps the hiring of a nanny. Money could be made to last a long time, she knew, if she gave up the love of luxury that Henry reveled in.

She knew the city summer had arrived because all the girls at the theater had taken to applying volumes of perfume to combat the pools of horse piss and manure that they negotiated on the way to work. All well and good, but once inside a stuffy changing room the sweet smell was overbearing. The stir of electric fans merely pushed the same stale air in circles. Katherine kept a small bottle of peppermint extract by the mirror to pass under her nose.

She spent too much time looking at her body's profile in mirrors, awaiting some sudden revelation. Every night, she seemed to dream of her child or at least her stomach. Dreamed that she would walk on stage thinking no one knew, and then halfway through the act, realize that she had the taut balloon of a woman almost due. And then they were all standing, all the men in the audience were standing, and she thought it was an ovation, but no, each was shouting that it was his child. But she stood there against them, because it was all hers, entirely hers.

The few times that she managed to see Dent, he seemed content but slightly wary, as if her presence might reverse the deal he had negotiated with Ben. She tried to keep him happy with flattering questions. When she asked after Arch, there seemed to be an independent glow about him, and she knew Henry's concept had worked well. He had already seen the glimpse of easy money that Ben was offering. Only once did Dent mention that he had seen Ben again, that they had taken lunch together in the country, and what a fine young man he thought he was.

"Ben hadn't told me," she said.

Dent shrugged. "It was lunch," he said. "Nothing important. I have to go back to Chicago on business for a few days," he continued, and raised his hand to her cheek in a gesture of pure insincerity.

"With Arch?"

"No," said Dent. "Nothing to do with Arch."

"Things are moving on," she smiled.

"Of course," he said. "Will you be here later?"

"I don't think so. I think I'll just go home to sleep before the theater."

"I'll be back at the end of the week," he said. "Friday, I think."

"What for?"

"The party? Remember. You said you'd accompany me."

"Of course," said Katherine, "I'll meet you after the theater."

He barely grunted in her direction. He was tiring of her. She could feel it. Perhaps her pregnancy had helped create his new sense of dominion. There was rarely any kind of relationship that could survive the sort of winning lottery ticket that Ben must be offering. She knew that soon he would be trying to find himself a new and improved version of herself. She'd seen men do it with their automobiles, a constant search not simply for the better, but for the new.

Knowing that Dent had been put on the send by Ben, that he had gone to Chicago for his money, was sweet and comforting news. She was happy for herself and decided that it was time to say her goodbyes to the Englishman. It was the first time that she had visited Ben's apartment. On entering, all the joy she had felt fled. The room was sparse, that of a man who had arrived a day and not months before. There were no signs of character, no bookcases, only bare walls and clothes neatly folded in a corner. Ben could have packed and left without trace in a matter of minutes.

"Your government doesn't keep you too well," she said, looking about her.

Ben shrugged. "I wouldn't describe myself as high ranking."

She took all of a minute to tell him that she would be returning to Westchester to have the baby and was canceling her engagement at the Eltinge.

"Just like that?" he asked. She was flattered to notice a rise of concern in his voice. "You're giving up?"

"I'm going to be with my family."

"I was meaning to take care of your child," he said. "I told your friend, Mr. Dent, that I would." He went over to a suit hanging from a nail in the wall and pulled out an envelope. "It's a thousand," he said, handing it to her. All of Dent's money, she thought, not even keeping a fee of his own. Inside, she was torn between thinking him sweet and wanting to laugh in his face. Sweet, she decided. How like a bunco man to be sharp in all things but love.

"I'm not sure I should let you go," said Ben.

"You're not my husband," she said.

"And if I were?" asked Ben.

"Then I'd deserve divorce for having been with another man."

"I'm not sure I can explain," said Ben, tapping his own chest. "But this doesn't sit well right here. It feels wrong to let you go."

She reached out to kiss him. He was a kind man. "I don't love Dent, if that's what you're asking." She ran her hand over her stomach. "Things are muddled. For a while, I just want it to be the two of us."

"You and me?" asked Ben with such sweet hopefulness.

"Me and my child," Katherine answered.

At the theater that night, a hand-delivered note arrived from Dent, reminding her to be ready at eleven. The original invitation read A SOIREE ON BEHALF OF THE INDUSTRIAL WORKERS OF THE WORLD. Only in this city, Katherine thought, do you get someone throwing a union a party on Fifth Avenue.

><

Was it odd for those invited? According to Katherine that evening, most certainly. The pained awkwardness of champagne and servants, the blatant ironies, so scarlet and obvious that no one was stupid enough to point them out.

Dent and Katherine were greeted by their hostess under her high ceilings, a heavy canary in a cream dress who flapped about the room chirping introductions. The wooden floor was painted forest green, and every chair and sofa glared in reds and yellows. An edenic mural of palms and baobab trees lined the walls. All who stood in such a setting were equal in their discomfort. Katherine was wondering why on earth Dent would want to be among such a mixed crowd when he gave her hand an explanatory squeeze.

"There he is," said Dent. "Come meet Quinlan Harvey."

In the corner, under the painted monkey hanging from the banana tree, sat a great magnet riveted to his chair, the whole room swaying toward him. Broad jaw, pug nose, jowls, but impressive, thought Katherine, in the same way that oversized statues in parks are impressive. Harvey rose on seeing Dent and crossed the room to greet him, then offered Katherine a roguish bow. His name meant nothing to her, never mentioned by Ben, let alone Henry. Whoever he was and whatever he did, Katherine would have no way to inform Henry of his existence.

They joined Harvey on his sofa and were brought glasses. A platter of salmon and lemon wedges on the bamboo table in front of them. As Harvey orchestrated the pouring of the champagne, Katherine turned to Dent.

"Is he Irish?" she whispered.

"Of course."

"At least he's not another of your Germans," said Katherine.

"Might as well be," said Dent with a smile. "Be a sweet girl and just let me speak to him alone for a moment?"

Katherine stood up again and moved away in search of more champagne. She hadn't thought of that. It had been in the papers last Easter, when up had sprung a thousand men in Dublin, rallying for freedom and the end to conscription in England's war. The British had rewarded the ringleaders with nooses. Even Sir Roger Casement, who had sought to run guns to Ireland from Berlin, found that his English title had not been coupled with English mercy. He was to be hanged soon. Yes, Katherine imagined the Germans had more friends than she had thought up and down the East Coast.

She wandered about the apartment, chatting with a small gathering of ill-dressed women who were discussing whether the fair sex ought to be allowed to smoke on the street. By the time she returned to Dent, she was amused to find Harvey talking to a young blonde sitting next to him, ignoring Dent. Katherine liked him all the more for it when she heard Harvey lower his tone to one of mock confidentiality, the unmistakable sound of the flirt, twisting the young blonde's Oriental parasol in his great hands. The temptation of the good life is so obvious, thought Katherine, biting into the salmon, that she wondered why the poor would not simply aspire to such luxury rather than all this loose talk of dragging everybody down.

Dent stood to excuse himself for the bathroom and Katherine took a seat beside Harvey to await his return. Favoring her above the blonde on his left, Harvey leaned over to bless her with his attention. His accent was music-hall Erin, thick with the countryside.

"You known Rudolph long?"

"We spend a lot of time up in Newport together."

"So you know Mr. Grayson as well?"

"Of course," said Katherine. "Arch takes me flying."

"Then he'll be glad to know all his problems with the planes are fixed."

"You mean the crash?" asked Katherine.

Harvey seemed to realize that perhaps he'd said more than he'd intended.

"I'm sure I don't know what I mean," said Harvey.

"Anything good for business and I'm sure Arch'll be thrilled," said Katherine, trying to keep the conversation alive.

"A dollar is a dollar," said Harvey. "The sum of all our wishes."

Dent pushed his way between a couple of women back toward them and offered Katherine a hand to help her rise. He waved at Harvey as he turned to leave.

"A pleasure as always."

"Is everything okay?" asked Katherine, fishing as they descended in the elevator. "You know, with your airplane company?"

Dent looked surprised. He waited until they left the elevator and its operator behind and had stepped into the street.

He took her by the hand. "What did Quinlan tell you?"

"Nothing," said Katherine. "Just that the planes had been fixed."

Dent let go of her arm.

"Was it about the crash?"

Dent nodded. "It was an engine problem."

"So did you lose all your money?" asked Katherine, suddenly worried again that Dent would not have enough left for her.

"Hardly."

"Are the engines insured?" she finally asked.

"Partially," said Dent. "Only a fool would insure them in the air, but on land or at sea, an aircraft's engine is safe as can be."

"That's good," said Katherine.

"Not really," said Dent. "Hardly good odds for air cadets in France. We have to presume the whole batch bad. If you have glanders in a barn, like it or not, you slaughter your herd."

"You have to get rid of them all?"

"Every last one."

"You'll lose a fortune."

"As I said," stressed Dent, bothered by her apparent stupidity, "they're already insured."

"And Quinlan?"

"He's the one who makes sure we get our money," explained Dent. "I suppose, if you were an insurance company, you'd call him an act of God."

"Hold on," said Katherine, stopping and putting her hand on her stomach. "I think he's kicking early."

As she predicted, Dent said nothing. She hoped he'd rather talk about anything than the thought of his unborn child.

"So what does he do to get rid of them?" she asked.

Dent looked at her. "I really don't want to know," he said. "Remember the U-boat? How orderly it all was ?"

"Sure."

"More of the same," said Dent reassuringly. "One more boat out of commission."

"An insured one?"

"Exactly."

"With a U-boat?"

Dent smiled. "That sort of thing."

Chapter Fifteen

SATURDAY, JULY 29, and the crowded city seemed to expand. The busiest centers, the Lower East Side, the Bowery, broke their banks and spilled their people through the streets. The paths of least resistance led to Central Park and, subsequently, Fifth Avenue. Regal residences, washed clean of winter soot and coal dust, had their summer views of Nature interrupted by the surge from downtown. Those lush green lawns that had lain almost empty in April were dotted now with picnicking clusters.

The views may have been marred, but there was no one to observe them other than housekeepers and skeleton staffs. The city summer was for the aspiring middle classes, subject to weekend commutes, and for the spreading lower populace. For them, Central Park was the forest glade, the piers on the Hudson the beachfront. The moneyed should, by all rights, be accompanying their families to cooler climes, Adirondack camps or Cape breezes. Dreams of Capri blue had been postponed by war.

Neither Grayson, nor Dent, nor even Katherine had any desire to know exactly how Quinlan Harvey hoped to destroy the engines. The act was considered a part of financial investment. Investments working in ways that none could see. And as long as they brought profits, why should any man be concerned with Quinlan Harvey's precise movements, such as his passage before dawn across the Hudson?

A few dollars cast at a poorly paid night watchmen ensured a lackadaisical attitude. That night they did not wander along the harborfront with electric flashlights, as ordered, but gathered in the heat of their cement huts to smoke. Harvey did not stride in, but slunk, face darkened by river mud, sweating through a black cotton shirt. In his pocket, two lead tubes, the size of cigars, both hollow but for a thin copper separation — on one side of the divide, picric acid, the other side, sulfuric. Katherine's memory of school would have been too vague to remember that both acids would corrode copper. If the copper was an inch thick, perhaps the acids would not meet for a year, but in the tubes Quinlan cast into the hold of the ship storing their airplane engines, the copper was as slender as a thumbnail.

The acids were intended to meet within the week, celebrating in a burst of fire that would set wooden boxes alight, ammunition aburst. And, at sea, captains were instructed to immediately fill their holds with seawater to douse any danger, ruining all mechanical cargo, including, for example, airplane engines. It was exactly what Harvey intended. He had done as much before, on behalf of other clients, ruining the cargo of at least half a dozen Allied ships over the course of the year. But if Katherine was not familiar with chemical properties, how exact would she have guessed Harvey's knowledge to be? Say the copper's thickness was not enough to wait a week; suppose the tubes were intended to be kept in a cool place, not the summer hold of a tin-hulled ship in July? Say they didn't last a week, but only a day, until a Saturday night. What if the ship of airplane engines was not alone at sea, but moored next to the single greatest store of munitions anywhere outside the theater of war?

Saturday morning, Katherine rose early and posted a coded note to Henry, then a telegram, in the hope that he had some way of breaking free of the federal Bureau to be warned of Dent's intentions. She knew from Dent that the airplane engines were already aboard a ship. At the very least, it might be information that Henry could pass on to the authorities. While exporting engines or armaments to Europe was perfectly legal, surely Dent might be held awhile on charges of insurance fraud? It might give them more time to claim his money.

><

She hadn't been able to resist one more afternoon with Ben, making love. Ben, she would miss. Dent would not be spared a thought. There she sat, knowing well that in his vault was a vast amount of cash. Dent did not worry about his money; it sat happily in the safe in his suite, ten floors above the city, guarded by the combination of houseboy, doormen, and hotel security, not that any of them knew of their proximity to thousands of dollars.

On her way to meet Dent for the last time, Katherine bought a copy of the *Herald*. She looked to see if the Cubs had won, knew that somewhere Henry would be checking the scores, and instead caught a blur of European news. She tried to imagine a war taking place in the summer. During the winter, she had presumed conflict a thing of rain, fog, and mists. A summer war did not adhere to her insistence that heat and languor lagged hand in hand. How could generals motivate men in sluggish July? Yet the newspaper had said something about a new offensive at the Somme. Perhaps the light was better at this time of year.

How to survive this heat? The real answer, she knew, was in leaving for the sea. Once their business was over, she had decided to cross the border in Maine and spend a month in Newfoundland, where she knew not a soul. Now that the day had come, all the decisiveness she had felt in the last month wavered. Henry was not a bad man, she kept telling herself. And to be alone? Pregnant and alone? Perhaps it's better to wait. But no, she countered, opportunity is sacred. Don't think a week ahead, think of the rest of your life.

After the party where she had met his friend Quinlan Harvey, Dent had taken her out to Churchill's for dinner and dancing. Then she had known for sure. They were dancing the Grizzly Bear to a *click-clack* modern beat and his hands were all over her, as they should have been, and she knew he didn't care for her anymore. There was no joy in his touch, he did not wish to explore, he did not wish to push against her stomach and upset her. She knew she would lose him any day now, con or no con. She had had no choice but to play her goodbye card.

It hadn't been a question of beauty. She was impeccably turned out, albeit in the same dress he had bought for their last foray to Newport. She supposed she was still trying to please him, with her coiffed hair, the look of thanks right into his eyes. Truth be told, she knew he couldn't wait to be rid of her.

Her news had surprised him. Sitting in their booth, away from the band, she had leaned over to him and said, "I'm going back home."
   He'd looked up at her and, to his credit, withheld a smile.
   "Is your Englishman going with you?"
   She nodded. "I hope he's coming out for the birth."
   She waited and didn't say anything, let him sit in his guilty silence.
   "I was hoping you'd allow me to give you something to help you set up a home."
   "I don't know Rudolph," she had hemmed weakly.
   "I insist."
   She reached out and touched his cheek, and he smiled for the good times that they had had together over the last months. "Thank you."
   He had no desire to be with her that night, but took her to the door of her hotel. She received a rather sad, paternal kiss on her forehead, the kiss of the last goodbye. "You can come and pick it up tomorrow."

Now, as she rode the elevator of the Hotel Astor for the last time, she wondered if she would miss the chandeliers in the lobby, or the streaks of red as bellboys clattered across the marble floors, or the bows of managers and gentle inquiries, all the illusions of respect. No, Katherine thought to herself, change is what I love, and what greater change could there be than motherhood? Katherine thanked the operator and turned right along the carpeted corridor toward Dent's suite. She knocked, her easy smile vanishing when the door opened.

Before her stood a Pinkerton agent. You could spot them a mile off. He was a boxy, red-cheeked man who looked like he had spent his life in uniform. Not a stiff military bearing, but an officiousness Katherine had only observed in tram and train conductors. There was nothing on him that was not highly polished, from the shine of his shoes, to the gleam of his spectacles, to the brilliant orb of his silver fob. He looked at her with disapproval. Katherine could see the bulge of his revolver riding high in his shoulder holster beneath his jacket.

"You must be Miss Howells," said the man, reaching for his pocket.

Katherine's heart thumped hard, but he simply withdrew an envelope. "Mr. Dent instructed me to give you this."

Katherine took the small packet and wondered how much he thought she'd been bought off for.

"Isn't he going to come and say goodbye?" she asked.

The detective was kind enough to shrug. "I'm afraid not."

Katherine reached up to brush an imaginary tear from her face. The agent did nothing but close the door gently on her. All things considered, the rudeness would be returned to Dent by midnight. Dent would be spending the night in a holding cell until the feds could be certain he had nothing to do with the crew of counterfeiters and bunco men. Only afterward would they believe his cries that the money, the real money, was all his. Unless her telegram had been forwarded to Henry in time, in which case, Dent might have significantly more explaining to do when his engines became submerged in brine.

Katherine went downstairs, hailed a taxi, and had him wait across the street, paying him by the hour, biding her time for Dent. It was late now, almost midnight. The envelope contained five hundred dollars. Pretty cheap in the end, she thought. She wondered for the first time if Ben and his syndicate had any idea that Dent was bringing an armed Pinkerton man with him. Henry wouldn't have a clue, but he'd be surrounded by feds. The sudden thought of too many guns in too small a place made her worry on Henry's behalf. She wanted him to be gone from her life, not dead. When Dent finally emerged, she had the taxi follow him far downtown to Warren Street, where he disappeared through the doors of a Chinese laundry. The Pinkerton man waited outside. Katherine had the taxi drive around the corner, then walked back and into a small bar across the street. She took a seat away from the window. Whenever the door to the bar opened or shut, she could see the Pinkerton man standing as motionless as a palace guard.

There was a rumble from outside, the sound of a large summer storm. Damn it, thought Katherine, I didn't bring an umbrella. She wondered if Henry had one. He couldn't be more than a hundred yards away. She ran her hands over the pleats of her dress, letting them brush her stomach, and thought she had not one, but two, to keep dry. But the rumble from above came again and Katherine knew it was not a natural sound; it simply ran on too long, too ferociously. Immediately she thought of the ships she had witnessed plummeting to the depths of the ocean off Newport, then of Quinlan Harvey and the fate of Dent's engines. She wondered if Harvey might have something to do with the buffeting thunder that made her glass shiver on the table.

PART FOUR

MR. BENEDICT CRAMB
June 1916

Chapter One

BEN HAD SOME memory of his early education, of British movement and conquest, but no one had ever told him about the wars of other countries, that somewhere along these streets he now walked the veterans of Shiloh and Bull Run still breathed stories that seemed fresh in the depth of their dreams. He didn't know America wasn't an innocent, that she had grown so fast that experience and memory had become hard nuggets hidden beneath the immigrant mountain, under the gloves at opera time, in the dark nickelodeons, along electric rails, and between subway carriages.

But, better than most men, Ben understood that Europe was not three thousand miles to the east, nor eleven thousand miles to the west, but an immeasurable distance, the breech of what could and what could not be imagined. He watched the gatherings of men in New York's Herald Square and they did not study the boards for war news, though war news sat there with the solemnity of an open casket. They came for the sports scores, posted quarter by quarter, inning by inning, following the Giants' winning streak, or Chick Gandil's winning bat, or Jess Willard's fists. Ben knew these contests were local, they were professional and sporting. Who should fathom, or care, for a fight halfway across the world?

Until the outbreak of Europe's war, America had been welcoming a million immigrants a year to her shores. Ben had heard enough of their stories to know. They were processed and poked, checked for black spots, and passed from the rock of Ellis Island and its booming halls of confusion to the strange familiarity of Manhattan. Where almost everything was different and yet, if you were Greek or Italian, a Pole or a Slav, German or Irish, Ben knew that you would find that under this crashing wave the shore was made up of what had come before and what had come before was you. And did immigrants leave New York? Many, but many stayed, a quarter of that million in 1915, and the same again the previous year. And where did they live? Ben was learning that if you were downtown, on the east or west, or even in the Camelot of Greenwich Village, once the weather was kind, it seemed as if they all lived in the streets.

Ben presumed that there were always firsts. Countries so small, so remote, that they had not yet thrown a body New York's way. Men who could not expect to find others who shared their knowledge. Ben had not stood in the lines of Ellis Island. He wondered if he had been unique in that he had had no dreams of New York, nor expectations of the city. When he had stepped aboard three months ago, he had not only failed to notice the name of the ship but had no idea of her destination. Had she dropped anchor at some South Seas port, he would have been much less surprised than when his eyes finally saw strange, lopsided Manhattan, the towers of its southern tip.

And now he had forged a new family of one kind or other. The boys were still there, not beside, but inside him. He would talk, they would answer, full of opinion. They agreed on much. To a man, they thought Katherine Howells beautiful. There was no consensus on McAteer. To Ben he was not a father, but an uncle, one who seemed to have his interest at heart. If nothing else, at least an employer who had saved him from humdrum piano playing and Bowery depths and allowed him to see the brightness of New York's possibilities. But the boys begged him not to trust the American. Why?, asked Ben. Not family. But then who is? You can't ask that much of me, said Ben. You can't ask me never to have another friend. No, said David, we can't. No, agreed Douglas. Chimer said nothing at all.

No matter what the boys thought, Ben was haunted by McAteer's original comment that all newcomers to his business were responsible for roping. Out of the eight thousand dollars taken from

Henry Jergens, almost three thousand were devoted to expenses: hotel rooms, office rent, train tickets, entertainment, and salaries for the various bit players, recruited from among McAteer's friends. That left five thousand, ten percent of which was automatically paid to their lawyers, and an exorbitant thousand for police protection. Out of the remaining three thousand five hundred, Ben's cut stood at four hundred dollars.

"My boy," said McAteer to Ben. "We've been let down." McAteer looked away from Ben, who wondered, not for the first time, if McAteer held him partly responsible for their predicament. Though Ben knew that his only fault lay in his newness to the game, he realized that that was enough of a deviation to shoulder a greater part of the blame. "They don't all bite, truly they don't," continued McAteer, "but once they bite, you'd like to think they bite harder than that."

He bought Ben an early dinner and raised the toast. "The next time will be our time. Dear God, put someone fat in front of us and let us *both* leave him skinny."

They clinked glasses.

"Expenses are cut," continued McAteer. "When we rope again, we play again, we pay again. Get a little work if you have to; prefer it if you don't. You go through your money, come see me. Even if we're not running a game, maybe someone else will have something small for you to play."

Ben interpreted the comments as strong encouragement in his search for money and a pointed reminder that, to some extent, Jergens's poor payoff had been laid at his door.

It was odd to be back in the apartment full-time, to the different noises of the city. He had become too accustomed to his midtown retreat, polite knocks on doors, doormen's whistles, rush-hour movement, the to and fro of cars and taxis. Now he was back among the low roofs of Greenwich Village and human sounds, the gutter noise of summer streets. From his second-floor window, he could not only distinguish individual voices but recognize them. He had made the mistake of jimmying open the back window and remembered immediately why it was sealed shut. The neighboring building was close enough to touch, and there, in the thin passage below, lay kitchen garbage from four floors of both buildings: chicken gizzards and vegetable peelings, a stench of rotting that attracted rat chatter and the flecked movement of cockroaches.

That afternoon, McAteer and Ben placed their summer boaters on their heads and headed downtown to Vesey Street, past the second-hand bookshops abutting the railings of St. Victor's churchyard. It was an odd street of lodging houses, barrow men hawking skinned rabbits, smelt, herrings, trays of pigeons.

They walked south down Church Street, passing by great sacks of nuts, barrels of olive oil. The warm wind carried the scent of roasting peanuts. At Broad Street, money dismissed the other smells. Curb brokers, dealing in their small odd lots outside of the Exchange, called from group to group. McAteer and Ben wandered among them, tipping their hats, searching for those who had the dazed look of a fresh arrival.

Steering and roping entailed looking for the affluent, the approachable, the malleable, the reasonably intelligent. There were men in town from Texarkana, Fez, Bismarck, Kiev, long steamship journeys. In town for a week, maybe a month or two, plenty of time to ripen and be reaped. While Jergens had been presented in an enclosed railway car and given to Ben, and though the same webs were still spread throughout the newspapers of the country, there was nothing wrong with the old-fashioned, direct approach. Either way, it was clear that the pressure was on Ben to produce the next mark.

McAteer had suitcases of unclaimed inheritances, gold bricks, and counterfeiting machines waiting for their matches. There was nothing new to any of their games; they were the same gifts wrapped in different, more appropriate paper. A man who knew the horses couldn't be taken on ponies, but what did he know about stocks? And a stockbroker, how familiar was he with Texas real estate? They wandered about the district, stopped for a sandwich in a bar conspicuously absent of money. All morning they had achieved little other than the erosion of shoe leather.

It was a compliment to McAteer that soon Ben began to stare at the strangers with green in his eyes. But for all the wealth that they had what he really wanted was their lives. He didn't tell Chimer, David, or Douglas, but what he wanted was to have been born with money in this country, with no responsibilities beyond those to your own parents, to have never seen what he had seen. Either that, or to be himself in London two years ago.

He had taken to buying week-old copies of the *Times* from London. He told himself that it was because he suffered from a touch of homesickness, but always his eyes turned to measure the length of the list of officers killed and wounded. He tried to convince himself that he was no longer English, yet he did not wish to be simply an immigrant, one of those who had traveled four thousand miles, who had lined up in Ellis Island, wept to be included in the new world, and then promptly rebuilt their villages on New York streets. Where was the freedom that they came for? Ben wanted the liberty of the rich individual and the peace of an empty mind.

"We're doing nobody no good," said McAteer.

They entered an Irish bar near the waterfront and occupied a low booth, the table scarred with engraved initials. There was the constant *click-clack* of dominoes coming from behind them.

"Tell me," said Ben, "did you learn how to rope and steer all by yourself?"

"Of course not," said McAteer. "You're learning from me, and I learned from the man before me. Right back till when the first of our kind sold Plymouth Rock to a passing Pilgrim."

"Where's your professor now?"

"He was a fat old son of a bitch," said McAteer. "They called him Gallon. One day I took everything the man had."

"You ran a con on him?" asked Ben, intrigued.

"Don't go getting ideas," said McAteer, wagging a finger at him. "Worse than that anyway. To my eternal shame it was simple thievery. Nobody on this coast talked to me for maybe five years and more. Took everything, *everything* he had."

"Including his woman?"

"Hardly his taste," said McAteer. "He was a bugger boy."

Ben must have looked away.

"And no, before you ask," said McAteer, "we didn't play drop the soap in a shared tub."

Ben shrugged. "Is he still around?"

McAteer shook his head. "I sent a man to his funeral, maybe twenty years ago. Open casket, otherwise I would have thought he'd be running something on someone. Maybe me. They say he was taken by a failure of the heart in flagrante delicto with a hundred-pound Finn."

Ben must have been listening to it since he had arrived, but only then did his concentration slip from his own conversation to notice. There wafted, over the sound of the familiar Irish brogue of the bar, a second language. At a table, in New York City, comfortably situated in the middle of the room, sat four sailors speaking in a tongue Ben had rarely heard. It made him catch his breath. Every country represented in this city, but he had not thought of this coupling of Irish and German.

"How about the girls Ben? How you doing on that front?" McAteer was asking.

There were very few occasions when Ben had heard the sound of German being spoken during his months in France. The first time was one of his earliest memories of the war. It was the usual stint of ten days or so in the trenches: three in the reserve, three in the support, three in the front line, a day of marching. They had been billeted on a farm, then torn out of that strange idyll, brought up to support the push at Loos they'd been listening to all night. The day before they'd been marched to a brewery and forced to bathe in one of the great vats, filled with cold dirty water, twelve at a time scrubbing the farm stench of compost and manure from their skins. On the march back to their stables, they'd stopped by a Trappist monastery. Captain Traven had allowed Douglas to buy a barrel of beer from the hole in the wall that served as a silent estaminet.

Marching to the front line the next day, Ben and Chimer had paused to steal pears off trees. Soon they'd passed splintered wagons and unburied horses, and just when a sense of trepidation was taking hold of them, there appeared a great band of men. Ben's company were ordered to stand to the side of the slim road and, four abreast, German prisoners trudged past them. At the head of the column was a group of German officers, arguing incessantly, behind them perhaps two hundred soldiers. At either end of the column, to the great amusement of Ben's company, marched a short, stocky Argyll and Sutherland Highlander. Despite the rain that fell about them, and the sounds of shelling ahead, they were happy and laughing together at the strange sight.

"One," said Chimer. "That's all it fucking takes."

"Can't weigh much more than you," answered Ben, "with a ton of Germans."

They had arrived too late at the greatest push, Ben had thought, but even as part of Kitchener's mob they could now claim some vague association with a decisive victory. Truth be told, Ben remembered, he had even felt peeved that they had not got there sooner.

Five minutes later, a more worrying spectacle came their way. Eight sergeants of the Gordons, walking down the road, helping one another along. All were affected by the gas, faces splotched scarlet and yellow and eyes squeezed shut in pain.

Ben's company had managed to retain a mild enthusiasm their first day on the front, fighting to peek through periscopes and proudly showing their new equipment to the London Divisions. At night, they played games with their gas masks. Chimer's made little flatulent noises with every exhalation. They even ate well, hot stew somehow cooked up for them. But up and down the line Ben noticed men walking with special brassards of red and white, the emblems of the Gas Brigade. It meant they were going over the next morning. They'd been shown the ground ahead of them in the reserve trenches, a football pitch–sized replica of topography to instruct them where they would burst through the German wire. But come the morning, all Ben could remember were the brigades standing by their great cylinders, leaking their gas. Despite the mist he could see it moving slowly toward the German lines, and then came the change of wind, moving slowly back to them, farther down the line. Over they had gone anyway and luck, pure luck, to follow another company and find a hole in the wire and for most to make it through with barely a scratch. They held the abandoned German trench for nearly an hour when, much to their dismay, they were whistled back again.

Coming off the line the next day, they understood how fortunate they had been. They did not walk with hundreds, but thousands of wounded, gassed men holding hands like schoolchildren, wandering back toward the reserve. Their small group seemed apart, returning to their original billet and the familiar stench of midden. Back they went to their local estaminet and talked hours of nonsense, but already, Ben felt he was a different man. While the others were comparing the minutiae of their day, Ben had stared at the serving maid. He had been attentive to her the week before, but only in his familiar manner, all flirtation and directness. She smiled at him as always, but he could only bring himself to nod in her direction. Later in the evening, just before Captain Traven turned them out so that the officers might have the place for themselves, she turned to pour Chimer more beer and Ben ran his hand up the back of her skirt. When she didn't flinch or turn, he pushed farther up until he held the cheek of her bare bottom in his hand. She hesitated for a moment, then simply moved away without even turning back to glance at him. Chimer had teased Ben about her on the way back to the farm.

"You'll never have a wife in your life," he'd said. "You'll never have a child. You'll fuck your way from one shell hole to another till the girls stop looking at you."

Ben remembered shaking his head in protest. "Don't you think this might change us?"

"Us? For sure," Chimer had said. "You? Never."

"Hey Ben," said McAteer. "Whatever happened to your actress? Any more time alone, you're going to have me thinking *you're* the daisy boy."

"I have my eye on her," said Ben.

"When are you going to see her?"

"She invited me to a party tomorrow night."

"Party?" said McAteer, with just a hint of jealousy. Perhaps, thought Ben, I should have invited him. "You think a guy is lonely," continued McAteer, clucking his tongue, "then you find he's been dancing the cakewalk."

Chapter Two

BEN HAD DRESSED up to attend the fund-raising evening at the Eltinge Theater. His socks with the small pinstripes. His wing tips and his dark blue suit. His red-patterned tie and light blue shirt, a new gold tiepin, boater girded by a sky-blue ribbon, to complement his eyes. He spent ten minutes trimming his mustache, then adding the right amount of wax.

Warm summer winds were rolling off the Hudson, charging their way through the Greenwich Village streets, blowing east one block, west another, until they found the comforting order of avenues and hurtled uptown. Ben leaned into the gusts, one hand on his hat. He climbed up the steps to the Sixth Avenue el, paid his nickel, and stood in the front car all the way up to Forty-second Street. The carriage still held the rush-hour warmth of vanished bodies, and Ben stared out into the passing tableaux of third-floor windows. He looked into the miniature myths of apartments flashing past and knew that he could no longer stand to be alone in his city box. No boys, he thought, not even with the three of you for company.

She appeared again, and Ben, one leg bent over the other, sat upright and listened to the first small speech of Katherine Howells. He liked the fact that he had come alone, that he had discovered her alongside Jergens, now long gone. It was as if she was now his secret. Nobody, not even McAteer, knew who she was. Her voice, thought Ben, was a touch deep for true femininity. What was Chimer's expression? Too much flesh, not enough veils. She wasn't wearing a corset, there was a looseness in the sway of her dress, the breasts moved. At intermission, there she stood on stage, helping the cast sell war bonds for the Allies. Beside her stood a soldier, an officer from the Lifeguards. But Ben did not have to speak; he motioned twice with his hand, won the bid at a hundred dollars, and received a wave and an excited smile of recognition from Katherine Howells herself. What I love and what I fear, he thought, standing side by side.

And he had followed her, shared a drink with her, strafed her with telegrams, and then waited in the bar for her to arrive. And she had come and held his hand in the cinema. In his mind's eye, it was Katherine up on screen, twenty feet tall, naked and soaked in oils, her hands running over her own body. She was Chimer's sister, and the girl at the estaminet, all that he could not have. The intermission card came up. Ben had had to position his hat casually over his erection before he took Katherine outside for a cigarette, hoping he didn't accidentally brush against someone and create a scene.

In the restaurant, Ben remembered the feeling. He might reach out, touch, be accepted in another's life. Holding a woman's hand for the first time and knowing that the agreement was already made. And then nothing but the wonderful anticipation. The expectation of touch. To know the excitement, the denial, the exultation that awaited. And did she feel the same?

He looked at her when she excused herself for the bathroom. Looked through that dress, the faint line of her undergarments. Nothing but desire. The thought of her, of her stripped before him, the joyful pushing apart of her legs, sliding between, the initial mutual gasp. He knew how he would be with her, could see what she would enjoy. This was a woman who for all the posture, all the sharp talk, all the deep stares, wanted to be pushed back down again. This was the aggressor who wished to be aggressed against. He had heard of hard work as the antidote to grief, but pleasure was the balm for anxiety. Keep busy, loud, involved. Do not look inward, try to stay up all evening.

She slept with him. Not unusual for Ben before the war, or of course, when such things were paid for. Still, there seemed something off — she took him back to the days of London ladies. Never anything serious, good humor was all that was counted on, no ridiculous promises, but the truth that life was a disappointment and only this should be bliss. He was slightly perplexed, as if he had expected himself to fall in love but had not stopped to think that it might not be reciprocated.

He knew that Katherine would be gone. The boys had already reminded him. Girls like that. Actresses. They moved about, in London they moved about, there was too much distraction. Fidelity was for the audiences, adulation for the actresses. There was the gentleman that he had met alongside Henry Jergens, there was Ben, perhaps there were others. She wanted money from one man, instruction from another, perhaps love from a third, laughter from a fourth.

Yet, it was a happy time for Ben. He acknowledged it to himself. Such an odd word to confess to. Of course he had smiled and laughed, even in France, even after he had ceased to care, had lost friends, but now he felt gloriously busy. Mornings with Katherine, afternoons roping with McAteer, conversations with the boys. At seven, he would walk Katherine to the theater. She would kiss him goodbye on the corner and meet him at a café after the show. He was, to the casual glance, the other half of a woman's life, connected to the neon side of the city.

Knowing that her cast was suspicious of her comings and goings, Katherine refused to introduce Ben. It was not a question of shame, she said, but simply of decorum. She did not wish to disrespect Ben, but neither could she afford to offend Rudolph Dent.

"Rudolph?" smirked Ben, in bed that night. "German name."

"Don't be jealous," said Katherine.

"How can I be jealous?" Ben replied, and reached over to plant a kiss on her bare nipple.

"You will be when he comes to town."

"Where's he from again?"

"Chicago."

"Is he terribly rich?"

"Horribly."

"What's his business?"

"The very worst," teased Katherine.

"Slaver?"

"Inheritor," said Katherine. "Barely does a thing. He says that if you inherit money *and* marry it, then working for it's just showing off."

"So you are . . ."

"Taken care of," said Katherine. "Is it that shocking? He pays for this apartment. My clothes, the bed we're in, the sheets. Rudolph."

"I suppose I should thank him."

"He probably wouldn't mind. He's terribly sophisticated. Probably got another girl in Chicago. Me, he only sees me a few days a month."

"Perhaps that's all he can handle," said Ben, rolling over, pushing her legs apart, and resting between them. "I, for one," he continued, "am exhausted. Absolutely exhausted."

Ben was distracted by her body. The dislocation that he felt between his concerns and his daily life drew together when he was with Katherine. Everyone was different, every woman preferred to be touched in different ways, but he had been alert to her desires, letting her lead him with approving murmurs. How do you wish to be touched? How do you wish to be kissed? What is the balance between our sheets? You like to bite. Do you now? How hard? You like your hands grasped at the wrists above your head. You like to be held about the hips, you like to look into my eyes, staring into me, as if you could read my thoughts. Are you making sense of me? How much of me can you stand?

When Ben rested, when the nightmares that he ignored in the pace of his life leaked out in his sleep to wake her, she listened. In the morning she would watch quietly as he stretched his mouth into yawns to release the tension in his jaw. She'd pop her clove gum in her mouth and chew and watch. Ben was glad she did not run from him, did not think him mad, did not seem to dislike or pity him for his dreams, though they were not good for her sleep. He knew he had her sympathy. And sometimes Ben dreamed of her, but mostly, blessedly, he dreamed of nothing at all.

The next Friday when Rudolph Dent telegraphed for Katherine to meet him in Newport, Ben did not think to bar the way. It had never crossed his mind that she would give up a source of income for him any more than that he should cease to work. She was undoubtedly a vital element in the continuing process of noise and distraction, but that was where he knew the attachment should stop. Yet he knew he was lying to himself if he did not admit to a tinge of jealousy. It was a trait he immediately buried, giving her his St. Patrick's Cathedral eyes, all distance and emptied of emotion, the attempt at Abu Abu, when in fact, his heart had stirred.

"How can a man do nothing?" asked Ben as she packed.

"They're different," said Katherine. "You ask me, when you get as rich as Rudolph, it takes half your day keeping one eye on your money. I mean, where do you put it?"

"Not in the bank," fished Ben. "I suppose you make investments."

"Who knows," said Katherine.

"So what does Rudolph invest in?"

"I think it's something about airplanes," said Katherine. "He helps sell airplanes to Europe."

Ben knew what that meant. Americans now used the word *Europe* as a euphemism for war. He said something banal in reply, didn't even hear himself. He had come all the way from those shores, and the man he shared her bed with was busy sending products back. So odd to think of airplanes in France. The high swooping whines over trench lines. All of their eyes following them and Chimer knowing the name of the plane before it even came into sight. Those flimsy vehicles cutting through the wisps of the skies. And they would all stay in France, whether crashed and buried in glutinous mud or corroding in some foreign airfield but here he was, breathing, not buried; busy, not rusted.

"Is that all he sells?"

"I doubt it," said Katherine.

"I wish you weren't going," said Ben softly. Though his mind was ticking in different directions, at least he knew he still meant what he was saying. Did we think of that, did we *ever* think of that?, he asked himself. Where it all comes from? What we drove in, what we carried, what we shot? It all comes from somewhere.

"Just for the weekend." She touched her hand to Ben's cheek. "You don't mind do you?"

"I understand," said Ben. "It's like having a second job, isn't it?" She looked at him.

"It's the American way. If you don't have two jobs, you have none."

"God," said Katherine, "I thought you were about to tell me what you do." She kissed him on the forehead and turned to go. "Listen," she said, "I know I'm gone this weekend, but will you be around in two weeks to spend some time with me? They're closing the theater for three days. It might be nice. I'd like you to meet my parents."

How normal a thing to be asked. He smiled brightly and accepted the invitation.

Chapter Three

McAteer seemed intent on the growth of his wallet and worked hard that Monday meandering with Ben through the wealthier parts of town. Ben noticed a conspicuous absence of McAteer's chatter. He presumed the old man's newfound sourness came from the lack of prospects, or perhaps expecting Ben to deliver a mark. Ben held Dent's name close to his chest all morning, waiting to see when best to deploy it. McAteer had admitted to having had six replies to various advertisements and lures throughout New England — four from Hartford, a shoemaker in Boston, a surgeon from Springfield, not one of which had given him any reason to smile.

The two men walked at their own leisurely pace while everyone else rushed, pushing between them, running after streetcars rather than waiting for the next one already rumbling toward them. What do you do with all these precious minutes now that they are saved?, thought Ben. They walked down the right roads — Exchange Alley and Broad Street — took coffee with well-dressed gentlemen in Herald Square. They loitered in the lobbies of the best of Manhattan's hotels, the Biltmore, the Navarre, the Cumberland, noting porters and bellboys struggling with steamer trunks. Ben watched McAteer's eyes trail women lit by jewels, then flicker back to his own face. Even this, thought Ben, would be more fun with Katherine by his side.

They started walking again.

"How much is a rope worth?" asked Ben.

"Fifteen to twenty percent," said McAteer. He examined Ben from the corner of his eye. "Look at you," he said. "You're itching with information."

Ben nodded. "I suppose I am."

"So why don't you give me a name?"

"Because I don't trust you."

"Only a fool would," said McAteer. "But what are you looking for? My word? A scrap of paper signed before lawyers? Would you trust those?"

"Of course not."

"So you might as well tell me," said McAteer. "If you've found a rope, maybe it's good, maybe it's not, but I guarantee that you're too raw to play it yourself. And a hundred percent of nothing is just air in a poor man's pocket."

"Then I'll have to settle for your word," said Ben.

"You poor man."

"His name is Rudolph Dent."

"Dent?" repeated McAteer. "Where's he from?"

"Chicago, I think."

"A Chicago Dent?"

Ben nodded his head. "She says they're an old family," said Ben.

"Who says?"

"My girl."

"The actress? What does she know?"

"Nothing about me. She's been with him for a few months."

"You met him?"

"Only briefly."

"They've got horses," said McAteer, straightening his back. "Plenty of horses. Good ones too. Now that could be worth a minor investigation. Where is he now?"

"Up in Newport," said Ben.

Once they had resumed walking, McAteer seemed more relaxed, companionable, as if all the bottled tension that he had been feeling toward Ben had fizzed harmlessly into the atmosphere.

"So we're at twenty percent?" asked Ben. "If this moves forward?"

"Of course," said McAteer. "Fifty percent right now. Fifty percent of nothing, or twenty percent, whatever you prefer."

><><

Ben spent the fortnight in anticipation of his weekend. Could he go with Katherine to the country, clasp her hand, fit a false ring upon her finger? Could he play her fiancé for a night? Otherwise her father would cut her off, and Broadway salary aside, she'd be in a precarious state. Ben could not think of a better role and during these days allowed himself to be content with little of Katherine's company, knowing that soon he would have her to himself, away from Rudolph Dent.

On the train out to Westchester, Ben leafed through the *New York Times* while Katherine could only stare out the windows. She looked a little sad, though he could sympathize. He could not imagine a similar ride again, knew he may never experience the odd trepidation of returning to a childhood house. All he was going to do, he thought, was to play a part so Katherine could gain approval, an amusing role. It was just a small con to bring acceptance, deference, and a flow of money for his girl, all through a simple lie.

He had been looking forward to this moment for two weeks, and now that it had arrived, it had a preternatural quality to it. A man was allowed an illusion. In France, when he had run his hand up the back of the serving girl's dress, what was that but a touch of empty promise, nothing but a willingness on that woman's part to give him some intangible dream. It was the same possibility with Katherine. She promised him nothing at all, but he could play as her fiancé, and for the temporary nature of the role, he was most grateful. And he thought of Dent, too; it seemed almost too perfect to have a rival and perhaps to take everything from him. But what would happen after? He might lose Katherine. Yes. For a while. But he could find her again. Dent, for instance, would associate her with the loss of money, no matter how good their turnoff was. Which would, in turn, leave her free enough to eventually return to him.

Ben watched her. She was not above vanity, and vanity finds beauty comforting, reaffirming the objective. Better still, he knew she thought of him as a handsome romantic, a veteran of the greatest of wars. He supposed it was almost like having a London star in town, as if war were a production and though it hadn't yet come to Broadway, it had run so long in Europe that all New York could recognize it. At least, he guessed that was how she was counting on her father seeing it.

He put aside the New York papers and picked up an old London *Times* he had bought at Grand Central. Ben was frightened by what he read. He'd known about the losses on the Somme from the American newspapers, but here was fresh news that it had been the Pals Battalions, from Leeds, Sheffield, and Accrington, that had lost between most and half their men in a single morning. He knew at once that the dead would be from selected streets, his kind of streets, his kind of friends. Ben thought of all the English fingers running over the lists, of blinds being drawn on narrow streets and bells tolling in every town. He folded the paper and felt stunned, as if he had just read an obituary for England herself.

Mr. and Mrs. Howells had brought their car to the station. Ben could think of nothing but his distance from England. The young couple sat in the back. Katherine held his hand. Ben flinched, but she steadied him with her stare and soon he let go of his thoughts of home. He had done well to leave, and knew he should be happy with Katherine. They wound their way through country lanes to end up before a large, freshly painted white clapboard house. It stood in the middle of an orchard, an American flag hanging from the balcony. A trio of crows sat on a branch looking over the flat lands. The car rattled up the long drive, and then the engine died.

Now the countryside was still. Ben had not even considered such a thing, so buoyed had he been in Katherine's company then so stunned by the news from France. It was a morning where the dew had been dried by the wind, the wind had died, and the country sat in silence before him. Every morning in France they had the advantage, the sun silhouetting belated German patrols as they slunk back; every sunset was cause for Allied concern. But you would rarely see the sun, only toward the height of day as it passed overhead, for vision was limited to the thin strip of sky visible from the safety of the trench. Dull, dull days, damp days, boredom, and the only thing worse was the constant shelling. In Ben's opinion, the main occupation of the infantry was to endure. After large bombardments, entire regiments would suffer from constipation, the latrines empty, duty easy.

There was the smell of roasted chicken, of singed skin that was rising in tasty blisters within the oven. Katherine was fortunate inasmuch as she looked like neither of her parents. Her father, McAteer's age, a scrawny rooster with a mustache as thick as a blackboard's duster. Mother, built like a well-fed hen, all plump with rolling breasts and little stockinged legs, busy about the kitchen. No one spoke, but all smiled as if smiles were a language, and perhaps they were but they made no noise. Ben clapped his hands together. "I am famished." But no one spoke back to him. "This is a treat," continued Ben, "an absolute treat, so rare to get out of the city. Katherine's been busy, and I'd hate to leave town without her." And on he went, rambling through the banal and inane, just artificial noise. The silence could not be stood for. How long could he talk? Should he pause and see if someone would step into the gap?

"Darling," said Katherine, "let's just take a small walk before lunch."

Outside Katherine asked, "Are you all right?"

"How do I seem?"

"Either anxious," she said, "or pretending to be anxious."

"I'm fine."

"You're overplaying the nervous suitor," she said with a smile, and rubbed his back as you would to warm a child. Ben was conscious of the maternalism of the act.

Over dinner, Mr. Howells kept up a particular Victorian tradition, which Ben guessed had barely even existed then, of ignoring women at the table. It was a ritual continued by those who thought every generation was necessarily more brutish than its predecessors. Mr. Howells was apparently blissfully unaware that fifteen miles away the streets were full of talk of women's suffrage and birth control. Women cook, men eat, women watch, men talk, women sit, men fight. Three perfectly good arguments, thought Ben, three reasons for women to be happy that men were busy exterminating themselves from the world.

"Apparently," growled Mr. Howells in his slightly accented English, "you don't work in the Exchange?"

"No, I don't."

"What do you do?"

"Cattle," said Ben. "I own an abattoir."

"Decent business?"

"Bloody business."

"Back in England?"

"Yes."

"I suppose you'll be taking her over there." Howells sent a half jab of his fork in Katherine's direction.

"Perhaps," said Ben, "but not until after the war."

Howells grunted. "God knows when that could be. Katherine going. Won't make much a difference to me and the wife. Don't see much of her anyway. Fifteen miles as good as a thousand."

"She cares about what you think," said Ben.

"Can't say I think she does," said Howells. "Else you two wouldn't be engaged so early in the first place."

Katherine flashed a full smile at Ben. It said, *Now you know. Would you have stayed a minute longer in this house than I did?*

"Times have changed," said Ben.

"Daresay they have," said Howells. "Must have, for her to find a man like you."

"I'm not much of anything special," said Ben.

"I can see that," said Howells. "It's what I like about you."

After lunch, as he walked alone with Katherine through the afternoon heat, Ben couldn't help but map out the countryside. He

knew how he would take the hill to the east. Where he would seek
cover for the rifle brigade, where they would have their machine
gunners. Ben had once seen a German machine gunner bow after
firing his last round. Stand and bow, and it was a theater of war, not
melodrama, not tragedy, but a constant farce perfect for the
Bowery music halls. Outside of La Bassée, he had visited the prop
shop of the War Department, seen imitation trees, sandbags, a fake
dead horse. There's no bloody difference, is there lads, thought
Ben, it's all a show.

"What was it like here?" asked Ben. "Tell me something about
growing up here. What were they like, your parents?"

So she began to talk, something about a pet cat and dead mice,
but Ben wasn't listening to the words, just the rhythm of sound that
forced silence and memory backward, and he thought how he
could love a woman like this, a woman with a voice just like this,
who could soothe him.

"Thank you again for coming out here," she said as they turned
down a narrow wooden lane.

"Oh that's all right," he murmured. He felt she suspected the
worst within him and all she did was rub his back. Not beg him to
talk, not try to push inside his mind, but simply to calm it down.

"You prefer the city though, don't you?" asked Katherine.

"I just like people," said Ben. "Lots of them."

She took Ben by the hand and pushed through the undergrowth
to the side of the lane. Ten yards in, Ben spread his jacket on the
shaded grass. They were totally enclosed by low branches, a green,
translucent cave. It felt different to Ben from all the other times
they had made love. It was affection, genuine when everything that
had come before seemed automatic in comparison. When they had
undressed each other, standing awkwardly, pushing clothes to the
ground until they were nude, Katherine took his face in her hands
and kissed him gently, then urgently, reaching down to grasp him.
They knelt. Katherine lay back and pulled Ben on top of her, inside
her. He looked up to steady himself and there were leaves bowing
down toward them and the sun speckled on their bodies. His mind

was filled with the scent of the forest, all full smells of rich soil, tiny seedlings birthing beneath. Ben felt holy, tantalized with tiny prickles where his bare feet pushed into the summer earth. Even when they dressed again, Ben felt the earth between his toes. He held her hand closely, walked back into her parents' house.

Chapter Four

"REMEMBER THE NAME you mentioned last week?" said McAteer on Monday morning as he stood before Ben in the Englishman's room. "Interesting enough. A tricky one for sure."

"Tricky as in, tricky enough not to give a roper twenty percent?" asked Ben.

"You haven't exactly roped him yet."

"But I can."

"Early days."

"You mean you're planning to put one over on me and just want to wait for my introduction," said Ben.

McAteer shuffled. "Something like that."

"I'd prefer to negotiate now."

"Hardly the right time, my boy," said McAteer. "As far as myself and the rest of the shop are concerned, there's around twenty or thirty thousand missing from the kitty thanks to Mr. Jergens. You're not the most popular man at the bar if you catch my drift."

"They blame me?" asked Ben.

"Always blame the new man. You should know that."

"I'm sure you encouraged it."

"Stoked it all I could," said McAteer. "Either way, we can always find another mark. Maybe not as promising a one as Dent. But it's a challenge to play a man like that. Bigger than rich that man. That's a hornet's nest. Won't necessarily work. We lose him we may end up with a percentage of nothing. Then we'd have to move again, except without you. And there you are, a bunco man without a team, without a friend, in a city you barely know."

"Very convincing," said Ben.

"It's my job."

"I'll take five thousand as a flat fee," said Ben.

McAteer offered his hand.

"Now what do you think you'll squeeze him for," said Ben.

"Best mark I've ever seen," said McAteer, smiling. "He might go for eighty, maybe more. If I were you, I'd have held out for ten."

Over the past two weeks, McAteer had sent telegrams to friends in Chicago, men ensconced for the season in fine lakeside hotels, mingling with the best of the out-of-towners, happy to provide information to one of their kind on one of their own. The recommendations returned quickly, and within days, McAteer began to amass impressive figures not simply about Dent, but about his wife's charitable endeavors, things that Rudolph Dent himself knew little about. Seven thousand dollars a year to both the Sanitary Commission and the Children's Aid Association. Ben read that Rudolph Dent, a graduate of St. Paul's and Yale, had been employed briefly by his father-in-law as a vice president in charge of sales in Carson Textiles. Yet, judging from the social registers, Dent was more inclined to summering in foreign climes than to the American work ethic. Best of all, said McAteer, was his list of acquaintances. For a man who was, by any standard of the world, very rich, his friends were names of nationally renowned wealth. A frequenter of the great Newport cottages, Dent was an intimate of Archibald Grayson, a man whose wealth was rumored to double with every six months of Europe's war. Ben had introduced a concept that made McAteer's brain whir.

Tickets were bought to Newport, reservations made for McAteer and Ben at the Bay View Resort, a vast white hotel topped by an American flag. It was exactly the sort of institution McAteer favored: large, but fairly exclusive, crawling with vacationing families hunting and pecking for invitations into Newport summer society. McAteer had never been to Newport in the summer. There was, he discovered, an appalling amount of money to be seen outside the hotel, yachts and yachtsmen, men who divided their days between lying down under the sun and inventing cocktails. Within an hour, he had learned that most of the local wealth passed through a dignified two-story, shingled building called the Newport Casino, though it had nothing to do with gambling. Their Bay View concierge, tipped a twenty, managed to arrange a prospect's tour for the two visitors the same morning.

Members of the Casino could choose among tennis, archery, billiards, bowling, dancing, tea parties, and theatricals. McAteer and Ben spent all morning waiting there to catch sight of Dent or Grayson, but they did not appear. But McAteer soon understood that even the elite had echelons and that Arch Grayson and his guests did not mingle, but sent for minglers.

At least the club was a center of gossip, and while McAteer chatted kindly with anyone who would share a minute of his or her time, most of the names thrown his way were unknown. However, when Grayson's name was mentioned, it was invariably with complaint. It seemed he spent a great deal of his time down at the airfield, had paid for most of its construction himself, and frequently buzzed his planes close to the yachts, drawing ire.

That afternoon, Ben and McAteer drove out to the local airfield between Newport and Jamestown. The place was empty, but in one of the hangars they found a young man, no more than nineteen, smoothing a propeller with sandpaper. McAteer walked up and down the closest airplane, running his hand over the chassis as if it were a favored mare.

"Like her?" asked the young man.

"I'm in the business myself," said McAteer.

"You know Mr. Grayson?"

"By reputation," said McAteer.

"He loves his planes," said the boy. "You fly?"

"I do not."

"He does," said the boy. "How about you?" he asked, addressing Ben.

Ben shook his head. "Feet on the ground," he said, ensuring that his accent was as unmistakably English as a pantomime duke's. "I was an army man."

The boy's eyes lit up. "In France?"

"That's right."

"You're English," he said, his tone little short of awe. "We're coming over soon. That's what I heard said, my brother says it's so, but Mr. Grayson says it won't happen yet."

"We'll be glad to have you when you get there."

"Is this a testing ground?" interrupted McAteer.

"Yes sir," said the boy. "Before anything is shipped to France, it's all run through here. Everything tested personally. I run the Penguins now. I reckon I could be up in a Spad by the end of the summer."

"Would you mind showing us around?" asked Ben.

As they followed the chattering boy, Ben recognized all the various planes from the skies over France. Voisins, Bréguets, Caudrons, Nieuports, Spads. For the first time he considered the insides of the machine, seeing past the painted markings and the shape that identified the chassis as friend or foe. Neither he, nor Chimer nor Douglas nor David, previously imagined that something complete could be constructed of parts delivered from other countries. Of course, now that he was thinking, he did not see how France was in a position to manufacture much of anything. But still, that airplane engines should come from the East Coast of America came as a shock. It was as if he had not fully escaped the war, but merely stepped from the stage to the prop shop. It made him feel immediately vulnerable again, to find that there was more cooperation and complicity between his real and adopted countries. That he might be offered up between the two with little fuss.

"There you have it," said McAteer after their tour as they walked back toward the ocean. "Right there."

"Where?" asked Ben.

"We have to make some presumptions for our work," said McAteer.

"First, does Dent know what kind of business Grayson is in? Even if he doesn't have some part of it, I'm sure he suspects how the man makes his money. If you know where a sure source of income comes from, wouldn't you want a part of it? Presumption number two, how much does he know about the intricacy of the business? In other words, which is your bait and which is your con? Do you bait him with the war and switch him to stocks or real estate, or vice versa?"

Ben shrugged. "You're biased," said McAteer. "You didn't like it, did you? You took one look at those planes and whoosh, your mind went traveling backward. Didn't it?"

Ben nodded. "It's all right for you," he said. "You can sit over here and you read your papers, and you see numbers and you don't think of faces. You don't think of faces do you?"

"Of course I don't," said McAteer. "Why the fuck should I?"

"Maybe you shouldn't," said Ben, his voice rising. "But I fucking do."

"You're being a fool," said McAteer, softly. He put his hand on Ben's arm. "Dent and Grayson already have something to do with the war. The joy of what you'd be doing is *pretending* to have something to do with it. Diverting funds. Money that would have been used to provide planes. Planes that drop bombs, report Allied positions, all the rest of it — you'd be stopping them from ever reaching France."

"You don't need to tell me," said Ben, calming.

"Yes I do," said McAteer.

McAteer sat in silence in the dining car as they traveled south to New York. He hadn't touched his tea, but had ordered a whiskey, obviously perturbed by their trip, steeped in thought.

"I'm not so sure," McAteer said. "Maybe you're right. Maybe it's too big."

"How?"

"Dent's connected to Grayson, Grayson to governments. If he rats, they seek, we're found. I'm in the stir, you're swung. And maybe you can't do it. Maybe it's too close to everything you've run away from."

"Why would he rat?" asked Ben, leaning forward, speaking softly to avoid reaching neighboring ears. "Not if we present our company as a competitor," continued Ben. "Grayson would be the last man that Dent would tell. Even after he loses his money. Dent's not desperate for cash. He'd swallow his loss without a word. That's what gentlemen do."

"I get it," said McAteer, looking closely at Ben, trying to figure his angle. "This is your gift. I turn it down, you still owe me the rope. You'd need to go looking for a mark all over again. You lose your five thousand."

"Of course," said Ben. "But yesterday you said Dent was perfect. Now you want to run. Who's right, you yesterday, or you today? I'll make you a bet. You wait till tomorrow and you'll agree with yourself again."

McAteer laughed. "I like that," he said. "That's good. You're getting better."

"At least work through the ifs," said Ben.

"What would you do," asked McAteer, "if he was your mark?"

"I'd find a way to get Katherine to introduce me, or introduce myself. I'd bring you to meet him, make him wait. I'd bait him with something obvious and simple, attractive to a Chicago man who likes to visit New York: Manhattan real estate, horse racing, nightclubs, a bit of East Coast glamour. Then I'd switch him to the war."

"War?" asked McAteer.

"That's what it is," said Ben, coldly. "I'd offer him engines, doesn't matter what kind, motors, things they need over in France. I should know that. We'd just have to figure what to show the man and where to find it." Stop one shipment, Ben thought, and perhaps save one life.

"Of course we're not going to let him go," said McAteer, plucking his whiskey from the tray. He took a long swig and watched Ben smile to know that he had merely been brought around to seconding McAteer's intentions.

Chapter Five

WITH RUDOLPH DENT in New York, Ben tacitly accepted Katherine's lack of time for him. During the day, he imagined Dent lying on the sheets Dent had bought, in the apartment Dent had rented, a new car parked outside. Dent lying on top of Katherine Howells and the pretense that he did not exist. And what he found himself dreaming of was not only the smooth skin of Katherine but the wallet of Rudolph Dent.

As McAteer advised, Ben followed their prospect as Dent visited with other women, but Ben did not consider telling Katherine. Not only would such knowledge be impossible to explain, but she was a pragmatist. Ben was sure that she would not care what a man did out of her sight. Dent eyed every woman he walked past, and occasionally the stare was returned. A very confident man. But when Katherine and Dent were together, Ben noted that Dent displayed the deference of a man in love, though she was just an actress, just beauty, enchantment. Ben knew he might lose this woman if they chose Dent as a mark. Yet he did care for her, at least to the extent that he worried about himself without her.

When Dent did not require her, Ben took Katherine out to dinner and watched her intently, waiting to orchestrate his introduction to Dent. There was no hiding in shady restaurants, the domain of urban affairs. They went about openly, and Ben regretted that the closest thing he had had to a normal life was about to be temporarily absorbed by one of McAteer's games. Katherine's was almost a fierce face, very proud, but it broke into an easy smile. Her deportment was perfect: ramrod back, elegant gait. Her face was strong-jawed, nose small, lips wide and always painted a bright red and set beneath a fashionably short cut, black hair swept backward. And yet when they were in bed together and she lay on her stomach and tilted her head to study him, Ben could see only the child in her. With everyone else, another age was on display, a willingness to convince others she was older than she seemed.

McAteer had told him that he would have to wait until the appropriate moment to finagle a meeting with Dent. Since Ben already knew about Dent, he believed he could ask Katherine for an introduction under the guise of business, or else orchestrate an accidental drink together, flashing faux medals or some other point of conversation, or return and rely on McAteer. Yet Ben did not have to rely on any such awkwardness. Two days later, he awoke to the sound of Katherine retching in the bathroom.

"What is it?" he asked.

"What do you think?"

Ben wondered if it could possibly be his child. Wondered if he might actually be able to create. Small waves of sympathy and possibility broke within him. He thought back to their afternoon in the woods near her parents' property in Westchester.

"If I'm going to have the child," said Katherine later that afternoon, "it might as well have a rich daddy."

Ben didn't argue, but thought for a moment. "Does Dent know you're with someone else?"

"Of course."

"He knows about me?"

"Sure," said Katherine. "He knows all about you. As much as I know."

"You talk about me?"

"You know about him; why shouldn't he know about you?" said Katherine. "He thinks it's normal. He's very sophisticated. I'm young, you're young, he's older. He's got a wife, you haven't. He's glad I have a friend. He'd rather I had one than two or three."

Ben paused in admiration. "Perhaps I should meet him?" said Ben.

"That's what he said."

"He did?" asked Ben. "He's a gentleman then, isn't he?"

Ben's nerves were running like a confluence of electric rails; he felt confidently alive. The past did not feel close. Before going up to the Hotel Astor, he watched trucks and wagons filled with glass panes arriving in front of a building's skeleton close to Sixth Avenue. Windows, wrapped in canvas sheets, were carefully pulled from flatbeds and carried inside. The wind that ran through the building would soon be shunned.

It had been a dreadful meeting for Ben. His nerves ran amok and yet the excuse was there. Katherine had confessed that she'd told Dent Ben had been in France. Everything about the apartment in the Hotel Astor had signaled a surfeit of money. The rich distanced themselves from noise, thought Ben. They wanted to hear only their own feet resounding across marble entrances. Servants wore soft-soled shoes to avoid disturbance. Windows were made of thick, expensive glass and carpets ran from wall to wall, muffling echoes. Ben decided that wealth and silence were synonymous and the epiphany rocked him.

He opened the windows, stirred the ice in his whiskey, put a disc on the Victrola, cranked it, and did much that could have offended the prospective mark. And he was torn between the wish to offend Dent now, to show that wealth and silence were opposite to his desires, and the greater need to perform perfectly, to tempt him so that McAteer might feast and Katherine be torn from him. But he played it well enough, waited for the offer he knew Dent would make, parlayed it quickly into a meeting with McAteer.

It was a spectacular automobile, a Jordan loaned to McAteer for the week by a friend at a dealership across the river in New Jersey. Sleek with lines usually reserved for cedar yachts, it was the color of a bruised berry, smelling strongly of polished walnut and padded leather with enough room in the back for a pack of foxhounds.

When Ben had been picked up, he noted the chauffeur was the

same Negro bandleader who had taken him for the extra ten dollars the night he first took Henry Jergens to Harlem.

"How are you?" asked Ben.

"Busy," called the man from the front of the car.

"Don't you owe me ten dollars?" asked Ben.

"For what?"

"From Sensie's."

"That was your money, was it?" he asked.

Ben smiled. "We could have split it."

"You got taken, not me," said the man.

When they arrived in front of the Hotel Astor, Rudolph Dent entered the automobile and stretched out his legs. "Quite a car, old man," he complimented. "Did your government lend it to you?"

"No," said Ben. "It's Mr. O'Keefe's. He likes a good motor on the weekends. Fussy about his comfort."

Throughout the remainder of the drive, Dent continued to inquire after Mr. O'Keefe. Ben repeated McAteer's tale of his alter ego. Since his wife's death from tuberculosis thirty years ago, O'Keefe had focused obsessively on making money from real estate and had only kept an apartment in New York since the outbreak of war in Europe. Dent never asked the obvious. If O'Keefe really had made his money in real estate, then why did he either employ, or at least work beside, Ben, a man whom Katherine insisted was working with the British government? The question hung over their conversation. Ben never addressed the matter and Dent was, as McAteer had expected, too much of a gentleman to inquire directly.

They talked occasionally of Katherine, agreeing not to mention their mutual business to her, but considered her in a good-natured way, talking about the strength of men and the unfortunate side effects of womanhood. Both agreed that a termination would be the best thing for Katherine, but if she insisted, then Ben agreed that the child should be his in name. Besides, he had already signed the paper.

"I'm glad it's over and done with," Dent had said. "A man like you. You're serious, Mr. Newcombe. I'm afraid I'm built for frivolity. I'm overly fond of the frolic."

It only confirmed what Ben already knew about himself. He had indeed changed. Chimer hadn't acknowledged it, nor any other of the lads, only American strangers. Ben remembered the day of his fight with Chimer, the only time they had come to blows in fifteen years of friendship. In France, they had all been obsessed by food. There had been too many flavorless days of cadging about. They called La Bassée the Egg and Chip Front since laying hens were as common as lice. The field cooks only had two large vats in which everything was prepared. Tea inevitably reeked of meat or eggs, or worse, it stank of the water it was made from, carried about in petrol cans that had the taste of a London bus. Chimer said he could taste the difference between Shell and BP tins. If that weren't bad enough, the cooks were under orders to purify the water with chloride of lime. All Ben could remember was the mild burn of chemicals in the back of his throat.

Ben had been popular earlier in the week. He had found a cellar in the farmyard where the farmer had hidden a cache of absinthe and brandy. He'd made a deal with the serving girl at the estaminet, swapping bottles for strawberry jam, when no soldier in France had tasted anything but plum and apple for months. And yet, while out trying to trade absinthe for a live chicken, Chimer had finished all their jam without him. When Ben had challenged him, Chimer had said, "What's the scene for? Why don't you just go ask the girl for more?"

That evening, they had been playing cards together, just the four of them, at a corner table in the estaminet. Ben had been treated royally. The serving girl kept their beer flowing. Among the boys they could barely speak a hundred words of French, but she hung about their table and entertained them with her fractured English. Chimer began the talk every time she left the table.

"Go on then, Ben," he had said. "Go on after her. She can't be worth more than a bottle of brandy."

Douglas had laughed. "You're slowing down," he had said. "Six months ago you'd already be wiping yourself clean."

"Asking if she had a sister," David had added.

"Go on, Abu," Chimer had continued. "Go stick a cork in her."

"Listen to the chattering virgins," Ben had said. He had smiled, took the ragging, but began to cheat at cards, directing every device he knew against Chimer. Within the hour, he had cleaned him of a month's wages. It didn't really matter, because no one went forward to the front line with money in his pocket. It was considered bad luck. They'd all wondered who'd thought that one up. The owners of the estaminets? But still, no one challenged the superstition, so what did it matter that he had taken Chimer's money? It was only for silent satisfaction. But Ben had felt aggrieved at how his friends thought of him. That he was still Abu Abu, the heartless man.

It did not occur to Ben until he saw Chimer eyeing the girl across the room that the true problem was that Chimer had fallen for her. He watched closely to be sure. It was a very unusual situation. Skinny, shy, and picky, Chimer never liked a soul. Every time she came close, Chimer would look away, then attempt a spasm of French, laugh with the rest of the lads, follow her figure as she left, and then immediately turn on Ben to cover his own interest. Ben waited until the sergeant blew his whistle and turned them out of the estaminet in favor of the officers, then walked up to her. Well aware that Chimer was watching, he took her by the hand in the emptying room. She smiled, so, catching Chimer's eye, he leaned in and planted a kiss on the side of her neck.

Chimer had been waiting for him outside the estaminet. Ben did not have a chance to say a word before Chimer swung and caught him in the mouth, bloodying his lip against his teeth. The others, confused, held their friend back.

"You know," Chimer had said, pointing at Ben. "You bloody well know what that was for."

Two days later they had gone to the front line. It made Ben want to weep to think that their friendship had not lasted out the war. They were all right that night in the open, in the shell hole; they'd been laughing, hadn't they? They'd been friends again. Ben couldn't really remember; he could only recall the argument and the sting of blood on his lips and the fury in Chimer's face. Why had such an unhappy memory etched itself so deeply? Why only the cruel words and not the love they had felt for each other? Chimer would have liked to have seen New York. All three of them would have had stiff necks from looking up. And Chimer would have seen that Ben had truly changed. But he hadn't even mentioned it in New York. Didn't believe that Ben could treat a woman without the pawing and the flirting, or that he could keep an interest in just one girl. For men could change. Ben was sure of it. Even a man like Dent could sense that they were not alike.

"Katherine's still a good girl," Dent was saying. "Really a fine-looking woman. Ziegfeld will snap her up. I bet you. If she gets her figure back. If it's the kind of thing she wants. You never know with a woman. I told you I'd been through this before. Last one was taken care of privately. So much easier hiring a trusted professional. Really, rather an easy operation."

Chapter Six

BEN FORCED DENT to wait another day for his meeting. When McAteer was finally introduced it was as Mr. Julius O'Keefe, an older gentleman, not too short of retirement, with a gold watch fob, spectacles, simple leather shoes, stiff white collar, and red bow tie. He wasn't supposed to seem as wealthy as Arch Grayson, but to retain a roughness to suggest he had worked slowly up the ladder and not been propelled shell-like. Still, McAteer was now the sort of man rich enough to wear silk suspenders even when he wasn't going to take off his jacket. Dent shook his hand as McAteer leaned heavily on a cherry cane.

"Delighted," said Dent.

McAteer grunted. The Negro chauffeur outfitted in goggles and brown peaked hat stood beside the Jordan. Dent slid into the backseat and Ben followed. The mahogany paneling gleamed; the pleated French leather smelled new. Ben watched Dent, but he didn't look twice and smeared the bottom of his feet against the Oriental rugs. He was entirely accustomed to this treatment.

That Sunday morning they honked and fought their way over the Brooklyn Bridge, and drove onward, past row after row of prettified suburbia, where the roots of New England had come all the way south, trying to broach Manhattan with white clapboard houses and recessed yards. Out past Bedford, the roadster pulled into a gas station. Two attendants came to fill the tanks and wipe the smear of insects from the windscreen. There were murmurs of appreciation for the Jordan. A pair of young men looked with admiration from the seats of their rusted Model A Ford.

><

A small hunting and bathing club situated lakeside, Pine Ridge was populated by a stolid mixture of stockbrokers and local inheritors, including an old colleague of McAteer's. The clubhouse was built from burnished oak and stood there for precious little reason other than that men liked to talk and drink away from women.

"So," said McAteer as they descended from the car and walked toward the club, "Sergeant Newcombe tells me that you've a friend in common."

"*Sergeant* Newcombe?" asked Dent.

"Me," said Ben.

Ben watched the emotions slowly pass across Dent's face. Since he had first met Ben, it must never have occurred to him that he might rank higher than private. Dent probably did not expect his maid to be a librettist, nor his cook a country alderman.

"You're going to have to forgive me," said Dent. "Katherine never told me you were a sergeant."

"Best she doesn't know much," said Ben.

Dent's admiration increased when the two men changed for the small beach. Ben undressed in front of Dent. Dent was presuming it was simply a British habit left over from school, but all thought disintegrated when his eyes ran across Ben's scars. Dent was polite enough to pretend to ignore them, but the current between them changed. How could a man doubt such cruel scars, or the story through which they were explained? In Dent's judgment, war had dragged an ordinary man upward and put him down on an equal plane. As Ben swam in the lake, Dent and McAteer leaned back in green Adirondack chairs and let the sun come down on them.

"What's Sergeant Newcombe doing in New York?" asked Dent.

"There's a war over here too," said McAteer. "You don't fight it with shells, but words and money. He's not out of the fight just because he got shot through."

"So Newcombe does work for the government?" asked Dent.

"Even soldiers make excellent salesmen," explained McAteer.

><

After Ben dried off, he joined the small party for a lunch of sand-wiches and beer served over chipped ice.

Dent asked the Englishman, "What do you do over here?"

Ben looked at McAteer for permission to speak.

Once he had received a nod, the Englishman explained, "What I do is compete for products needed in Europe."

"Compete with whom?" asked Dent sitting upright in his chair. Ben presumed he was wondering if they strove directly against Grayson.

"The firm we run works under the name 'Bowman and Company.' Bauman, Bowman, a common enough switch at Ellis Island, German to American. This attracts people you would not necessarily wish to attract."

"Germans," said Dent.

Ben nodded. "I am sure you know that there are German ships blockaded in New York Harbor until the end of the war. Well, ships entail ships' crews. They still arouse a lot of sympathy for their cause."

Ben paused to sip his beer and let McAteer take the reins.

"For a year now, we have made false sales to German agents. It is common enough," said McAteer. "They do the same to us. They buy, they pay, we do not provide. The company closes, declares bankruptcy, opens again under a new name and looks for new German buyers."

"And now?" asked Dent.

"Our commission from the British government is almost up," said McAteer. "But we still have the original merchandise. The bait, as it were; what the German agents see before they make their bids, what they never get."

"Why isn't your equipment returning to England?" asked Dent.

"That was never its purpose. We have not been paid in over a year," said McAteer.

"Governments are unreliable," concurred Dent. "Never more so than in times of war."

"But we believe," said McAteer, "that the time has come when we deserve payment. Perhaps my own country will soon become involved. Perhaps we shall be forgotten about altogether. We would like to take some satisfaction from our work before it is all over."

"What are you looking for?"

"Not just a buyer," said McAteer. "That's easy enough. We need a seller. We're too well known within the circles."

"What are you selling?"

"A large array," said McAteer vaguely. "Mostly mechanical, practical, the indispensable. If you were interested, I'd be happy to give you the details."

"How much are we talking about?" said Dent.

"That depends," said McAteer. "We have considerable amounts of merchandise. Our deal was to either sell it forward to the English at the end of our tenure or to repay them at cost. Originally, it was valued at a hundred thousand dollars. What London doesn't know is that the market cost has risen considerably in New York over the last year. If we could repay them their money, we would be free to sell it forward at market value. Perhaps double that."

"How much have you raised?" asked Dent.

"My own accounts are monitored," said McAteer. "Mr. Newcombe is investing five thousand dollars. I have another twenty thousand in a more discreet account. I would like to split the rest of the payment between no more than two investors. It will be a very fast transaction. It can be paid off in one day, sold on the next. Your return will be anywhere between sixty and one hundred percent."

Ben could read Dent's face. Too cautious to speak definitively and too curious to let go. They didn't push. On the way back in the Jordan, Dent said, "Let's go have a drink together." McAteer excused himself on business.

"What do you say Ben?" insisted Dent.

They drank beer together back in Manhattan early in the afternoon. Beer paid for by Dent and not a mention was made of engines or armaments. Dent's attitude toward him had changed. He was now a veteran soldier, an automatic hero. Ben felt Dent trying to forge some vague brotherhood between them, if not over business, then over Katherine, all in search of intimate knowledge of war.

He tapped a finger on the back of his hand, then pointed at Ben. "How did you get that scar?"

"Which one?"

"The one on the hand. Was it in the war?"

Ben nodded.

"A German?"

Ben nodded again.

"Mouth-to-mouth combat?" asked Dent with the suggestion of a smirk.

Ben managed to smile.

"Sorry," apologized Dent. "I can't imagine." He looked Ben in the eyes. "I don't think I'm going to continue in our deal."

"Why's that?" asked Ben, not allowing the panic to show on his face.

"It's a money deal," said Dent. "They almost always go wrong. *In and out* normally becomes *stuck for a year*. Basically, one has to ask oneself, can one spare the money, and then, does one need the money? And then, why me?"

"Why you?" asked Ben. "Probably because I don't know many that have the money to take on a large piece and I thought you could afford it."

"I can afford it," said Dent.

Ben shrugged. "I'm not twisting any arms. I know I'm just a sergeant but I'm getting my dues one way or another."

Dent nodded. "That I can understand. We'll talk more about it. At dinner, say tonight?"

Away from Dent, McAteer was visibly energized. Back in his frayed blazer and pale trousers, his O'Keefe potter had been transformed into the vigorous strides of the determined.

"You're still for it?" asked Ben.

"Of course."

"Even if he isn't?"

"He's moaning?"

Ben nodded. "Do we go ahead and get things organized anyway?"

"We'll take the risk," said McAteer. "Besides, I believe I can run the whole shop for a couple of thousand dollars."

"How?" asked Ben.

Later that day, down on Mulberry Street, the mint man passed by McAteer, the fresh scent from the crushed leaves momentarily dismissing the omnipresent city reek of warm horse piss. McAteer sat on a stoop, one step beneath Ben. He bit into a fresh baked sweet potato. In front of him was a man selling squid from large tin buckets. Whenever they frothed, he sprinkled them with a watering can. Occasionally Ben caught the briny whiff. In the one block between Grand and Broome Streets stood the debris of the Saturday Bazaar. Lazy crowds walked past women clutching infants, young men in pairs linked at the arm. Italian women moved about bareheaded, or in lace scarves, or three-cornered shawls, returning home before the dead Catholic quiet of Sunday evening descended. McAteer looked south, past gutters filled with purple cabbage leaves and the gleaming foil of candy wrappers.

"There he goes," said McAteer, and they rose to follow.

Ignazio Mincione was a lank-haired man with a bony face and a choleric disposition. He had the look of one who took sick too easily, one suspicious of what he could see and afraid of what he could not. McAteer had known him for over twenty years, and while most of his family had remained in the building trade they had worked in Abruzzo, Mincione did not wish to work outside. Instead, he had learned how to handle a truck, employed by De La Rosa and Sons, driving munitions consignments down from upstate to the depot of Black Tom Island, across the Hudson in New Jersey. He had not seemed surprised to see McAteer and offered his guests the two chairs in the tiny, dark apartment. For five minutes he sat listening before finally saying, "I'm not going to give you my truck."

"We don't want your truck," said McAteer. "Have you ever made a delivery late?"

"Sure," said Mincione. "I blew three tires coming down from Saratoga."

"How late were you?"

"Eighteen hours."

"What did they do?"

"They docked me half a day."

"What's that worth to you?" asked Ben.

"Five dollars."

"Say you were a whole day late, what would they take?"

"The whole day, eleven dollars."

"I'll pay you thirty for being late," said McAteer. "Better still, you'll spend that night at home."

"What happens to the merchandise?"

"That's the beauty," said McAteer. "Not a thing. You get it back the next morning as you had it. My word on that."

The happy, bobbing heads of the two colleagues joined the thousand other hats moving up and down, streaming through the streets.

"The place where Mincione drops it off," said Ben. "what's it like?"

"You're going to love it," said McAteer. "Everyone loves it. It's right under city hall."

"Under?" asked Ben. "Underground?" Ben didn't like the sound of it. Beneath might mean silence, darkness, a host of experiences Ben wished to deter. He could hear the lads right beside him. But they didn't say a word either.

"Wait till you see it," said McAteer.

Chapter Seven

WHEN DENT HAD mentioned having dinner, Ben had presumed it would simply be the two of them. Even when Dent had reminded him to dress formally as they said their goodbyes, Ben had not altered his expectations. A tuxedo was no stranger in Dent's world than a cloth cap in Ben's. They shared a taxi from the Astor to the Navarre. Dent rolled the windows down to let a small breeze keep them from dampening their collars. To start an evening with a dark collar was as unforgivable as ending the night with a clean one.

"I think you'll enjoy my friends," said Dent.

"Friends?" asked Ben, leaning forward to let the wind ruffle his hair. The taxi stopped and the summer suffocation descended with all the thickness of the traffic.

"Just a few of us. Men only," said Dent. "A small dinner I'm giving on behalf of the deputy ambassador."

"From England?" said Ben, in shock.

"From France," said Dent.

Ben passed a block in silence. He was not ready, not composed. He wondered what Dent suspected. Was this a test of his own position, or was he being brought along as a fellow ally in the war of exportation currently being waged on the East Coast? Perhaps Dent already knew that Ben was a fraud, that this would be a public humiliation. Or was Dent merely trying to impress him? Ben realized that he might prove the undoing of the entire con. He was glad, at least, that he was there alone, and that McAteer would not fall with him. Either way, if Ben came up with an excuse to stop the taxi and beg off dinner, Dent's suspicions, if he had any, would be confirmed.

><

"Is the deputy ambassador a friend of yours?" asked Ben.

"Acquaintance," said Dent. "We've done business before, with a mutual friend." Archibald Grayson, thought Ben. "I told him you were in the war. Said you were now fund-raising this side. Let's leave it at that, shall we?"

"Of course," said Ben.

"Maybe you should have worn your uniform," said Dent. "Don't most of your lot put it on when they're rattling the pot for change?"

Ben shook his head. "Not in our regiment," he improvised. "Besides, strictly speaking, my business is unconnected to the government."

Dent shrugged. "Here's to the long life of the tuxedo as the American uniform."

At dinner, a tidy party of eight, Ben shook the hand of the deputy ambassador firmly. A small, elegant man, wearing silk gloves and a top hat, the deputy ambassador had arrived with pleasant rings of smile lines surrounding his mouth. He had, to Ben's relief, not the slightest semblance of military bearing but was scrupulously polite. Ben could see how he must have many variations of smile and paid close attention to determine if he could differentiate the meaning of one from another.

"Monsieur Newcombe," he said, with the twitch of a grin that suggested he already knew all that he needed to know. "It is a pleasure to meet you. Allow me to introduce you to . . . but perhaps you already know each other. Our new arrival from London. Major Sanderson? We have one of yours over here."

Ben froze, took a sharp breath, and managed to nod at the approaching man. Tall and slightly emaciated, Major Sanderson could only have looked more aristocratic had he worn a monocle.

Sanderson dipped his eyes from over the constellation of medals attached to his breast pocket and surveyed Ben as the deputy ambassador turned to greet another guest. "Your name?"

"Newcombe, sir," choked Ben.

"We haven't met yet? Have we?"

"No sir. I fear I rank a few notches beneath you. More in the field than most."

"Good, good," said Sanderson. "And Mr. Dent tells me you were in France."

Ben could feel a large bead of sweat creep slowly down his spine. "Yes sir."

"Where?"

"La Bassée," said Ben. Don't let him have been there. Don't let him know a thing.

"Who was your CO?"

"Captain Traven, sir," said Ben.

"Jonathan Traven?"

"Yes sir."

"How is Captain Traven?"

"Dead sir, near Loos."

Major Sanderson nodded. Ben breathed out quietly. He saw Dent approaching and turned his body to allow the American to enter the conversation. "Shall we have some dinner?" asked Dent.

Sanderson seemed satisfied enough, even slightly disturbed by his news. At least Ben looked the part, deferential, the answers were right, for in truth, Ben had barely lied.

Dinner was a formal affair, eight men at an oblong table, Ben sitting on one end. To his own relief, he could take little part in the conversation, since it was conducted, for the most part, in French. He caught the occasional word that he had picked up during his months near La Bassée, but he soon realized he had learned only imperatives: "Give me a beer." "Wash these clothes." "Sit on my lap." He decided to keep quiet. He heard Grayson's name mentioned often, along with the words for *thanks* and *planes*. Sanderson's French was heavily accented, but Ben thought deliberately so, as if he had made a conscious decision to speak a foreign language while remaining identifiably English.

><

Occasionally, the deputy ambassador attempted to draw Ben into the conversation. Wary of Sanderson, Ben lowered his eyes when he spoke and did his best impression of a man humbled by the elegance of company he found himself among. It was an easy enough stance, buffeted as Ben was by courses of consommé, *pommes parisienne*, Camembert, and cognac. He could feel the boys around him, each holding their breath on his behalf. There were many toasts, all to the end of war. Ben drank copiously. There were no pledges against the Germans, nor did any man use the term *Hun*. In an odd sense, Ben felt he had more in common with all these men than with English civilians that he had encountered on leave. A total absence of bellicosity.

The only time conversation did turn toward the subject of Germany, Ben was fascinated.

"What can you do here in the city?" the deputy ambassador addressed the table. "There is too much money moving at too high a speed to know precisely where it is coming from."

Ben was both worried and excited to hear it. Dent would not be surprised at the pace of their own business. He suddenly began to feel confident. If he could only negotiate his path safely to the end of dinner, Dent would never have reason to doubt McAteer.

"I am not sure about the exact figure," said the deputy, "but we think there is somewhere in the region of one hundred and fifty million dollars moving from Germany to America. Now that the Germans have no transatlantic cable, it will be hard for them to know how to distribute it. Is it for sabotage? Is it to fund strikes? Is it to buy munitions?"

The rest listened to the politician talk.

"Please excuse me for saying so, Mr. Dent, but the Americans are of little help. The agencies lack, how do you say, funding? This is a continent with the sensibility of an island."

Major Sanderson coughed in agreement and then turned the

conversation back into French with his broad accent, alienating Ben from the intricacies that followed.

The conversation did not turn back to English until after cigars were passed and smoked.

"Will you join us for a sail?" asked the deputy ambassador as they stood, addressing Ben.

"When?" asked Ben.

"Now," said Dent.

Sanderson and the rest of the gentlemen excused themselves, thanking the deputy ambassador for his generosity. As they left the Navarre, the deputy ambassador linked his arm in Ben's. He had seen the custom often enough in France, but still, it seemed most strange to Ben to be walking arm in arm with another man, let alone the deputy ambassador. "I did not mention it in front of the other men," he now said. "I have to presume that you lost many friends. I, too, have lost two sons." He looked Ben in the eye and Ben nodded.

"What will happen next?" asked Ben. "Will America come over?"

The Frenchman shrugged. "We can only hope. Pacifism makes so much sense until your own house is occupied. Even you cannot know how that feels. You have land in England, perhaps a house?"

Ben shook his head.

"A wise man. Now we shall show them all Black Tom," said the deputy ambassador, as if Ben knew exactly what he was talking about. But Ben had not been in New York long enough to know. He had heard the name before, from both McAteer and the truck driver Mincione, knew it was where deliveries bound for Europe passed through, but no more. Instead, he gave a knowing, silent smile and continued walking westward, no longer arm in arm, to where a chauffeur waited beside a limousine.

They were driven to the piers of the Hudson, just opposite Thirty-fourth Street. The launch they took skirted the western edge of Manhattan, passed by eighty interned German vessels, and swept toward the New Jersey shore. Ben was fascinated by the strength of the electric bulb that carved into the lapping darkness, barely noticing their path as it seemed to take them toward the triangular shape of lights that marked the railroad terminus. Only when the boat boy threw his rope over the stanchion on a pier of Black Tom Island, a half mile from the Terminus, did Ben bother looking up.

Attached to the Jersey shore by a series of heavy wooden piers, the island was a man-made construction. Shallow-bottomed barges the size of football fields were moored alongside Black Tom. Tracks had been run to the end of the pier, behind which lurked a rail yard of locomotives, some of which were still warm to Ben's passing touch.

"Evening," said the deputy ambassador.

Two men dipped their hats. "*Bon soir.*" Their party was expected.

"Have you been here before?" asked Dent, dropping back to walk beside Ben.

Ben shook his head. "Mr. O'Keefe is always here, but they've never allowed me over."

Dent seemed pleased by the information, as if he had been able to give a treat to a favored nephew.

They passed through the doors of one of fourteen great warehouses, covered in an inky tar paper that blocked the moonlight.

"Russian, English, or French," explained Dent. "No Germans allowed. They check your breath for bratwurst at the gates." He waited for Ben to laugh, but his new friend was too absorbed in the new sights. The warehouse was quiet. Only a group of stevedores remained, sitting outside a small concrete guardhouse.

"Is that bombproof?" asked Ben.

"Hardly," said Dent. "It's where the men go for a smoke. Can't have them tossing butts into any old passing barge. Airplane engines in the back," explained Dent. "This isn't just carbines and ammunition. This is the entire operation of a war."

They passed along one of the great aisles of the warehouse. Every hundred yards brought a new variation of packaging. Great cardboard boxes, canvas-covered containers, metal cases sealed with red straps. "See," said Dent, pointing to one pile. "Tents, twelve thousand pairs of boots. Fifty thousand spades. It's hard to make real money on what everyone understands. There are a lot of men in this world who know what a boot is worth."

"Of course."

"But if you didn't do what you do, I could look you in the eye and tell you an airplane costs ten thousand dollars and you wouldn't know any better."

"Doesn't a flier know any better?"

"There's an army for the ground, a navy for the sea, but nothing for the air. Not over here, not yet. Regulation is rather loose. The ambassador knows better. Unfortunately. Here," said Dent as they walked between the vast rolling doors through to the neighboring warehouse, "this appeals to the boy in me."

It was one of the stranger sights that Ben had seen. On one side of the vast warehouse, nothing but countless sacks of sugar. On the other, endless ordered rows of ammunition. Small-caliber arms, eight-inch, ten-inch shells, the great Jack Johnson shells, half as high as a man, stacked as shiny individuals. Three-quarters of the ammunition for the Western Front passed through Black Tom Island. Fuck, said Ben, look at that. *Look* at that. Christ all-bloody-mighty.

"You could buy every last shell in this warehouse today and it would be filled by the weekend," said the deputy ambassador, turning toward them. "Endless demand — Italian, Russian, English, French. Each of us with an open checkbook."

Ben was horrified. He felt a deep panic take hold in his stomach, like the automatic revulsion after taking a swig of curdled milk. The war wouldn't end. All sympathy he had felt for Dent and his toast for peace evaporated immediately. This was not about bringing a quick end to hostilities, this was a corner grocery store, stocked from floor to ceiling, knowing a mob of customers had their noses pressed against the windows. Dent's engines were in the back, and what else did he push? What had Katherine said, that German U-boats were in Newport? What did Dent and Grayson sell them? And what was Ben doing? Was he helping or hindering the war? Was he profiting from his own pain? He was furious. He walked out of the warehouse before anyone could turn and notice his reaction. Dent looked over his shoulder, the deputy ambassador held up his hand to wave him back, but so determined was Ben's walk that neither protested.

Outside he didn't know what to do. He walked among the loco-motives, then back to the doors of the warehouse, trying to make sense of the sight. Calm yourself, he thought, do nothing but calm yourself. He thought of Chimer and the rest of the boys, and others like him, sole survivors of their tiny groups. He thought of his counterpart in Germany, a man like him, with his doubts and wishes, and bore him no ill will. But who to blame? Who to harm? It was an impossibly large conflagration, an over-whelming feeling of finding nothing good and nothing evil about you. Ben could no longer differentiate war from nature. All the anger flowed from him, alchemized into a desultory sense of having been set adrift.

He waited a few more minutes, then wandered back into the ware-house toward Dent and the deputy ambassador, both engrossed in conversation amid the glimmering beauty.

"Everything all right?" asked Dent.

"Just the boat trip," explained Ben, putting his hand to his stomach. "A bit on the queasy side."

Dent smiled and Ben looked upward, his eyes attracted by the shimmering studs in the ceiling high above.

"A system of sprinklers," said the deputy ambassador, following his gaze. "It would be, how do you say? *Ce serait une situation inquié-tante*. Mr. Dent, a translation?"

"Like pissing against a forest fire. Near every shell that heads to Europe comes through here," said Dent in hushed tones of awe.

"Nearly," said Ben, and Dent allowed himself a small conspirato-rial smile.

"How do we sleep at night?" mused the deputy ambassador, pointing out toward Manhattan. "I would like to move the embassy a little farther east. Perhaps Bermuda."

>●<

For the first time that evening Ben began to think what a wonderful thing it would be to take money out of the hands of those who were spending it on arms. Perhaps, in a small way, he would do more to save a life in France than if he had stayed three thousand miles away in the mud and guts of Flanders.

Chapter Eight

THE HEAT IN the city had become so intense that night that even Ben was beginning to wish he were somewhere else. He looked up at the skies when he heard the familiar distant drone and traced the passage of a small plane through the blueness. Airmen always bundled up. He imagined the coolness of the altitude, the cold wind drying skin. He remembered training, before going on the line, all of them huddled in their bell tents in France and the sudden sound of an airplane, the first break of a blast, and John Chandler wounded before he was even on the line. Back in England with some infected scratch, a day after coming to France, pierced by a tiny fragment of a dropped bomb. Ben remembered the soldier had been disappointed.

There followed swampy days when the sympathy of strangers in the city was aroused by the common tragedy of heat. Deaths and prostrations were announced daily on the front page of the *New York Times*, and Ben spent his early mornings in a tub of water as warm as English beer, head lolling back, forehead hot. Again and again, he talked his situation through with Chimer, Douglas, and David. Among them, they agreed that nothing was to be done but to press forward.

No child slept through the night. All the mothers in his neighborhood were turning their days inside out, taking the children walking at dawn and dusk, the sidewalks full of red-faced babies, weeping in protest at the endless heat. On the few trips Ben had made to the stifling theater, he had watched Katherine's makeup melt during the evening's show. The whole cast seemed to teeter between good humor at the impossibility of performance and bad-tempered snapping at the backstage boys. Wherever you went in the city, the smell was of men and horses and garbage. Every jacket that Ben owned now held the musty smell of wet wool, the revival of odor. And those who had to move, to work, did so with regret, for even money seemed heavier, danker, soggy green notes that captured the perspiration when passed from hand to hand. Ben began to practice the art of sitting still in shadows, calculating down to the last step the amount of energy he needed to trace Rudolph Dent.

As Ben was emerging from the tub, McAteer rapped on the bathroom door and entered, not waiting for an invitation. Ben dried himself with a raggedy towel as McAteer peppered him with questions about his tightrope walk with Major Sanderson and his brief tour of Black Tom Island.

"What's in there?"

"His engines. Munitions, tents, boots, sugar, spades. Anything that you can think of. Everything that I used to think of. Socks. You can never tell when you're going to need more socks."

McAteer looked at him strangely as Ben pulled his shirt over his head.

"And there was a stack of jerkins. Good ones. Beaver or something. We could have done with some of those."

"But what do you think?" said McAteer.

"I think he'll buy anything you put in front of him if you give him the right price. Why wouldn't he?"

"So what's wrong with that?"

"If he goes for it, it's too easy," said Ben.

"Sometimes easy is easy," said McAteer.

"And sometimes it's a fucking disaster."

"If he goes for it, it's too easy. That's a contradiction. If he doesn't go for it, it's hardly likely that it's easy, now is it? You do your part," said McAteer, taking his leave. "I'll take care of the rest. If you're having trouble falling asleep at night, just count to five thousand, one dollar at a time."

At the bathing club, Ben remembered, he had undressed in front of Dent as McAteer had instructed. Let his eyes see those scars, McAteer had said. Ben had nodded. He had understood. Big lies can be carried inside small truths. And Dent's eyes had absorbed the white marks on his torso and Ben felt he could have told a dozen lies in a single sentence and Dent's head would have bobbed up and down. Despite the surprise of the deputy ambassador, Ben was still sure that he was liked by Dent, though the feeling was not reciprocated. Ben thought Dent the sort who reckoned the world just rolled happily from one generation to the next, as it had for his family. He looked as though grief and pain were like lice and rickets, afflictions for the lesser.

Once again, Ben decided he did not like the sense of their con. As if the war weren't close enough, as if it didn't chase him, and now they were creating the illusion of arms. It was a bitter con to be pulling but he knew how convincing he had been just broaching the subject with Dent. He could see Dent rapt by his own inquiries into the dreary muck of soldiery. What if all this talk led Ben back to the war?, he thought. What if luck required discretion and here he was dabbling again when he had run cleanly from France? Would war come again for him? Would they come to drag him back to it?

More disturbingly, in the last day or so Ben had begun to see people, friends from the war. Not Chimer, Douglas, or David, but men he did not know were dead or alive, but here they were, in army greens, gathered on New York street corners. No one else noticed them of course. They did nothing to Ben but stare as he passed. Silent stares, no outright accusations. Not even from the ones he was pretty certain were dead. And they were mixed in with others: his father and mother came walking out of a shop, Doctor Willis from Osborne House read a newspaper next to him on the subway. Even Henry Jergens had passed by on the other side of the street, and Ben had stared and then quickened his step to hide. They only came, he noticed, when his mind wandered. If he kept about himself, concentrated on anything, whatever was at hand, then all was well. But let himself drift, or worse, find himself amid silence, and a stream of these dreams began to invade his waking life.

As Ben left the building, he knew his paranoia was growing. He had had the lie of the embassy man squashed by McAteer at Miner's months ago. But twice now he was convinced he was being followed. He wondered if it was Major Sanderson. Perhaps the major had asked around at the embassy, found that no one had ever heard of a Ben Newcombe. Ben knew he should feel under threat, but he was confused about what was real and what was not. He had stopped buying the English papers. To read the casualty lists had done him no good. The commuting hordes heading toward the terminals at the end of the working day would suddenly all be dressed in drab army green, marching in step.

It was a growing fear, but he was not entirely sure what was coming after him. He felt himself starving for something, capable of rash acts. Full of flinches and the very thing that he had thirsted for, all that noise, was now beginning to spin him. What if he needed silence? He would go mad. But the apparitions had invaded the city. They didn't object to Klaxon and footfalls. The precious defenses of noise and preoccupation were melting in the summer heat. You keep yourself together, said Chimer. Do you hear us? You stay where you are, nice and cushy. If you lose your head, we're all gone. You understand that? Everything we've ever done is lost.

He felt himself leaning on McAteer and the process of business to ensure his sanity. He was absorbed by the minutiae of the con. They knew that Dent would take precautions, would have McAteer's story investigated, and there were the papers and previous transactions that McAteer would produce in evidence. All the papers ran under different names, placed newspaper clippings from the *New York Herald* carrying the announcements of the bankruptcy of their various companies. It was, thought Ben, a balance to what Dent and Grayson did. Dent actually put arms out there.

Ben and his boss only pretended to. They were not actual dealers but phantoms. And while Dent and Grayson traded again and again, feeding war, theirs was a single transaction. Better, this deal sided with the majority opinion of the American public in favor of the Allies. It would be a major investment that allowed Dent to move in and front a company that would not even exist in a week. In Bedford, McAteer had already shown Dent a telegram implying that British interests would offer one hundred and eighty thousand for the equipment. All Dent had to come up with was the seventy-five thousand dollars that would free their equipment from its original owners so that they might trade for profit.

McAteer had suggested the Russians might offer more, but Dent had said that if he chose to come in with them he would prefer to sell to the French. He could tell that Ben approved. Dent, the main investor, would reap a very quick eighty percent profit. Only four hours ago, Ignazio Mincione had arrived and his stock had been unloaded by every man that McAteer trusted in the city. Had Ben not been sent to shepherd Dent toward their meeting with McAteer, he would have seen a familiar cast of their expansive company. From the busboy at Reisenweber's to the deputies at their law offices — even the plugger, Neville, who had recited "I Know What's Good for You." They came, they carried, soaking through their shirts amid grumbles. They earned good money.

Chapter Nine

ADMITTEDLY, IT WAS hardly ideal weather to head underground. Entering Gracy's, a tailor shop and laundry on Warren Street, Ben was as mystified as Dent. McAteer was obviously well acquainted with the owner, a broad-hipped Chinese lady. Her English was so poor that Ben presumed McAteer had picked up a word or two of Mandarin in his travels, until he realized that McAteer had dropped into pidgin English. Dent made a half-hearted bow of vague Oriental inclination and followed McAteer to the back of the shop.

All the men left their jackets hanging from iron hooks in the laundry and walked through a trapdoor in the back of the shop in their shirtsleeves, a parade of tipins, cuff links, and shiny brows. Together, they descended. Ben had never encountered such stillness. He used to ask where the wind came from. "Air," said his father, "is rushed by the speed at which the world turns." Ever since, he had believed it, thinking that on stormy days the world spun faster and when there was no wind, the earth stood still.

The steps led to a second trapdoor, but this one was iron, airtight, heavy, like those that separated chambers on a dreadnought. A hiss seemed to accompany its opening, and a dampness wafted over the men, the musty biscuit breath of an octogenarian. McAteer flipped a switch and waved Dent and Ben ahead of him. He picked up a flashlight from the ground, a precaution against the summer's electric flutter or a full-blown blackout. Ben paused at the lip of the entrance. A broad staircase disappeared into the brightly lit silence.

"I don't think I can do it," whispered Ben to McAteer. Dent turned around and stared.

"What?"

"Go down there."

"What do you mean?" McAteer reached out a hand on Ben's back. "Put it away, whatever you're thinking about, put it away," he whispered. More gently, McAteer added, "Hold the flashlight, it'll feel better that way."

Ben made his way slowly down until he could see Dent standing in a long warehouse, really a glorified tunnel, filled with crates and boxes. Dent could discern the contours of a fountain and another series of descending steps.

"What the hell is this?" asked Dent.

"A subway station," said McAteer. "Before there were subways."

Ben stared at the ground and watched how Dent left footprints in between the boxes like a man walking across a frost-lined field.

"It was a pneumatic subway," continued McAteer. "They built it forty years ago." He jerked his hand behind him. "There was the big turbine up that end. You switch it the one way, it blew the car down the tracks, flip it the other, and it sucked it back."

"What happened?" asked Dent.

"Boss Tweed, he didn't like it," said McAteer. "Didn't much matter anyway. Cost a fortune to fuel the engine and everything had to be sealed perfectly. If you don't have the vacuum, you don't get the pressure. No pressure, no movement. Then came the electrics, goodbye to the air."

"Must have been strange," whispered Ben. "Must have barely made a sound. Like a sailing ship."

"Three blocks from city hall," said McAteer. "You can't ask for a more central warehouse, can you now, Mr. Dent?"

Dent turned around and smiled, looking at the hundreds of marked crates before him, staring all about him in the ugly electric illumination. "This city," he said, in the tone of a man who still enjoyed surprises. Full crates were at the front; at the back, where it would have taken twenty men to dig to, lay stacks of unmarked, empty boxes. They had had no say in what Mincione had brought, only the knowledge of who he worked for. He had arrived with an uneven mix of motorcycle engines, rifles, ammunition, and boots.

Dent rummaged through the boxes, dismissive of boots, pushing his fingers against the cool metal of the engines, unaware of exactly what they were. But he knew his rifles. He had Ben prise open crate after crate, sifting through straw to eye the weapons. He pulled one out, a well-oiled barrel, a shiny stock. He held it up to his shoulder and peered down its length, then found a crate of ammunition.

"Is it all right if I have a pop?"

"Too much ammunition down here," cautioned Ben.

"Go ahead," said McAteer.

Dent leveled the gun and prepared to shoot it along the length of the tunnel, which ended in a simple brick wall. None of them was prepared for the report of the rifle. To Dent's ears, it was loud enough to be heard by his wife back in Illinois. He was grinning as he handed the rifle back to Ben. "You have a shot, Sergeant," he said.

Ben knew Dent did it deliberately, that he was handing a gun to a man who had been shot through several times. Or did he want to see how a supposed expert handled a weapon? Underground, Ben felt the sickness of premonition. Not nausea, but the queasy knowledge that it soon would come. The boys weren't saying a word. Silence, a terror of mounting emptiness, he whistled, hummed, but when Dent pushed the rifle into his hands, Ben had wanted nothing but to commit whatever meaningless horror was needed to extract himself from this underground. To turn the gun, push it into Dent's soft eye, and trigger the back of the man's head off, or to jam the gun under his own chin, to stretch and drive a round through the top of his head. Instead he had shaken, humiliated, and shot a bullet into the darkness at the end of the tunnel. And then Dent had offered him a clean white handkerchief to wipe his brow. Ben had looked at it in amazement and remembered their sergeant passing among the men a year ago, replacing all white handkerchiefs with pink-dotted substitutes. Fabrics that could never be mistaken for signs of surrender.

"Think you missed the target," said Dent.

"Where was it?"

"A joke," said Dent. "I couldn't have hit a subway train. Hot as hell, isn't it?"

Ben could only nod.

Dent was talking again at McAteer, inquiring as to rates and numbers, general information. Ben was ignored.

"I don't have to tell you the demand there is for anything of this kind," said McAteer. "I've got Italians, Russians, English, French. From good conscience on Ben's behalf, I can hardly turn it over to the Germans, though I've had my chance. We can arrange everything for you, if you come in with us. Transport, papers for transaction, these are all the things that our firm provides."

Ben could hear, but he was not listening. This was New York, not the Piccadilly post at Loos, or Trafalgar near La Bassée. Thousands of miles away from panic and fear. Ghosts couldn't cross moving water. Not theirs, not his. Dark, sonorous echoes seemed to hum through Ben's body. McAteer was talking again, but Ben was spinning backward through the year. Every attempt he made to focus on the present was jarred by a succession of memories. This is a wall. Do you remember your friend Douglas Carvey? Do you remember what happened to him? This is Warren Street, New York City. Do you remember Chimer? Do you remember the red gleam of his blood, its warmth when it ran across your hand?

McAteer was waiting for an answer to his last question. Ben's tongue suddenly felt swollen, a fluish uncertainty blocking his mouth.

"Are you listening to me, Sergeant?"

"Can we leave?" asked Ben weakly.

He stood, walked a yard, then stopped. He sank to the floor and put both his palms against the cool tiles, telling himself to stay steady, to remember the now. His breathing became shallow, he was only vaguely aware that McAteer was fumbling beside him. Shallow breaths, barely mud-covered, in confusion. Upside down, drooling, arms reaching out to find the wet ground beneath his feet, blood running from his wounds, leaking through his trousers. Pressed to the sodden earth, under the earth, silence pushing down, worse than a year of pounding shells, each blast eroding the walls, out and in. It was on top of him, all this silence and the overwhelming voices, pushing down; it might bury him, he was the instrument, Ben could bury himself.

"Shit," said Chimer.

"Thunder," said Douglas. "It's coming again. Heads down."

"Two days in a row."

"A whistler."

"Any rum left?" asked David.

"Ben," said McAteer. "You all right?"

Ben couldn't speak.

"Christ," said Dent as he bent over to drag Ben upright.

McAteer helped hold Ben's weight, and the men struggled upward into the afternoon. Both could feel the helpless shivering of the Englishman's body. McAteer kept up a continuous flow of comforting words as they huffed out the door.

"Is he all right?" asked Dent.

"Thanks for your help," said McAteer. "He'll be fine. Just some fresh air."

Dent waited beside them on the street. Two children rolled empty milk cans past them to a dairy on the corner, filling the air with the hollow metallic clang of theatrical thunder. McAteer pinched Ben's cheek.

"Okay, pal, we're out again. Fresh air. Everything good, just fine. You okay?"

Ben managed a nod and inhaled deeply.

"You want to talk about it?" McAteer was looking at Ben differently. Ben didn't even shake his head.

"Talk about it," encouraged Dent, staring down at him. "Do you some good."

McAteer gave one of the passing children a dollar and sent him for a tot of rum. Dent took McAteer by the arm. "Is that why they sent him over here?" he whispered to McAteer. "Can't take a pop or two?"

"I suppose," said McAteer.

Dent shook his head sadly. "Wouldn't have guessed he was that yellow, would you?"

Within minutes, Ben managed to stand, but he remained shaken for the rest of the day. Such a charged memory made him doubt the movement of time. It should move forward, always forward, not disturb a man in darkness by leaping into the past, threatening to dissolve his progress. It was as if the boys had sprung out of his head and he had not been able to force them back inside. Alone, when first deserting, Ben felt that he had drifted too far from the course of expectation. Friends, work, family no longer existed. He had been alone. He knew he existed, but no one else in this country did.

Ben was petrified to find that the fear had not lapsed, it was still alive within him. He was no longer terrified of men who could bring him back to the war, but that the war itself might seek him out. That it would contaminate the very ground he walked over, that Manhattan gutters would be transformed into trenches, that the rumble of subway cars would become the shudder of artillery, that women would disappear, hats become helmets. Had it not just happened?

He knew that it was not guilt that McAteer felt, but extreme awkwardness at having witnessed his collapse, the sudden shattering that had seemingly come from nowhere. No one wanted to believe that such weakening demons might inhabit a friend. It was easier to welcome back the shell, help Ben rebuild it with kindness, with the correct dose of attention. Besides, professionally, thought Ben, McAteer has need of me. Had he not already helped to bring money to their company? Be patient with me, prayed Ben, not only because I am your friend, but because I'm about to make you money.

Chapter Ten

ON A WARM Saturday afternoon Ben was forced to cede Katherine to Dent. It was their last meeting before her move back to her parents' house. He wished he felt better for her, having little energy, drained by his collapse the day before, uncertain about what was true and what illusory. The boys hadn't talked to him all day. He'd called for them, but they weren't there. Were they out walking, thought Ben, alive with the rest of the dead, wandering the streets of the city?

Katherine stood in her bedroom door in her tailored covert suit, a white broadcloth collar bright with embroidery. Katherine, a firework, streaking across the sky, gorgeous but perhaps short-lived, more like him, a warped reflection. He could tell Katherine so many things that she didn't know. Of another man's life he had once lived, of a soldier he had been, of what he now did for a living.

"Where are you meeting him?" Ben asked.

"Uptown," she said.

"I'll come with you," he said. "Just to drop you off."

"This one or this one?" she asked, asking him to choose between a straw hat with a stick-up of roses or a brimmed sailor's hat.

Ben clicked his teeth together and said quickly, "Wear the roses."

"Why not?" she had answered with a smile.

She was perfectly dressed, camera-ready, when he kissed her. She let her kiss linger, then kissed him again and sucked his lip to bite it. In truth, he had begun to feel the pity she felt for him. A half hour later she was getting dressed again, and Ben was happy for a moment, naked, fidgeting through his clothes, looking for a cigarette.

He watched her and wondered and knew that he wanted to be loved by her. Love me, and accept what ever I can give in return. Friends, you could hear anything from them, but romance, that was a precious balloon, needing a precise atmosphere, and Ben couldn't imagine a quicker way to deflate it than to share his visions of hell. Yet, at the same time, he couldn't think of a surer way to draw Katherine into his confidence, to be drawn into hers, then by telling her everything.

At least his conscience was clean. He'd given her every dime that he'd accepted from Dent for supporting the child, and he was sure that she'd made money out of Dent on the side, if she'd been smart enough to save it. Her parents would care for her. He knew where she'd be. He could find her after he had made his five thousand dollars, show that he could be depended upon.

The period of invincibility that the act of sex lent Ben soon disappeared and silence loomed. As Katherine dressed, he rested in bed, amid her scent, smoking cigarette after cigarette. A free afternoon reminded Ben of those precious hours of leisure between marches when they found themselves in a decent-sized town, wandering with hours of open possibility before them, only now he could barely stand it.

Last autumn, just behind their lines lay a copse of hazels and beeches. Ben remembered hiding from the heat in their shade, and the morning smells were still about, the mold and leaves lending their dampness to the stolid air. Sitting there with his friends amid the ignorant birds and distracted insect hymn, waiting for the sergeant's whistle. Knowing that peace would be interrupted, that routine awaited, and that days like this New York day were beyond the imagination.

>●<

They rode uptown in a taxi. Ben stopped it on the corner of Fifth and Fifty-ninth, by the park. He reached out to take her hand. The park seemed green, peaceful, even as a baize table. Such danger, but he knew he would be well close to her. Do you know what can happen to me in silence? What would she say if he told her that right now, a company of Highlanders were crossing the park behind her, boots caked in mud. His nostrils were filled with the odors of soldiers' feet. Yet he still withstood the park's relative quiet. He found that he was not panicking. Perhaps silence aided communication. Perhaps things flowed more quickly between people when words were lacking.

Not far from the chimes of the carousel, Ben wandered over to a small patch of wildflowers and plucked a half dozen, gripping them into an improvised bouquet.

"Is that legal?" Katherine called out.

"It's a public park, isn't it?"

"Are you a member of the American public?" she teased.

Ben realized that he was not. He handed them to her quickly. She inhaled deeply and asked. "Do you ever think of the future?"

"No," said Ben, tracing the path of the soldiers over her shoulder.

"I think of me," said Katherine, "and then I think of the future me. I try to do her favors. Things she'll appreciate."

"And the past you?"

"I don't pay her any attention," said Katherine. "What's done can't be helped."

"To do yourself favors," said Ben quickly, "do you have to know where you're going to be?"

"I don't know," said Katherine. "Do you know where you'll be?"

"Here," he said. "Waiting for you. Do you have to go home?"

She gave him a sweet peck on the check.

She wouldn't find another to love her so, thought Ben. Not with a child. She was a fool if she really believed Dent would care for her. He'd throw her over for the next pair of long legs that high-heeled past him. When should a girl like that make the trade, Ben wondered. Turning in her beauty and youth for stability. Perhaps not until the applause died down. Then he would be there; then he would show the depth of his capability. Right lads? No answer at all.

"I know where to find you," said Ben.

"There's no escaping you," said Katherine. She kissed him again on the mouth.

Chapter Eleven

THERE WERE OTHER subways that ran near city hall; you could hear them rumble through the silence, and the sharp squeal of braking traffic traveled downward. All had remembered handkerchiefs for their second visit. Ben watched the way Dent dabbed at his face. The sort of behavior taught by well-dressed mothers. The rest mopped at their brows, dragging the rag like they were scrubbing at decks. All was so smooth this night. Ben was excited; he was aware of everything about him. It was running as it was supposed to run. He was whistling to himself, lips almost closed, music contained in his own mouth.

His eyes surveyed the naked bulbs that hung from the low ceilings, and when Ben looked back at Dent, his face was surrounded by a burning halo from the afterglow. All the words that were being spoken seemed warm, voices that had been slowly heated, until they had begun to melt and slur. Ben tried listening but could not differentiate the breath that separated one word from another. He was doubting his own mind. Nod — you are minutes from success. A prickly heat rose in his legs. He must stand, not quake or fall.

He remembered the sergeant who worked for the Midland Educational in civilian life. He had jabbed a thumb and selected Ben for night patrol, those useless sallies through cold and darkness to listening posts. Always lying quietly next to corpses in the hope the Germans would think you too were dead. Ben remembered the croaking frogs and lack of fear, just resignation. He'd put his hand through a corpse's stomach. It had taken days to scrape the smell from under his fingernails. They waited, they listened. They did not, they could not trust their ears. All they could trust was their ears. The damned silence, and the magnitude, the comparative earthquake of an unseen rodent shuffling past. All senses are heightened, for this is your life. Your ears have become your life, so listen closely.

There are no flares, none of the random shots that usually mark the night. You know your patrol have had this thought, or are having it, or will have it in the silence any moment. It means only one thing. That the Germans also have a patrol out, somewhere about you. And oddest of all, when you are barely breathing, trying to scrape sounds from the darkness with your ears, a voice whispers in English. It comes from the lip of the German trench, and very clearly it says, "If you don't go away now we shall have to shoot you."

Ben laughed out loud.

"What's the joke, Sergeant?" asked Dent.

A schoolboy's fear descended quickly, the dread of being stared at, that made Ben hotter still, the fear of weakness being shown to all, to reveal the real man that lurked behind Newcombe, back beyond soldiering, beyond pianos and cousins' floors, back to the child that Chimer knew.

"Nothing," muttered Ben, wiping at his brow. "Just thought of something from way back."

But even then, there was a distraction, there was a task at hand and men were making investments and Ben was returned to the present because he remembered the insides of the mind do not matter.

Yes, Mr. Dent. Transportation at your direction. Wherever you wish. A certain gentleman at Black Tom. Of course it can be arranged. Ben could feel the hundreds of tiny sweat beads summoned by his nerves. They were trying to betray him. It was Dent who had chosen to meet down here, who had brought a bodyguard, left aboveground, and others were about, McAteer's bogus accountants, making figures, estimates of transportation costs. Perfect, McAteer had said, to meet so late at night. Makes Dent think he's taking a risk or two for his profit. And there he stood, Rudolph Dent, carrying the oversized leather wallet he had brought back from Chicago with seventy-five thousand dollars.

Mincione had come back again, for double the first day's pay, and they had filled his truck with identical merchandise. It had all come together to release Ben. Five thousand dollars was absolute freedom. And what was there to stay in New York for? Why not convince Katherine and depart, away from the edge that pointed toward Europe, and head into the middle of the country?

When all were satisfied and handshakes had been ceremoniously swapped, they made their way to the top of the steps. McAteer had a calm smile, the small gratitude of business concluded to mutual benefit. Ben pushed against the trapdoor and swung it open into the laundry. In came that comforting smell of starch and powders. Ben offered his hand to McAteer, who struggled up through the steps, Dent's oversized wallet now gripped firmly to his side. A surprisingly mild night, thank God, thought Ben, as they walked into the darkness, grateful he had survived underground. Had he entered a swampy humidity perhaps his head would not have cleared. It was clear, wasn't it? Those oppressive thoughts trying to lean through the past and touch him underground, they were going now. Gone.

There was a group of men across the street. They walked toward Ben. A strange and familiar shadow among them. But more men and the gleam of guns. It took Ben a moment to think of the money, for a moment his mind had tried to trick him, to tell him that guns came with night patrols and with soldiers came war. But Ben could see the outline of boater hats. He paused. McAteer paused beside him. Dent and the accountants were talking among themselves and had failed to register the shadows. There was a low rumble of thunder. In the light of the street lamp, he thought he saw the face of Henry Jergens approaching.

Chapter Twelve

BEN SQUINTED THROUGH the darkness, glanced across at the group, saw more standing behind, perhaps a dozen in all. There were rifles aimed at them. The man in glasses was speaking to them but Ben could barely hear, "Arrest . . . the counterfeiting of . . . fraud . . . investigation." And another voice, an English voice calling out his true name. The sky turned white above them and Ben hardly noticed, presumed it was the insides of his own head coming to rest, but why then, would all of them, those holding the rifles, revolvers, badges, even McAteer beside him, why were they all looking up at the night?

There is that strange moment, brief and infrequent, where dreams, no matter how unlikely, are reflected outside the sleeping body. Perhaps the physical world has entered the imagination. Perhaps the mind has altered its surroundings. Ben knew he was in America, in New York, three thousand miles away, but shells burst within him and outside, the sky was illuminated within the dome of his head and above in city night. The booming noises of his mind echoed the thunder of the street.

Ben followed the gaze of the men about him as the pressure wave hit, sweeping across the Hudson from Black Tom Island. It snapped at the ears, invisible and violent, like a breaker on the beach but made of one burst of wind, and it slammed them all into the street. Rifles went skittering like matchsticks across a pub floor and off tumbled McAteer's precious wallet. All but one of the street lamps shattered. It cast its light as a promise that nothing was wrong, that all remained intact. Across the river, minutes ago, it had merely been one small fire started by Quinlan Harvey in a ship filled with airplane engines. That was all it was supposed to be, a single ship aflame in open water. But now the fire was burning through the flat-bottomed ferries, up through the rail yard, into the warehouses. McAteer raised himself to his knees, his head scratched and bleeding, and stared after the bag. Ben could see his intensity was only matched by that of Henry Jergens, looking for something he'd dropped.

To most eyes, it was a street of glass, a dangerous black menace of wicked shards balanced at all angles. But two sets of hands were already sorting through the sharp shadows about them, their ears deafened, but hands at work, each looking for the comfort of a black wallet. They could not see it, but they could imagine it; they would know the weight of the money. Ben saw McAteer crawl one way, Jergens not ten yards from him. And both found what they were looking for. Each hand gripped a heavy bag in the darkness. Disappointment for McAteer could only come with light.

The first plate of glass dropped to the street just as men were testing their ears with deliberate yawns and prodding fingers. Three panes from a building above came slicing down through the air and cracked against the pavement close to one of the Bureau's men. He turned from the glass, but it came at him, little pieces cutting through his thin summer jacket into his back. And then it truly began, a second blast, another wave of air, not as strong as the first, and this time not one pane of glass but dozens, loosened and crashing onto the street. Ben watched them staring upward, saw Henry Jergens with his head tilted in expectation. A glass plate knocked him to the wall, slicing deep into his arm, entering at the elbow. A soldier ran to him. No, it wasn't a soldier. But beside the man a woman appeared. She looked like Katherine Howells. And she didn't pause to see to Jergens's wound, but grabbed at a bag lying by his side and turned away. And Jergens smiled, as if the coming and going of this thieving apparition was a good thing. A man was seeing to him now. No point, thought Ben, a wound like that and you'll lose that arm. Then the last street lamp surrendered, blowing out its sides, extinguishing all light.

There were lamps still shining to the north. Ben got to his feet and began to move toward them. No one seemed to be stopping him. The priorities of the city had shifted between one second and the next. What to do? Ben was sure he was awake. A block from Warren Street he knelt amid the glass and squeezed a shard, watched the cut bleed and he could feel it. And he turned away and turned back and still he bled and there was no miraculous cure of his dreams, no shattered soldiers whole again, just the quick drip of blood and the continuing boom.

To every other soul in Manhattan, the panic was palpable, but Ben walked through, the only one familiar with the chaos, the only man to whom this was nothing but the looming threat of an assault. Only Ben thought he knew what was happening. How they had dreamed of this sitting in their trenches, dreamed of wars coming to cities to bring an understanding, to impose fear, to share their cruelties, and to let the world know that war had come and war had won and war would stay. If you sent your men away, they might not come back, but war would, because it lived.

Walk north, thought Ben. Get swept with the tide toward the reserve trench, to the support, hide yourself in the middle, let yourself be carried in this rush. It is not yet mud, it is paving stones and sidewalks. Bundle with the civilians, avoid the falling glass. The Jack Johnson shells and their impossibly deep whistle and the shrill whine of speeding rounds and the flashes of munitions all up in the sky and all inside his skull.

  Ben's heart beat hummingbird-fast. He could not know what he looked like, how little different he seemed from the rest. All eyes were sharp and maddened. Nobody knew what this was. Every alarm in the city was ringing from the quake of the first blast. Every telephone line was either occupied or down and all that was known was the rush of shouts and rumors. People were waking as far away as Philadelphia, listening to the distant turbulence. The Statue of Liberty was pierced again and again. Men were preaching calm in New York's streets with strained voices. There are tears, you can hear tears, there are voices breaking, thought Ben.

Something great had arrived. Julius McAteer, sixty years old, was curled against a dirty street curb as if it were deep enough to hide him. Henry Jergens was clutching one arm with the other, smiling through the pain. Bureau men had tumbled toward walls and then back into the middle of the streets, away from the falling glass. But Ben was moving between the shells visiting the northern buildings and the fire from the south. So much glass was breaking that it seemed to fall down then up, like monsoon rain. He moved from his knees, stooped, and ran, past the people huddling under fire escapes.

Four, five, a dozen alarms were ringing. Ben was running, not fast, but at a sustainable rate, as if prepared to run all night. The war had reached him. The canyons of Manhattan were the deepest trenches ever dug. And all was shuddering in thunder and Ben's two worlds that should never have met were being slammed together like cymbals. Suits were uniforms, umbrellas were rifles, officers were beside him, and Chimer, Douglas, and David, dead for nine months, were giddying him up. As he ran past civilians braced against the walls, they stared at him in wonder for the boldness of his movement.

The glass was crunching beneath his feet. The open wheat fields in France and the mayflies, born without mouths, who flew for a day and then died soft along the mud trucks. And you could walk on them, back from the front in your boots, and hear the slight bony grind beneath.

There, two blocks from Warren Street, he thought he saw Katherine Howells again, standing at a bar behind shattered glass. Ben didn't blink for her; he was waving on an invisible army behind him. Chimer, Douglas, and David were on either side, hurrying him on. Shells were landing and glass was falling like winter hail.

Other blasts sent palpable winds rushing up the avenues. The Brooklyn Bridge swayed from the constant buffeting. Nobody understood. Telegraph lines were severed, bundles of them lying flat across streets. Only the citizen herd reacted; it moved generally eastward, generally north, away from the noise. Rumors were running fast: Black Tom Island was alight, a fire was spreading through the warehouses, but Ben did not need to listen to them because he recognized the sound of every shell. He moved north, through the flooded blocks around Forty-second Street, broken mains pushing a foot of water into the streets. His shoes, his trousers were now soaked. Up at the edge of Central Park, people were congregating, as if Nature were the borderland of hell. Ben burst through the gates of the park, pushing through the people, making his way up to Belvedere Castle, accompanied by the distant burst of shells, to the familiar place he had spent his first night of peace in the city.

Epilogue

IT SEEMED AS if, within days, New York had put aside the last days of July. The city moved. The August streets were teeming with newcomers, crowded in the shade, escaping the bottled blackness of the tenements. There was talk about, coming through the windows, talk of what should be bought, calls of caution to galloping children, endless loops of language. There was no purpose in considering Black Tom Island. That was why there were historians and laureates and scribes. They sat there waiting for the present to fall into the past. Everyone else was getting to work.

Seven dead in Manhattan: a fisherman who had been blown out of his boat and drowned; Mr. Cook, killed on Delancey Street by falling glass. A night watchman lay where he fell on Black Tom Island, burned of flesh, the heat so keen that his bones had broken and crumbled. There was no stoker to encourage the fire, and his remains were mixed with falling ashes from the warehouses and ruptured canvas tents and leather boots, of mud from the riverbed and the churning earth. The very dreams that had haunted Ben for months were now hiding in New York, accidentally unleashed by Dent and Grayson's actions to secure the insurance for their airplanes.

Ben lay prone under the humid shadows beneath Belvedere Castle. Where's Katherine?, he thought. For three days he had lived in the park, torn between the desire to go and find her and the fear of being found. Hearing his real name read aloud had shocked him into immobility. He had not known where to go, could barely think. Buying bread and bottles of soda on Broadway, Ben kept returning to the park, making his home in the thick foliage of the Ramble. It was unbearably hot. The newspapers he slept on top of were soggy come the morning, dampened by a mixture of dew and sweat. The sky was far above him, a sheen of white clouds blurring the sun. Summer was all he could smell, thick air and cut grass.

He could hear voices through his sleep, the hum of circling bees, the sound of dogs barking and rustling through the bushes to where he hid. But Chimer, Douglas, and David were nowhere to be heard. On August second, Ben got to his feet, walked to the top of Belvedere Castle, and looked down upon the park and the shocking normalcy beneath him, the vast greenness beyond the reservoir, dotted with picnickers, strollers, lovers. His eyes ached, as if he had stared too long into electric lights. His memory began to tick into action.

His own first thought had been not of capture, nor of McAteer, nor of his money, but of Katherine. But was McAteer alive? If so, had he been arrested? Or had he taken every cent of Dent's money and decided he did not need Ben again? Ben stared upward at the sky above New York, ensuring it was free of Very lights. Now that his head was clearing, he knew he shouldn't remain in the city, that he should head for a station, a boat, a taxi away. It was probably what McAteer had done, had he made it from Warren Street without being arrested. The need for movement worried Ben of course. He looked in his pocket. He still had the remains of their take from Henry Jergens, less than a hundred dollars. And he had seen Jergens, that was true, was it not? Not some fragment of his past? It was true. Jergens had come back to have them all arrested.

He read through the newspapers he used to lie on at night, noting all the reports on Black Tom Island. How there was nothing left there but a crater under the water in the Hudson. Rumors had abounded for a day or two. Mismanagement, sabotage, sparks. Ben knew that it didn't matter, that it was the signal for war. Perhaps not today, but America would come to the war and the war would come to America, sooner or later.

On August third, Ben walked over to a barber on Lexington Avenue and had his face shaved clean of his mustache. He ran a finger over the smoothness of his top lip and knew he looked like a newsboy. Next he walked into a secondhand clothes shop down by the East River and swapped his forty-dollar suit from Lord and Taylor for a cheap summer seersucker with blue stripes. The subway carried him down to Spring Street, where he walked west to within a few blocks of his old apartment. He gave a small boy a nickel to go to Mrs. McAteer's apartment and ask if there was any mail for him, promising a dime for a quick return. Ben sat in the shadow of a stoop and waited, glancing up and down the street anytime more than one man at a time walked toward him. Ten minutes later the boy returned with a single letter. Ben gave him his dime. The child tipped an imaginary cap in his direction as Ben pulled open the letter.

My Friend,
Please join me in the Grand Hotel in Columbus,
Ohio, 10th August.
— JM

Ben smiled and wondered if it was true. Such a short note, yet containing both warmth and promise. What did Ben expect of McAteer? If McAteer didn't have the money, then why ask him west? Yet, if he did have the money, Ben knew how it worked. Whatever your intention, once you held a man's share awhile, it became yours, harder to give up. Unless McAteer wanted to work with him again, but had he not ruined the chances of that? McAteer knew that there was too much Ben was incapable of, underground, silence. Either way, the meeting was a week away and Ben knew he should find a place outside of New York as soon as possible.

⊱⊰

Ben knew of only one location that no one would think to look for him. Telling himself that he could be back later that afternoon, yet knowing that he might not be back at all, Ben headed north in a taxi, not trusting Grand Central, but opting to take a train from a station in the Bronx. By the time he paid for his round-trip ticket, he had less than eighty-five dollars to his name.

Katherine Howells should be there. She had said her goodbyes the previous weekend, had left to have her child with her parents in Westchester. On the train, ladies nodded in his direction. The conductor treated him with abject indifference. He took a taxi to the Howells' house, not wishing to seem impecunious. Yet, when he knocked, there was no answer. Beneath him the summer seemed to have passed from greenness and the grass was tinged with burnt yellow. The shimmering sounds of cicadas filled the air, that permanent sizzle of water hitting the skillet. Wherever he trod the sounds seemed to retreat, as if the insects moved in organized battalions. He walked around to the back of the house. In the corner of the herb garden stood Katherine's father, in gardening boots, contemplating a row of tomato plants. Walking closer, Ben saw it was not Mr. Howells at all, but perhaps a gardener.

"Excuse me," called Ben. "Are Mr. and Mrs. Howells about?"

The man bent over and brushed dirt from his knees, then took a step toward Ben.

"Mr. and Mrs. Who?"

"Howells?"

"And who would they be?"

"The owners of the house."

"Owners don't come back till September," said the gardener, staring hard at Ben. "You can rent it by the week if you choose. You talking about renters?"

"When did they leave? When did the owners leave?"

"Last day of May," said the gardener. "That way you can get money for all of June."

"You're sure of this?" asked Ben. "You've never heard of a family called Howells?"

"Been working for the Atkins for a dozen years. Can't be much surer than that."

Ben tipped his hat and turned around. He walked to the front of the house and sat on the stoop in the shade. Katherine was a liar. She was not simply a liar, she had invited him into a lie. A performance in which he had been like a mark. A great swell washed over his brain.

Why had she treated him that way? What had he to take? He knew he'd been played, but for what? He thought all the way back to when he had first met Katherine. Who had been present in the theater? Rudolph Dent, who had been fleeced of seventy-five thousand dollars, and Henry Jergens, who had introduced him to Katherine afterward. My God, Ben thought to himself. And when did we next meet? At the coffee shop. And who was there? Henry Jergens. Who had cut his commitment from thirty thousand dollars to eight? And the night of Black Tom, when he had run through the streets. Who was there again? Jergens. Ben could not quite trace the path, but knew that a link existed. He remembered now, Jergens cut and bleeding and Katherine beside him on the sidewalk. Could he have imagined that? No, it had been real enough.

She worked with Jergens. If she worked with Jergens, used the rules of the con, then the two of them were flimflammers like McAteer. She had introduced Ben to Dent, and yet Jergens was there on Warren Street that night, with what looked like a host of Pinkertons. Had he convinced them he had been robbed and intended to rob them back again, taking Dent's money from them? Was that it, or close enough? Who else could he not trust? Was even McAteer telling him the truth?

The Ben who traveled back into New York City was a sharper man, brain roiling as if finally jolted awake from the night of Black Tom. His stomach felt empty, yet he had no wish to eat. Abu Abu without a heart, Ben sat with a raw throat, unnerved and uncertain of everything about him, wishing, needing to be anchored by something familiar. Are you there? Is anyone there? Nothing. The boys were gone. Ben was on his own.

He walked back down to King Street, not approaching McAteer's building but waiting across the street the rest of the day, watching. Was McAteer really in Ohio, or was Ben supposed to follow him on a goose chase? Perhaps he just wanted to speed away from the city; perhaps their friendship had meant nothing to him. Ben did not think of entering, fearful that either Dent would have hired Pinkertons, or else his own embassy would still be looking for him. There was little other than a suit or two of his in there. Nothing personal at all. He waited for McAteer all that night and all the next day. Eyes peeled for that shift of walk, ready to interpret him through any costume or disguise. Not even knowing whether or not he was on a fool's errand.

Ben didn't notice her at first, so concentrated was he on men of McAteer's height. The woman had walked down the street and entered the building, then emerged five minutes later. Katherine Howells was looking for him. His heart gave a sudden burst of recognition, like an engine igniting. All the bewilderment he had felt in Westchester was balanced by the simple joy of looking at her. She wore a pale blue dress that hung softly against her hips.

He maintained the advantage of watching her, undetected. Why had she come for him? Had they failed to make off with Dent's money? Did McAteer actually have it? But then, Ben noticed that the dress was new. Would you buy a dress if you had just lost money? Her manner seemed slightly anxious to him, as if she were curious to find him, but not desperate. Why is she here?, he asked himself again. If she didn't have the money, perhaps she presumed that Ben did. Perhaps that was it — she's still after the money. McAteer must have it after all.

He was about to step in front of her, but realized that a little patience might deliver many answers. Instead, he watched her pause, then walk back toward the subway. He followed her down, bought a newspaper, and got into the car behind her. She emerged at Fifty-ninth Street and walked east to a small hotel for women. Across the street stood a tiny, neat diner called Carl's. He sat there until midnight, when they asked him to leave. He returned at six in the morning, watched her door until she emerged at eight. Back down into the subway she went and he followed her until, once more, she entered McAteer's building. Not once had he seen her talk to anyone, and, more importantly to Ben, she had never headed to a hospital. It meant that she and Jergens were not as close as he'd presumed. Just professional colleagues? Even if Jergens had died (and the wound had not looked so serious) then surely she'd either have left town or be visiting funeral parlors. When she left McAteer's, he followed her uptown once more. Before she entered her own hotel, she bought one bagful of groceries.

Ben waited an hour and then entered the hotel. There was a horse-toothed concierge sitting at a small table in front of a row of letter-boxes. She was about fifty, her shoulders draped in a maroon opera cloak despite the heat. He had seen her there all day yesterday, chatting for minutes to the postman, the deliverymen, the telegraph boys. Ben had decided that she'd be a willing talker.

"Good morning, sir," she said as he entered the stucco lobby. "How can we help you?"

"I'm looking for some information about one of your guests," he said.

"And you are?" she asked, smiling.

"I'm from Scotland Yard," said Ben. "We're the . . ."

"You're English," she said. "I know what Scotland Yard is. How can I help you?"

"Nothing too exciting, I'm afraid," said Ben, leaning over the counter toward her, doing his best to exude a professional weariness. "It's just a small matter of stolen property. Just one or two questions."

"I hardly see how I can help you," said the woman.

"We're looking for a young Englishwoman who might have some documents belonging to the government."

The concierge sat up, nodded and bent an ear. Much more exciting, thought Ben, than her usual day.

"Have you any young Englishwomen staying here?"

"I'm afraid I don't."

"Any new tenants in the last few days?"

"Yes," she said. "We've two."

"Either of them about five-foot-four with straight black hair?"

"Yes," said the lady. "Miss Newcombe."

Ben almost lost his composure. She'd used his own false name. What did that mean?

"Have you seen her with anyone?"

"No one at all," said the lady. "She seems a very quiet person."

"She's had no visitors at all?"

"Not a one," said the woman. "I keep a close record. Not a one for Miss Newcombe."

"One last question," said Ben. "Does she have a scar down her right cheek?"

"No, no," said the lady. "She has perfect skin. A very pretty young lady."

Ben huffed in disappointment. "Not our girl. I'm terribly sorry to have wasted your time."

"Not at all, Mr. — ?"

"Atkins," said Ben. "Chief Inspector Atkins."

Why is she after me, Ben asked himself, walking back toward Central Park. She couldn't have known he had been following her. What if this was truth? What if, despite weeks of lies and falseness, now that it was over, she had decided that she wanted to see him again? What have I to offer her? If it's the money, then she'll think I was in for ten percent or so. That I have eight or twelve thousand dollars to my name. Do you trust her?, he asked himself. No, of course not. But do you love her?

➤●◄

The next morning, Ben was up early and stationed across the street from his old room. She arrived just after nine, this time in a plain white dress, almost bridal, but discreet, with a blue sash tied in a bow around her waist. Again, she entered the building, and when she exited two minutes later, he was waiting for her on the side of the street.

It took her a moment to register his face, to see beyond the strange suit, the absence of a mustache.

"I've been looking for you for days," she said, a wide smile breaking across her face.

Ben nodded, but said not a word of what he was thinking, nor a word of what he knew.

"Such an unsettling time," said Katherine. "I didn't even know if you were all right."

"Are you at the theater tonight?" he asked sweetly.

"No," she said. "You know I quit the job."

"Why so soon?" he asked.

She patted her stomach. "I was about to show. Better than being fired."

"Sure," he said.

What a pair we are, thought Ben. He thought of the child for the first time in days. Maybe she wasn't involved with Jergens. Perhaps the child wasn't Dent's. Maybe, after all, it was his.

"It's good to see you," said Katherine, his strange openness now affecting her. They still hadn't even kissed hello. "Can we have dinner later in the week?" she asked suddenly.

"I thought you were living out with your parents," said Ben, his voice filled with kindly concern.

"Yes," she said, "I was. But Mother's feeling poorly, and I can't put this on top of them as well." She looked earnestly into his eyes.

"In Westchester?" he asked.

"Of course."

"I was out there visiting," he said.

"You were?" asked Katherine, a note of panic in her voice.

Ben nodded and said, very pleasantly. "They asked me to send you their love."

She was nervous immediately. Finally Katherine was herself, thought Ben, off balance, unsure of what to say. She turned away from him and began to walk up the street, brushing her hand through her hair. He followed her and it felt familiar to him, being the one with all the knowledge, back in charge.

"You're only walking away," he said, keeping pace at her side, "because you haven't rehearsed this scene. Why don't we practice a little improvisation."

Katherine shook her head while walking, her arms crossed tightly before her.

"You're not quite sure what to think," he said. "I've thought it through for you."

"Have you?" she said. She looked at him at last and saw a wide smile on his face. He held her gently by the wrist, slowing her down until she stopped to turn to him.

"Yes," said Ben. "I've had longer than you to think on this."

"And what did you decide?" asked Katherine, her eyes moving from side to side, wondering, perhaps, if other members of his shop were about.

"It's just me," said Ben.

She looked up at him.

"What do you want?" she asked.

"The same as you," he said.

"What's that then?"

"Dinner," said Ben.

She looked around again. "How do I know you're not playing me?"

"You're not going to know," he said, "until you appear at eight o'clock at the Hotel Ferguson."

"And you're going to be there?" she asked, her voice filled with challenge and doubt.

"Of course."

"I don't even know that hotel."

"That's because it's in San Francisco," said Ben.

Katherine laughed. "Are you being serious? That's three thousand miles away."

Ben tipped an imaginary hat at her and walked farther down the block. He turned around to look at her and she was there, but smiling herself now. Perhaps she was seeing it as he was seeing it, that the game he was playing had nothing to do with money, but the older game of courtship.

"That's a long way to go for dinner," she called after him.

"You don't have to travel alone," said Ben, and waited to see if Katherine would take a step toward him.

Author's Note

While *Dizzy City* leans heavily on the events of 1916, it is in no way to be confused with history. Obviously the Western Front is well trodden ground, but researching *Dizzy City* meant studying the Great War from both sides of the Atlantic. I have to confess that, for the purposes of the plot, various events have been shifted in time. German submarines didn't reach Newport for another three months. While the Broadway play *Cheating Cheaters* was performed at the Eltinge during the summer, Griffith's *Intolerance* didn't have its New York premiere until September. The pneumatic subway tunnel, completed in 1870, was destroyed in 1912. The explosion at Black Tom Island did take place on July 30, 1916. However, it was not until the 1930s that it was confirmed as an act of sabotage.